A CHRISTMAS
Seduction

PASSION UNDER THE MISTLETOE!

A CHRISTMAS Seduction

MERRY CHRISTMAS
by
Emma Darcy

MISTLETOE MISTRESS
by
Helen Brooks

CHRISTMAS WITH A STRANGER
by
Catherine Spencer

MILLS & BOON®

*All the characters in this book have no existence outside the imagination
of the author, and have no relation whatsoever to anyone bearing the
same name or names. They are not even distantly inspired by any
individual known or unknown to the author, and all the incidents are
pure invention.*

*All Rights Reserved including the right of reproduction in whole or in part
in any form. This edition is published by arrangement with Harlequin
Enterprises II B.V. The text of this publication or any part thereof may not
be reproduced or transmitted in any form or by any means, electronic or
mechanical, including photocopying, recording, storage in an
information retrieval system, or otherwise, without the written
permission of the publisher.*

*This book is sold subject to the condition that it shall not, by way of trade
or otherwise, be lent, resold, hired out or otherwise circulated without the
prior consent of the publisher in any form of binding or cover other than
that in which it is published and without a similar condition including this
condition being imposed on the subsequent purchaser.*

*MILLS & BOON and MILLS & BOON with the Rose Device
are registered trademarks of the publisher.
Harlequin Mills & Boon Limited,
Eton House, 18-24 Paradise Road, Richmond, Surrey, TW9 1SR*

A CHRISTMAS SEDUCTION
© by Harlequin Enterprises II B.V., 2001

Merry Christmas, Mistletoe Mistress and *Christmas with a Stranger*
were first published in Great Britain by Harlequin Mills & Boon Limited
in separate, single volumes.

Merry Christmas © Emma Darcy 1997
Mistletoe Mistress © Helen Brooks 1998
Christmas with a Stranger © Catherine Spencer 1997

ISBN 0 263 82780 1

05-1201

*Printed and bound in Spain
by Litografia Rosés S.A., Barcelona*

Initially a French/English teacher, **Emma Darcy** changed careers to computer programming before marriage and motherhood settled her into a community life. Creative urges were channelled into oil-painting, pottery, designing and overseeing the construction and decoration of two homes, all in the midst of keeping up with three lively sons and the very social life of her businessman husband, Frank. Very much a people person, and always interested in relationships, she finds the world of romance fiction a happy one and the challenge of creating her own cast of characters very addictive.

Emma Darcy is the author of more than 70 novels including the international bestseller, THE SECRETS WITHIN, published by MIRA® Books.

She enjoys travelling and often her experiences find their way into her books. Emma Darcy lives on a country property in New South Wales, Australia.

**Look out for
Emma Darcy's new trilogy, Kings of Australia
Coming soon in Modern Romance™**

MERRY CHRISTMAS

by

Emma Darcy

CHAPTER ONE

"Uncle Nick? You asked me what I want for Christmas?"

Kimberly's belligerent tone was forewarning enough that Nick was not going to like it. His twelve-year-old niece could be as difficult and as trying as a fully fledged teenager. She'd been sulking in her room ever since Rachel had arrived for Sunday brunch and this sudden, dramatic challenge, fired at him from the doorway to the balcony, was not a promise of peace and harmony. The plot, he deduced, was to demand something totally unreasonable and stir contention.

"Mmmh?" he said non-committally, staying behind his newspaper in the hope of taking the sting out of the bait.

Rachel's newspaper rustled down. Undoubtedly she was looking at Kimberly with a brightly encouraging smile, doing her best to win the girl over. An increasingly futile exercise, Nick thought gloomily.

"I want my *real* mother."

The shock of it almost wiped him out. The wallop to his heart took some absorbing and his mind totally fused. Fortunately his hands went into clench mode, keeping the newspaper up in cover defence while the initial impact of the surprise attack gave way to fast and furious thought.

Her *real* mother…was it a try-on, a fantasy, or sure knowledge? Impossible to tell without looking at her. He composed his face into an expression of puzzled inquiry and lowered his newspaper.

"I beg your pardon?"

Fierce green eyes scorned his bluff. "*You* know, Uncle Nick. The solicitor would have told you when Mum and Dad died. You couldn't have become my legal guardian without knowing."

Still he played it warily. "What am I supposed to know, Kimberly?"

"That I was adopted."

Absolute certainty looked him straight in the face. It threw Nick into confusion. Kimberly was not supposed to know. His sister had been almost paranoid about keeping the secret. After the fatal accident last year, Nick had thought it best to keep the knowledge from his niece until she was eighteen. After all, losing both parents in traumatic circumstances and learning to live with an uncle was a big enough adjustment to make. Any further erosion of her sense of security did not seem a good idea.

"I have a *real* mother," came the vehement assertion, her chin tilting defiantly, her eyes flashing resentment at Rachel before pinning Nick again. "I want to be with *her* for Christmas."

He folded the newspaper and set it aside, realising this confrontation was very serious, indeed. 'How long have you known, Kimberly?" he asked quietly.

"Ages," she tossed at him.

"Who told you?" It had to be Colin, he thought. His sister's husband had been a gentle man, dominated by Denise for the most part, yet retaining an innate personal dignity and integrity that would not be shaken over matters he considered "right."

"No one told me," Kimberly answered loftily. "I figured it out for myself."

That rocked him. Had he conceded confirmation too soon? Too easily? How on earth could Kimberly figure it out for herself?

If someone had actually worked at matching a child to a family to ensure an adopted baby looked like natural offspring, Kimberly would be a prime example of outstanding success. She could easily be claimed by his side of the family.

She was long-legged and tall, like himself and his sister. Her black hair had the same springy texture and she even had a widow's peak hairline, a family feature that went back generations. The eye colour—green instead of brown—was easily explained with Colin's eyes being hazel. There were untraceable differences—every person was uniquely individual—but if his sister had declared her adopted child her own flesh and blood, Nick would never have doubted it.

So why had Kimberly?

"Would you mind telling me what gave it away to you?" he asked, trying to keep his voice calmly controlled.

"The photographs," she said as though throwing down irrefutable proof.

Nick had no idea what she was talking about.

She flounced forward and picked a cherry off the fruit platter he and Rachel had been sharing, popped it into her mouth and ostentatiously chewed it, hugging her budding chest, aggressively holding the floor, waiting for him to comment. Her green eyes had a fighting gleam.

Rebellion was in the air, from the swing of her ponytail to the brightly checked orange-yellow shorts teamed with a lime green tank top. Kimberly was making statements; right, left and centre. She was not going to be ignored, overlooked or left in the wings of anybody's life.

Nick glanced at Rachel who had tactfully withdrawn any obvious interest in the family contretemps. From the balcony of his Blues Point apartment, one could take in a vast sweep of Sydney Harbour. Rachel's gaze was fixed on the water view but her stillness revealed an acute listening and suddenly Nick didn't want her hearing this, despite their intimate relationship.

"Rachel, this is a very private family matter..."

"Of course." She rose quickly from her chair, flashing him an understanding smile. "I'll let myself out and leave you to it, Nick."

There was so much about Rachel he liked...very capable, highly intelligent, shrewdly perceptive about most people, though his twelve-year-old niece frequently flummoxed her. Even their careers dovetailed, she an investment advisor, he a banker. They were both in their thirties. As a prospective partner in life, Rachel Pearce looked about as good as Nick thought he was going to get, desirable in every sense, yet...the magic connection was missing.

As she stood up, sunshine glinted off her auburn hair, turning the short hairstyle into a glorious, copper cap. Good-looking, always chic, sexy, comfortable with men, her sherry brown eyes invariably warm for him... Nick wondered what more he could want in a woman?

Nevertheless, it didn't feel right for her to be privy to such sensitive family secrets as Kimberly's adoption. It involved delving into lives that only he and his niece had known and shared. It was not Rachel's business. Not yet.

He rose from his chair at the same time, intent on taking command of the situation. "Thanks for your company, Rachel."

"My pleasure. I hope..." She glanced at Kimberly who was helping herself to another cherry, stiffly and steadfastly ignoring her, then with a last rueful look at Nick, she shrugged her helplessness and turned to leave.

"Even if my real mother doesn't want me, I won't go to your old boarding school anyway," Kimberly shot after her. "So you needn't think you can get rid of me that easily."

Rachel froze in the doorway to the living room.

Nick's heart sustained another breathtaking blow. His mind, however, did have something to clutch on to this time—his conversation with Rachel last night. Kimberly should have been in her room asleep but she must have eavesdropped. This current mood and stance had clearly been fermenting ever since.

"It's not a matter of getting rid of you, Kimberly," he said tersely. "It's a matter of what's best for you."

"You mean what's best for you," she retorted. "And best for her." Her eyes flared fierce resentment. "I'm not stupid, Uncle Nick."

"Precisely. Which is why I'd like you to start your secondary education at a good school. To give you the best teachers and the best education."

"Most girls would consider it a privilege to go to PLC," Rachel argued with some heat. "It's certainly been advantageous to me."

"Well, you would say that, wouldn't you?" Kimberly retaliated. "Anything to shunt me out of the way. You think I don't know when I'm not wanted?"

"That's enough, Kimberly," Nick warned. Rachel had tried to reach out to his niece. There just didn't seem to be any meeting place. Or she wasn't granted one.

"Why boarding school, Uncle Nick?" came the pointed challenge. "If it's only education you're thinking of, why couldn't I go as a day pupil? PLC is right here in Sydney."

"You're on your own too much, Kimberly," he answered. "I thought the companionship of other girls would round out your life more."

"*You* thought?" An accusing glare at Rachel. "Or Ms. Pearce suggested?"

"I was going to discuss it with you after Christmas."

The accusative glare swung onto him. "You told her to go ahead and try to get me in."

"That's still not decisive, Kimberly. And you shouldn't have been eavesdropping."

"If Mum had wanted me to go to an expensive, private boarding school, she would have booked me in years ago." Tears glittered in her eyes. "You don't want me. Not like Mum and Dad did."

The recognition of unresolved grief was swift and sharp. His stomach clenched. He couldn't replace her parents. No one could. He missed them, too, his only sibling who'd virtually brought him up, and Colin who'd always given him affectionate support and approval. It had been a struggle this past year, trying to merge his life with a twelve-year-old's, but not once had he begrudged the task or the responsibility.

"I do want you, Kimberly," he assured her gravely.

She shook her head, her face screwing up with conflicting and painful emotions. "I was dumped on you and now you want to dump me somewhere else."

"No."

She swiped her eyes with the back of her hand, smearing the wetness aside. "You won't have to do anything if my real mother wants me. You can give me up and have your lady friend free and clear of somebody else's daughter." She glared balefully at Rachel. "I don't want to be stuck with you any more than you want to be stuck with me, Ms. Pearce."

Rachel heaved a sigh and rolled her eyes at Nick, powerless to stop the hostility aimed at her.

"Just go, Rachel," he advised quietly.

"Sorry, Nick."

"Not your fault."

"No, it's my fault," Kimberly cried, her voice rising toward shrill hysteria. "I spoil it for both of you. So I'm the one who should go."

The arm Nick swung out to stop her was left hanging uselessly as she rushed to the doorway and ducked past Rachel into the living room. He swiftly followed her but she ran full pelt to the front door, pausing only to yell back at him.

"If you care anything at all about me, Uncle Nick, you'll do it. You'll get my *real* mother for me for Christmas! Then maybe it could turn out right for all of us."

CHAPTER TWO

IT HADN'T come today, either…the letter from Denise Graham with news of Kimberly and the photographs spanning another year.

Meredith Palmer struggled to fight off a depressing wave of anxiety as she entered her apartment and locked the rest of the world out. Again she shuffled through the stack of mail she'd just collected from her box; Christmas cards, bank statement, an advertising brochure. She opened the envelopes and extracted the contents, making doubly sure there was no mistake. Nothing from Denise Graham.

The packet usually came in the last week of November. It had done so for the past eleven years. Today was the fourteenth of December and the uneasy feeling that something was wrong was fast growing into conviction. Denise Graham had come across to Meredith, even in her letters, as a very precise person, the kind who would live by a strictly kept timetable. Unless the packet had somehow been lost or misdirected in the volume of Christmas mail, something had to be badly wrong in the Graham household.

Illness? An accident?

The tight feeling in her chest grew tighter as disastrous possibilities flew through Meredith's mind. Not Kimberly, she fiercely prayed. Please…not Kimberly. Her little girl had to have a wonderful life ahead of her. Only by believing that had Meredith managed to repress the misery of not having kept her daughter.

She shook her head, fighting back the worst-case scenarios. Maybe something had happened to the solicitor who had handled the legal aspects of the adoption and subsequently become a conduit for the annual updates to Meredith. Whenever she'd had a change of address she had contacted him, at least half a dozen times before she'd saved enough money to invest in this apartment at Balmoral. Each time she had received a note of acknowledgment and nothing had gone wrong. Nevertheless, it could be that someone else was now handling his business, someone not as meticulously efficient.

She walked across her living room to the writing desk which spread across one corner, linking two walls of bookcases. Having automatically sorted her mail for future replies, she dropped it into in-baskets, then opened a drawer and took out her address book. It was too late to contact the firm of solicitors today but she'd do it first thing tomorrow. It made her feel better, simply copying the telephone number into the notebook she always carried in her handbag.

Despite having set herself a constructive course of action, Meredith still found it impossible to stop worrying. She switched on the television set to catch the evening news but didn't hear a word of it. The glass of white wine she poured herself was consumed although she had no conscious memory of drinking it. After opening the refrigerator and staring at the contents of the shelves for several minutes without connecting anything together for a proper meal, she gave up on the idea of cooking and settled on cheese and pickles and crackers.

The problem was, she didn't have a legal leg to stand on if Denise Graham had decided, for some reason, to break off the one promised contact with her. It had been a matter of trust, her letting Meredith know about their daughter's life once a year…one mother's word to another…an act of compassion in the face of Meredith's grief at giving up her baby. If the solicitor told her there was to be no more contact, there was nothing she could do about it. Absolutely nothing.

A sense of helplessness kept eating at her, robbing her of any appetite, distracting her from doing anything purposeful. When the doorbell rang, she almost didn't answer it. A check of her watch put the time at a few minutes past eight. She wasn't expecting anyone and wasn't in the mood to entertain a visitor. Only the thought of a neighbour in need prompted her to open the door.

Living alone had established automatic precautions. The security chain lock on the door only allowed an opening of a few centimetres. It was through this space—like a long crack in the fabric of time—Meredith saw the man she had never expected to see again.

His eyes caught hers, triggering the weird gush of feeling that only he had ever evoked...the wild whoosh from her heart to her head, like the sea washing into her ears, followed by a fountain of excitement shooting, splashing, rippling through her entire body, setting up an electric tingling of expectation for the most special connection in the world.

It had been like that for her thirteen years ago. As she stared at him now, the shocked sense of her world reeling backward was so strong, all she could do was stare and grip the doorknob with painful intensity, needing some reinforcement of current physical reality.

"Miss Palmer? Meredith Palmer?"

His voice struck old familiar chords that had lain dormant so long Meredith had forgotten them... chords of pleasure, of some sixth sense recognition, a deep resonant tone that thrummed through her, a seductive beat of belonging drawing on her soul.

Yet he didn't know her. She could see he didn't. He would have called her Merry. It had been his name for her...Merry...Merry Christmas...the best Christmas he had ever had.

"Yes," she said, affirming her identity, her heart

still bleeding over what his sister had sworn to her was the truth when she'd denied Meredith access to the father of her baby all those years ago. An accident had wiped out all memory of his summer vacation. He would have no recollection of her. Since he'd already left for the U.S. on a two-year study grant, Meredith had no possible way of testing if what his sister claimed was fact or fiction.

Now the evidence was in front of her. Not Merry. Miss Meredith Palmer with a question mark.

Yet shouldn't there be a gut memory? Shouldn't he feel at least an echo of what she was feeling? It hadn't been one-sided back in the summer of her sixteenth year.

"My name is Nick Hamilton..."

There was a pause, as though he had to regather his thoughts and concentrate them on his purpose for coming to her. Since it wasn't prompted by any memory of her—nerves tightened around Meredith's stomach—it had to be related to Kimberly. Had he found out Kimberly was his daughter? Had something happened to her? Was he the carrier of bad news from his sister?

"...I'm Denise Graham's brother," he stated, identifying the connection that gave him credentials for calling on her.

"Yes," Meredith repeated numbly, painfully aware of all the ramifications of that relationship. "You must have come about Kimberly. The packet..." She swallowed hard, a sickening wave of fear welling up over the emotional impact of seeing him again. ''...I should have got it over a fortnight ago.''

''So I understand,'' he said sympathetically. ''May I come in? There's a lot to explain.''

Meredith nodded, too choked up to speak. This man and his child had dominated the course of her life for thirteen years. To have him physically in front of her after all this time was both a dream and a nightmare. Her fingers fumbled over the chain slot. Her mind buzzed with the thought of letting him in...to far more than her apartment. And what of his child—her child—who had to be the reason he was here?

''Is Kimberly all right?'' The question burst from her as she shakily drew the door wide for him to enter.

''Yes. Couldn't be healthier,'' came the quick assurance. He stepped inside, pausing beside her as she sagged in relief. His brow creased in concern and he made an apologetic gesture. ''I'm sorry you were worried. Your daughter is fine, Miss Palmer.''

The acknowledgment that she had a daughter brought tears to her eyes. No one in her current life knew. It had always been a painfully private part of her, not easily shared. Who could understand? There'd been so many forces pushing her into letting her baby go—for the best, they'd all said—but sometimes the mourning for the child she could never hold in her arms was overwhelming.

''Thank you,'' she managed huskily.

Agitated by Nick Hamilton's nearness, his understanding and his sympathy, she waved him on to her living room and made a prolonged business of relocking the door. Being situated on the fourth floor of this apartment building gave her some protection against break-ins and burglaries but Meredith was always careful. A woman on her own had to be in the city. Though it was impossible to protect against everything. She had opened her door and the past had rushed in on her tonight. Impossible to know at this point, whether it was good or bad.

''Nice place you have here.''

The appreciative compliment strove to put this meeting on an ordinary footing. It almost provoked a hysterical laugh from Meredith. She took a deep breath, struggling to keep her wildly swinging emotions under control, then slowly turned to play gracious hostess to this gracious guest. Following a polite formula was probably the best way of coping with untenable dreams.

''Thank you,'' she said again, her voice steadier, more natural.

He stood mostly in profile, looking back at her from the end of the short hallway that led past the kitchenette to the living room. For a heart-catching moment she saw the twenty-two-year-old Nick Hamilton, as enraptured by her as she was by him, the air between them charged by a heightened awareness that excluded the rest of the world.

Her heart started to thump erratically. Stupid to think nothing had changed. He was still tall, dark and stunningly handsome, but his superb physique was now clothed in an executive-class suit, there were threads of silver in his glossy black hair, and the lines of his face had a mature set to them, harder, sharper, stronger. Life moved on. He was probably married. With other children.

She'd thought that thought a thousand times before, so why did it hurt like hell right now? Because he was here, she answered herself, and his eyes looked exactly the same as when he'd looked at her in the summertime of their youth, combining the slowly feasting sensuality of dark chocolate with the overlying shine of intense magnets, tugging on her soul.

But what was he seeing? She wasn't so young anymore, either, and she was suddenly acutely aware of her appearance. Her make-up was probably looking tired after the long day she'd put in at her office, mascara smudged under her eyes, lipstick faded to a pencilled outline. While her smooth olive skin didn't have blemishes to cover, the matt powder she used to reduce shine would have worn off.

Not exactly putting her best foot forward, she thought ruefully, and was instantly reminded she was standing in her stockinged feet, having kicked off her shoes when she'd come in. Not that it made much difference. She only ever wore little heels. Her legs were so long she always felt her tall, slim figure looked out of proportion in high heels. Nevertheless, the omission of shoes left her feeling even more ungroomed.

And her hair had to be adding to that impression. He'd once described it as strings of honeycomb and treacle—words of smiling whimsy. It was undoubtedly stringy tonight. It hadn't been brushed since this morning and it was so thick and fine it tended to look unkempt after a few hours, billowing out into a fuzzy cloud instead of a smooth curtain on either side of her long neck.

At least her dress would have retained its class. The silk linen chemise was mostly printed in a geometric pattern, black, white and sand, with stylish bands of each colour running around the lower half of the skirt. It was very much an adult, career-woman dress, she thought wryly, no shades of the teenager in skimpy beach wear. Life had moved on for her, too.

He broke out of his stillness, his shoulders visibly squaring, chin lifting in a dismissive jerk. "Forgive me for staring. It must be the likeness to Kimberly. The eyes. Same unusual shade of green. It feels...uncanny," he said in an awkward rush.

"I thought she was more like..." *You.*

The word teetered on her tongue. She barely bit

it back in time. Her heart somersaulted. Did he know? He wasn't supposed to know. Meredith had no idea what it would mean to his life if he did. She quickly shook her head, dismissing the subject.

"I would have remembered if I'd ever met you," he blurted out with emphatic certainty, his gaze skating over her, taking in the line and length of her, each finely drawn feature of her face. His brow puckered over the sense of recognition. "It has to be the eyes," he murmured more to himself than her.

No, it's all of me, Meredith silently cried, fiercely wishing she could say it.

He shot her a smile that dizzied her with its appealing charm. "I have to confess this situation is like none other I've ever been in. I'm not usually so gauche."

"Please…go on and sit down. Make yourself comfortable," she invited, forcing herself to move to the kitchen doorway. Easier to cover the strain of this meeting with social conventions. "Can I get you a drink? I've opened a bottle of white wine if you'd like a glass, but if you'd prefer tea or coffee…?"

He hesitated, then with an air of playing for time, asked, "Will you have some wine with me?"

"Yes." Why not? She wanted time with him, too, however futile and hurtful it might be.

He nodded. "Thank you."

She took the bottle from the refrigerator, glad to

have something to do. His presence had her nerves jangling. What did he want here? Why had he come?

He didn't sit down. He prowled around, glancing over the contents of her bookcases, taking in the twilight view of the ocean beyond Balmoral Beach from the picture windows behind her lounge suite, eyeing the floral arrangements she'd done for herself, matching them against her furnishings. She'd been pleased with their artistic simplicity. Was he impressed? she wondered. What was he gleaning from this detailed observation of her personal environment?

Strange to think she would never have become a florist but for being pregnant so young, having to drop out of school and being shuttled out of sight to her stepmother's sister in Sydney. Ironic how one thing had led to another, the unpaid apprenticeship in her stepaunt's shop giving her the interest and training to develop a talent she had eventually turned into a successful business.

"Do you share this apartment?" Nick Hamilton asked, tense and ill at ease with the question but asking it nonetheless.

"No," she replied. "It's all mine," she added with a touch of pride, knowing that the home she'd created here proved she was a woman of independent means.

She'd taken her time, selecting what she wanted to live with. The deeply cushioned, squashy leather sofa and chairs were cream so she could dress them up with the multicoloured tapestry cushions she'd stitched over many lonely nights. The wood of the bookshelves and desk was a blond ash, as were the sidetables and her small, four-chair dining suite. The carpet was a dusky pink mushroom.

She'd wanted everything soft and light, uplifting and cosy. It suited her. She fiercely told herself whatever he thought didn't matter. He'd dropped out of her life thirteen years ago and had no right to walk back into it and be critical of anything.

She pushed his glass of wine across the kitchen counter which was open to the living area. "Your drink."

"Thank you. You haven't married?" His eyes were sharply curious and calculating as he came toward her to pick up the wine.

The highly personal inquiry niggled Meredith. He'd spoiled her for any other man and she resented the implication she might have had a free ride on a husband's income. "No. I didn't get this place from a man, Mr. Hamilton," she answered tersely. "I've made my own way through a lot of hard work and a bit of luck. Did you achieve whatever you've got through a woman?"

In a way he had, his sister protecting him from even knowing about a responsibility he had incurred. He'd been left free to prosper in his chosen career instead of being saddled with a young wife and baby. Denise Graham had not only ensured he had every chance to succeed, she'd kept his child for him, too.

He looked abashed. ''I didn't mean to suggest…''

Resentment over his intrusion in her life now—far too late—brought a surge of impatience with his purpose. ''Just why are you checking me out?'' she demanded bluntly. ''What answers are you looking for?''

He grimaced at her directness. ''I guess you could say we're both faced with a highly delicate situation. I'm trying to ascertain what your attitude might be toward a meeting with Kimberly. Whether it would intrude negatively on the life you have now.''

Her mind reeled at the incredible import of what he was saying. A meeting with her daughter? She'd barely dared to hope for it some time in the future when Kimberly was old enough to be her own person. How could this be when she was only twelve?

''Your sister will allow it?'' Her throat had gone so dry her voice was a raw croak. Her eyes clung to his in a torment of doubt.

''My sister and her husband were killed in a car accident a year ago. Just before Christmas,'' he stated quietly. ''Kimberly has been in my care ever since.''

Shock rolled through her in mind-blowing, heart-wrenching waves. Denise and Colin Graham dead. Since before Christmas last year. And all this time she'd been thinking of them, picturing them going about their lives in their family unit, enjoying all she couldn't enjoy with their daughter. A year! Her daughter had been without a mother, without her adoptive parents, for a whole year!

"I was appointed her legal guardian," Nick Hamilton went on, apparently still unaware he was Kimberly's natural father. His gaze seemed to tunnel into her mind as he added, "I didn't know about you. Didn't know there was any contact between you and my sister."

Meredith closed her eyes. She couldn't bear his non-knowledge of her. And death could have sealed those secret, intimate links forever. It made her sick to think of it.

"Only today did I get your address from the solicitor." His voice strained now, strained with all he didn't know and the fear of the unknown. "He didn't want to give it to me. He argued that Denise's death closed the personal connection between the two of you. He advised against my picking it up."

Fear of the consequences...dear God! The roads that had been travelled to this point! And he was afraid of letting her in to their lives!

"Why did you?" she asked faintly, trying to suppress the bitterness of having no legal rights. Even when the adoptive parents were dead, she couldn't make a claim on her own child.

"For Kimberly. She wants..."

Meredith lifted her lashes enough to see his grimace. He didn't like this. Didn't want it. He'd come against the solicitor's advice, against his own better judgment. His chest rose and fell as he expelled a long, ragged sigh.

"She wants...her *real* mother...for Christmas," he finished flatly.

For Christmas.

Only for Christmas.

A limited encounter...just like with her father. Limited...time out of time to cherish...treasure...haunt. The pain of the limitation sucked the blood from her brain. She clutched at the kitchen counter but couldn't summon the strength to hold on as she slid into dark oblivion.

CHAPTER THREE

NICK picked her up from the kitchen floor and cradled her against his chest. A pins and needles sensation attacked his whole body. It wasn't the effort of carrying her weight. She was not a big woman despite her above-average height. It was the way she seemed to nestle in his arms, her head dropping onto his shoulder as though it belonged there, her long hair flowing across his throat, skeins of silk somehow entangling him with feelings his brain couldn't compute at all. They didn't make sense. At least...not a sense he was ready to acknowledge.

It was too crazy...too beyond rational explanation. He hadn't met her before. He knew he hadn't. Her eyes being the same as Kimberly's was not the answer, either. Kimberly was a child. Meredith Palmer was a woman. How did a woman he didn't know get to walk through his dreams? And to have her materialise in front of him...real flesh and blood...every line of her hauntingly familiar to him... Nick was hopelessly distracted from establishing what he'd come here to do.

He should have approached the salient facts more obliquely, been more sensitive to their impact on her. It was obvious she'd been stressed at not receiving the packet from Denise and his appearance on the scene must have agitated her further despite the reassurance he'd tried to give. Here she was in a dead faint, all because he'd responded without giving enough thought to how it would affect her, and he was still caught up in how she affected him!

Instead of standing in her kitchen like a dumb ox, holding her in his own personal daze, he should be doing something constructive about bringing her back to consciousness. He forced his mind to focus on practicalities.

The sofa in her living room was only a two-seater, not large enough to lay her out comfortably. Bedroom and bathroom had to be nearby. A door stood slightly ajar near one of the bookcases. He carried her to it and manoeuvred her into what proved to be her bedroom.

She was beginning to stir as he lowered her onto the bed, her head rolling restlessly, as though in blind search of something lost. A low moan of longing or some deep inner torment issued from her throat and tugged at his heart. He grasped her hand, his fingers curling tightly around hers, pressing his warmth and strength, wanting to impart she was not alone.

Thinking he should probably get her a glass of water, he glanced around, looking for a door into an ensuite bathroom. And shock hit him again.

The walls were covered with photographs of Kimberly!

Montages of each year of his niece's life hung in frames, interspersed with blow-ups of what were particularly good shots of her, capturing a highly expressive look that seemed to bring her personality stunningly, vibrantly alive in this room.

It was eerie, seeing Kimberly in such close focus from babyhood onward. Nick had seen most of the photographs before at various times, but never in this kind of concentration. The collection, so overwhelmingly displayed, suddenly seemed to smack of unhealthy obsessiveness.

Kimberly's plea...*if my real mother wants me*...became an absurd understatement in the face of so much visual evidence of *wanting*. Nick's head buzzed with a confusion of moral and legal rights. Kimberly was family to him, yet how much more was she to this woman who had given her birth? What if Kimberly's desire to meet her was capricious? What was he setting in motion here?

The warning given by Hector Burnside, Denise's old solicitor, started ringing in Nick's ears. *Leave well enough alone. You don't know what you might be walking into. It could be dangerous ground.*

Maybe he should have heeded the advice of a man who had seen all sides of human nature in his line of work. Nick shook his head over the dilemma he now found himself in. He'd promised Kimberly an answer from her real mother. In choosing to follow that course, he wasn't sure if he'd stepped into a dream or a nightmare. Either way, it was too late to walk out of it.

CHAPTER FOUR

HE WAS holding her hand.

The physical link generated a flood of warm feeling that drove away the chilling fear of the unknown and soothed the whirling chaos in her mind. She hadn't died and moved on to where impossible things were possible. She wasn't dreaming. Nick Hamilton's hand pressed solid substance in a world that had shifted too fast for Meredith to retain a grip on it herself.

The initial confusion of finding herself on her bed, with him sitting beside her, quickly cleared as she remembered what had gone before. "I must have fainted," she croaked in surprise.

Her voice startled him out of the private reverie he'd fallen into. His head jerked around to face her. His eyes had a dazed look. "Yes," he said, his focus sharpening. "You still look pale. Would you like a drink of water?"

She started to prop herself up on her elbow. The room reeled. She fell back on the pillows, hopelessly dizzy. "Yes, please. It might help." She closed her eyes, fighting a wave of nausea. "Sorry…"

33

"My fault." His weight shifted off the bed. "Be right back."

A combination of shock with too much wine on an empty stomach, Meredith reasoned, wishing she'd had the sense to eat properly. She didn't want Nick Hamilton thinking she was sickly and unable to cope with difficult situations. He might think better of her meeting Kimberly for even a short time.

The longing to see her daughter in the flesh rose so strongly, it overrode every other consideration. To actually see her, watch her in action, listen to her, hear how she felt about so many things...it would be worth any amount of heartache.

Fearing that the opening Nick Hamilton had offered might be withdrawn if his impression of her was negative, Meredith swung her legs off the bed and bent her head down to her knees, determined on regaining her equilibrium. By the time he returned with a glass of water, she had steadied enough to drink it.

The weight of liquid helped settle her stomach. As she put the emptied glass on the bedside table, she glanced up to thank him, only to find he wasn't watching her. He was staring at the photographs on the wall and the grim set to his face did not reflect any pleasure in them.

Her heart sank as she realised what an overwhelming effect the display might have on someone who hadn't seen it, who didn't live with it. She didn't expect others to understand her need for these all too few windows on the life of her lost child and she instinctively recoiled from having that deeply driven maternal need exposed.

"I didn't invite you in here. I don't invite anyone in here," she burst out defensively.

The look he turned on her was so wary it made Meredith feel frantic. Was he in retreat from her? She made a floundering gesture at the photographs.

"I mean all this…it's private," she cried, desperate to win a sympathetic hearing. "You probably take Kimberly and everything about her for granted, having her around you all the time. This is the only way I have of seeing my child grow up."

He shook his head, an appalled expression in his eyes, as though, until this moment, he hadn't begun to comprehend the immense loss she'd borne since Kimberly's birth.

"I gave her up because I thought it best for her. That doesn't mean I love her any less," Meredith asserted with vehement passion, trying to appeal to his sense of fairness.

"I'm sorry," he said gruffly. "I had no idea…no appreciation of…" He gestured apologetically. "I beg your pardon for not being more…prepared."

The father of her child, appearing out of nowhere to suddenly hold out the chance of a reunion—more of a reunion than he knew—how could he have any idea what it meant to her? She ached all over just looking at him, having him near, bringing back the memories of her double grief.

He backed off a step, his face creased in pained concern. "I didn't mean to invade your privacy by bringing you in here. It was only to help. If you'd prefer to recover alone now…"

Anxiety sank its claws in. Was he seizing an opportunity to escape from a situation he was finding too fraught with emotion? Had she just ruined the one chance she might ever have of meeting her daughter? The last thing she wanted was to drive him away. So much was hanging in the balance. She sought frantically for ways to plead her cause and all she could come up with was to beg a stay of judgment.

"Please don't go. I won't collapse on you again."

An aeon seemed to pass as his eyes bored into hers, searching, sifting, undecided as to what was right or wrong. His tension made hers worse. Every nerve in her body was strung tight, willing him to stay and talk until a more favourable position was reached.

"I'll wait in the living room," he said, clearly discomforted by the walls of photographs, the stark evidence of deprived motherhood and the over-charged atmosphere that had risen from its confrontation.

An intense wash of relief brought a hot flow of blood to Meredith's cheeks. Hopefully it gave them a healthy-looking flush. "I'll come with you," she rushed out, afraid to let him out of her sight in case he had second thoughts. "It's food I need. Once I've had something solid to eat I'm sure I'll feel much better."

She quickly pushed up from the bed, swaying slightly before finding her balance. He was beside her in an instant, ready to lend his support. Her eyes pleaded for belief as she assured him, "I'm not usually fragile."

"Take my arm." It was a firm command. "I'll see you seated on your sofa. Then you can tell me what to do in your kitchen to assemble a meal for you."

"I can manage," she protested, intent on proving it.

"So can I," he insisted, intent on taking control.

The need to show independent strength suddenly lost its importance. If she kept him busy with her now, she gained the time to impress him as a responsible person whom he could trust to act both sensibly and sensitively when it came to a meeting with Kimberly. It had to come to that. Had to.

She hooked her arm around his and felt his muscles harden as her hand slid over them. It made her feel skittish, uncertain if he was inwardly recoiling from her touch or reacting to it in the way he once had. Though it was madness to think of that now when so much else was at stake. Besides, the quickly sparked desires of youth hardly fitted into this picture.

Nevertheless, she couldn't help being extremely

aware of him as he matched his steps to hers in their walk to the living room. Her upper arm was tucked against the warm wall of his chest and their hips and thighs brushed, arousing little shivers of sensitivity that sharply reminded her of how intimate they had once been.

Breathing in his aftershave lotion—surely the same tangy scent he'd used then—tickled her nostrils, evoking the memory of how he'd brought all her senses incredibly alive that summer. Every smell had seemed exotic, every colour brighter, every sound magnified, every taste heightened, every touch…Meredith fiercely clamped down on that line of thought. It was stirring feelings she couldn't afford.

It was a relief when Nick Hamilton deposited her on the sofa and dropped all physical contact with her. He took off so briskly for the kitchen, Meredith suspected it was a relief for him to have some distance between them, too, though his reasons were undoubtedly different. Getting on with the business he'd come about would be very much on his mind.

She watched him taking inventory of the contents of her refrigerator and called, ''A sandwich will do. There's bread in the fridge.''

Decisive and efficient in his movements, he set out a loaf of bread, butter, a packet of sliced cheese and tomatoes, then switched on the griller at the top of the stove. He was certainly kitchen trained,

Meredith thought, and wondered how much he fended for himself. Was he married?

However pertinent the question was in the circumstances, Meredith shied away from it, reluctant to picture him with a wife. Then she remembered the misery of trying to get along with her stepmother and wondered if Kimberly was suffering the same problem, having lost the parents who had brought her up and then been landed on a woman who had no deep caring for her, a woman who was only there because she was attached to Nick Hamilton.

Meredith knew from first-hand experience how unwanted a girl of Kimberly's age could feel, given such a situation. And it stood to reason that something had to be prompting the desire to meet her real mother. It also stood to reason that a man as attractive as Nick Hamilton would not be without a woman.

Another question sprang to mind. How did Kimberly know about her? Surely it would be uncharacteristic of Denise Graham to reveal anything about Kimberly's *real* mother to the child she was bringing up as her own daughter. It struck Meredith that Nick Hamilton might have more to answer for than he'd like to admit.

"How long has Kimberly known she was adopted?" she asked, feeling the knowledge had to have come after the death of her adoptive parents.

"She found out a week before the car accident that killed Denise and Colin," he answered flatly.

Found out? Dear Heaven! Had the resulting upset contributed to the accident?

Nick Hamilton's dark gaze lifted briefly from the bread he was buttering, a heavy sadness dulling his eyes. "Apparently Denise was sorting through photographs and discussing with Colin which ones to send to you. Kimberly overheard them and pieced the information together." He frowned. "She has a bad habit of eavesdropping. Perhaps being an only child...no sibling to talk to..."

"Did she confront them with it?" Meredith broke in anxiously, imagining the guilt her daughter might feel if there'd been arguments.

He shook his head. "She wanted to think about it. Work out what it meant to her."

A lot of inner turmoil there, Meredith thought, though it was a relief to learn there had been no open conflict for which Kimberly might blame herself.

"Then her world came crashing down," Nick Hamilton continued, "and there were so many changes for her to take on, I guess she clung to what was safely familiar rather than pursue what probably seemed like an intangible dream."

"So *you* didn't talk to her about it?"

"I thought it better not to. She had enough trauma losing one set of parents, let alone two." He grimaced. ''She kept it to herself until a few days ago.''

Holding such a big secret all that time…holding it in reserve, Meredith thought, and wondered how often her daughter might have fantasised about another life as she tried living with the man who had been legally appointed her guardian, a man who was only an uncle by adoption. Or did Kimberly instinctively feel more closely bonded to him…her *real* father?

Was there an innate tie of blood, whether it was known or not? Would her daughter feel she was a total stranger or would there be an instant, intuitive link between them? The need to know pounded through Meredith, bringing a wave of excitement, of almost unbearable anticipation. It was difficult to contain it but she sternly told herself she had to while a meeting was still not settled.

She watched the only man she had ever loved place the sandwiches he was intent on toasting under the griller and tried to imagine what he was feeling about Kimberly's request, coming virtually out of nowhere. He would not have been *prepared* for that, either. But Nick Hamilton was no dodger of delicate issues. He faced them and dealt with them according to his sense of rightness. It was that very quality of character Meredith had implicitly believed in when she had found herself pregnant.

''You think a rich college boy is going to stand by you?'' her stepmother had mocked. ''He skipped out fast enough when I told him your age. A guy like that doesn't want to be shackled to a sixteen-year-old country girl who was no more than a Christmas vacation fling to him.''

He hadn't *skipped out*. Meredith hadn't thought it then and she didn't think it now.

It had shocked him when her stepmother had confronted him with how young she was. Meredith had let him assume she was older, knowing she could easily pass for nineteen and desperately wanting to go with him wherever he wanted to take her. She'd argued to herself that love had nothing to do with age.

But Nick had faced the issues squarely and laid them out to her. She still had two more years of school plus tertiary education after that, if she wanted it. There was so much more for her to do and experience and think about before tying herself to anyone or anything. She should be free to make the choices that would best suit her. The love they felt for each other could be recaptured when she was older. He didn't feel right about taking up her life while she still had so much in front of her.

He had given her his address and suggested they send each other Christmas cards if they both wanted to keep the connection going. No commitment. But there was no harm in maintaining a friendly communication once a year. When she was twenty-one…

''Isn't eighteen old enough?'' she'd protested,

devastated at the thought of waiting so many years before they could be lovers again.

"It wouldn't be fair," he'd answered ruefully. "Any more than it would be fair of me to stay on here, Merry. The more deeply we get involved the harder it will be to part."

He'd gone that very day, the day after her stepmother had discovered them making love on the back veranda and created such an ugly scene, accusing Nick of taking advantage of a girl who was barely past being a minor. Despite his shock, Nick hadn't allowed her stepmother to turn what had been beautiful into something low and dirty. And though he had left her, it wasn't without the promise of a future for them...if their love held true. Giving her his address was proof of his good faith. He wouldn't have done that if he was *skipping out* on her.

Meredith had known her pregnancy would come as another shock to him. He'd taken precautions every time they'd made love. How they'd failed she didn't know but she'd had no doubt Nick would stand by her. He was kind and caring and responsible and honourable. She couldn't imagine him letting her down.

It hurt, even now, thinking back to the Christmas after the birth of their baby. Secretly, she'd been so sure a Christmas card would come from him. Even though he was overseas in America, he would think of her and write and then she'd have a contact address and be able to write back, telling him what had happened. She had dreamed of him flying home and reclaiming their child from his sister. They'd be married and…but no Christmas card had come from him.

The only communication had been the first promised packet of photographs from his sister.

So had begun the painful process of accepting that Denise Graham had told the truth about his losing all memory of the time they'd spent together. Or that Nick had put her out of his life. Either way, it was too late to change her mind about giving up her baby daughter. That decision was irrevocable.

But some dreams refused to die. A year later she'd succumbed to the temptation of going to the address Nick had given her, the Grahams' address, hoping to see him since his two years in the U.S. were up, wanting the chance to know for certain how matters stood between them. The Grahams had moved. None of their neighbours knew where they'd gone. The one avenue she'd had to him was closed.

She'd told herself to get on with her life, and she had, but for a long, long time the dream had persisted that he would turn up one day and make everything right again. And here he was, but with no memory of her, and trying to make things right for the child he thought of as his niece.

He emerged from the kitchen, carrying a plate of toasted sandwiches, and Meredith steeled herself to keep a calm composure, determined on convincing him she would do what was best for Kimberly, the welfare and happiness of her daughter being her first consideration. But she couldn't stop her eyes from wandering over him, nor could she quell the wish for some sign of the love they had once shared.

Her pulse quickened with each step he took toward her. As he bent to set the plate on the coffee table in front of her, her eyes feasted on his face, admiring the long thick sweep of his eyelashes— their daughter had inherited them—and retracing the sensual contours of his mouth, remembering the explosive passion of his kisses. Her muscles clenched, wanting the release he had once given them, and Meredith savagely berated herself for being unable to suppress the desires he stirred.

"Are you married?" she asked, driven to know if he was out of bounds to her. If he was, maybe she could put this intense distraction aside and concentrate solely on establishing time with Kimberly.

"No." He flashed a sharp look at her before moving to settle in the armchair on the other side of the table.

Meredith struggled to maintain a natural air of inquiry. That one brief word eased the terrible tightness in her chest. It was like a song of hope in her ears. For a moment or two her mind danced with wonderful possibilities. Then the realities of today's

world crashed in, reminding her of the common-
place arrangements that didn't require marriage.

"Do you live with...with a partner?" She
couldn't bring herself to say *lover*.

"No." He sat facing her, watching her, and
Meredith could only hope he couldn't see she was
giddy with relief. His expression was carefully
schooled to give nothing of his thoughts away as
he slowly added, "I employ a woman to come in
weekdays and be there after school hours. She also
looks after Kimberly whenever I'm out in the evening. She's with her now. They get on quite well."

He was assuring her his guardianship was not at
fault. A smile burst across her face. "That's good,"
she said, wildly understating what she really felt.

He stared at her so long the smile stiffened and
faded as self-consciousness swept in, along with the
worry she had overstepped some line he'd drawn
in his mind.

"Eat," he commanded.

She quickly pounced on a toasted triangle, glad
to have something to do until he showed more of
his hand. Never had she enjoyed the taste of melted
cheese on tomato so much. It was as though her
whole body zinged with a new appreciation of life
and a greed for all it could offer.

Nick Hamilton was with her again.

He had their daughter in his safekeeping.

And he wasn't tied to any other woman.

CHAPTER FIVE

NICK couldn't get her smile out of his head, her face lighting up like a Christmas tree, jolting him anew with the sense of recognition. He didn't believe in all that New Age stuff about having known each other in previous lives. He had no answer for what he was feeling and it was bugging the hell out of him. Even the touch of her made him jangle with the tension of hormones running riot, body chemistry leaping out of control.

He watched her eat the toasted sandwiches he'd made, brooding over why this woman—this stranger—should affect him so strongly. On the surface she was no more attractive than Rachel. In strictly physical terms, she was slimmer, not as curvy, not as pretty. Yet more striking, more…electric somehow.

He was finding this encounter so damned disturbing he wished it was at an end. In fact, there was no reason to prolong it since there seemed to be no serious impediment to the meeting with Kimberly.

Only God knew where that would end. It was impossible for him to judge.

All he knew was Kimberly was not about to let it rest until it happened and he didn't feel right about keeping them apart. Let the pieces fall however they would, he thought, glumly acknowledging that the outcome would most probably be out of his control, as well.

"Would lunch this Saturday suit you?" he asked.

Another smile. It had the kick of a mule.

"Any day at all. Any time," she answered eagerly.

He frowned. It sounded too carefree. "Don't you work?"

"I run my own business. I can arrange my time as I like," came the ready reply. A touch of pride, as well.

"What do you do?" Kimberly would want to know and his own curiosity was piqued.

"I have contracts with hotels and restaurants to supply their floral arrangements. My company name is *Flower Power*."

Impressive. He glanced at the clever piece of floral art on the coffee table. He'd admired it earlier...just three perfect blooms at different heights set in an interesting variety of leaves...very simple yet very pleasing to the eye. "Your work?"

"Yes. Do you like it?"

He nodded. "A fine dramatic touch. Did you study art?"

She looked pleased. "No. All hands-on experience."

"Probably the best teacher anyway," he conceded, warming to her warmth. "Though you must have an innate talent for it."

"I enjoy the work." Her mesmerisingly familiar green eyes sparkled with delight. "Flowers give so much pleasure and they can light up a room."

You can, too, he thought, wondering if there was a man in her life. She didn't have a husband or a live-in lover but that didn't mean she wasn't attached to someone. As he was, to Rachel. To Nick's further confusion, something in him strongly wanted to reject both their involvements with other people, no matter how well-founded they were. Again, the irrational nature of the feeling prompted him to finish up here as fast as he could.

She'd eaten the sandwiches and appeared to have fully recovered from the faint. He could leave with an easy conscience. "Do you know the Harbour Restaurant underneath the opera house?"

"Yes."

They could sit out on the open deck under an umbrella, he decided. The pleasant venue with the wide view of the harbour and the passing parade of people should provide a relaxed atmosphere, if anything about this first mother-daughter meeting could be relaxed.

"I'll book a table for twelve o'clock." He stood

up, softening his leave-taking with a rueful smile. ''I doubt Kimberly will be able to wait to a later time. And I mustn't keep her waiting any longer now. She won't go to bed until I return with news of you.''

''Of course. I hope…'' She flushed as she rose quickly from the sofa to see him out. Her eyes filled with an eloquent appeal that tunneled straight into his gut. ''Please tell her I'm looking forward enormously to our meeting.''

Compassion forced him to a kindly warning. ''Don't bank too much on it, Miss Palmer. Kimberly's a good kid at heart but she's a bit mixed up about future direction at the moment. She'll be starting high school next year and choosing what school has become an issue. You seem to have become part of that issue. She *is* only twelve. I don't think she comprehends…the larger picture.''

Meredith Palmer drew a deep breath and sighed in wry resignation. ''Whatever happens, at least I'll have a little while with her. Thank you for allowing it, Mr. Hamilton. I'm very grateful to you.''

Any crumb from the table was better than nothing.

That depressing thought stayed with him as he drove away. It was wrong for so little to mean so much. The walls of photographs in her bedroom kept flashing through his mind. He'd never given any consideration to the effect on a woman who gave up her baby for adoption. It had to be traumatic...a wound that never healed.

He wondered what forces had played a part in Meredith Palmer's decision, whether she'd been in her right mind at the time or pressured beyond bearing into a sacrifice she had regretted ever since. Had her family been straitlaced, shamed by their daughter falling pregnant, denying her the chance of keeping her baby by withholding support?

She must have been very young. It was difficult to tell a woman's age but Meredith Palmer looked to be only in her twenties now. At fourteen or fifteen, possibly suffering post-natal depression, a baby must have seemed an overwhelming responsibility, the problem of coping properly with it insurmountable if her family wasn't prepared to help.

I gave her up because I thought it best for her.

Such sad, hopeless words.

He should have asked what connection there'd been to his sister for the private adoption to be arranged. He must remember to do that. He wanted to know.

Until Kimberly had told him about the photographs and he'd subsequently tackled Denise's old solicitor about them, he had assumed the adoption had taken place through normal channels. Denise and Colin had talked often of having applied to the government agency. Their names had been on a waiting list. When they'd written to him in the

States to tell him of their new baby he had simply thought the wait had ended. They had not enlightened him otherwise.

Why the secret?

Why the photographs?

Some kind of guilt on his sister's part?

In the face of Meredith Palmer's yearning for her child, he felt guilty himself for having her in his keeping. Yet Kimberly was his family and had been all her life. He'd always had a soft spot for her. He strongly recoiled from the idea of giving her up...even to go to her real mother.

Perhaps a sharing arrangement could be made.

That, of course, would depend on how the meeting turned out. At this point he couldn't predict how Kimberly would react to it. He didn't know what she was secretly expecting or wanting, beyond satisfying the need to see.

She fell upon him the moment he entered his apartment. "What's she like? Is she pretty? Does she want to see me? Did you set up a meeting?"

"Yes to the last three questions. Now please hold on a moment!" he commanded, pulling her hyperactive body back off him and setting her a pace away.

She radiated excitement, hands waving like a baby, ponytail swinging, her face aglow with wildly impatient anticipation, her glittering green eyes— Meredith Palmer's eyes—stabbing into him, desperately eager for information. "Don't be a stodge, Uncle Nick! I'm dying to know all about her."

"Let me pay Mrs. Armstrong first, Kimberly." He turned to the woman who was packing up her knitting, ready to leave. "Any calls, Fran?"

"Only the one, from Rachel Pearce. She asked if you'd return it tonight at your convenience." Having gathered up her belongings, she headed toward them and the front door, a smile of caring concern sweeping them both. "I do hope this business with Kimberly's mother turns out well. It doesn't always, you know. I've read so many stories in magazines…"

"I guess life is about taking chances, Fran," Nick cut in, his smile appealing for no negative comment. It served no good purpose at this point.

She nodded, an obliging soul, always prepared to ride along with what he wanted. A widow in her fifties, her children had grown up and flown the home nest, leaving her with no role to play until they gave her grandchildren. Her hair was unashamedly grey, permed tightly for tidiness, her face and figure pleasantly plump, her clothes matronly, and she knitted soft toys interminably. She dearly wanted to be a doting grandmother. Looking after Kimberly helped to fill that hole in her life and Nick was grateful she was so good at it.

He added a tip to the usual fee.

"You are a good man," she said warmly. "I'll

see you tomorrow, Kimberly. Don't be dancing around all night, there's a dear girl. You need your sleep.''

"Good night, Mrs. Armstrong. Thanks for being here. I'll settle down after I dig everything out of Uncle Nick,'' Kimberly promised breezily.

Dig was the operative word. She attacked again the moment the door closed behind her minder, bubbling around him with avid curiosity. Feeling in need of a stiff drink, Nick moved across the dining area to the liquor cabinet as he answered the first burst of questions, trying to give the detail Kimberly demanded. He opened a bottle of port and poured a generous measure into a glass. The fortified liquor seemed highly appropriate for these circumstances.

He carried it over to the lounge, finding himself sweeping a critical gaze over the furnishings he'd lived with for years; black leather upholstery on both dining and lounge suites, glass tables, blue-grey carpet, black fixtures for the television and hi-fi system, a few sculptured pieces he'd fancied, some provocative modern paintings he didn't really look at anymore.

He'd liked her living room. More warmth. More individual, personal touches like the colourful, hand-stitched cushions and the flowers and the books…the sense of it all being an integral part of her. Then the intensely private, secret life in the bedroom revealing the deeper side of her, not shown to anyone. He shouldn't have seen it, but he had, and now he couldn't forget it.

He sank onto one of the sofas and made himself comfortable for the important task of instructing his niece on what would be acceptable behaviour with her *real* mother. Kimberly sprawled on the sofa opposite his and kept prodding and prying, extracting all the information he was prepared to give on Meredith Palmer, then fell into musing on what she should wear on Saturday, keen to make a positive impression on the woman who had given her birth. Nick mentally girded his loins and plunged in to the more sensitive aspect of the meeting.

"I appreciate you find this very exciting, Kimberly," he said quietly, "but you must understand it is strictly a getting-to-know-you meeting on Saturday. Don't turn it into a battleground, playing Miss Palmer against me..."

"I wouldn't do that, Uncle Nick," she cried earnestly.

"...Or against Rachel."

She flushed, her eyes wavering from his.

"You'll be meeting a person with highly sensitive feelings about having given up her child," he went on gravely. "It would be wrong to embroil her in an argument about a school. Don't make her feel you're using her, Kimberly."

Discomfort on that point clearly showed as she

plucked at one of the blue decorator cushions on the sofa. Then her gaze flashed up in belligerent challenge. "Wouldn't she care how I feel about it?"

"Yes. She'd care. And you would make her feel unhappy and helpless because she has no say in it. She lost her right to have any say in your life when she agreed to your adoption."

"But that's not fair!" she burst out. "She's my real mother."

"Do you want to know her...or do you want to use her, Kimberly?" he bored in.

She gestured an agitated protest. "Of course I want to *know* her..."

But she had been nursing other items on her agenda.

Nick followed up relentlessly. "I would hope you wouldn't be so petty or so mean and selfish as to complain about your personal problems when meeting you is the fulfilment of a dream to her."

"A dream?"

"She had the photographs to build a dream of you, Kimberly. I'd like her to feel proud of the person you are now. If nothing else, you owe it to the mother who loved and cared for you since you were a baby to show she did a good job of bringing you up."

Her face puckered. "Mum wouldn't mind me meeting her, would she, Uncle Nick? I mean, she did send the photographs so she must have wanted her to see how I was growing up.''

"I think this meeting would have her blessing, Kimberly, but I also think she'd like it best if Miss Palmer met you and thought she couldn't have done a better job of teaching you good manners and being nice to people. You know your Mum set a lot of store by that.''

Tears glittered in her eyes. "I'll be good, Uncle Nick.'' She came off her sofa in a rush and landed on his lap, her arms flung around his neck and her head nestling on his shoulder. "I'll make Mum real proud of me. I promise,'' she whispered huskily.

He hugged her and rubbed his cheek over her hair, loving the child she still was and deeply moved by her uninhibited affection. She belonged with him. She was the only family he had left. Yet he knew every time he looked at her now he would be reminded of Meredith Palmer and her enduring love for the child she had given up. He felt caught in a hopeless quandary.

"I think your real mother will think you're wonderful,'' he murmured. "The best Christmas present she's ever had.''

A deep sigh. "I want her to like me.''

"I'm sure she will.'' He dropped a kiss on her temple. "Best off to bed now, Kimberly. Sweet dreams.''

"Good night, Uncle Nick. And thanks for everything.'' She pecked his cheek and was off, pausing at the hall to the bedrooms to say, ''I've dreamed about her, too. My real mother, I mean. Ever since I knew I was adopted I've been dreaming about her.''

She didn't wait for a reply. It was simply confiding the truth to him. Nick was left thinking of his own dreams, wondering how his subconscious had conjured up the image of Meredith Palmer. Perhaps he'd seen a photograph of her. If his sister had known her she might have had a photograph.

But why didn't he remember it? And why of all the women in the photographs his sister had taken over decades, had *she* become a dream-woman to him…a figure that called to him yet remained tantalisingly out of reach.

He'd figured it was symbolic of his disappointment in being unable to strike a soul mate amongst the women he'd met and dated. Symbolic also of a need to believe there was someone still out there for him, and if only he persisted long enough he would find her.

But for the fantasy figure to match up to someone in real life… Nick clenched his teeth. He was not going to consider supernatural stuff. The coincidence had to have a rational explanation. And the effect Meredith Palmer was having on him…that was mixed up with her matching a dream. Naturally, something so unexpected triggered confusion. The power of her impact would be much less when they met again on Saturday.

Determinedly pushing aside her lingering influence on him, Nick pushed up from the sofa and went into the kitchen to call Rachel. It was almost eleven o'clock but he knew Rachel rarely went to bed before midnight. Besides, she'd asked for him to call and talking to her might restore his sanity.

When her voice came over the line, he was vexed to find himself comparing the bright, brisk, matter-of-fact tone to Meredith Palmer's softer lilt. "It's Nick," he said quickly.

"Dear Nick, I'm so glad you got back to me." An injection of warmth that should have lightened his mood, but didn't. "I have an invite to Christmas cocktails on Harvey Sinclair's yacht. Saturday evening. Six o'clock start. Want to partner me?"

Harvey Sinclair was a big fish in the financial world. Rachel was bound to be eager to go. Good contacts would abound at such a party. Normally Nick would have given an automatic yes, but he found himself hesitating, looking for a way out of it.

"I'd rather not," he said honestly. "Can you find someone else to go with?"

A pause, her shrewd mind sifting signals. "Some problem, Nick?"

He sighed over his own unease. "I've set up a meeting between Kimberly and her real mother on

Saturday. I don't know how it will turn out, Rachel.''

''And you want to stick around. Understandable, Nick. Tricky business.''

''Very.'' He appreciated her quick grasp of the situation. He rarely had to explain much to Rachel. It made conversation flow so easily.

''Not to worry,'' she assured him without a trace of feeling put out. ''I don't mind going by myself. I intended to circulate anyway. I'll tell you all about it when next we get together.''

''I'll look forward to it.''

''I hope the meeting…well, I hope it helps Kimberly.''

''Thanks for your caring, Rachel. I'm sorry about her attitude toward you. I wish…''

''Hey! She's had a lot on her mind. Maybe she'll give me a break when some of it's been lifted.''

He smiled at her ready good humour. ''Well, have a good time Saturday night. I'll see you soon.''

It was a comfortable note on which to end the call, causing Nick to reflect that his relationship with Rachel was comfortable. It was effortlessly companionable, easy, undemanding.

What it lacked was passion.

The thought struck Nick forcefully and stayed with him long after he'd gone to bed. Rachel was always reasonable. So was he. Two eminently reasonable human beings, feeling no great highs but no great lows, either. Safe.

Passion was a roller-coaster, an explosive force, a whirlwind, and he suddenly knew that was what Meredith Palmer represented, what he'd felt caught up in while he was with her...passion in all its range and dimensions.

It was pervasively disturbing.

And intensely alluring.

CHAPTER SIX

MEREDITH strolled slowly along the wide promenade that edged Circular Quay, filling in time since she was far too early for the lunch appointment with Kimberly and Nick Hamilton. If she'd stayed any longer in her apartment she would have undoubtedly changed clothes again, succumbing to the frenzy of anxiety that had forced her into four different outfits, dithering over what would be most appropriate and appealing for this critical meeting with her daughter.

She had tried to think what a twelve-year-old girl might want her mother to look like; smart and classy, soft and feminine, casual and approachable, bright and boldly chic…there were so many looks one might present. She'd swung through the lot; dress, suit, jazzy separates, tailored slacks, jeans. What she had finally chosen was probably too formal but at least she always felt good in it.

The colour suited her—a lemon-yellow floral print on white pique cotton. The short-sleeved, figure-hugging jacket had a wide, white collar with dramatic lapels, setting off her long neck and providing a sharp contrast to the dark blond fall of her hair. The narrow skirt was a trendy length, ending just above her knees. Low-heeled lemon-yellow shoes and a matching handbag added the fashion touch that lifted the outfit into top class. It had invariably drawn compliments.

The plain truth was, Meredith admitted to herself, vanity had won out in the end. She wanted Kimberly to feel proud of her mother. And however foolish it might be, she wanted Nick Hamilton to take a second look at her...a long second look.

Although she knew next to nothing about him now—how his character had developed over the years or what turns his life had taken—the long-cherished memories of their young love had resurfaced, tantalising her with possibilities that kept burrowing into her heart. Some dreams didn't die easily. Not even in the bright light of day.

It couldn't be brighter than it was at the moment, she thought with wry humour. The sparkling waters of the harbour reflected the clear blue of a cloudless summer sky. Sunshine glittered off the tiled roofs of the opera house, accentuating the effect of sails billowed to full stretch. Boats and ferries left a wake of frothy waves, trails of brilliant white bubbles. It was the kind of day that made people feel it was great to be alive.

Happy tourists were out en masse, a river of colour streaming around her. Christmas was everywhere; gaudy and glorious decorations, street-sellers pressing their wares as gifts, Santa Claus greeting children. Buskers provided entertainment, well-loved carols being the obvious favourite. Gaiety and goodwill were in the air and Meredith no longer cared that Kimberly had only asked to see her for Christmas. It was a start...and who knew where it would finish?

She skirted groups posing for photographs against the background of the huge coathanger bridge that spanned the harbour. So many smiling faces. They made her smile, too, lifting her spirits. Anything was possible.

Although Nick Hamilton didn't remember it, today was the anniversary of when they'd first met, thirteen years ago. If he could only see her with the same eyes as then, the magical connection could happen again, couldn't it?

It was still ten minutes short of noon when she arrived at the large apron deck on the harbour side of the opera house, but she wasn't the first to arrive. Despite the milling crowd enjoying the view from this marvellous vantage point, she spotted Nick Hamilton immediately. He was standing in profile, leaning on the railing near where the water taxis drew in to set down or pick up theatregoers.

Meredith instantly halted, needing to catch her breath and give her heart time to recover its normal beat, or at least an approximation of it. Her gaze targeted the girl beside him. She faced the water, her back turned to Meredith, but it had to be Kimberly...her daughter...her baby grown to girlhood.

She was tall for her age, with the supple slenderness of a fast-growing child. Her long legs were encased in lime green jeans which she'd teamed with a white T-shirt patterned with orange and lemon and lime squiggles. A bubbly lemon band circled her black ponytail and she wore lemon sneakers on her feet. White socks.

She obviously liked bright colours. Meredith felt a wave of glad relief that her own colour choice in this instance fitted her daughter's taste.

A movement caught her eye, Nick Hamilton's head turning toward her. She looked back at him, her pulse racing again. He stiffened as his gaze connected with hers. The impact moment of recognition seemed to screech along every nerve in Meredith's body. Did he know her this time? Had she struck some chord in his memory? He stared at her as though she were a mirage he couldn't quite believe in.

Then he visibly shook himself out of the hypnotic fixation and touched Kimberly on the shoulder. His mouth formed words Meredith couldn't hear. The effect on the girl was instant. She swung around, her vibrant face lit with eager anticipation, her eyes swiftly scanning faces, her body tense with excitement.

The tug on Meredith's heart was so strong, her feet started forward, walking fast, faster, the need to close the distance between them urgent. She wanted to sing out, "I'm here!" She wanted to sweep her child up and hug her in an ecstasy of loving, in a wild celebration of both of them being alive, being able to touch and feel and know that their coming together was real.

Nick Hamilton's hand lifted, pointing direction. Perhaps he said more. Kimberly's gaze zeroed in on Meredith and stuck, her eyes rounding in stunned surprise, her mouth falling open. She didn't move. It was Nick Hamilton who moved, stepping out as though in warning to Meredith to hold back a little, approach more slowly.

The impulses surging through her wavered as caution caught at them. Sober reason clicked into her mind driving back the wild rush of emotion, insisting that too much too soon was not a wise course in these circumstances. She was a stranger to her child, a stranger who had to win her trust and love.

Tears blurred her eyes as she struggled to contain the tumult of feeling. A smile, she thought. At least she could show her love in a smile. Her legs obeyed her command to come to a halt beside the man who had initiated this meeting and she gave her daughter the brightest smile she could dredge up, knowing it wobbled but trying her utmost to hold it and inject it with all the warmth of a welcome that had been waiting so terribly long.

"Kimberly…this is your mother…Meredith Palmer," came the gentle introduction from Nick Hamilton.

Kimberly closed her mouth and swallowed hard. Her eyes clung to Meredith's face.

"I'm so very happy to meet you, Kimberly," Meredith managed huskily.

"You're beautiful," came the awed whisper.

"You are, too," was the only answer that came to mind. It was true. The combination of her green eyes with Nick's black hair was stunning. She'd inherited their best features in a pleasing amalgamation that was uniquely her own.

"You could say hello, Kimberly," Nick prompted in a kindly, indulgent tone.

She flushed, quickly offering her hand for Meredith to clasp. "Hello," she echoed. "I'm really glad you came. I'm sorry I got so dumb. Uncle Nick said you were pretty, but you could be a model. Honest!"

The awkward, eager words tumbled out artlessly. Meredith's smile threatened to wobble again as she curled her hand around the smaller one of her daughter's, such soft young skin, warm flesh and blood, solid and real. Her mind swirled around the heady sensation of touch. It was hard to drive it into making conversation.

"Not a day has gone by that I haven't thought of you, wondering where you were and how you were doing," she said softly. "It always helped that I knew you had good parents, Kimberly, and I'm sorry you lost them." She couldn't resist squeezing the small hand as she added, "I wish I could have been there for you then."

"It's okay," came the shy reply. "I had Uncle Nick. He's pretty good really."

"That could be the best compliment I've had for some time," Nick drawled in a teasing lilt. "Maybe I should get it in writing. Will you witness it, Miss Palmer?"

It lightened the emotion-charged atmosphere and served as a warning for Meredith to ease off.

"Oh, come on, Uncle Nick!" Kimberly rolled her eyes at him. "I only say you're a stodge when you're being a stick-in-the-mud." She withdrew her hand to gesture a reproof. "We're supposed to be saying good things today."

"I stand corrected," he said with mock ruefulness. "From here on in I'll tell Miss Palmer you're a perfect angel."

Kimberly sighed in exasperation.

Meredith laughed, happy to see the easy rapport between the two, the love that was taken for granted. It was obvious her daughter was fine and Nick was taking good care of her.

Kimberly gave her a look that appealed for understanding. "I'm not a perfect angel..."

"None of us are," Meredith assured her with a grin. "On the other hand, it's such a perfect day, let's enjoy it all we can."

"Starting with food," Nick popped in. "I don't know about you, Miss Palmer, but the nervous energy that's been swirling around me this morning seems to have drained my stomach. I'm starving."

He was handling this so well. No constraint. Smoothing the path. Her eyes thanked him, loving him for caring to make it as right as he could. "Lunch would be good," she agreed, half turning and holding out her left hand for Kimberly to take if she wanted to, smiling encouragement.

She took it. "Uncle Nick said this restaurant served super food. I hope you'll like it." Eager to impress.

"How could I not? It has such a lovely position." *And I've got the best company in the world.* Her heart was so full it was difficult not to pour out her feelings. Only the thought of overwhelming the child stopped her. She forced herself to hold her hand lightly as they walked along together, chatting about food preferences.

Long tubs of shrubs formed a demarcation line between the outside dining area of the restaurant and the public domain. A waiter took Nick's name and ushered them to a table by the water. A wide umbrella overhead provided welcome shade, lowering the glare and protecting them from the harmful rays of the sun.

They had an unrestricted view of Fort Denison, the small island in the harbour where the worst criminals were marooned in the early convict days. *Pinchgut,* it had been commonly called, because the men had been left for lengthy periods with only very small rations. Like her with Kimberly, Meredith thought, remembering the long emptiness in between the once-a-year photographs and the subsequent craving for more.

She watched her daughter covertly as they settled into their chairs, secretly feasting on the wealth of detail that photographs could never impart; the way she moved, the wonderful mobility of her face as her expressions changed, the bright intelligence in her eyes, the fascinating dimple in one cheek, the holding-her-own tilt of her chin as she bantered with the man she believed was her uncle.

A jug of ice water was quickly brought, menus handed around. The business of selecting their orders helped to set a more relaxed mood, though Meredith noticed Kimberly took every discreet opportunity to eye her in more lingering detail. Meredith fiercely hoped she liked all she saw.

The menu was a blur of choices. It didn't matter what she ate. It was highly doubtful she'd even taste it. When the waiter returned, Kimberly ordered bat-

tered fish fillets and chips and Meredith said she'd
have the same. Nick decided on a chicken dish and
added a green salad for three as an accompaniment
to their meal. He asked if she'd like to share a bottle
of wine but Meredith declined, not wanting her per-
ceptions even slightly fuzzied. They all requested
soft drinks.

"Uncle Nick said you live at Balmoral. Do you
like the beach?" Kimberly asked.

"Very much. I was brought up in Coff's Harbour
on the far north coast." She flicked a glance at the
man who had met and known her there. His expression held speculative interest, no personal reaction to the name of the seaside town. "The beach
used to be my playground," she added to Kimberly.
"Since I came to Sydney I've always lived somewhere near one."

"Because it reminds you of home?"

No, not home, Meredith thought, shaking her
head. Her stepmother had never really provided a
home. "More because it offers so many free pleas-
ures," she answered. "Walking along the shore,
breathing in the fresh sea air, surfing. What about
you? Do you enjoy swimming?"

"Mmmh." Pride in her achievement danced in
her eyes. "I'm fairly good at it actually."

"School champion for her age this year," Nick
said dryly. "She's a regular mermaid."

Kimberly laughed, bubbling over with pleasure.

"Uncle Nick's going to teach me windsurfing over the summer holidays."

"That sounds wonderful," Meredith enthused, her heart turning over as her mind suddenly filled with the memory of learning the same skills from him thirteen summers ago; catching the wind, skimming over the water, riding the waves, the exhilaration of it made even more intoxicating because he was watching, sharing, enjoying it with her.

The ache for what she had had and lost welled up in her. She was glad Kimberly had such a good relationship with her father, but seeing it, experiencing it, made the hurt of being shut out of their lives all these years so much worse. What she had missed…and could never have…because the time that could have been spent together was gone and the memories belonged to them, not to her.

"Miss…Miss Palmer?" Kimberly called hesitantly.

Miss Palmer…a stranger.

Meredith had automatically veiled her thoughts and it was an effort to lift her lashes and summon a smile. "Yes?"

Kimberly searched her eyes worriedly. "You were looking so sad. Did I say something wrong?"

"No." Meredith's smile turned wry. "It's just…I wish I could have been there to cheer you on when you won the swimming championship."

"Mum always used to come and watch me."

Mum... It was like a stab to the heart. But Denise Graham wouldn't be there to watch her adopted daughter windsurfing. The past was gone and Meredith silently berated herself for brooding over it. She had to concentrate on the future.

"I'm sure she was very proud of you," she said as warmly as she could.

Kimberly shifted uncomfortably. "It's sort of weird. I know you're my real mother...but Mum was Mum...and you look so young..."

"Are you worried about what to call me?" Meredith put in helpfully.

It triggered an instant appeal. "Uncle Nick said maybe your first name...if that was okay by you. It feels a bit stodgy, calling you Miss Palmer."

"Try Merry." The special name slipped out before Meredith thought better of it.

"Merry...short for Meredith," Kimberly mused. "Is that what your friends call you?"

She hesitated, glancing quickly at Nick Hamilton. He looked back at her quizzically. The name had no relevance to him. Somehow that painful truth goaded her to say to their daughter, "Only one other person has ever used that name for me."

"Your mother?" came the quick guess.

"No."

"Who then?" Curiosity piqued.

There was almost a savage, primitive satisfaction in relating how it had been, knowing that Nick

Hamilton was listening, unaware she was speaking of him. "It was your father, Kimberly. Your real father. When he met me he said it was like all the Christmas lights in the world switching on inside him and when he asked me my name and I told him, he shook his head and said…"

Suddenly she choked, the memory so vivid, and here she was, all these years later, sitting with the heart-wrenching outcome of the one love affair of her life…with a daughter she didn't know and the lover who didn't know her.

"What did he say?" Kimberly prompted avidly, caught up in the story about her real father, her eyes begging to be told.

She had to go on. Impossible to retract or retreat. Meredith was intensely conscious of Nick Hamilton listening…sitting very still and listening as she forced the words past the lump in her throat.

"He said…not Meredith. Merry. It has to be Merry. I laughed and asked him why…"

"Yes?" Kimberly urged.

Meredith took a deep breath to steady her voice. "It was Christmas time, you see. Just as it is now. And he looked at me, his eyes sparkling so much it felt like I was in a shower of beautiful fireworks. I've never forgotten the moment or the reply he gave me."

She paused, fighting back tears.

Kimberly was breathlessly hanging on hearing it all.

Nick Hamilton remained still and silent.

"Merry..." she repeated softly, hugging the poignant memory to herself as she turned her head away from both of them and stared out across the endlessly shifting waters to the old stone fort that had once served as a prison. History, she thought. It's past history. Old history. Forgotten history. Only she remembered the words. She could still hear them, just as they had been spoken, and the long echo of happy pleasure furred her voice as she added, "...*Because you're my Merry Christmas.*"

CHAPTER SEVEN

LIKE all the Christmas lights in the world switching on inside him...

Nick found himself captivated by that image, realising it was uncannily accurate. He sat staring at the woman who'd conjured it up, wishing he could read her mind, wishing she was not such a disturbing enigma to him.

He hadn't even tried to define what he felt when he'd spotted her amongst the crowd. She'd been standing still, her whole being concentrated on him, an energy force that zapped across the distance between them and set off a host of electric charges through his nervous system. The impact had stunned him for several seconds.

She was still affecting him. Not only was the physical attraction disconcertingly strong, his mind was being continually teased by the sense of recognition. He figured the only way to deal with that was to wait for her to reveal more about herself, hopefully something that would explain the inexplicable to him.

Whoever Kimberly's real father was, he'd undoubtedly been a smooth-tongued bastard to come up with that apt and evocative description. It was all too clear that lover boy had taken his *Merry Christmas* and left her pregnant, the fanciful words just so much tinsel when it came to a test of integrity and commitment.

Looking at the sad wistfulness on her face, the memory of him lingering in her mind, Nick had no trouble believing she'd fallen for the guy like a ton of bricks. Then the harsh realities of being left with a baby must have fallen on her like a ton of bricks.

She couldn't have been much more than a kid; innocent, naive, trusting, caught up in romantic excitement, falling in love for probably the first time. The odd part was, she didn't sound bitter about the lover who hadn't stood by her. It was almost as though she cherished the memory.

Kimberly heaved a huge, sentimental sigh over the romantic story. "I think that's lovely," she softly gushed. "Thank you for telling me, Merry."

Her mother's face lightened as she swung her attention back to his niece...her daughter. "It was the best Christmas of my life until now. Meeting you today is the most wonderful thing that's happened to me since."

"But you must have had good times in between." Kimberly was appalled at the idea of twelve Christmases going by with not much to say for them. They had always been a big deal for her.

''Don't you have a family to go to?'' she asked in concern.

A sad shake of the head. ''My mother died when I was eight. My father remarried when I was twelve. He was swept off rocks by a big wave while fishing and drowned when I was fourteen.'' She grimaced. ''Which left me with my stepmother.''

''You didn't like her?'' Kimberly popped in.

''We didn't get on very well.'' The reply was clearly understated.

Kimberly flashed a pointed look at Nick. The message was loud and clear. She didn't want a stepmother. If he was thinking of marrying Rachel he'd better take notice.

Rachel, however, had never been further from Nick's mind and the idea of marrying her had slipped into limbo. His thoughts were constantly revolving around the woman sitting opposite him.

Having shot him her warning, Kimberly persisted on the subject with her *real* mother. ''I bet she didn't want you with her.''

''You're right,'' came the ready concession. ''She made me feel like leftover baggage from her marriage to my father. The last straw for her was my getting pregnant at sixteen. She called me a lot of nasty names but none of them was true.'' Her expression softened. ''I loved your father, Kimberly. He was the only one.''

The warm feeling in her voice curled around

Nick's heart and squeezed it. An irrational jealousy burned his mind. The guy who'd let her down didn't deserve being loved and cherished. He'd had something precious and wasted it. Something in Nick fiercely rebelled at that man being *the only one* in Merry's life.

Merry... Damn it! The name had an insidious attraction. Nick silently vowed not to use it. It might give Kimberly a happy sense of being linked to her *real* father, which was fair enough, but Nick instinctively recoiled from using *his* special name for her. Meredith, he thought, forcefully stamping on the strong appeal of *Merry*.

"What happened?" Kimberly's question snapped Nick's attention back to her. She was frowning, looking puzzled, worrying over her mother. "I mean...he shouldn't have left you. How could he? Especially when you were going to have his baby."

No wool pulled over Kimberly's eyes, Nick thought with approval. She'd gone straight to the crux of the matter. It would do Meredith good to see the past from a less rosy-eyed, emotional perspective.

"Sometimes things happen that we have no control over, Kimberly."

The rueful reply twisted him up again. "What things?" he demanded, more harshly than he meant to. His insides writhed with embarrassment.

Meredith Palmer's personal past was none of his business. It was okay for Kimberly to ask about it but he should be keeping his mouth shut.

Those soul-tugging green eyes fastened on his and he had the weird sensation they were drawing on his mind, looking for an answer that would make sense to him.

"He was twenty-two," she said quietly. "When he found out I was only sixteen, he thought he should wait until I was older. We parted on the understanding of contacting each other at Christmas each year."

"But when you found out you were having me, didn't you tell him?" Kimberly queried. "Wasn't that more important than waiting for the next Christmas?"

Nick felt a sense of release as Meredith Palmer turned her gaze to his niece. It was like a cobweb of tingling threads being withdrawn. So conscious was he of the extraordinary effect, he barely heard her reply.

"I tried. Circumstances had changed for him. He'd gone overseas and I had no way of making contact."

"What about when the next Christmas came?" Kimberly pressed. "Did he write?"

A wistful shake of the head. "Not to my knowledge. If he wrote, the letter went astray."

Kimberly was visibly distressed by the tragic outcome of that possibility. She searched for a way around it. There was none, yet the pleading for some other resolution was in her voice as she cried, "He didn't ever come back to you?"

It was wrong for him not to. So obviously, hurtfully wrong. Kimberly needed some mitigation for his abandonment of her mother. It was all too plain to Nick that to her young, trusting mind, a love such as Meredith had described, should have an answer. He should have come. But that emotional certainty didn't change anything. It only raised a tension that tore at all of them.

Meredith Palmer summoned a wry smile in an effort to dissipate it. "Time moves on and people move on, Kimberly. They meet other people."

The philosophical reply didn't satisfy. Nick found it too tolerant and forgiving. Kimberly heaved another sigh, this one of deep discontent. She didn't like the story left dangling in no man's land.

"But you're so beautiful, Merry!" she protested. "I don't see how he could forget you."

Nick saw the flicker of pain on Meredith Palmer's face and suffered a wave of guilt for having encouraged this line of questioning. Of course she would feel obliged to answer Kimberly, wanting her daughter's sympathy and probably frightened of condemnation. But on their part, shouldn't curiosity take second place to compassion? God only knew how rough a time she'd been through. They should let the past rest and get on with the present.

And the future.

He quickly inserted, "There could have been other reasons why your real father never came back, Kimberly. Since none of us know, let's leave it at that, shall we? I'm sure Miss Palmer would like to talk of happier things."

"Oh!" Kimberly squirmed as her mind flashed through other scenarios, probably remembering last year's fatal car accident. "Uncle Nick said you run a florist business," she said in a gush of relief at having seized on a less sensitive subject. "What's your favourite flower?"

Flower Power provided bright conversation. Nick sat back and let it flow, discreetly observing the fascinating play of expression on Meredith Palmer's face, the eloquent body language encompassing the listening tilt of her head, the graceful hand gestures, the concentrated interest, the warm inviting smiles. Her whole being was reaching out to her child with every breath she took, every word she spoke.

Kimberly was entranced.

Nick wondered what it would be like to have all her passionate intensity focused on him. He fought a constant battle against a tightening in his loins. Desiring a woman so much on such little acquaintance was a new experience and he wasn't sure he liked it. Being in control was second nature to him. Around this woman, the laws of nature didn't seem to apply.

Again he was tantalised by the question of how her image had been branded on his subconscious and why it emerged in his dreams. She *was* beautiful, though it was more the power behind the beauty that teased Nick's mind. Kimberly had a point in blurting out, *I don't see how he could forget you!* On no acquaintance at all, Nick had found Meredith Palmer so unforgettable she haunted his dreams! Any way he looked at it, that teetered on the supernatural.

He was glad when lunch arrived. Eating was an ordinary human habit. Not that she ate much. Nick forced himself to consume everything on his plate and the lion's share of the salad, as well. It proved, at least to all outward appearances, he was handling everything with ease.

Occasionally Kimberly called on him to comment on some point of the conversation but Meredith Palmer never once tried to draw him into it. He sensed she was wary of him, guarded, perhaps overconscious of his power to call a halt to this meeting and take Kimberly away from her. Or was she as acutely aware of him as he was of her, and hiding it in case it created a problem in future meetings with her daughter?

He was still speculating on this possibility when Kimberly turned to him, her face transparently eager as she asked, "Uncle Nick, is it all right for Merry to come over to the apartment tomorrow? I could show her all my stuff."

"Would you like to, Miss Palmer?" he asked, wanting to make her look at him full-on again. For the past hour he'd received no more than brief, courteous glances, frustrating his need to know if he was right about a mutual attraction.

Her eyes met his and his stomach contracted. Hope burned in their luminous green depths, an anguished hope that begged more from him than a casual invitation. "Yes," she said simply. Then as though belatedly recognising it might be an imposition on his generosity, she flushed and added, "If it won't inconvenience you, Mr. Hamilton."

"You're welcome." It was the truth. On more levels than he cared to examine. He wanted her. Not in his dreams, but in his flesh and blood life. She held the promise of things that demanded exploration.

"Thank you."

Her smile was radiant, bathing him in a pulsing glow of happiness. "Call me Nick," he commanded on a sudden rush of blood to the head. He didn't want distance between them. He wanted... God! It was almost impossible to clamp down on his rioting feelings but he managed some semblance of it, smiling back at her and asking, "May I call you Meredith?"

The sparkling light in her eyes momentarily receded, as though sucked back to some dark place in her soul. It burst on him again so quickly, the slight falter was erased and Nick was showered with pleasure.

"Yes. Please do."

The soft lilt of her voice sang through him, stroking chords and striking harmonies that filled him with a glorious sense of well-being. The sense of starting out on a path that had always been waiting for them was overwhelming.

Kimberly reclaimed her attention, working out the details of tomorrow's visit. Nick didn't care what was arranged. Something special had started between him and Meredith Palmer. He knew it in his bones. The determination to pursue it as far as it could go was burning in his heart. Tomorrow was the next step.

Meredith…maybe when he'd called her by her full name she'd momentarily remembered the guy who'd called her Merry, but she'd come back to him with a burst of positive signals. Nick was fiercely glad that her one great love had walked out of her life and never returned, elated that he had this chance at something unbelievably unique in his experience.

Surely she could put that man behind her now.

Thirteen years had passed. Though she hadn't forgotten him. But Kimberly had hit the nail on the head. How could he have forgotten her? The man had to be a shallow fool, probably breaking hearts wherever he went on his very convenient trip overseas.

Nick reflected, with some irony, that he'd been twenty-two himself, thirteen years ago. And he'd gone off overseas at the same time, having won a grant for further studies at Harvard University in the U.S.

Strange, the little coincidences in life…the man who'd left her…and the man with her now. Had the two of them met? he wondered. Had he been shown a photograph of Merry?

He couldn't recall any such incident.

It didn't really matter.

The woman of his dreams was with him in reality. He didn't care what had happened before. The future was his to make.

CHAPTER EIGHT

MEREDITH took three deep breaths in a vain attempt to calm her nervous excitement before ringing the doorbell to Nick Hamilton's apartment. Its Blues Point location, with views over the harbour, made it prime real estate, way beyond her income bracket. She was about to step into a world of wealth and class and it was difficult not to be daunted by it.

She reminded herself it had always been Nick's background, though she hadn't realised it until she'd gone looking for him at the address he'd given her. Denise and Colin Graham had lived in a magnificent home at Pittwater in those days. It was one of the reasons she'd given up her baby to them, wanting her daughter to have all the privileges she couldn't provide, the same privileges her father had.

Nevertheless, wealth and class couldn't provide mother love and that was what Kimberly wanted now. There was a need to be filled and Meredith was determined to fill it as far as Nick Hamilton would allow. Surely this Sunday brunch had to mean he was willing for them to establish an on-going relationship.

Ever since they'd parted yesterday she'd been

hugging his "You're welcome" comment to her heart.

Welcome in *his* life, too? Was he attracted to her again? Maybe it was too much to hope for. Dangerous, too, if it got in the way of forging a future with Kimberly.

Caution had to be exercised. He'd unbent enough to invite her to call him Nick, but Meredith was not Merry. He didn't remember what they'd shared and it was no use wanting him to. She had to take it from here...whatever came.

Despite the three deep breaths, her pulse was wildly fluttering as she pressed the doorbell. Kimberly must have been prowling near the door, impatient for her arrival. Meredith had barely touched the button before her daughter was in front of her, the entrance to her home swept wide open in eager welcome.

"Hi!" It was a breath of delight, accompanied by a grin from ear to ear. "You made it here in time!"

In time for what? Meredith puzzled. Nick had said brunch was casual and arriving any time after eleven would be fine. Feeling somewhat confused, she asked, "Was I supposed to be here earlier?" A quick check of her watch showed eleven-twenty.

"Oh, no! Everything's perfect," Kimberly assured her and grabbed her hand to draw her inside. "I love that outfit, Merry."

No problem there. Her stretch tights were lime green, printed with white daisies and teamed with a loose white T-shirt. Meredith had chosen her outfit for its appeal to her daughter and bright colours were certainly the order of the day. Kimberly was in orange shorts and a matching midriff top.

"I love what you're wearing, too," she said, smiling warm approval. It would be marvellous to take her daughter shopping one day. Was it too soon to suggest it?

The compliment didn't really register with Kimberly. "They're just old things," she dismissed, hustling Meredith inside and pushing the door shut. Clearly pumped up with excitement, she danced ahead, pulling on Meredith's hand to urge her forward. "Do come on, Merry. They're out on the patio."

Hit by the ultra modern and expensive decor in the open plan living room—black leather, streamlined chrome and glass, collector pieces of art, carpet so plush footprints showed up in it—Meredith was slow to pick up on the critical word. Then a frisson of unease ran down her spine. She stopped dead, halting Kimberly's headlong rush past the designer class dining suite.

"Who are *they?*"

She hadn't been told there would be other guests this morning. She wasn't prepared for it.

Kimberly shrugged as though it was nonconsequential. "It's only Uncle Nick and the woman he goes out with. She dropped in about half an hour ago. Her name is Rachel Pearce."

A lump of lead plunged into Meredith's heart. He was involved with someone else. With a woman who felt comfortable enough in their relationship to drop in whenever she wished.

"I want her to meet you."

No...o...o...o. The silent wail echoed down the chasm that had opened up in Meredith's mind, swallowing the hope she had nursed and spilling an ink-black darkness into her soul.

"It will only take a minute," Kimberly offered persuasively. "Then I'll show you my room."

She had to drag herself out of the pit to focus on her daughter again, seeing her own green eyes looking back at her, wanting her compliance, not realising what was asked had any import to Meredith beyond a casual meeting of two people who didn't know each other.

Her daughter...whom she wanted to keep seeing...so meeting the woman in Nick Hamilton's life was inevitable. Seal off what cannot be, reason dictated. Get on with it. "Do you like her, Kimberly?" Meredith asked softly, needing to know what she was walking into so as not to blunder onto sensitive territory and do herself a damage.

"She's okay, I guess," came the half-hearted reply. Her nose wrinkled expressively. "She sort of

talks down to me but she's not nasty or mean.''
Then realising her words might be off-putting, she
hastily added, ''You don't have to worry, Merry.
She'll be nice to you. Uncle Nick wouldn't like it
if she wasn't.''

Her daughter was no fool, Meredith thought
wryly. She was certainly wise to the ways of a
woman who wanted to keep a man's good opinion.
Curiosity, on her daughter's behalf, helped push the
pain aside. An assessment of the woman who might
be playing a big part in Kimberly's life was necessary if she was to understand the situation and be
of any help.

''Well, I guess I'd better meet her,'' she said,
practising a smile.

''Great!'' Kimberly enthused. ''She'll probably
be dead jealous when she sees how beautiful you
are.''

Meredith wasn't sure if her daughter was proud
of her or intent on stirring up trouble. Either way,
she had little time to think about it. Kimberly was
on the march again, pulling her past a luxurious
lounge setting to the glass doors that led out to the
patio.

A profusion of purple and cerise bougainvillea
grew from huge earthenware urns and spilled over
the safety wall that edged the spacious outdoors
area. Casually arranged on a lovely blue-green
slate-covered floor were a dining suite, a couple of

occasional tables and three sun loungers in white lace aluminium, comfort provided by royal blue cushions.

Nick Hamilton and a red-haired woman sat at the dining table, cosily chatting to each other. Their heads swivelled at the sound of the doors sliding open and both of them pushed their chairs back and rose to their feet as Kimberly led Meredith out to them. Wealth and class staring her in the face, Meredith thought, mentally building herself a thicker protective wall to ward off their effect on her.

Nick was dressed in a smart, casual Jag ensemble, the steel blue shorts revealing the powerful muscularity of his legs, the loose tomato-red top emphasising the broadness of his chest and shoulders. He was definitely *at home,* albeit in designer leisure wear.

Rachel Pearce, however, could have stepped out of *Vogue* magazine. She was style from head to toe, making Meredith feel like a dropout from a chainstore.

Beautifully tailored white linen trousers teamed with a matching halter-neck top that moulded a perfectly curved figure. The jacket that completed the outfit was hooked over the back of her chair. Silver bracelets adorned her arms and silver hoops hung from her ears, dramatic against the shining copper of her hair and the make-up that emphasised pretty features and polished sophistication.

Her suitability for a man of Nick Hamilton's status and her sex appeal were heart-wrenchingly obvious to Meredith, and that comprised only surface attractions. No doubt she had other qualities that appealed to the man beside her.

"This is my *real* mother," Kimberly announced to the woman, her voice ringing with triumphant satisfaction, as though the reality of a mother could displace any ambitions Rachel Pearce might have for fulfilling a maternal role. Unfortunately, relationships didn't fall into neat black and white patterns.

Nick sighed and gestured a reproof at his niece. "Kimberly, a proper introduction would be appreciated."

"She's all excited, Nick," his companion excused indulgently, one hand touching his arm in a soothing squeeze, a claim of familiarity that spelled out her position. Her smile to Meredith could not be faulted. It was open and friendly, her eyes dancing with interest. "Hello… I'm Rachel Pearce," she said with easy warmth, offering her other hand invitingly.

Meredith took it, adopting the "we aim to please" air she used with a prospective client. "Meredith Palmer. A pleasure to meet you, Miss Pearce."

"Rachel…please," came the laughing reply. "Nick has been calling you Meredith. I hope you don't mind if I do."

Establishing their coupling.

"Not at all." Conscious of not having really acknowledged Nick Hamilton as yet, Meredith made the effort to shift her gaze to him and say, "Good morning, Nick," as lightly as she could.

She caught him perusing her long legs, faithfully and emphatically outlined in lime green. On the instant of hearing his name, his gaze flicked up, the dark eyes sharp and alert and boring into hers with an urgent intensity that made no sense to Meredith. What was he thinking? That she might side with Kimberly against the woman he wanted? Clearly there was a conflict area which needed delicate negotiation. Maybe he was trying to discern if she would be his ally or his enemy.

"Another beautiful day," he said. "It's good to see you, Meredith. Would you like to join us or…"

"Merry wants to see my room," Kimberly answered for her. "I've got all the photo albums laid out on the bed and my swimming trophies and…"

"I see the first claim has been made," Nick broke in dryly.

"Yes. If you'll excuse us…" Meredith said quickly, flashing an appealing smile from him to Rachel Pearce.

"Of course. You must want to catch up on everything,'' Rachel said, her eyes sympathetic, not the least bit jealous of Kimberly's attention.

"We did invite Meredith for brunch, Kimberly," Nick reminded her. "Don't get so involved with showing off that you forget we're supposed to eat, too.''

"I've got a bowl of cherries and a big bag of chips. Give us a call when you put on the barbecue, Uncle Nick,'' she answered breezily.

He rolled his eyes and shot a grin at Meredith that pierced her shield and hammered into her heart. "Doomed to cherries and chips. Be assured I will rescue you.''

She managed a laugh, nodded to his companion and took her leave of them with Kimberly, fiercely telling herself once again the past was gone. The love of her life could not be rescued.

"What did you think of her?" Kimberly demanded in a confidence-inviting whisper as they traversed the living room, heading for a hallway.

Meredith instantly adopted neutral ground, wary of repercussions. "I don't know her, Kimberly. If you want my first impression, she's smart and pretty and has a very pleasant manner.''

It drew a huff and a grimace. "I don't want Uncle Nick to marry her. He'll have no time for me if he does.''

Meredith frowned. "I'm sure that's not true. He cares very much about you.''

''She brought over the enrolment forms for PLC. That's *her* old school. She's got Uncle Nick thinking it would be good for me to be a boarder there.''

''It is a top-class school,'' Meredith commented cautiously, aware it was also a highly expensive private school that carried a lot of status, both socially and academically. Students there were definitely privileged, which was what she had wanted for her daughter, though not at the cost of her being unhappy.

''I don't want to be a boarder.'' It was a sulky, belligerent statement. ''She wants me out of the way so she can have Uncle Nick to herself.''

That might or might not be true. In all fairness, Meredith had to reserve judgment. She tried to take a middle line. ''I thought most boarding schools allowed their students to go home at weekends.''

It didn't work.

Kimberly shot her a doleful look.

''What would be the use? She and Uncle Nick go out most Saturday nights. Mrs. Armstrong comes to mind me. I might as well be at the school with the other girls who stay in.''

''There is Sunday,'' Meredith reminded her.

Another grimace. ''It's not the same with Uncle Nick when *she's* here.''

Kimberly fell into brooding silence as they walked along the hall. Meredith didn't feel equipped to break it in any constructive way. The situation had changed dramatically from what she had imagined it to be earlier this morning.

A prospective stepmother.

Rumblings of discontent from Kimberly.

Areas of conflict rising from the intermingled relationships.

Was she supposed to supply a solution?

What if Nick Hamilton wanted her to establish a good relationship with Kimberly so she could provide a happy alternative to coming home to a stepmother who seemed only to stir resentment?

They came to the room at the end of the hall. Kimberly had her hand on the knob, ready to open the door when she paused, turning to eye Meredith speculatively.

"You know what would be really good?"

"Tell me." Safer to invite than to guess.

She hesitated a moment, then seemed to pick her way carefully as she said, "Uncle Nick is going to invite you to spend the Christmas holidays with us at Pearl Beach. It's on the Central Coast, about two hours from here. Can you come, Merry?"

Christmas with her daughter. She wouldn't let anything get in the way of having that joy. She smiled. "Yes. I'd love to."

"You'll be in the same house with us," Kimberly said with satisfaction. "It's right on the beach, so you'll like it."

"I'm sure I will."

"And Ms. Pearce won't be there."

Meredith made no comment. The Machiavellian glint in her daughter's eyes was disquietening. It was a relief when she grinned and her expression changed to mischievous conspiracy.

"It would be really good if we could get Uncle Nick to marry you instead of her…wouldn't it!"

CHAPTER NINE

THEY strolled along Pearl Beach in the darkening twilight—man, woman, child—and Meredith let herself pretend they were together in the idyllic sense. After all, it didn't matter what she dreamed as long as neither Nick nor Kimberly knew.

It was their first night here, the first of nine nights they would spend in this beautiful place with no one else to please but the three of them. The three of them for Christmas. Tomorrow was Christmas Eve. Tonight was simply for the pleasure of feeling their normal lives were left behind in Sydney and this was the start of a special time.

For her it was, anyway.

This was her family…her child…and the father of her child.

After these holidays…but she wouldn't think about what might happen then. Better to treasure every moment she had with the only two people who were especially dear to her.

Although Nick had brought provisions, now stacked away in the kitchen of the holiday house, they'd gone to the take-away shop in the village and dined on hamburgers and chips, just like any other family who didn't want to bother with cooking after a long, busy day. The walk home along the beach was Kimberly's decision. Meredith suspected it was part of her daughter's plot to promote romantic situations between her and Nick.

She skipped ahead of them, dancing around the scalloped edges of dying waves, still very much a child, perhaps enjoying the fact that her parents were following her, watching her antics, caring about her. Not that Nick knew he was her father, but being her legal guardian was more or less the same. Meredith wondered what he was thinking...feeling.

He was walking beside her, as they'd walked so long ago, sand squelching under their feet, the splash of waves slapping onto the shore, whooshing up and being sucked back, the underlying thrum of the sea in constant motion, a breeze flicking their hair and teasing their nostrils with the fresh smell of salt.

She could feel the heat of his body, almost touching hers. His strong maleness stirred an acute awareness of her femininity and the need to have it complemented. They had once been perfect together. The memory clung, arousing desires she hugged to herself, secretly wishing they could be expressed.

It was strange. The thought of Rachel Pearce had tormented her all week, yet here...maybe it was the sense of distance or the magic of the night...the woman who belonged to Nick's city life just didn't seem real. Only the three of them were real...walking together...listening to the same sounds, all their senses alive to a different world.

"Look at the stars! There are so many!" Kimberly remarked in awe.

"No pollution dimming our view of them," Nick commented.

"That's so unromantic, Uncle Nick."

"Simple truth."

Kimberly huffed her exasperation. None of her matchmaking efforts had borne any fruit so far. Meredith found them intensely embarrassing and Nick pretended he didn't notice the hints and manoeuvrings.

"We're almost home," Kimberly pointed out.

"So we are," Nick agreed dryly.

Their holiday home was a rambling old weatherboard house with verandas running around all four sides of it. Built before any council regulations came into force, it faced directly onto the beach with no reserve in front of it. The foundation pylons were high, ensuring the body of the house remained above shifting sand dunes. Quite a steep flight of steps led up to the veranda overlooking the sea.

"I think I'll go straight to bed," Kimberly announced. "I'm really tired out and I want to get up early tomorrow."

"Bed sounds a good idea," Nick tossed back at her.

She rounded on him. "Not for you, Uncle Nick. It's too early for you." Most emphatic.

"Aren't I allowed to be tired?" he teased.

"You always say you need to wind down first," Kimberly sternly reminded him. "It'd be good for you to have a nightcap before going to bed."

"Mmmh…" Noncommittal.

"One of those Irish coffees you sometimes make," Kimberly suggested enthusiastically. "You could take it out to the veranda and watch the stars and listen to the sea and really wind down."

"That certainly should be relaxing," he mused.

"And Merry could relax with you. She's been busy, too, getting all the flowers organised for Christmas before coming away. You'd like an Irish coffee, Merry."

Not a question. This was pure and simple manipulation.

There was a laugh in Nick's voice as he turned to her and asked, "Would you care to join me in a nightcap on the veranda, Meredith, counting the stars and being lulled by the sound of the sea until we're ready to fall asleep?"

The light tone made it sound harmless. Why not? she thought, wanting to indulge in her private pretence a little while longer. "I'd enjoy that," she answered, smiling to show she understood there was nothing personal in it on his part. It was no more than an agreeable way of ending the evening.

"That's settled then," Kimberly declared with gleeful satisfaction. She literally pranced up the beach toward the house, apparently re-energised. There was no sign whatsoever of being so tired she had to go to bed.

Nick slowly expelled the breath he'd been holding. At last some time alone with her! No woman had ever shielded herself from him so determinedly and consistently as Meredith Palmer. He'd never felt so intrigued nor frustrated in any other person's company. At least tonight he had the chance to get her to unwind with him.

Thanks to Kimberly, the little minx, prodding and plotting to push them into rearranging their lives to give her what she wanted in the most convenient way possible. Her motivations stuck out a mile. One day he would have to teach her about subtlety. With her too obvious schemes she'd been driving Meredith away from him not toward him, as well as forcing him into maintaining a laid-back attitude to counter any feeling of being trapped in an untenable situation.

Now that Kimberly had gone on ahead he decided to tackle the problem so it wouldn't continue to be a running issue. "It's only natural, you know, for her to see us getting together as a neat solution," he said casually.

A perceptible rise in tension. "I'm sorry. It must make things so awkward for you."

"I can ride it. Kimberly's a good kid. She usually sees sense in the end."

An apprehensive look. "Please don't think I'm encouraging her in this…this fantasy."

"Meredith, it's very plain to me you're not," he said dryly.

"I never meant to make trouble for anyone."

He found the anxiety in her voice painful. "You aren't," he quickly assured her. "Please stop worrying."

No relief flashed at him. The silence as they walked on was heavy. He tried to think of what other assurance he could give to ease her concerns. More than anything he needed her to open up to him. Then he'd have something to work with.

"It's easy for you to say that." Her voice was quiet, not accusing yet strained with inner torment. "You have the power to take Kimberly away from me again if it gets too much for you."

The shock of what had been playing on her mind halted him. She stepped ahead. His hand automatically lifted, clasping her shoulder to halt her, too. "You can't think I'd be so heartless!" The words burst from him in horror. He wasn't aware of his fingers digging into her flesh in reflexive recoil from her view of him.

She stood still, absolutely still for several seconds, long enough for him to recollect himself and realise she was holding her breath, frightened to move. He hastily loosened his grip, sliding his hand to her upper arm as he strode forward and wheeled to face her, compelled to dispel her fears.

"Meredith…" Her eyes were unfocused, unseeing, staring straight through him. He grasped her other arm, tempted to shake her, barely restraining the turbulence she stirred in him. "Meredith…"

"What do I know of you…of the man you are now?" Her voice sounded eerily hollow.

An uneasy feeling crawled down Nick's spine. What did she mean…*now?* Had they met in some other life? He shook off the wild idea. Be damned if he was going to get befuddled over supernatural stuff again! This was now and he had to get through to her.

"I'm the same man who came to you ten days ago, wanting to find a way to reunite you and your daughter," he stated vehemently.

Her gaze suddenly sharpened, fastening on his with blazing intensity. "Why? For her sake or yours? It couldn't be mine. I'm a stranger to you. And I don't know what the end is."

The agony of doubt in her voice hit him hard. She had shown him, shown both him and Kimberly where she was coming from, and he hadn't answered her need to know where they were going to. A woman without any legal right to her child, afraid of being cut off again...it sickened his soul that she'd been in such torment while he and Kimberly breezed on with their lives, including her as they wished.

"It wasn't for my sake, Meredith. I came for Kimberly, for a child who wanted to meet her real mother. I didn't know the end then and I don't know it now. It's what you and she decide."

Rejection of his claim twisted across her face. "You know I have no control over this. It all depends on your generosity."

He dropped his grasp on her arms to cup her face, to hold it still, to force her to look into his eyes and see his sincerity. "Then take it from me. I'm prepared to be generous."

"Why?" came the anguished whisper.

"Because I care."

Her eyes searched his in tortured uncertainty. "Care...for me?"

It was on the tip of his tongue to say she moved him as no other woman ever had but he knew it wasn't an appropriate answer at this raw moment. She needed reassurance, a sense of security. Very gently he fanned a finger across her cheek and smiled a soft appeal.

"Is it so impossible for you to believe that I can

feel compassion for the loss you've felt? To want you to know what you should have known as a mother?''

Her lashes swept down. Her throat moved in a convulsive swallow. He sensed her struggle to come to terms with what he'd said. The breeze flicked tendrils of her long hair across the back of his hand. He couldn't resist tucking them back behind her ear. She didn't seem to notice.

''It was good of you to invite me here with you,'' she said stiltedly, as though pushing the words out, reciting them as a grateful and well-mannered guest might. ''I'll try not to be a…a burden on you.''

The sense of displacement that haunted her twisted his heart. ''Meredith…just be yourself,'' he implored, trying to instil some confidence in the beautiful person she was. ''Enjoy this Christmas.'' He hoped it would go some way to making up for all the empty Christmases she'd had.

She bit her bottom lip. Her shoulders rose and fell as she inhaled deeply and expelled the long breath. Her lashes slowly lifted. Tears glistened in her eyes. ''Is it only for Christmas?'' she asked huskily.

He didn't know what she meant. He frowned, trying to follow her thoughts. ''I hope you'll enjoy the rest of your life, Meredith,'' he said, genuinely wanting her to be happy, distressed that he'd inadvertently given her cause for tears.

''No. You said…Kimberly wanted her real mother for Christmas.''

''And you thought…'' Horror at his blind insensitivity struck him again. ''Oh, hell! It might have started like that, Meredith, but I honestly see it going on for the rest of your lives.''

The tears spilled down her cheeks.

He couldn't bear it. He wrapped her in his arms and hugged her to him, wanting to comfort, wanting to impress on her that the terrible loneliness she had known was over. The silent weeping broke into convulsive sobs, her body trembling as she fought to stifle them.

''It's all right,'' he murmured, stroking her hair, easing her head onto his shoulder. ''You've held too much in for too long. It's all right to cry.''

The stiffness collapsed. She sagged against him as though suddenly released from unbearable strain and the weeping was deep and uncontrolled.

Nick ached for her, hating the burden she'd carried around in her mind. The urge kept surging through him to tell her she'd come home now and there was nothing more to worry about. He'd take care of her. He'd take care of everything for her and she'd never be unhappy or alone again.

Madness.

But it didn't feel mad. It felt right. Maybe it was the protective male being fired in him, but he'd never felt anything so strongly before. He was holding her and the desire to hold on to her forever suffused his entire being. Meredith, he thought, the woman he'd been waiting for. She'd finally come to him, out of his dreams and into real life.

Merry…the name slipped into his mind, tantalising with its emotional pull, yet too associated with her love for another man for him to use. He wished…no, he couldn't unwish the past. Without Kimberly they might never have met.

God! He'd forgotten Kimberly!

The lights were on in the house. She'd gone inside. If she'd witnessed this scene she'd be more than happy to leave them to it. Not that it meant what she probably thought, but what the hell! He'd sort it out with her tomorrow.

Meredith's needs demanded all his concentration right now. He suddenly realised she had stopped crying. Probably too drained to move. Or maybe it felt good to her to be held. By him. He hoped so.

The thought of making love to her crept into his mind and triggered a sharp awareness of how her body was fitted to his, the warm feminine softness clinging to his chest and belly and thighs. The temptation to run his hand over the curve of her bottom and press her closer was almost overwhelming. He had to fiercely will the growing tension in his loins to ease off. It was imperative to soothe Meredith's fears, not raise more. The last thing he wanted was to alarm her into being skittish with him again, shying away from any contact.

"Kimberly!"

Her head jerked back as the name exploded off her lips. Agitated hands pushed at him as her gaze swept the area up to the house, her face mirroring shock at having forgotten the presence of her daughter.

"No problem," Nick assured her. "Kimberly didn't stick around. She put the house lights on for us and has probably taken herself off to bed by now."

"Oh!" Her eyes fluttered at him in embarrassment. "I'm sorry…"

"Don't be. I'm sorry we put you in such stressful turmoil. I had no idea you saw yourself on trial. That's not how it is, Meredith, I promise you."

She sucked in a deep breath and expelled it on a long, shuddering sigh. "I completely lost it." Still embarrassed, she started shifting backwards, creating distance between them again.

Rather than lose all contact with her, Nick dropped his embrace, sweeping one arm out as a directive to the house and dropping the other to catch her hand and hold it in a companionable grasp as he started them walking again, smiling encouragement at her.

"What you need is an Irish coffee to unjangle all

your nerves. I can highly recommend it as a re-
storative as well as a relaxing agent.''

It teased a wobbly smile from her. ''You're very
kind.''

''Hold that thought!'' he admonished her with
mock gravity. ''No more making me out a callous
monster. Okay?''

''Okay.''

She was tagging along with him, letting her hand
rest in his. He kept his grip steady, elated at this
small victory. ''Once we're settled on the veranda,
we'll talk about what you'd like to have with
Kimberly. Get it sorted out as best we can.''

Another wobbly smile. ''Thank you.''

''You know, last year with Denise and Colin
gone and their deaths happening so close to it,
Kimberly and I had a fairly miserable Christmas.
This year, because we have you with us...'' A
family again, he thought, his grin unashamedly
showing delight in the idea. ''...We'll have a merry
Christmas.''

Her feet faltered. She stared at him, an arrested
look on her face, and Nick started to tingle...everywhere...as though all the Christmas
lights in the world had been switched on inside him.
Then he realised what he'd said...Merry
Christmas...and the primal male inside him rose

rampant, determined to fight his way to her heart.

Me.

Not him.

Me.

CHAPTER TEN

NICK released her hand to let her precede him up the steps to the house. Meredith's heart was pumping so hard her temples throbbed. She grabbed the banister to keep herself steady. It was an act of will to force her quivery legs into the required climbing action.

The way he'd looked at her just now, when he'd said "Merry Christmas"...it was as though time had tunneled backward. But he didn't know. He hadn't realised. Yet how could he look at her like that without feeling what he'd felt all those years ago? Was it happening again?

Her mind whirled with the eruption of desires from their long, dormant state. Impossible to tuck them away again. They were running rampant, demanding release, demanding expression, crying out against the containment she had enforced. If she just turned, reached out, they would surely be met and answered by the man who'd answered them so magically before.

Then the insidiously dampening thought of Rachel Pearce wormed its way through the chaotic impulses holding reign. However unreal the other

113

woman seemed right now, she did exist in Nick Hamilton's life and they had most likely been lovers for quite some time.

The image conjured up was miserably deflating. But it didn't have to mean he couldn't be attracted to me, she fiercely argued. Or were her senses distorted from wanting him so much? Maybe she had a fevered imagination from having been in Nick's embrace again, wallowing in the sense of belonging to him.

She reached the veranda and started for the door.

"Why don't you stay out here while I make the coffees?" Nick suggested. "Just relax. It'll be my pleasure to serve you."

He was being kind, giving her time to recover her composure after her crying jag. She nodded and managed another smile. "Thank you, Nick."

"Won't be long," he promised.

She watched him go inside, a man who cared about others' feelings, a kind man, no different from the Nick she'd known so intimately. She should have realised those ingrained qualities of character wouldn't change. Had anything, apart from the one vital loss of memory?

Hopeful thinking, she cautioned herself. Rachel Pearce might be left behind in Sydney. It didn't mean she was forgotten. By Kimberly's account, Nick was very much involved with her. It was indicative of trust and confidence that Kimberly's future educational direction was discussed between them and the choice of Rachel's old school had a ring of family continuity about it. While there didn't appear to be any formal engagement, marriage was probably on their minds.

Nevertheless, they weren't married yet.

Was it bad of her to think that? To want another woman's man?

A fiercely primitive wave of possessiveness tore at the uncomfortable scruples as her mind filled with the thought...*he was mine first!*

And he wasn't indifferent to her. Apart from his words of caring, the way he'd held her while she'd wept had demonstrated a very real caring. Then taking her hand afterward, looking at her with that special sparkle in his eyes...her stomach curled, just thinking about it.

What would happen if she told him Kimberly was his child?

Meredith brooded over the question as she wandered down the veranda and settled in one of the cane armchairs they'd brought out from the house earlier this evening. Was it fair to lay that on him? Was it fair that he'd left her with a baby and wasn't there to stand by her when she'd most needed him?

Not his fault, she savagely reminded herself.

It would make him feel guilty if she told him. Did she want him to turn to her out of guilt?

No.

It had to be with love, given freely.

She knew in her heart it wouldn't work otherwise.

If it was going to happen, it would of its own accord, she decided. All she had to do was wait. Having set her course once more, and having been assured by Nick there was no cut-off point with Kimberly, Meredith switched off her mind, letting the sound of the sea fill it with a rhythm that soothed with its constancy, the repetitive roll of water upon land.

"Two Irish coffees coming up."

The announcement heralded Nick's return to the veranda. Meredith's hard-won sense of peace instantly shattered. Her body sprang alive with a prickling awareness as Nick loomed closer, carrying a tray holding two long mugs. Her mind pulsed with irrepressible needs. She tried desperately to get herself under control as he set the tray on the table next to her and subsided into the chair on the other side of it.

"This is the life," he declared with deep satisfaction. "Far from the madding crowd, no pressure decisions to be made. Sun, sand and surf. Can't beat it for a holiday."

That hadn't changed for him, either.

"Is it very stressful, being a merchant banker?" she asked, grateful for his lead into a safe conversation.

"It has its moments. The money markets need to be carefully watched. But I don't let it get on top of me. It's what I'm trained for,'' he answered with the easy confidence of a man who had a long record of success in the financial world.

"Then it was worthwhile going to Harvard.''

His head snapped around. "How do you know I went to Harvard?''

Meredith's heart kicked into a panicky beat. The comment had slipped out and now she had to answer for it. She quickly busied herself, stirring the layer of whipped cream into her coffee while her mind frantically sought an acceptable explanation.

If she said Kimberly had mentioned it… Too risky. He could check with her. Impossible to claim reading it in an article. She had no idea if any story had ever been printed on him. What else would serve…except the truth?

"Your sister told me,'' she said flatly, evading his sharply questing gaze, sitting back in her chair and holding the mug of coffee to her lips, ready to sip.

"Denise? Why would she tell you about me?''

Meredith's brain moved into crisis mode, darting around danger areas with incredible speed. "I wanted to know about the family that would become my baby's family,'' she said, keeping her tone eminently reasonable.

"I've been meaning to ask you about your connection with Denise. As I see it, this adoption could not have gone through regular channels. Normally there's no contact between the parties.''

He wasn't going to leave it alone. She had to satisfy his curiosity without revealing his paternity. Ruthlessly monitoring every step made toward the adoption, Meredith plunged into telling him the barest of facts.

"My stepmother sent me to her sister in Sydney so my pregnancy wouldn't shame her with her friends. The doctor who did my check-ups was also your sister's doctor. I was booked into a hospital which was a regular channel for adoption through a government agency. Your sister knew the person who could arrange for my baby to be adopted by her."

"Are we talking bribery here?"

"I don't know. You asked for the connections. Those were certainly some of the connections made," she stated carefully.

"Go on," he invited tersely, not liking what he was hearing.

"At first, I didn't want to give up my baby."

"Are you saying my sister and this person coerced you?" he broke in again, clearly upset.

Meredith shook her head and sipped the strongly flavoured coffee, needing a suffusion of warmth. He was shocked, angry, and there seemed no point in stirring bad feelings. It was too late to change anything and Denise and Colin Graham had been good parents to Kimberly.

"They put their case," she explained. "I listened and gave it a lot of thought. I couldn't have let my baby go to someone I didn't know anything about. I trusted your sister to do the best she could for my daughter. She agreed to send me the photographs so I'd know something of her life. And that was it. I signed the adoption papers, knowing my baby was going to a better home than I could give her.''

''You were talked into it,'' he muttered, his sense of fairness still frayed.

''I made the choice, Nick,'' she said quietly.

''Denise could be very domineering.''

''She did all I wanted her to do for Kimberly.''

He ruminated on that for several minutes. ''I guess she did,'' he finally conceded. ''Denise was good at mothering. Our parents died when I was a kid and she was more a mother to me than a sister.''

I know, Meredith thought, but she didn't make the mistake of voicing the give-away words this time.

''She and Colin...they were good people,'' he mused sadly.

He was letting it go. She'd done it! He was satisfied.

His gaze swung around to her, dark and disturbed under frowning brows, making her pulse skitter again.

''All the same, it was wrong to keep bargaining with you when you were so vulnerable. As much as Denise craved a child of her own, she shouldn't have done that.''

Meredith took refuge in sipping some more coffee. When no comment was forthcoming, Nick turned his gaze broodingly out to sea. There was a time and a tide for everything, Meredith thought, and the events Nick was questioning were long gone. Nothing could be gained by chewing over them.

"You said we could talk about Kimberly and the future," she softly reminded him.

"Yes." He brightened, sitting up in his chair and reaching for his coffee, his eyes pleased with the new subject. "Tell me what you'd like to do," he invited warmly.

Relief and pleasure danced through her. He was a beautiful man and her heart swelled with love for him. Her whole being clamoured for a resolution to all the unfinished business between them.

"It depends on what plans you've made," she offered cautiously. "Kimberly said you were thinking of sending her to PLC."

"Ah!" He grimaced. "Do I detect some more manoeuvring and manipulation by my devious niece? Has she been bending your ear about being banished to boarding school?"

"Not really." Meredith saw the opportunity to clarify the situation and took it. "She seems more concerned about how she'll fit into your life if you marry Rachel Pearce."

"Marry Rachel?" He frowned. "It's not on. I never said it was on."

Her pulse went crazy. He wasn't committed. She

gulped some more coffee in the hope it would settle her down again.

''In fact, Rachel dropped by last Sunday to give me the enrolment forms for PLC and let me know she'd just remet the one big love of her life the night before.''

''Oh!'' That information put a different complexion on the picture. Maybe it was pride saying marriage had never been on. On the other hand, if Nick had been deeply wounded last Sunday he'd been amazingly good at hiding it. ''That must have come as a shock to you,'' she said, watching intently for some sign of the effect on him.

''More a surprise.'' He shrugged. ''I was happy for her. The man in question was married the first time around and she'd been fairly cut up about it. He's now in the throes of divorce and wants another chance with her. Rachel was on her way to meet him for lunch when she called in.''

So that was why she'd been dressed to the nines! And Nick was now absolutely free of any sense of commitment to her! Meredith was dizzy with elation. It took an enormous effort to concentrate her mind on finding out if he was also heart-free.

''Were you...very attached to her?''

''You mean, did it hurt?'' he said bluntly.

''Well...'' She winced sympathetically. ''You couldn't have been expecting it.''

''We were good friends.'' He smiled without any chagrin whatsoever. ''We're still good friends. I would expect Rachel to call on me for a favour and I'd do the same, if need be.''

"That's nice," Meredith murmured, feeling weak with relief.

"She's a nice person. Unfortunately, she tended to rub Kimberly up the wrong way. No natural knack with children.''

This past year would not have been an easy time to win acceptance, Meredith thought, with Kimberly still feeling the loss of the parents she'd known. Rachel had probably met a brick wall resistance.

"Besides which, I think Kimberly had you on her mind," Nick remarked.

The insight surprised her yet instantly made sense. "The other mother figure," she murmured.

"Precisely. She wanted you. And she finally came out with it.''

Meredith sighed her contentment. It was wonderful to feel wanted by her daughter. If only Nick wanted her, too, her life would feel complete.

"She's very happy with you," Nick assured her.

"Yes." She smiled at him, almost bursting with pleasure. "Though no doubt we'll have our differences in times to come.''

He grinned, his dark eyes dancing again, making her heart trip over itself. "Little storms do blow up now and then. It's a matter of weathering them," he dryly advised. "Tell me what you think about sending her to PLC.''

They talked for hours, plotting—as parents do—what might be best for their child, with the reservation that the plans met with Kimberly's approval. They agreed the most important thing was for her to feel secure about them always being there for her. On the other hand, selfish and unreasonable demands were not to be encouraged nor catered to.

It was marvellous, being invited to share the responsibility of parenthood with Nick. Meredith revelled in it. The time passed so quickly she was shocked when he mentioned it was almost midnight and Kimberly would undoubtedly be up early, excited and full of energy.

They went inside together. Excitement and energy were not reserved for tomorrow, Meredith thought ruefully. Her whole body was tingling with the electricity of being super alive. Sleep looked like being an impossibility for quite a while.

She paused at the door of the bedroom allotted to her and smiled at the man she loved. "Thank you for being so generous. Good night, Nick."

"Sweet dreams," he answered, his eyes the colour of dark chocolate.

They will be tonight, she thought as she murmured, "You, too."

Parting from him was a wrench, but they were under the same roof, in harmony with each other, and there was tomorrow, as well as sweet dreams.

CHAPTER ELEVEN

NICK lay on his bed in the darkness, wondering why he was questioning the sense that something incredibly special had entered his life. Meredith Palmer seemed to offer him everything he'd ever wanted in a woman. The problem was, he couldn't be sure how much the dreams of her were influencing him. Was this compelling attraction wish-driven or substantially real?

The feelings she evoked in him were so strong and happening so fast, he'd barely held back the temptation to push the connection as far as he could tonight. He'd grabbed the excuse of Kimberly's early rising tomorrow to keep his desires in check, but holding control of himself had been a close run thing at her bedroom door.

He wanted her. He wanted to hold her and taste her and absorb every part of her and it was killing him to clamp down on the urges raging through him. If there were only the two of them to consider, nothing would hold him back, but Kimberly was involved too closely with this relationship for him to make hasty moves.

The wisest course was to wait. Meredith was not

about to go away. He had to be sure that whatever he did was right for all of them. It was definitely the sensible thing to do. Recklessly throwing caution to the winds was hardly commendable in this situation.

On the other hand, she emitted a power that made nonsense of caution. Each time he was with her he felt drawn into a vortex of passion that stimulated his body and intoxicated his mind. Pulling back to take stock of where they were was more and more a violation of the flow.

Sweet dreams.

The irony was he'd wanted the magic. Now he was feeling it, the experience was both an exquisite pleasure and a torment. For a moment tonight, when she'd mentioned Harvard, he thought they might have met there. However unlikely it was that he could have forgotten it, at least it would have been an answer to how she'd come to infiltrate his dreams.

And there was the other thing she'd said that had struck him as oddly out of place... *What do I know of the man you are now?* Perhaps it referred to what Denise had told her about him, yet it had felt too personal for merely second-hand knowledge. All his instincts were screaming there was something he should know about Meredith Palmer and if he just reached out far enough it would come to him. Yet it hadn't, regardless of how much he twisted and turned in his search for it.

The click of a door opening interrupted his train of thought. Had he imagined it? No. There was the sound again. He listened for the creak of the floorboards along the hall. The old house didn't lend itself to silent walking. The creak came. Someone was afoot. Kimberly or Meredith?

He listened for bathroom sounds. None eventuated. A visit to the kitchen seemed a reasonable alternative. He lay very still, straining to hear the slightest noise that would affirm his guess or identify some other normal activity. The house was quiet and continued to be quiet. No creak in the hall from footfalls returning. The silence stretched on and on, playing on his nerves. Curiosity turned to concern. Nick rose from his bed to investigate.

No lights were on under any of the doors in the bedroom wing. There didn't appear to be any glow of light coming from the living areas, either. He was crossing the main hall that bisected the house when he noticed the front door slightly ajar, letting in a sliver of moonlight.

A sense of unease drew him on. Had an intruder been in and out of the house? It didn't occur to him he was only wearing the boxer shorts he normally slept in, the concession to modesty he'd made when Kimberly had come to live with him. The need to know if it was Kimberly or Meredith or someone else on the move was imperative. Very quietly he opened the door far enough to slide around it.

No one was on the veranda. He stepped out, listening for any movement. Nothing impinged above the sound of the sea. He crossed to the railing, intent on scanning the beach. A figure standing on the waterline directly down from the house caught his eye. *And* stopped his heart as the sense of deja vu swamped his mind.

It was a scene from one of his dreams...the woman standing as still as a statue at the frothing edge of dying waves, her back turned to him, the dark, moody mystery of the sea in front of her, a black velvet sky studded with stars sweeping around and above her. Only the flying strands of hair, flicked out by the breeze from the long fall over her shoulders, added life to her stillness.

As though the breeze carried the essence of her to him, Nick could feel her waiting, yearning for someone to come to her, to join with her and end her long loneliness. The poignant passion of her need swirled into the empty places in his soul and tugged, inexorably pulling him toward her.

Nick was barely conscious of leaving the veranda, his legs automatically pumping down the steps, feet churning through the dry sand of the dunes. His heart was pounding, his mind filled with the compulsion to answer the siren song that he felt was calling to him...only to him...from her.

It was the dream, yet not the dream. This time he could smell the sea, feel the breeze slapping against him and the sand squeezing between his toes...real sensations, exciting him with the promise of a tangible ending. Still there was the eeriness of the action being the same.

As he closed the distance between them she either heard him or sensed him coming and she started to turn, slowly, as though not quite believing he would be there, drawn almost against her will to look…hair whipping across her face, a soft garment wrapping itself around her thighs, her breasts briefly silhouetted, tilted in tantalising womanliness, lending an infinite seductiveness to the sylphlike figure.

Of their own accord, his legs slowed their approach, waiting for her to come full face, waiting for the dream to follow its normal course, anticipating the flash of recognition, the widening of her eyes, the look of wonderment, the joyful welcome that would light her features, shining for him, beckoning him on.

It all happened, as he'd seen it happen countless times, like a video playing over and over in his mind in the dead of night, emerging from some secret place he could neither find nor control.

First the jolt of actually finding he was not a phantom of her mind, then the quiver of delight running through her body, the strong surge of happiness setting her face aglow, her mouth falling slightly open, giving a fuller sensuality to her lips, her eyes huge pools of green, dazzling drowning pools that sucked at his heart.

Now would come the barrier, he thought, the invisible wall he always strained against but couldn't break. Never had he been allowed to reach her.

A clammy sweat broke out on his brow. His hands clenched. The muscles in his legs tautened with all the power he could drive in to them. His heart drummed wild determination. If this was real, nothing could stop him tonight.

He surged forward.

She didn't fade away.

She stood her ground.

He reached out, his hands curling around her upper arms, warm flesh, solid flesh, giving flesh. His chest heaved, fighting the constriction of what felt like steel bands around it. His lungs filled with air. He was alive. And she was alive.

"Who are you?" he cried, his voice hoarse and alien to his own ears, as though possessed by his own dream figure and struggling to emerge into the reality of this night.

She didn't seem to understand. Or the question was irrelevant to her. Her eyes roved his face as though matching it to every detail of a beloved memory, savouring it anew.

He'd reached her, yet in some indefinable way he hadn't reached her. "Who are you?" he cried again in a torment of frustration.

Her eyes fastened on his, wanting him to know, aching for him to know. "I'm Merry," she whispered, "Merry…"

CHAPTER TWELVE

SHE saw the confusion in his eyes and her heart bled for the memory that had been lost. He'd approached her with such an air of purpose and passion, she'd thought it had all come back to him. But it wasn't important. Only the feeling was, and it pulsed from him with a strength that demolished the barrier of time.

Past, present, future...none of it had any meaning. It was all blotted out by the unleashed need surging between them. For Meredith, the magic of coming together again was an irresistible lure. She lifted a hand to his face, instinctively using touch to wipe away the distraction of a name he didn't relate to.

"I couldn't sleep...thinking of you," she murmured, her eyes mirroring the love that was his to take.

"Me? Was it me you were thinking of? Or..." He struggled with the doubt she'd inadvertently put in his mind.

"You, Nick. Only you," she assured him, sliding her other hand up over his bare chest, craving the physical contact she had missed for so long.

The flare of desire in his eyes poured a flood of warmth through her veins. He cupped her face, fingers spreading into her hair above and below her ears. His head bent. Her mouth opened to meet his, wanting to feast on his kiss, so hungry for it she went up on tiptoe to accelerate the yearned-for intimacy.

He tasted her eagerness, revelled in it, plundered her mouth with devouring intensity, pent-up need exploding in a passion for every exciting sensation that could be derived from the fierce foray into finding each other, finding and knowing and exulting in the pulsing reality of dreams being fulfilled.

She hung on to his head, fingers clawing through his hair, gripping to keep him with her, driven to a frenzy of possessiveness now that she had him again. He wrapped his arms around her, scooping her into full body contact, electrifying every nerve with an acute awareness of their sexuality...man and woman...wanting what each could give, straining to feel the promise of it.

His hands slid down the arched curve of her back, clutched and kneaded the rounded flesh below it, moulding the softness, fitting her more closely, achingly close to the swollen hardness thrusting from his loins. Her thighs quivered against the taut power of his as desire swirled through her, sensitising her breasts, curling her stomach, stirring the throbbing need to feel him inside her, to hold him there so he would never think of leaving her again, never want to.

His mouth lifted from hers long enough to murmur, "I want you."

"Yes," she answered, her sense of urgency as great as his.

"Now."

"Yes."

"Not here. The grit of sand…"

"Wherever you want."

"The sleep-out on the veranda. We'll be comfortable there."

"Yes."

He broke away, caught her hand, and they ran together in an exhilarating burst of energy, knowing what was to come, the ecstatic freedom of no restraint in their loving, time to explore their pleasure in each other and savour every moment of it. They could have plucked stars from the sky, their spirits were soaring so high, and behind them the sea boomed and crashed in counterpoint to the drum of their hearts.

Nick paused her at the foot of the steps to wash off the sand under a tap positioned there for that purpose, his hands stroking her calves and ankles, caressing her feet and toes. She bent to do the same for him but he grew agitated with her ministrations, quickly turning the tap off and lifting her up, his eyes dark and turbulent as they tensely searched hers.

"You make me feel…"

"What?" she encouraged.

He shook his head. "I want this to be…let me make love to you, Meredith."

A need for control, she thought, but when he swept her off her feet and cradled her against his chest, she wondered if it was some deeply felt male need to claim her as his woman, to impress himself upon her and wipe out any thought of what she'd felt or done with anyone else.

She curled her arms around his neck and nestled her head close to his throat, soaking in the sense of belonging, of having at last come home after years in the wilderness. "I thought you'd never come, but you did," she sighed on a warm gush of happiness. Then, wanting him to know how special he was, "You're the man I've been longing for, Nick."

"Yes." The word burst from him like a shot of steam, pushed from a maelstrom of emotion. His arms tightened around her. "No more waiting, Meredith. That's over."

His voice rang with triumph, as though he'd finally won a hard battle, and like a victor carrying off his reward, he charged up the steps and strode exuberantly around the veranda to the section that had been enclosed for extra sleeping quarters.

The room was stuffy. Nick laid her on the bed,

which was covered with a cotton quilt, then hastily swept around the louvred windows, opening them to the fresh night air. Meredith smiled at his caring for her comfort but her smile was swallowed by a tidal wave of tingling excitement when he dropped his shorts and straightened up, breathtakingly male in his nakedness.

She quickly pushed herself into a sitting position, her hands scrabbling at the short silk shift she'd worn to bed earlier in the night. Wanting to be free of all barriers between them, she dragged it off and hurled it aside, just before he reached her.

He swooped to lift her up, standing her on the edge of the double bed, hooking his hands into the briefs she'd put on before going down to the beach. He paused, breathing hard, his gaze fastened on her breasts, so enticingly close to his face.

Her nipples instantly puckered in response. They were level with his mouth and the temptation to lean forward, to feel his lips encircling them… She moaned with pleasure as he took them, one and then the other, licking, sucking, tugging, drawing on her desire and embellishing it a hundredfold with his.

Excitement pumped from her breasts and streamed wildly to the apex between her thighs. She clutched his shoulders for support as he drew her briefs down, frantic to work her legs out of them so he wouldn't have to bend, wouldn't have to stop the glorious momentum of intensely satisfying sensation.

Her breasts had been made for this and she'd missed having it with the baby she'd borne him, the natural bonding she'd been denied. But Nick wasn't denying her. He was loving her as she'd yearned to be loved, no holds barred, completely and passionately. She cradled his head, cherishing him, caressing the nape of his neck, pressing kisses over his hair.

His hand softly cupped the silky mound below her stomach and she rejoiced that her legs were now free to move apart for him, to invite and welcome his touch, needing it, wanting it, seething with anticipation for it. He stroked her with exquisite gentleness, slowly, seductively, arousing a sensitivity that quivered and craved for more. The slick sweet caresses became unbearable and she clawed his back in a fever of urgent need.

"Nick…"

The groaned plea was enough. An arm crushed her close as he knelt on the bed and lowered her into position for him. Then he reared back, looming over her, his magnificent body taut, every muscle strained with the power of his manhood.

His eyes blazed with a wild exultation as he thrust himself inside her, tunneling fast and deep, and she arched to entice the whole glorious fullness of him, loving its passage, loving the thrilling sensation of its intimate journey to the centre of her inner world.

Only he had ever joined her there and when he reached the innermost rim of it, she wound her legs around him to hold him there, squeezing tight in an ecstasy of possession.

A guttural cry of fierce satisfaction broke from his throat. His arms burrowed under her shoulders, raising her. His mouth came down on hers with ravaging force, invading, possessing, passionately pursuing the deepest sense of union with her. It was wild, beautiful, intense, the penultimate sense of mating.

When her muscles relaxed he pulled his mouth from hers and concentrated all his energy on repeating his first climactic entry, sliding back to plunge again and again, building a rhythm that threshed her into another peak of sweet bliss, and still he went on, riding from crest to crest, pushing the pleasure up a scale of intensity until no more was possible and he spilled the driving force of his need for her, filling her with the exquisite warmth of final fusion.

She took his spent body in her arms, stroking the shuddering muscles into gentle relaxation. Flesh of my flesh, she thought, remembering the baby they'd made and wondering if it would happen again. Would he like it to? Was she assuming too much from one night of loving?

No, it was more than that. Much more. She was certain now he felt all that she did. It hadn't gone away. It had been waiting for her.

Merry... The name kept echoing through Nick's mind as though it belonged to this moment, belonged to the incredible magic of their coming together.

"Meredith..." he said out loud, trying to drive away the echo, override it.

"Yes?"

The husky answer forced him to think of an appropriate reply. Surely to God she'd given him more of herself than she'd given to any other man. It was wrong to confuse this with the spectre of her lost love.

"I could not have dreamed what we've just shared," he murmured, raising himself from her embrace to brush his lips over hers in tender tribute to her generous loving. "It goes beyond dreams."

He rolled onto his side, taking her with him, tucking one arm around her so she lay on his chest, her legs still entangled with his in close intimacy. She felt so right, perfect, as though she'd been made especially for him. How could she have loved another? There'd never been any other woman like her for him.

"It's a miracle," she whispered, her warm breath fanning his skin, making it tingle. "A Christmas miracle.'' He could hear the happy smile in her voice.

Christmas…

Merry Christmas…

The special name stirred an unease, a sense of wrongness he tried to resist, but it persisted. He remembered watching the grieving look on her face, hearing the sad heartache in her voice as she'd recounted how Kimberly's real father had come to call her *Merry.*

How was it then that she'd said to him tonight, *You're the man I've been longing for?*

They'd only met a little over a week ago.

Yet her other words to him also suggested waiting for a much longer span of time…

I thought you'd never come.

Haunting words…focused on him, yet not making any real sense in the context of their short acquaintance.

Her being in his dreams all these years made no sense, either.

He stroked the long silky hair he'd seen so often in those dreams and never been allowed to touch. He played it through his fingers, real hair, as real as she was. She snuggled into a more comfortable position and sighed her contentment. After passion, the peace, he thought. Sweet dreams…

He ran his fingertips over her back, loving the satin texture of her skin, the soft curves of her body.

She was beautiful, inside and out, just as he'd always felt she would be, his fantasy woman come to life. And still he didn't know how the fantasy had begun.

He cast through his memory, trying to recall how far back it had gone. Not school days. Not during his years at Killara Business College. Then there was that blank spot before he went to Harvard, due to that damned surfboard cracking his skull.

It had taken him a while to get his brain back in order to continue his studies for the career he'd been aiming for, trying to recollect things he knew he should know. And yes, he remembered now. The dream had been part of that. He'd put it down to some subconscious manifestation of his frustration. Over the years he'd interpreted it differently, linking it to other things, but it had started then.

After the blank spot.

A nasty little frisson ran down Nick's spine. His mind instinctively shied away from the thought that hit it. But it stuck.

The blank spot incorporated the Christmas period.

Thirteen years ago.

CHAPTER THIRTEEN

A TAPPING on the door woke Meredith. She came alert with a jolt, her head whipping around to find Nick. He wasn't with her. Then she realised this wasn't the sleep-out on the veranda. She was back in her own bedroom. Alone.

"Are you awake, Merry?" Kimberly's voice!

Awake and stark naked! If Kimberly took it in her head to come in... Meredith's agitated gaze finally fell on the nightie and briefs lying across the foot of the bed. She snatched them up and quickly pulled the nightie over her head, struggling to get her arms into the holes. "Yes?" she called, shoving her briefs under the pillow.

"Uncle Nick said if we're to buy a decent Christmas tree, we'd better get moving or the best ones will all be sold."

Nick was up and about! What time was it? She checked her watch. Five to nine. Shock galvanised her into action. She threw off the bedclothes and raced to the wardrobe.

"Sorry I overslept, Kimberly. I'll be right out. Is the bathroom free?"

"Yes. We're all ready."

Almost nine o'clock. Kimberly had probably been up since six. Or earlier. If they'd still been in the sleep-out... Thank heaven Nick had thought of what might happen in the morning. She must have been dead to the world when he'd carried her back here.

She shoved her arms into the silk wraparound that matched her nightie, then quickly grabbed fresh underclothes and the yellow shorts and top she'd planned to wear today. Flushed, her heart racing, she dashed to the door, wrenched it open, and almost ran straight into Kimberly who was still lingering there.

"Oh! I really am sorry, Kimberly. You should have woken me earlier," she rattled out.

"It's okay." A happy grin flashed across her face. "Uncle Nick said you were up really late talking." Her eyes danced with how pleased she was with such promising proceedings from her artful manipulation. "Did you have a good time, Merry?"

Meredith's flush deepened, burning her cheeks. "Yes, I did. I'd better hurry." She sidestepped and headed for the bathroom, acutely aware that the musky smell of their lovemaking was still clinging to her.

"Uncle Nick said it was the best time he'd ever had," Kimberly crowed triumphantly.

Meredith paused with her hand on the knob, her

heart leaping with joy. She smiled back at her daughter…his daughter. ''That's nice.''

''Yeah,'' she drawled feelingly. Her eyes sparkled. ''And he said he wasn't going to marry Rachel Pearce, so things are going really good.''

''Well, I'm glad you're relieved of that worry,'' Meredith said lightly.

Kimberly surveyed the mussed state of her mother's hair with a critical eye. ''You can take your time, Merry,'' she advised. ''We'll wait for you.''

Meredith sailed into the bathroom on a wave of pure happiness. *The best time he'd ever had.* Her, too. The very best. Better than before because there was nothing in the way now. Not her age. Not his career. No disapproving family from either side. And their daughter was only too eager for them to come together. It couldn't be more perfect.

Mindful of not spending too long under the shower, Meredith, nevertheless, took a deep, sensual pleasure in soaping her body all over, remembering the magical feelings Nick had aroused in her last night. Sometimes, over the years, she had wondered if she was making the memories better than how it had really been. It wasn't so. If anything, they had dulled. What she had experienced with Nick last night was everything she had remembered and more.

Having switched off the shower and towelled herself dry, Meredith wasted no time in dressing. It was a big bathroom with plenty of bench space and she'd stored her vanity bag in the cupboard under the washbasin. She quickly pulled it out and unzipped it, removing the items she needed.

Kimberly had been right about her hair. The salt air and the breeze had made a mess of it, forcing her to wash it. She wielded a hair dryer and brush to best effect as fast as she could. Lipstick and a touch of eyeliner was enough make-up for the beach.

Confident she was now presentable enough to satisfy her daughter's need for her to look attractive, she raced back to her bedroom to dump her discarded clothes and pick up her camera. Buying their first Christmas tree together was too important an event not to capture on film. Meredith wanted to record everything about this Christmas.

As she crossed the hall she heard Kimberly and Nick bantering with each other in the kitchen. Meredith smiled over their easy give-and-take manner. Little storms might blow up now and then, as Nick said, but they shared a solid familiarity and an understanding that would not be shaken for long. She reminded herself to re-open the PLC issue with Kimberly, now that Rachel Pearce was no longer a factor in the equation.

When she stepped into the kitchen the conversation stopped, two pairs of eyes instantly swinging to her, making her pulse skip into a faster beat with the keen intensity of their interest.

"Oh!" Kimberly beamed approval at her. "You look lovely in yellow, Merry. Doesn't she, Uncle Nick?" An arch look at him.

"Better than sunshine," he obliged, smiling, but Meredith sensed an element of strain behind the smile, a volley of questions that couldn't be asked in front of Kimberly.

"Thank you," she said brightly to both of them, then directly to him, "And thank you for being so considerate of me."

He relaxed a little, his eyes softening with a caring that curled around her heart. "You were obviously exhausted. I hope you slept well."

"Too well. I wish I'd woken earlier." With you, she telegraphed to him, flushing a little as she mentally stripped his navy shorts and white T-shirt, remembering the magnificent power of his body and how it had felt, joining with hers.

"We have many days ahead of us." It was a blazing promise. "There's coffee simmering on the hotplate. Would you like a cup?"

"We kept you some muffins, too," Kimberly chimed in, rushing to set a plate for her.

"Is there time? I don't want us to miss out on a good Christmas tree," Meredith said quickly.

"Looking after you is more important," Nick declared, and the determined look in his eyes brooked no argument.

He waved her to a chair at the kitchen table and Meredith took it, happy to be looked after. She had been looking after herself for so long, she revelled in the feeling of being part of a family—her very own family—who cared about her.

"Uncle Nick and I are going to make this Christmas really special for you, Merry," Kimberly announced, giving her two muffins as Nick poured the coffee. "It's to make up for the ones when you didn't have anybody."

A rush of emotion brought tears to her eyes. She hastily blinked them away and smiled at her daughter. "It's already special."

The best, the very best, she thought blissfully, lifting her gaze to Nick as he set her cup of coffee beside her plate. His eyes mirrored the memories of last night's lovemaking, stirring an embarrassing but secretly exciting range of physical sensations.

The inner muscles that had held him so intimately spasmed in remembered delight and she barely stopped herself from squirming on her chair. She could only hope her bra hid the sudden hardening of her nipples. At least the quiver of her stomach was something that could be settled. She picked up a muffin and munched through it, sipping coffee to wash it down.

Nick engaged Kimberly in conversation while

Meredith was busy breakfasting. Watching the two of them together, so alike in more ways than they realised, it occurred to her she should re-think her decision to leave the past in the past. It felt wrong for Nick not to know he was Kimberly's father. She shouldn't keep such a special, flesh and blood bond from him. From either of them. They both had a natural right to know.

Telling him was not going to be easy, particularly after she had skated over the facts of the adoption last night. Her reasoning for holding back had seemed right at the time, not wanting to burden him with a truth he'd find disturbing and painful, considering the part his sister had played in taking responsibility from him, the long-played deceit that had denied him his true relationship with his own child.

However, the circumstances were different now. Nick felt the same about her as he had all those years before. Rachel Pearce was out of the picture. Meredith decided she wouldn't be putting any sense of obligation or guilt on him now they had come together again. No blame was attached to him for what had happened. He would surely understand that.

He would help her tell Kimberly. Doing it together—both of her real parents—would probably be the least traumatic way, with explanations smoothed by putting more emphasis on the future than the past. She would discuss it with Nick to-night. After they made love. Meredith smiled to herself. Nothing could go badly wrong when the feeling between them ran so strongly.

"Have you had all you want, Merry?" Kimberly asked eagerly.

Meredith promptly rose from her chair and picked up her camera. "Ready to go."

"Great! Let's move!" She took Meredith's free hand and led her toward the door. "Come on, Uncle Nick! We can get a bigger tree this year because there's three of us to carry it back."

Meredith shot him a laughing glance and was surprised by the grim look on his face. His eyes caught hers and he instantly lightened his expression, though not quite enough to completely erase the dark turbulence she saw in them. Something was troubling him. Something he didn't like. She wondered about it as they left the house and took the walk through the nature reserve to the village.

By the time they reached the esplanade she'd dismissed any concern over it. Kimberly was trying to tease out of Nick what he'd bought her for Christmas and he had them both laughing over his outlandish tales of shopping for the perfect gift.

He'd decided against the five thousand piece jig-saw because Kimberly was bound to lose some pieces in the jungle that was her bedroom. Since she had never shown an interest in stitching a fine seam, the super-duper sewing machine seemed bound to be wasted. And so on and so on.

A table-top truck, loaded with Christmas trees, was parked directly opposite the general store. A range of sizes had been propped against the vehicle and an enterprising salesman was doing a brisk trade. As soon as one tree was sold, a helpmate lifted another down to take its place. Meredith was reassured the choice had definitely not been left too late.

Kimberly and Nick strolled slowly down the row, assessing the merits of the trees on display, pausing here and there to stand trees upright, wanting to look at their overall shape. Meredith hung back and snapped photographs of them until Kimberly protested.

''Gosh, Merry! You're as bad as Mum, taking millions of photos of everything. You're missing the fun of choosing.''

The words rolled out naturally and Meredith thought nothing of them, content to put her camera away and join them. Nick, however, reacted strongly.

''Take as many photographs as you want, Meredith,'' he commanded, the dark turbulence flaring into his eyes. He turned sharply to Kimberly. ''You know about the packet of photographs Denise sent to Meredith.''

She nodded, disturbed by his abrupt change of mood.

"Denise sent them every year. So once a year, your real mother received an update of your life. Just once a year, Kimberly. And that's all she knew of you."

The emotional emphasis laced through the words struck Meredith dumb. She hadn't realised he'd been so deeply affected by the arrangement she'd made with his sister.

"The walls of Meredith's bedroom in her apartment are covered with those photographs," he went on, relentlessly beating out the truth of what she'd missed in giving up her baby. "The best of them are enlarged to see you all the better, everything about you…"

"Nick…" It wasn't necessary to tell Kimberly this, to make her feel guilty for something she wasn't a party to.

An almost savage tension emanated from him as he threw her a fierce look. "She should know how it was for you."

"It was my choice."

"At sixteen?"

"Please…" Her hand fluttered an agitated appeal. "It's over now." She looked at her daughter and smiled to take away the distress Nick had stirred. "You're right, Kimberly. It's better being with you than having photographs."

It was true. She didn't need photographs anymore. She had the real-life experience to enjoy. She walked over to her daughter, put her arm around her shoulders and gave a gentle hug. "Which tree do you like?"

Soulful green eyes looked up at her. "I thought of you, too, Merry. All this year. Ever since I knew of you. I wished I had a photo to see what you looked like, but I didn't have anything."

"I know. It's awful, not knowing, isn't it?" Meredith said in soft sympathy.

She nodded. Her expression turned anxious. "Don't be mad at Uncle Nick for telling me. I'm glad he did, Merry. Now I know you always cared about me."

"I'm not mad at him, Kimberly. He was just showing he cared." She held out her hand to him and willed him to take it. "Thank you, Nick."

He sighed, his eyes wry as his fingers curled around hers and his thumb stroked over the hyperactive pulse at her wrist. "A loving mother deserves no less. How about lending me your camera and I'll take some photos of you and Kimberly choosing the tree? *I'd* like them."

She laughed and handed him the camera, relieved that peace and goodwill had been restored.

Nevertheless, it concerned her that he'd been so upset about the photographs. How much more upset might he be tonight if she told him the full truth? It was Christmas Eve. She didn't want this Christmas spoiled. Maybe it was better to leave telling him everything until more time together built a comfort zone and the past was less sharp than it was now.

Or would that make it worse?

How could she continue to be intimate with him while hiding such a big secret?

Meredith fretted over the decision while she and Kimberly selected a tall tree with the most symmetrical shape. They posed on either side of it for Nick to take his photograph. Once the tree was paid for, they set off for home again, the three of them holding part of the long trunk to keep the branches off the ground.

A family, Meredith thought.

Except two of them didn't know it.

The sense of family was such a happy feeling, the kind of feeling everyone should have at Christmas time. She'd keenly felt the loss of it over the years. Nick and Kimberly must be feeling loss, too, with Denise and Colin Graham gone. Would revealing the truth make it better? Letting them know they still had a very real family? Or would she be destroying memories they held dear?

It's awful, not knowing... The words she'd spoken to Kimberly slipped back into her mind. It was the ultimate truth.

She had to tell Nick.

Tonight.

Then they could both figure out how to tell Kimberly.

CHAPTER FOURTEEN

IT WAS killing him, not knowing. Twice now he'd unsettled Meredith with his brooding over it. Not that she knew what was eating up his mind, and he couldn't just blurt it out. If he was wrong, she would think him mad, connecting himself to the lover who'd fathered Kimberly. He didn't want to confuse her feelings for him. But…he had to know!

Nick paced the living room, impatient for the necessary time to himself to try telephoning his old friends. If anyone would know the critical details of what had happened to him that Christmas thirteen years ago, Jerry and Dave had the inside track. As far as he knew, they'd been with him from start to end of that long vacation.

The tree dominating the corner of the room caught his eye and he stopped, struck by the irony of it all. Another Christmas. Tonight they'd be hanging the decorations on it, making merry.

Merry…

He shook his head, wanting this burden lifted. As soon as Meredith and Kimberly reappeared in their swimming costumes he would send them off to the beach ahead of him. And damn his old friends to hell if they could not be reached!

"Great tree, isn't it, Merry?"

Nick spun around. They were in the doorway. The sight of Meredith in a body-hugging white maillot, cut high to her hips, took his breath away. Her skin was tanned to the colour of golden honey and glowed like silk, compelling the need to touch. And her legs, her beautiful long legs…the feeling of them winding around him, tangling intimately with his was instantly triggered again, setting his heart pounding, pumping desire into a flood of wanting.

"You haven't changed into your swimmers."

Kimberly's accusing voice dragged his gaze to her. "I put them on under my shorts earlier," he answered distractedly.

"Well, come on then," she urged.

"I'll follow you. I've just remembered a call I should make."

She groaned. "Not business on Christmas Eve!"

"I won't be long."

"But we need you to bring the windsurfer down."

He shook his head. "Not enough breeze for it yet. Best to wait until after lunch. We'll try it then."

A disappointed sigh.

Meredith's hand gently squeezed Kimberly's

shoulder. "Let's not hassle Nick. I'm dying for a swim."

Kimberly's face broke into a cheeky grin. "Last one into the water is a rotten egg."

She dashed off with Meredith in laughing pursuit.

Nick was inexorably drawn to follow as far as the veranda, watching the two of them pelting over the sand. Meredith...the woman of his dreams, gloriously real and tangible and part of his life now. Kimberly...her black ponytail swinging, so many likenesses to his side of the family. Was she his daughter?

He watched them run into the surf, squealing and laughing and heart-wrenchingly happy with each other. If Meredith had missed out on this for all these years because of... Nick's hands gripped the veranda railing hard as a savage sense of loss tore through him.

He had to know.

He strode back into the house, heading straight for the telephone in the kitchen. There'd been no answer from either of the calls he'd made in the early hours of this morning. With it being the Christmas weekend, Jerry and Dave could be anywhere.

None of them was in regular contact, Jerry's work having taken him to Melbourne, and Dave having married in England and settled in London. They exchanged Christmas cards and met for a drink or dinner on the rare occasions they were in each other's cities. Nevertheless, the old sense of mateship was always quickly revived and Nick knew they would help if they could. He fiercely willed for one of them to be home.

He tried Jerry's number first.

No answer.

Frustration rose several notches. He mentally calculated the time in London. Around two in the morning. He didn't care. The need to know overrode every other consideration.

He dialled the international digits and waited, tension screwing up his stomach as the calling beeps repeated their pattern an excruciating number of times. Relief whooshed through him at the clatter of a receiver being fumbled off the hook.

"Dave?" The name exploded off his lips.

"Yeah. Who's this?" Voice slurred with sleep.

"Dave, it's Nick. Nick Hamilton. Sorry to…"

"Hell, man! Do you know what time it is over here?"

"I know but I couldn't get through before."

"Christmas…lines are jammed." The resigned mutter was followed by more alert interest. "So what's up?"

"This is very important to me, Dave. I need your help."

"Right! You've got it." No hesitation.

Nick took a deep breath. "Remember the trip we

went on when we finished college? The one where I ended up in hospital with a cracked skull.''

''Sure I remember it. We hit all the great surfing beaches, right up the coast to Tweed Heads, which was where you copped it.''

''Tell me the beaches, Dave.''

''You ring me up in the middle of the night to find out about beaches?''

''No, it's more than that. I need you to fill in that time for me. It's a blank to me, Dave. Help me with it. Please?''

''Okay. Let me think. Umm…first we stopped off at Boomerang near Forster. Great surf. We even had a school of dolphins swim in one day…''

''Next beach,'' Nick pressed.

''That'd be Flynn's at Port Macquarie.''

''After that?''

''South West Rocks, east of Kempsey.''

''And then?''

''Sawtell. Near Coff's Harbour.''

Coff's Harbour!

Nick swallowed hard. ''Dave, did I get tied up with a girl in Coff's Harbour?''

''Ah-ha! Woman trouble! Come back to haunt you, has she?'' Salacious interest.

Nick closed his eyes. Dave couldn't have spoken a truer word than *haunt*. ''So there was someone,'' he pressed on, determined to pin everything down.

''Sure was! You were head over heels, man! No

way were you going to leave her. You told us we could travel on if we wanted, but you'd found something a hell of a lot better than surfing beaches, and wild horses couldn't drag you away.''

''So why didn't I stay?''

''Her old woman told you she was only sixteen. A bit young for what you two were getting up to, old son. In the end you saw sense and we travelled on. Put a spike in your usual good humour, though. You shouldn't have taken that spill at Tweed Heads, you know. Your mind simply wasn't on surfing after Coff's.''

It fitted. Yet still he needed the final clincher. ''What was her name, Dave?''

''Her name…damned if I can remember.''

''Try. Try very hard,'' Nick urged, his heart hammering painfully.

''Don't know that I ever knew,'' Dave mused. ''You had a special name for her.'' He laughed. ''Certainly wasn't her real name.''

''Do you remember it?''

''Sure!'' He laughed again. ''A good one for this time of year, Nick.''

''Tell me.''

''Merry Christmas. That's what you called her. Merry Christmas.''

CHAPTER FIFTEEN

NICK jotted down the score, gathered up the playing cards and shuffled them. He looked tired. He'd been rather quiet—almost distant—all evening, only rallying out of his abstraction to respond to Kimberly's demands on him. Meredith hoped he wasn't too tired to stay up with her after Kimberly went to bed.

It had been an active day; swimming, windsurfing, setting the Christmas tree up and decorating it. Besides which, he couldn't have had many hours' sleep last night. He'd been up early with Kimberly this morning. What would she do if he suggested they retire early?

"This is definitely the last hand, Kimberly," he warned as he dealt the cards around the table. "Win or lose."

"But I'm much too excited to go to bed yet, Uncle Nick," she protested, jiggling around in her chair.

The gin rummy score had been seesawing between them and Nick was in the lead at the moment. Meredith was not in the running to win. Her playing had lacked concentration. She was too distracted, thinking about how best to reveal the truth to Nick.

"You've had more than a fair go," he pointed out. "You asked to stay up until *Carols By Candlelight* was finished on the TV, remember?"

"It's only just finished."

"A deal is a deal, my girl."

She huffed and sorted her hand of cards. "I'd better win, then."

Much to her delight, and Meredith's secret relief, she did. Or Nick let her. Either way, there was no more argument about bedtime. She danced around the card table, crowing triumphantly about her victory, gave Nick a hug and a kiss good night, did the same to Meredith, looked longingly at the presents piled under the Christmas tree, then broke into a chorus of "Jingle Bells" as she headed off to her bedroom.

"Hardly a lullaby," Meredith commented, expecting Nick to smile.

He didn't. "Let's clear up," he said quietly. "Get it out of the way."

She was instantly aware of tightly held restraint. The relaxed air he had maintained with Kimberly was gone. The inward tension coming from him was so strong, it plunged her into a turmoil of doubt. Was he regretting rushing headlong into an involvement with her?

She looked searchingly at him but his gaze was

hooded, looking down at the cards he was packing into their case. He stood to return it to the games cupboard, carrying the writing pad and pen, as well. It prompted her to get moving.

Her hands shook a little as she collected the dirty glasses and took them out to the kitchen sink, her mind racing over what might be wrong. This was the first time they'd been alone together all day. She'd been waiting for it, half in dread, half in eagerness. Now it had come, Nick showed no sign of taking pleasure in her company. Quite the opposite.

She rinsed the glasses and left them on the draining board to dry, feeling driven to return to the living room and confront whatever was on his mind. Her heart fluttered with apprehension but she stuck to her earlier conviction. Better to know than not know.

He was standing, staring at the Christmas tree when she walked in. He swung around at hearing her and gave her a travesty of a smile. "Will you come out to the veranda with me? I don't want Kimberly overhearing us."

Meredith nodded and led the way, extremely conscious of him following her and closing the front door after him. When she turned questioningly, he waved her on to the cane armchairs where they had sat and talked the previous evening. He certainly didn't have making love in mind. Any desire he might be feeling for her was rigidly repressed.

It occurred to her he could be concerned that they had acted recklessly last night. Maybe he wanted to know if she was protected. In the heat of the moment, neither of them had considered consequences. Meredith supposed she should regret the carelessness. Somehow it didn't seem important.

He waited for her to settle in one of the armchairs, clearly too ill at ease to sit beside her. She saw his hands clench. He moved over to the railing, looking out to sea for several moments before turning his gaze to her.

"I know now that Merry was my special name for you," he said very quietly. "It was me you were speaking of when you explained it to Kimberly."

Shock rendered her speechless. He *knew*. She didn't have to tell him.

"Were you aware I had no memory of it?" he asked.

The pain in his voice squeezed her heart. Her mind was still in chaos, wondering how and when he'd realised this was not their first involvement. Nevertheless, it was paramount that she answer and answer truthfully. It was what she had wanted…to let him know. Though not for one moment had she anticipated he would preempt her in opening up the past.

She searched for appropriate words, delivering

them haltingly. "Your sister told me. She explained about your accident. Then last week, when you came about Kimberly, it was obvious you had no memory of me."

His hand jerked out in a hopeless little gesture. "I still don't remember."

That shocked her anew. "Then how...? I don't understand..."

"I called Dave today. Dave Ketteridge. He was with me that summer."

One of Nick's friends. She remembered them. The other one was called Jerry. Jerry Thompson. The three of them had been mates for years and obviously still in contact since Nick had called Dave today. Which meant he'd known he was Kimberly's father when he'd joined them in the surf, known all afternoon, all evening. It was amazing he'd hidden it as well as he had, waiting and waiting to get her alone without fear of interruption.

"Why didn't you contact me?" he asked, stress straining his voice. "At least, let me have the chance to...to..." Pent-up feeling exploded. "Damn it, Merry! It was my child you were carrying. I should have been told."

There was no way to avoid giving him pain and in justice to herself she had to tell the truth. "I did all I could to reach you, Nick."

"You met my sister." The accusation shot from him, carrying a load of anger and frustration.

"Yes. You'd left me her address. To write to you if I wanted to after a year had gone by. When I found out I was pregnant, my stepmother..." That was irrelevant. She took a deep breath and went on, concentrating on keeping her tone quiet and calm. "I caught the bus from Coff's Harbour to Sydney..."

"Your stepmother threw you out?"

Meredith winced. "Not exactly. Her sister said she'd have me if I worked in her florist shop. I was supposed to be coming to her in Sydney, but I went to your address first."

"And I wasn't there."

"No. Your sister said you'd been invited to go to Harvard and wouldn't be back for two years."

"You could have asked her for my address in the U.S."

Still accusing. Still critical. Meredith looked squarely at him and said, "I did. I was distressed. I made the mistake of telling her I was pregnant to you."

"Mistake! What do you mean 'mistake'?" he demanded tersely.

Meredith paused. There was no kind way of saying this. She sighed and recited the facts as they'd been put to her. "She didn't want your prospects of a great career ruined. She didn't want you coming home to a girl you'd forgotten, a girl who'd hang a baby on you when you weren't in a position to take the responsibility of it, a girl who wasn't old enough or accomplished enough to be a suitable wife. I'd be like an albatross around your neck.''

''She said that?'' He was shocked, horrified.

''I guess it was reasonable from her point of view.'' Meredith answered flatly.

''So what happened then?''

''I didn't believe her. I thought…she doesn't want me.'' She looked at him, her eyes aching with the memory. ''But I couldn't believe you wouldn't want me, Nick. I thought she was lying about your forgetting me.''

His chest heaved with a sharp intake of breath. He released it on a long shuddering sigh. ''It was true…yet not true. I dreamed of you. I dreamed of you so many times over the years, when I first saw you at your apartment…'' He shook his head. ''It's been driving me crazy.''

Enlightenment dawned. ''So that's why you rang Dave.''

''That and other things…things you said…the way I felt…''

Was he saying he felt the same as he had before? Or had that changed now, with harbouring a sense of betrayal since his call to his friend. He wasn't coming near her, didn't want to touch. His dark brooding didn't invite her touch, either.

Sick at heart, Meredith said, ''I tried to find

Dave, Nick. And Jerry. They were my only other leads to you."

He stiffened. "Jerry knew where I was. I wrote to him."

"There are five pages of Thompsons in the Sydney phone book," Meredith informed him. "I tried Ketteridge first."

He frowned. "Dave went backpacking overseas that year," he muttered reminiscently.

"His father told me they were lucky if he sent a postcard now and then. The last one was from Turkey. It said Dave was heading for India. They knew you were in the U.S. but didn't have an address. I was given Jerry's home number."

"And Jerry didn't help?" Sheer incredulity.

"His mother answered the phone. She curtly informed me he'd moved away from home and she was sick of girls he'd left behind ringing him up. If he wanted to contact me he would. I managed to get in a question about you and she said as far as she was concerned, the same principle applied."

He groaned and pushed away from the railing, pacing the veranda to the steps and back, then throwing out his hands in an aggressive appeal. "You could have tried a letter to Harvard University."

The question cracked on her like a whip. Her head snapped up. "Could I, Nick?" She pushed out of the chair to face him on a more equal level, her eyes blazing a challenge to his assertion. "I'd had every door shut in my face. Your sister said you'd forgotten me. Mrs. Thompson scorned me for running after you. It had been months since you walked away from me. Skipping out, my stepmother called it."

"I didn't," he swiftly defended. "It was for your sake I left."

"You weren't there to tell me that," she shot back at him.

"God damn it!" he exploded. "I still had the right to know."

"Rage at your sister then." Her voice shook with the emotional torment she'd been put through. "*She* judged for you. *She* knew you best. *She* made the decision."

He closed his eyes and rubbed his brow, shaking his head. "I'm sorry. I keep thinking…all these years…all these years… I should have been told."

"And I'm the only one you've got to blame. Is that it, Nick?" she mocked in a surge of bitterness for all the lost years.

"No!" His eyes flew open in a flare of anguish. His hand came down in a clenched fist, smacking into the palm of his other hand for emphasis. "I need to understand…to get the facts straight in my mind."

"To understand," she repeated derisively. She shook her head and swung away from him, moving over to the railing and looking bleakly at a sea that had been silent witness to her sorrows many, many times. "You couldn't imagine in a million years how it was for me."

A heavy sigh. "I do realise Denise has a lot to answer for," he quietly acknowledged. "I don't blame you, Merry. I just wish…"

"You think I didn't wish?"

He'd scraped the old wounds raw again, making her voice harsh. She swallowed hard and lifted her gaze to the stars, brilliant, distant dots in a universe of worlds that were unreachable. Like him, when she'd needed him most.

"I gave up my baby to your sister because she was your family, and at least you would know our child. And love her for me. But I still wished… I ached for you to write to me that next Christmas. As you said you would, if your feeling for me hadn't changed."

She turned to fling her own anguish at him, her heart throbbing with all the painful doubts and the painful decisions she'd had to make. "I didn't believe you'd forgotten me. But I didn't know if you wanted me. He'll write if he still does, I told myself. He'll write. And then I can write back and tell him about our baby. He'll come home and make everything right if he truly wants me. We'll be together."

Her passionate outburst hung in the air between them, the understanding he'd demanded weaving its stinging tentacles of truth, inescapable, devastating in their power to set his mind straight.

"But I didn't write," he said hollowly.

"No. And then I realised I really had given my baby up." The dead despair of that moment hollowed out her voice. "And there was no turning back the clock."

He said nothing.

An ironic laugh broke from her throat. "It haunted me so much, when your two years at Harvard were up, I went back to your sister's place, determined to see you. Just to see…had you forgotten or didn't you want me?"

"They'd moved," he answered for her. "As soon as Denise got the baby, they bought a new home."

Meredith's mouth twisted. "For all I knew she'd told you everything anyway. I was only hurting myself, not letting go." She shrugged. "At least she kept her word, sending me the photographs."

"Which eventually led me back to you." He sounded tired, spent, a long, long way from being happy about it.

Tears welled into her eyes. "I thought you'd come for me, you know? For a moment, when I opened the door to my apartment and saw you standing there…I thought you'd come for me."

"God!" He shook his head despairingly. "What do I say to you?"

That you love me. That you'll hold me tight forever and never let me go again.

Her whole body ached for him to say the words, to take her in his arms and press them home to her.

The click of the front door opening startled both of them out of their painful thrall. Nick spun around to see. Meredith watched in tense helplessness as Kimberly stepped out onto the veranda, a forlorn little figure, throwing anxious glances at both of them, uncertain of her welcome yet forcing herself to brave facing them.

"What are you doing out of bed, Kimberly?" Nick snapped.

"I couldn't sleep." Her voice wavered. "I got up to look at the presents again."

"Spy on us, you mean," he said grimly.

"Nick…" Meredith protested.

He flashed her a tormented look. "Kimberly has a habit of eavesdropping."

Meredith looked at her daughter, seeing her torment, too. "Did you eavesdrop, Kimberly?" she asked softly.

A grave nod. "I didn't mean to, Merry. The window was open and you were saying…saying…" She gulped and looked at Nick, her eyes huge and shiny with tears.

"Damn it, Kimberly! This is none of your business!" he thundered, too upset to realise how wrong he was.

It was her business. Kimberly had the right to know, too. Meredith watched in helpless dismay as in the artless, direct way of children, her daughter put the question straight to him.

"Are you my real father, Uncle Nick?"

CHAPTER SIXTEEN

TEARS rolled down Kimberly's cheeks but she seemed unaware of them. Her eyes clung to Nick in silent, desperate pleading for him to put things right for her. One of her hands was twisting the soft cotton of her T-shirt nightie, fretting at it in a sub-conscious need to hold on to something. Her hair, released from its ponytail, hung in a bedraggled fashion around her face. She looked like a lost waif, bereft of all that had had meaning to her, and Meredith ached to gather her in her arms and hug comfort and reassurance.

But it was to Nick her daughter looked for what she needed, and Meredith painfully held herself back from rushing in. She simply wasn't in a po-sition to offer some secure platform from which they could all launch into a rosy future to replace the past. Nothing was really resolved between her and Nick. It was up to him to answer his daughter. It was up to him to answer all the questions now.

Yet Nick looked as lost as Kimberly, stricken by the realisation of all she might have overheard; the role her adoptive parents had played in taking her from Meredith, in preventing Nick from knowing

171

about his fatherhood, ensuring he didn't link up
with her mother again, and keeping the knowledge
of her real parentage from her.

The world they had known had been torn up and
the pieces couldn't be put together again. No matter
what was tried, it wouldn't be the same. Couldn't
be. The recognition of it made it all the harder to
come up with the right thing to say. Or do. The
moment had come upon them too fast. None of
them was ready for it. Yet it was so important to
get it right.

To Meredith, waiting on extreme tenterhooks, it
felt like aeons before Nick moved. His face softened as he stepped over to the child waiting to be
claimed by him. He squatted in front of her, his
eyes on the same level as hers, and he took her
hands, gently fondling them.

"Yes, I am, baby," he said softly. "I am your
real father."

Kimberly bit her lips and shook her head, too
distressed to speak.

"I didn't know, love. I didn't know until today,"
Nick went on. "But now that I do know…"

"How could you forget Merry?" It was a cry
from the heart, carrying the sense that he'd let her
mother down, let them all down.

The caring from her daughter moved Meredith to
tears. *My child, fighting for me…* How quickly the

bond had formed! Or had it always been there, waiting to be tapped?

Nick sucked in a deep breath, exhaling slowly as he reached out and gently smudged the tears on his daughter's cheeks. "I didn't forget her, Kimberly. I suffered a head injury soon after I left Merry all those years ago, and the weeks before the accident became a blank to me. I didn't remember meeting and falling in love with her, but I've dreamed of her ever since. I didn't know she was a real person. In my dreams, I could never reach her, but I felt if I ever did, she'd bring a special magic into my life. And she has. She's given me a daughter I didn't know I had."

More tears welled and overflowed, both from Kimberly and Meredith, though thankfully no one was looking at Meredith.

Kimberly swallowed convulsively. "Would you...would you have come back...and married her?"

"Yes." No hesitation. "I would have wanted to be a father to you, Kimberly. And as soon as I saw Merry, I would have fallen in love with her all over again."

Meredith's heart turned over. Was Nick expressing what he felt now? Or was he simply appeasing Kimberly's sense of rightness?

"Why did Mum keep her from you?" It was a

wail for what might have been. "It wasn't fair, Uncle Nick. It wasn't fair!"

Kimberly burst into sobbing.

Nick sprang up and hoisted her against his shoulder, hugging her tightly. She flung her arms around his neck and wept, her small body racked with the devastation of faith in the parents she thought had loved her, whom she had loved. Nick carried her to the closest cane armchair and sat down, cuddling her on his lap and gently rubbing her back.

Meredith could only stand helplessly by, waiting to give what assistance she could, when and if it was called upon. She fought a silent battle with her own tears, afraid she would distress Kimberly even more if she saw them.

Eventually the sobbing diminished to the occasional hiccup. Kimberly remained huddled against Nick's shoulder, limp and drained, accepting his silent soothing like a kitten, needing to be petted and loved.

"Kimberly…" Nick called softly. "What your Mum did was wrong. It was wrong for me and wrong for Merry. But she and your dad loved you very much. They didn't know how it had been between Merry and me. They thought they were doing the best for you. And they did, Kimberly. They did their best to give you a happy life."

Nick lifted his gaze to Meredith, his dark eyes anguished, apologetic, appealing for her understanding. She responded instantly, moving to crouch beside the child on his lap and rub her legs, chilled now from the cool night air and her enervated state.

"Kimberly…all the photographs your mum sent me year by year showed me a very happy child," she assured her. "I loved looking at them. As Nick told you, I have them all over the walls in my bedroom. Please don't let those years be spoiled for you now, my darling. You wouldn't be the wonderful girl you are if your mum and dad hadn't given you a very loving home."

A woebegone face peeked at her around lank strands of hair. "You would have loved me, too, Merry."

"I do love you. You're my own precious child. You always were and you always will be. Nothing changes that, Kimberly," Meredith promised her.

"But Mum took me from you. You said…"

"No. You've misunderstood, Kimberly," she broke in quickly. "I gave you to your Mum because she could look after you better than I could at that time. And she and your dad looked after you beautifully. Even if Nick had come back to me, I don't know if we could have done better."

Kimberly thought that over for a while before saying, "I would have had my real parents."

"You have them now." Meredith stroked the damp hair away from her daughter's pale little face, smiling as she tucked it behind her ear and said, "Aren't you the lucky girl, with two sets of parents loving you?"

There was a perceptible brightening of expression before a frown marred it. "You and Uncle Nick were angry at each other."

"No." Meredith shook her head, the smile still lingering on her lips. "Nick was upset because he couldn't remember and I was upset having to explain everything to him. But that's over now." She glanced up for his support. "Isn't it, Nick?"

"Yes. We've got it all sorted out, Kimberly," he assured her.

It stirred Kimberly into sitting upright so she could look Nick in the eye. "Have you fallen in love with Merry again?" she asked with disarming directness.

Meredith held her breath. Nick's gaze turned to her, telegraphing so many emotions they were difficult to decipher. A plea for forgiveness? Need for her understanding? Anguish at having been put on the spot?

"I never stopped loving her. Even when she was only in my dreams, she touched my heart."

Dear heaven! Was it true?

"Are you going to marry her now?"

The clear line logic of a child! It left nowhere for Nick to go. He was trapped within the integrity of what he'd already said in his efforts to soothe his daughter's distress.

His gaze did not leave Meredith's. It begged her response as he said, "If she'll have me."

Kimberly turned, her eyes full of hope and expectation. "Merry?"

She stood up, her legs trembling under the weight of decision. Two pairs of eyes were pinning her to a response here and now. Meredith's heart was pounding. She wanted to say yes, but was it right to do so when the question had been asked under duress? Did it matter? If Nick was truly willing for the sake of their daughter, why was she even hesitating?

"Yes," she said firmly.

Kimberly hurtled off Nick's lap and hugged her. "It's what I've been dreaming, Merry, for you and Uncle Nick to get married so I could have both of you all the time," she babbled.

Nick rose from the chair with the air of a man who had just had an enormous burden lifted from his shoulders. If he felt any weight from the responsibilities he had just taken on, it certainly didn't show. He oozed confidence, as though his world was under control again and what he had was what he wanted.

Meredith fiercely hoped so. She hoped she wasn't fooling herself into seeing what she wanted to see.

He gave her a grateful look and gently squeezed his daughter's shoulder. "Let's drop the uncle bit, Kimberly. Just call me Nick, as Merry does."

"Oh!" She swung around to beam at him. "Okay, Nick."

He tapped her cheek, smiling indulgently. "Off to bed, little one. It's Christmas tomorrow."

"And you and Merry want to kiss and make up," she replied with her own form of indulgence.

"You could be right about that."

She giggled.

Meredith was amazed at the resilience coming to the fore with the assurance of having both her real parents established in her life.

"Have a good night, Unc…I mean, Nick." Her grin was extended to Merry. "A very good night."

"Sweet dreams," Nick prompted.

"Yes. Sweet dreams," Meredith echoed, hoping her own dream was really coming true.

Kimberly walked jauntily to the front door, pausing before she made her exit to sweep them both with another grin, her eyes twinkling like stars. "Merry Christmas," she called very pointedly. Then off she went down the hallway singing, "I wish you a Merry Christmas, I wish you a Merry Christmas, I wish you a Merry Christmas and a Happy New Year!"

CHAPTER SEVENTEEN

As KIMBERLY'S singing receded down the hallway, Nick's hands slid around Meredith's waist and turned her to face him. Her heart was fluttering so wildly she felt almost sick, apprehension and excitement warring inside her.

"Thank you," he said quietly, his eyes a swirl of dark chocolate, meltingly warm. "Thank you for being you, for having my child and giving her to me. But above everything else, thank you for waiting for me, Merry."

"Oh, Nick!" Relief gushed through her. The love in his voice was unmistakable. "I'm sorry I gave up on you. I…"

"No…" He placed a finger on her lips, hushing the stream of regret. "I was wrong. You don't have anything to answer for." The finger softly stroked down to her chin and dropped, his hand moving to curl around her neck and caress her nape. "God knows I've seen enough, been with you enough to appreciate, in some small measure, how it's been for you. I'm sorry I got so screwed up about being left out."

The fluttering eased. She managed a wry smile.

179

"Well, at least I'm not too young for you any-more."

He frowned, pained by the reminder. "I don't know that you ever were. Some feelings go beyond any sensible reasoning. Dave said if I'd had my mind on surfing, the accident wouldn't have happened. Maybe I was thinking of coming back to you and that was what the dream meant."

Twice he'd spoken of dreaming about her. Meredith's curiosity was piqued. "What happened in your dream?"

An ironic smile cleared the frown. "It was mostly like last night, you waiting on the beach for me, facing out to sea. You never spoke, yet I'd feel you were calling me. I'd set out to reach you and when I got close, you'd turn around as though you'd heard me coming and your face would light up in welcome." He sighed. "Then my legs wouldn't move any more. I'd stand helplessly, watching you fade away."

"How strange!" she murmured. "Sometimes, especially after a walk on the beach, I'd have a restless night. I'd lie in the dark, thinking of you, how I used to stand at the water's edge, watching you ride your board or windsurf. I guess, in my heart, I was calling to you, Nick."

They stared at each other, awed by the need that had spanned time and distance, calling from soul to soul.

Nick sighed, his eyes turning rueful. "I wish I'd known how to answer. But for Kimberly finding out about you and wanting to meet her real mother…"

"She's wonderful, isn't she?"

He smiled. "Very much like her mother."

"And her father. She's got your hair…"

"Your eyes."

She laughed, happiness bubbling up and brimming over. "Isn't it marvellous we can now be her parents? Oh!" She winced as the thought of Denise and Colin Graham hit her. "I didn't mean…I wasn't being glad about what happened to your sister and brother-in-law, Nick. It was just…"

"I know." He pulled her closer, warming her with his body. "It was good of you to say what you did to Kimberly, considering the selfish judgment Denise made."

"It wasn't entirely selfish," Meredith quickly protested, so happy to be where she was, nothing else mattered. "Your sister was thinking of you, wanting you to be a success."

He shook his head. "She was thinking of what *she* wanted for me, not what *I* wanted, Merry."

"Still, you've been very successful with your career," she argued, not wanting him to harbour ill feelings toward a woman who had given him and Kimberly so much. "You must be pleased about that. You like your work. I can tell."

''*You've* been very successful with your *Flower Power*. Did it make up for what we missed?''

She slid her hands over his shoulders and around his neck, her eyes earnestly pleading her case. ''That time is gone, Nick. Let's not waste now in mourning it. And we've got so much to look forward to.''

His face softened and suddenly broke into a grin, his eyes twinkling like Kimberly's. ''You can take charge of the flowers for the wedding.''

Her stomach felt as if it was twinkling. ''Are we going to have a wedding?''

''We most certainly are,'' he answered with fervour. Then he laughed. ''Kimberly would accuse us both of being stodges if we did her out of it.''

''You really want to marry me?''

''Did you doubt it?''

Not now. The sense of coming full circle was far too strong. But it was fun to tease him, confident of a love that would go on forever, regardless of any obstacle or tribulation.

''Well, Kimberly did, more or less, force your hand,'' she said archly.

''Only getting to the heart of the matter more quickly, my love. And you are my love.'' His eyes searched hers with urgent intensity. ''You don't doubt that, do you, Merry?''

She smiled, glowing with certainty. ''You're calling me Merry.''

"I wanted to before. It sounded right. Felt right. But I kept thinking it was *his* name for you and I didn't want you to associate me with the lover who'd let you down." He grimaced. "There's some irony for you."

"I'm sorry you don't remember, Nick, but it was the same as it is now. I never stopped loving you, either," she said softly.

"Merry…"

He choked up. His head bent. His lips moved over hers in a slow, sensual tasting. She felt his desire to savour every nuance of her physical reality and his intent to treasure the magic of this coming together. And it *was* magic, the touch of love, the sureness of it coursing through them, swelling their hearts and warming their souls.

With the deepening of their kiss came the need for every closeness, all the intimacy they had shared the night before, heightened by the joy of knowing the long yearning for each other was over. They were one again and the desire to express that in every way was too strong to delay.

"Share my bed with me," Nick murmured. "I want to be with you all night."

Blissful thought…yet they weren't entirely alone. "Is it wise with Kimberly? If she finds us in the same room in the morning…"

"It will cement her happiness," he answered

confidently. "She feels our marriage is long over-due."

Meredith sighed. "You know her better than I do."

He smiled, tucking her close to him for the walk inside. "You're catching up fast and you have the advantage of being female. Like minds…"

She laughed, sliding her arm around his waist and snuggling closer as they strolled to the front door. "You're good with her, Nick. I've loved watching how you are together."

He pressed a soft kiss on her temple. "She's part of you. I guess it shone through. She's always been a special child to me."

Special…

The sense of it sang in Meredith's mind and hummed through her body all during their love-making. Nick was special. Their child was special. The feeling they had for each other was special. And this wonderful Christmas had to be the most special of all.

CHAPTER EIGHTEEN

"I've got one more present to give," Kimberly declared, her eyes sparkling with the anticipation of surprising them.

Nick wondered what she had up her sleeve. They'd cleared the bundle underneath the Christmas tree. Three piles of gifts were now on full display, their discarded wrapping littering the floor around them.

"But there's nothing left," Merry pointed out.

Kimberly laughed. "I thought of it last night. You'll never guess."

"Are we allowed to play twenty questions?" Nick asked, happy to go along with the teasing.

He couldn't remember ever feeling so happy. The three of them were sprawled on the carpet in the living room, surrounded by the trappings and spirit of Christmas. It was a perfect day outside and everything was right with his world. Beautifully, wonderfully right.

"Animal, mineral or vegetable?" he tossed at his daughter, revelling in the knowledge of their true relationship.

"It's an idea, not a thing," she smugly announced.

Nick rolled his eyes. "Then I give up."

"Me, too," Merry said, shaking her head. "An idea makes it far too tricky."

"I knew you'd never guess," Kimberly crowed triumphantly. "I've decided to go to PLC as a weekly boarder. It'll give you and Nick lots of time together, Merry. Like a really long honeymoon. Just the two of you."

"Oh!" Merry flushed, still a bit self-conscious over Kimberly's pleasure in finding them together this morning. "It's a lovely thought, Kimberly, but is it what you want to do?"

"I don't mind at all now I know I'll have you both at the weekends. It'll be fun being with a whole lot of other girls, doing the same stuff."

"Sure about this, Kimberly?" Nick asked, touched by her caring for them, yet reluctant to lose the sense of family he felt so strongly this morning.

"Absolutely!" she replied decisively. "Merry can help me shop for the right clothes and I'll have lots of exciting things to tell you at weekends." Her brow puckered. "There's one thing though…"

"You can always change your mind," Nick prompted.

"No. It's Mrs. Armstrong. She's been really nice, minding me. I don't like the thought of putting her out of a job."

Nick felt a swell of pride in his daughter. The kind concern for Fran Armstrong showed a generosity of spirit that had been sadly lacking with Rachel. On the other hand, grandmotherly Fran was hardly a threat to the place Kimberly had secretly earmarked for Merry.

"Don't worry about Mrs. Armstrong, Kimberly. I'm sure we can come to some arrangement. I promise you she won't lose by it."

Relief spread into smile. "That's good. She's still waiting on a grandchild. Her daughter's been trying to have a baby, but no luck yet."

A baby, Nick thought, and looked at Merry, remembering their conversation earlier this morning. It had shocked him when he realised he hadn't thought of using any form of contraception. On both nights his need and desire for her had obliterated any normal consideration of consequences. It was Merry who'd thought of it afterward, asking if he minded if they had another baby. As if he'd mind!

She caught his gaze and the soft look in her eyes and her smile told him she was thinking of the same conversation. A Christmas baby. Like Kimberly. Though if it happened, he wouldn't be missing out on the birth this time. He reached out and took Merry's hand in his, squeezing it as he silently promised he'd be there for her. Be there for everything.

"I know!" Kimberly said brightly, drawing their attention. "Why don't you two have a baby? Mrs. Armstrong would love that."

The suggestion popped out so unexpectedly, it caught them both by surprise. "How would you feel about it if we did, Kimberly?" Nick asked.

"Really?" she squealed excitedly.

He laughed at her. "Yes. Really."

She clapped her hands. "I've always wanted a sister or a brother." Her eyes glowed at the prospect. "If you got to work on it straight away we could have a bigger family next Christmas."

Merry laughed, her cheeks burning even more brightly.

A Christmas family, Nick thought. What could be better?

"But you must promise to do all the baby shopping with me," Kimberly demanded of her mother. "I mean that's real mother stuff and I want to be in on it."

Her real mother…

Kimberly loved having her.

Merry was right. It was a miracle the three of them had come together and everything had turned out right.

He feasted his eyes on the very special beauty of the woman he loved and would always love. It was true. She made him feel as though all the Christmas lights in the world had been switched on inside him.

His Merry Christmas.

No. His and Kimberly's.

Their own special Merry Christmas.

Helen Brooks lives in Northamptonshire and is married with three children. As she is a committed Christian, busy housewife and mother, her spare time is at a premium but her hobbies include reading, swimming, gardening and walking her two energetic, inquisitive and very endearing young dogs. Her long-cherished aspiration to write became a reality when she put pen to paper on reaching the age of forty, and sent the result off to Mills & Boon®.

**Look out for
THE GREEK TYCOON'S BRIDE by Helen
Brooks in Modern Romance™, March 2002**

MISTLETOE MISTRESS

by
Helen Brooks

CHAPTER ONE

'HEY, what's with all the long faces? There hasn't been a major disaster while I've been away, has there?' Joanne's bright smile dimmed and then faded altogether as her antennae picked up the waves radiating from her office staff.

'You...you haven't heard?'

'Heard what?' Joanne's wide honey-brown eyes narrowed slightly as she repeated, 'Heard what, Maggie?'

'About what's happened.'

'*Maggie.*'

'About the takeover, and Mr Brigmore, and... everything.' Maggie wriggled slightly in her typist's chair and half turned in the seat to include the rest of the office of six, all of whom patently ignored the silent plea for help, their faces clearly stating that Maggie had started this and she could finish it.

'The takeover? Maggie, I haven't got a clue what you are talking about,' Joanne said as patiently as she could. Brusqueness never helped with Maggie; she flustered very easily. 'And where does Mr Brigmore come into all this?'

'He doesn't, not any more.' Maggie's plump plain face was very earnest, and Joanne knew she wasn't deliberately trying to be obtuse, but something of the urge she felt to wring her junior's neck must have shown on her face because Maggie added hastily, 'Mr. Brigmore's gone—early retirement or something. It all happened last Thursday, when the takeover was announced; he went the same day. I left a message on your answer machine—'

'I haven't been back to my flat yet; I stayed overnight with a friend…' Joanne's voice trailed away as the enormity of what Maggie was saying hit her. 'Are you telling me Mr Brigmore was axed?' she asked faintly. 'Because if you are I can't believe it. Who's stepped into his shoes, then?'

'A relation of the mogul who now owns the firm.' Maggie's voice was full of meaning and Joanne nodded silently to what remained unsaid. So, nepotism was alive and well at Concise Publications, was it? And all this had happened during the month she had been gaily back-packing round Europe on a reunion with old university friends?

She had heard about these savage 'off with the old, on with the new' mergers, where the new ruling directorate were merciless in their desire to sweep clean, but she had never actually experienced one first-hand in her eight years of working life. And Charles, of all people…

Suddenly the anger was there, hot and fierce. Charles was the fatherly figure who had given her the sort of chance, five years ago, that she had been craving since leaving university, choosing her above a host of other more qualified applicants who had been eager for the post of publishing assistant to the managing director of Concise Publications.

He had been her mentor, her champion, but most of all her friend—he and his wife, Clare, taking her under their parental wing and giving her her first real glimpse of family life. And he had been replaced? By some young upstart, no doubt, who probably didn't know one end of a book from another.

'Male or female?' Her voice was quivering, but it was with sheer fury, not weakness.

'Male.' Maggie knew how much her superior thought of their ex-managing director, and she took a deep breath before she added, 'His name is Mallen. Hawk Mallen.'

'Hawk Mallen?' Joanne's voice was scathing, her emotion blinding her to the fact that Maggie had suddenly become very still and very quiet, her eyes no longer focused on Joanne's angry face. 'What sort of name is that?'

'*My* sort of name, Ms...?'

The deep male voice was not loud, but the timbre was such that Joanne felt liquid ice run over her nerves. She didn't turn for a good thirty seconds from her position just a few inches into the room, and when she did move it was with the knowledge that she had blown it—good and proper, as Charles would have said. And she cared. Oh, not because of her job, precious and important as it had been to her up to this minute in time, she told herself bitterly, but because she had wanted to fling her resignation into the lap of this faceless bureaucrat and walk away with her head held high—not be caught out like a child telling tales out of school.

'Crawford.' Her chin was high, her golden eyes shooting sparks as she looked up into the hard dark face of the big man standing in the doorway behind her. 'And it's Miss.'

'Ah...yes, of course. Charles's elusive publishing assistant. How nice to meet you.' On face value the words were polite and courteous, but, spoken as they were, in a dark cold drawl that was both menacing and patronising, they were anything but. 'Perhaps you'd like to come through to your office so we can discuss recent events in comfort?'

He meant without the twitching ears and avid interest of the outer office, Joanne thought tightly, but for once the professionalism she prided herself on had flown out the window. 'Is there any point?' she asked stiffly, knowing she was glaring but quite unable to help herself.

The suit this man had on would have paid her salary for months, she thought bitterly, and was indicative of his sovereignty somehow. He *reeked* of wealth and power; it flowed out of every pore and was in every gesture he made. This was a man who was used to being obeyed without question. Well—tough. There was no way she was going to be intimidated by the man responsible for sacking the only person she had any real affection for in the whole wide world. Well, there was Clare too, she qualified hastily as a little stab of disloyalty to Charles's wife made itself known; she loved her too, but Charles was Charles...

'Every point, Miss Crawford.'

When, in the next moment, her elbow was taken in a firm, uncompromising grip and she found herself all but flying through the outer office and into her small but comfortable little oasis, she was too surprised to make a sound. Until the door closed behind them, that was. 'What the hell do you think you're doing?' The explosion was in line with the vibrant chestnut-red of her hair, its glowing colour a clue to the volatile temper she had battled with all her life. 'How dare you manhandle me—?'

'I'm trying to stop you making a bigger fool of yourself than you have done already,' he said with a grimness that was insulting.

'Now look—'

'*No, you look, damn it!*' It was more of a pistol shot than a bark, and as her eyes widened with shock he pushed her none too gently into the seat in front of her desk, propping himself against the dark wood and staring down at her with blazing, piercingly blue eyes. Beautiful eyes, she thought inconsequentially, before the rage took over again. 'I'm trying to do this the nice way—'

'Like you did with poor Charles?' she cut in testily, the colour in her cheeks vying with her hair.

'Give me strength...' He shut his eyes for an infinitesimal moment, raking a hand through his jet-black, very short but expertly cropped hair before saying, in a tone that was very flat and very hard, 'Do you want me to gag you? Because so help me you're a moment away from it.'

'You wouldn't dare.' But he would—she knew, without knowing how she knew, that he would.

'Try me. Just open that delectable mouth one more time before I finish saying what I want to say and try me. The pleasure, as they say, would be all mine.'

She opened her mouth to fire back an equally caustic reply, glanced at the blue silk handkerchief he had just drawn out of his breast pocket, and shut it again. The pig! The arrogant, overbearing, stinking swine—

'And I dare bet I fit most of the names that are swirling through your head right at this moment,' he drawled easily, temper and composure apparently perfectly restored, 'but unfortunately that's where they'll have to stay—in your head. Now, where were we? Oh, yes, I was trying to save you from looking ridiculous...'

She spluttered, gulped, but was forced to admit silently to herself that she didn't dare call his bluff.

He had raised dark eyebrows at her mini paroxysm but when no verbal abuse was forthcoming smiled nastily before continuing, 'Charles has left messages for you over half of Europe, there is a letter explaining the full details of the merger with Mallen Books sitting on your doorstep at home, which is repeated at length on your answer machine, but I presume, from your rather undignified outburst out there, you haven't received any of them?'

She didn't reply, and he didn't seem to expect one as he went on, 'I suggest you go home and read the letter, pop round and see Charles, do whatever it is that women do to cool down, and then we'll go from there.'

'You're dismissing me?' she asked with icy hauteur.

'Don't you ever listen?'

She had got under his skin. For all his apparent equanimity she had definitely got under his skin, she noted with some hidden satisfaction as she watched him take a deep hard pull of air before shaking his head slowly.

'You're a very intelligent woman, Miss Crawford; I know that much from your file and all that Charles has told me about you. I've seen some of your work and it's impressive, damn impressive, so what's happened during this jaunt round Europe to that noteworthy brain of yours? Are you really determined to throw your job—and the considerable salary that goes with it—to the wind on little more than a whim, a temper tantrum, because you weren't in the know when all this happened? I know Charles respects both your work and you as a person, but he had to make a fast decision on our offer and you simply weren't around to confer with. Okay?'

He thought her reaction was petulance because she hadn't been consulted about the merger? She stared at him in amazement, unable to believe she was hearing right.

'Okay?' he said again, his voice cool and biting.

'Mr Mallen, I couldn't care less if you took over this firm and a hundred others besides every day for a month,' she said furiously. 'That's not the issue here.'

'Really?' He smiled a smile that wasn't a smile at all.

'Yes, really.' She had never wanted to wipe a smile from someone's face so violently before. 'The only thing that concerns me is the way you've got rid of Charles. This firm was his lifeblood, his reason for living, and don't tell me I don't know what I'm talking about,' she warned testily as he opened his mouth to interrupt. 'I know Charles—I know him better than you for a start—and to leave this firm would be like leaving his own child. He built Concise Publications up from nothing, sacrificed for it, lived his life around it, and now you sweep in and throw him out as though he's nothing.'

'You've got this all wrong—'

'Oh, spare me.' He wasn't used to being spoken to like this, and his displeasure was evident in the narrowing of the brilliant blue eyes and hard line of his mouth. A sensual mouth, firm and full, with a sexy bottom lip— She caught the thought as it materialised, shocked to the core at its inappropriateness, and it made her voice harsh as she went on, 'You've got rid of Charles and I don't doubt for a minute that he won't be the last to go. Well, I'll make it easy for you, Mr Mallen, and resign right now. I've no wish to continue working under the new administration, okay?'

The last word was said with exactly the same emphasis he had placed on it a few moments earlier and spoke of her utter disgust more strongly than anything she had said before.

'I don't believe I'm having this conversation.' As Joanne went to rise he pushed her back down in the seat with a mite more force than was necessary. 'And sit still, damn it,' he growled angrily. 'I haven't finished yet.'

'But I have.' This time when she rose he let her, his eyes unblinking as she smoothed down the pencil-slim skirt over her hips and tugged the matching jacket into place with shaking hands. He was a brute of a man, a cold, arrogant tyrant. She'd seen plenty of the same since coming to London from her university in Manchester eight years ago, and had never stopped thanking the guardian angel who had led her to Concise Publications and the Brigmores. She couldn't have wished for a better boss, and Clare had become more than a friend, almost a mother...

'How can someone who looks so fragile be so impossible?' he asked with a quietness that had all the softness of tempered steel. 'I've met some troublesome females in my time but you take the biscuit hands down.' He had straightened as she'd stood, and now she became fully aware for the first time of his considerable height and bulk, his broad-shouldered, lean body towering over her five feet six inches in a way that made her feel positively minute. And she was aware of something else too, something…undefinable, magnetic that pulsed from the hard male frame with a drawing power that was formidable, and it was this that made her swing round on her heel and make for the door without another word.

'Is that it?'

In any other circumstance, with any other man, the look of utter surprise on his face as she turned round would have made her smile; as it was she stared at him for a moment before she said, 'There's no point in continuing this, is there?'

'You really intend to throw in the towel because you consider Charles has been hard done by?' He surveyed her cynically, his mouth hard. 'What sort of relationship did you have with your departed boss anyway?' he added silkily, his meaning plain.

'I don't even intend to acknowledge that with the favour of a reply,' she said icily, her eyes wishing him somewhere very hot and very final as she glared at him one more time, before opening the door and sweeping into the outer office with a regality that wasn't lost on Hawk Mallen as he watched her go.

He liked her style. He watched her cross the outer office and exit without turning her head or faltering in her purpose. Yes, whatever else, she had one hell of a way with her.

Once in the corridor outside, Joanne set her face in a practised smile and made for the lift, passing the other offices on the exalted top floor of Concise Publications without looking to left or right. There were three floors in all, and as the lift took her swiftly downwards Joanne found she had gone into automatic, her whole being concentrating on getting out of the building and into her car without the humiliation of breaking down. One of Charles's editors—no, not Charles's any more, she corrected herself painfully—was in Reception and raised a hand to her as she passed. 'Everything all right?'

'Fine, fine.' She smiled and nodded but didn't stop, her mind registering the stupidity of her reply in the circumstances.

Once in her snazzy little red car she sat for a whole minute just breathing deeply before she could persuade her shaking hands to start the engine. Her whole life, the interesting, vital life she had fought for so hard, had just been turned upside down and the shock waves had her head buzzing.

She should have phoned Clare and Charles last night—she had meant to—but her flight from France had been delayed and when Melanie had offered her a bed for the night, rather than her having to drive right across London in the rush hour to her flat, she'd accepted gratefully. And then she had had a bath, and they'd eaten, and consumed one of the bottles of wine they'd brought back between them…

'Damn, damn, damn…' She turned and glanced at her huge rucksack in the middle of the back seat, surrounded by bags of wine and boxes of Belgian chocolates she'd brought back as presents, and then slipped off the jacket to the suit she had borrowed from Melanie and flung it on the seat beside her as she started the engine. Well, it was too late now; she had quite literally walked into the lion's mouth and definitely come off the worse for wear, but the main thing was to touch base with Charles and see how he was. It was so ironic that all this had happened during the first real holiday she had had in years, she thought miserably as she steered the car out of her reserved space in Concise Publication's small car park, and on to the busy main road.

The urge to see Charles was overwhelming, and as his

house in Islington was on her route home she headed for there, forcing herself to concentrate on the morning traffic rather than her jumbled thoughts that were flying in all directions. The September day was balmy and mellow, the warm sunshine pleasant but lacking the fierce heat that had characterised July and August, but Joanne was oblivious to the weather as she drove through the London streets in a turmoil that made her soft full mouth tight and stained her creamy, sun-tinted skin an angry red.

It was ten o'clock when she drew up outside Charles and Clare's large three-storeyed terraced house in its wide and pleasant street, and by five past she was seated in a cushioned cane chair in the garden with a box of tissues at her elbow and a steaming cup of coffee in front of her. 'I'm sorry, I didn't mean to cry on you...'

Clare, who was sitting on the arm of Joanne's chair, pulled her closer to her maternal bosom as Charles tut-tutted from his vantage point opposite. 'It's our fault, Joanne; it must have been such a shock to you,' Clare said worriedly. 'But apart from leaving a message for you to ring us when you got home, and the letter, of course, we didn't know how to contact you. The postcards kept coming from somewhere different every few days. Did you have a nice time?' she added as an afterthought.

'Lovely.' Joanne dismissed the month of fun and laughter in one word.

'And you only found out about the merger when you went in this morning?' Clare enquired anxiously.

Joanne nodded. She had only been able to blurt that much out on the doorstep before bursting into tears, from which point it had been all action.

'And did Hawk Mallen explain it fully?' Charles asked now. 'I couldn't have refused, Jo; offers like that don't come every day. Besides which...' He paused, glancing at Clare who nodded encouragingly. 'I haven't been too well recently and this seemed to present itself as a chance to get out of the rat race and have a few years enjoying ourselves before we're too old.'

'What do you mean, not too well?' Joanne knew Charles; he would rather walk through coals of fire than ever admit he was less than one hundred per cent fit. It was something she and Clare, along with the couple's three children, called his obstinate streak.

'We haven't told the children, for the same reason we didn't tell you—you'd all worry yourselves to death. But that time three months ago when Charles had a week off with flu—it was a minor heart attack. Very minor,' Clare added hastily as Joanne's eyes shot to Charles's sheepish face, 'but I've persuaded him to take it as a warning, and when this offer from the Mallen Corporation came along it seemed like the answer to everything.'

'Why didn't you tell me about the heart attack?' Joanne asked faintly. 'I could have helped.'

'*I* wanted to,' Clare said quickly, 'but you know Charles. He loves you like one of our own, Joanne, and he didn't want any of you worried—'

'Or fussing,' Charles cut in wryly. 'Clare did all the fussing that was necessary, believe me.'

'How long has this takeover been in the offing?' Joanne asked numbly, feeling as though the ground was moving under her feet. Charles was ill, with heart trouble? *Charles?*

'There has been the odd feeler there for a couple of months,' Charles said quietly, 'but the thing only crystallised the week you left for Europe. The Mallen Corporation is huge—I don't know if Hawk explained to you, but the publishing side is just one of their interests. When the offer became concrete I jumped at it, it's as simple as that really, and I decided to cut the umbilical cord in the process.

'Hawk Mallen is old man Mallen's grandson and right-hand man; apart from knowing everything there is to know about publishing, he's a brilliant businessman and entrepreneur—something I've never pretended to be,' he added drily. 'He's the future, I'm the past; if I had stayed I would have got in his way and that wouldn't have been good for either of us. He's a ruthless so-and-so, but he's got what it takes, Jo; you can't fault the man on business acumen.'

'I see.' As Charles went on, explaining the details of the transaction and the part everyone had played in it, Joanne's heart sank deeper and deeper.

It had been Charles who had insisted on the opt-out clause, Charles who had wanted to walk away at once without any long-drawn-out and heart-rending, mentally exhausting valedictions. And she'd accused Hawk Mallen of... She inwardly squirmed as she remembered the exact charges she'd laid at his feet. Oh, what a mess, what a terrible, almost laughable mess. Thank goodness she could rely on Charles for a good reference because she sure as eggs wouldn't get one from the eminent Mr Mallen.

If he wasn't as mad as hell at her, he'd be laughing his head off, and of the two options she'd much prefer the former, she thought painfully as a pair of piercingly blue cold eyes set in a hard, uncompromising face swam into the screen of her mind. But fortunately she'd never know one way or the other anyway, having burnt her bridges so completely.

And now she would have to tell Clare and Charles... They were upset, horrified, bewildered—blaming themselves, Hawk Mallen, anyone but Joanne—but by the time she left their tranquil home, after an alfresco lunch under the clear September sky, she had their solemn promise not to try to get her reinstated in any way.

She had made her bed and she would lie on it, she

thought determinedly on the drive home, and maybe it was time for a change anyway. She was twenty-nine years of age, and after the years of exams and striving for her degree she had only had two jobs—one of which was Concise Publications—and had hardly seen anything of life. The trip round Europe these past weeks had opened her eyes to the fact that there was a big wide world out there, just waiting to be explored, and perhaps this was the nudge she needed to get moving?

She had been happy and safe the last few years, Charles and Clare's open-armed drawing of her into their family going some way to heal the hurts of the past, but whilst she was cocooned in such a protected environment she would never reach out for more. And she wanted more.

The thought was a surprise, opening her eyes wide for an instant as she considered it. But it was true. Not the bonds of matrimony or a husband—she felt the panic and fear that accompanied such a possibility wash over her before she thrust them back behind the closed door in her mind—but she wanted to travel, to see new places, new cultures, work in different environments. And she could do it; *she could*. As Charles had said, the umbilical cord had been cut, nothing would be the same again, so *now* was the time.

Her spacious one-bedroom flat on the top storey of an old renovated house overlooking myriad rooftops and a wide expanse of light washed sky welcomed her as she opened the front door, the large terracotta-tiled balcony where she ate most of her meals during the spring and summer causing a momentary hiccup in her plans. Could she leave it? This, her first real home where she had been so happy, so secure?

She opened the French windows from the high-ceilinged lounge and walked out on to the flower-bedecked balcony, noting that most of the plants fes-

tooning the walls and floor were alive and thriving, for
which she had to thank her neighbour on the floor below
who had promised faithfully to water them each evening.

She was brought from further musing by the strident
ringing of the telephone in the room she had just left
and hurried back indoors, lifting the receiver and speaking breathlessly as she gave the number, fully expecting
it to be Clare making sure she had reached home safely
after the emotion of the day.

It wasn't Clare.

'Miss Crawford?' The deep dark voice was unmistakable. 'This is Hawk Mallen.'

'I... What...? Yes, Mr Mallen?' Oh, pull yourself together, for goodness' sake, she thought scathingly as she
heard her faltering voice with a burst of self-contempt
that was humiliating. What *did* she sound like? But she
sat down very suddenly on the little pouffe next to the
phone, her legs turning to jelly.

'Are you in full possession of all the facts relating to
the takeover of Concise Publications by Mallen Books
now?' the male voice, with its almost gravelly texture,
asked expressionlessly.

'I think... I think so, and I just want to say I didn't
realise... That is, I know I spoke out of turn—'

'Miss Crawford, I didn't ring for an apology, if that's
what you are thinking, although it is acknowledged and
accepted.'

She blinked a little, even more glad she was sitting
down as her stomach turned over with a shuddering jerk.
He was terrifying—in spite of the miles separating them
that dark, formidable aura swept into the room along
with his voice and caused her nerves to go haywire.

Once Charles had accepted she was serious about not
going back he had related numerous stories about the
Mallen empire, most of them featuring Hawk Mallen,
and as she had listened she had known that even if today

had not happened she could not have worked for this single-minded, utterly frightening, ruthless tycoon. He was the original workaholic according to Charles—cold, untouchable, his reputation built purely by his own efforts and having nothing to do with his grandfather's name. As Charles had gone on the main element to her emotion was sheer wonder that she had dared to say all she had to this walking legend. No wonder he had looked so amazed as she had left; it was doubtful if anyone had ever spoken to him like that before, or walked out on him either.

'Miss Crawford? Are you still there?'

She realised she was sitting in a kind of trance and jerked to life with the voice in her ear. 'Yes, yes, I am.' Breathe deeply, talk coherently, *act your age*. 'Thank you—'

'I would like to see you privately; I think the office staff have been entertained enough for one day,' he said silkily, his voice so smooth and bland that for a moment the import of his words didn't strike home. 'And preferably before the day starts tomorrow. Would this evening be convenient?'

'This evening?' Her voice was a squeak of horror— she knew it and he must have heard it, and now she began to gabble in an effort to cover up. 'I don't think so. I've just got back from holiday, you see, and there are things to do. I really can't—'

'Shall we say eight o'clock?' The silkiness sheathed cold steel, but in spite of his intimidation a little spurt of anger at his arrogance rose, hot and fierce.

'I honestly don't think there is any point, Mr Mallen.' Her voice was firmer but she was still glad she was sitting down. 'I can call by the office at your convenience to pick up my salary cheque and clear any outstanding matters you might need my assistance on; I'm quite prepared to help—'

'In that case you will see me this evening,' he said coolly. 'I'm not asking you for a date—' there was a moment's pause when she felt herself flush bright scarlet '—merely suggesting we discuss certain business matters over dinner.'

'But—'

'That's settled, then. Eight it is.' And the phone went dead. She stared at it for a full minute—the deep voice with its faint American accent still ringing in her ears—before she slowly replaced the receiver, but even then she made no effort to stand. He was taking her out to dinner? Hawk Mallen? Taking *her* out to dinner? She couldn't; she just couldn't.

She picked up the phone again and dialled Charles's number, her hand shaking.

'Charles Brigmore?' His voice was so reassuringly familiar she wanted to cry again, but checked the impulse firmly. She couldn't remember the last time she had cried before today, and now she couldn't stop.

'Charles, you'll never guess what's happened...' There was complete silence at the other end of the line as she went on, and as the silence lengthened when she had finished she said hesitantly, 'Charles? Say something.'

'You've agreed to go out to dinner with Hawk Mallen?' Charles asked bemusedly. 'But...why?'

'I didn't exactly *agree* to anything,' Joanne said a trifle testily. 'I told you. He just sort of...told me.'

'Well, untell him,' Charles said with a surprising lack of grammar. 'You don't know what you are getting into, Jo.'

'I *do*.' She paused, and moderated her tone as she continued, 'I've an idea anyway; that's why I'm ringing you to discuss it. I don't know why he wants to see me, but after my little outburst today it can't be for anything good. He wasn't too pleased when I left.'

'I can imagine.' Charles's voice was very dry.

'He can't hold me to anything, can he, with my contract?' Joanne asked anxiously. 'I know it says three months' notice, but surely in the circumstances he'd be prepared to be reasonable?'

'I don't think "reasonable" is a word that features in Hawk Mallen's vocabulary,' Charles said slowly. 'Look, ring him back and ask him exactly what he wants to see you about. That's only sensible, and if you're still not happy...'

'I shan't be happy; of course I shan't be happy,' Joanne said flatly. 'Would you be happy going out to dinner with Hawk Mallen after speaking to him the way I did? He's probably after my blood.'

'As long as that's all he's after,' Charles said darkly.

'What do you mean?'

'Joanne...' Charles's voice held the patience that characterised his relationship with her. 'I know you don't preen and powder like the average female but you must look in the mirror sometimes, surely? You're a very attractive woman, and Hawk Mallen is definitely very much a man. I didn't say this this afternoon, but he doesn't only work hard, if you get my meaning; the play is done pretty energetically and with great effect too.'

'No, he made it clear it wasn't a date, Charles; he actually spelled it out. Besides which I hardly think someone like Hawk Mallen would look twice at me.' She smiled to herself at the thought. 'He must have his pick of women.'

'No doubt,' Charles said drily.

'But I will phone him back. I can't see any point in meeting him,' she said resolutely.

'Ring me if there's any trouble.'

There was trouble, but she didn't ring back, deciding that it was her problem, not Charles's. Hawk Mallen wasn't in the building, Sue on Reception told her politely, and no, she had no idea where he could be contacted. She could give her the name of the hotel where he was staying at present if she'd like to ring there? Joanne did like, but he wasn't there either. She left messages in both places for him to contact her if he returned, and then paced the floor for the rest of the afternoon waiting for the telephone to ring.

By six o'clock she was panicking badly; by seven she had had a bath and washed her hair, and a feeling of inevitability had settled over her like a blanket. Whether he'd got her messages or not he wouldn't ring; she should have known, she told herself resignedly. He had made up his mind he was going to talk to her tonight, and that, as far as he was concerned, was that.

What did one wear when going out to dinner with a megalomaniac? she asked herself helplessly as she surveyed her wardrobe. Especially a fabulously wealthy, dark, attractive one, who frightened her half to death and was probably gunning for her blood? Was he going to prove awkward? Take pleasure in telling her he was going to put the knife in with future employers and so on? Or was he going to hold her to every last day of her contract? She could leave anyway—it would just mean a loss of salary and other benefits—but it wouldn't look too good with prospective employers.

The carefree days of the last month seemed like another lifetime as she glumly pulled a high-necked, long-sleeved cocktail dress in crushed black silk off its hanger. The dress was expensive but the style demure; it gave the impression of a controlled, capable woman in charge of her own destiny, which was exactly what she wanted for the night ahead.

Her hair was trimmed in a sleek bob just above the nape and she normally wore it loose, but she needed the extra sophistication having it up would give her, she decided nervously as she glanced at her reflection in the mirror. She was all fingers and thumbs, but eventually it was secured in a neat chignon at the back of her head, a pair of tiny gold studs her only jewellery, and a touch of mascara the sum total of her make-up.

There—calm, cool and competent, she decided silently as she looked into the long full-length mirror in her bedroom, seeing only the elegant dress with its matching shoes, and quite missing the beauty of her glowing red hair and honey-brown eyes which complemented the black silk perfectly.

Hawk Mallen missed neither when Joanne opened the door to his knock at exactly eight o'clock, her colour high again as she saw him framed in the doorway, big and dark and lazily self-assured.

'I've been trying to contact you all afternoon.' It probably wasn't the best of opening lines, but her brain seemed to scramble at the sight or sound of this man.

'And now you have.' He smiled easily, but it didn't reach the riveting blue eyes and she knew instantly, without a shadow of a doubt, that he had received her messages and guessed the reason for them.

'I...I was just going to ask what this was all about.' She had raised her chin slightly as she spoke without being aware of it, and the subtle gesture spoke volumes to the man watching her so closely.

'All in good time.' He gestured to the room beyond. 'Do you have a wrap, a jacket...?'

'Yes. Oh, come in.' She stepped back so hastily she nearly pivoted on the three-inch heels which were much higher than those she normally wore, recovering herself just in time and feeling her face grow even hotter in the process. This was going to be a riot of an evening, she told herself desperately, walking carefully through the tiny square hall and into the lounge where she had placed her jacket and handbag. She couldn't even stay upright, let alone impress him with her woman-of-the-world persona.

'Nice flat.' He had followed her, and as she turned the room immediately shrank in deference to his presence, his impressive height and build seeming to fill the pleasant light surroundings.

'I like it.' She couldn't for the life of her manage her normal social smile as she stared at him before moving hastily away, her face still flaming, and busying herself adjusting the brilliance of the wall lights. She reached for her jacket and bag. 'Shall we?' She nodded to the front door but he didn't move, surveying her with cool, narrowed eyes for a long, heart-thudding moment.

'I'm not going to eat you, you know,' he said softly. 'You're not Little Red Riding Hood and I'm not the Wolf. Well…' He paused, his eyes narrowing still more. 'You're not Little Red Riding Hood anyway,' he added sardonically.

'I didn't say—'

'You didn't have to.' He interrupted her before she could finish and again the incredible self-assurance hit a nerve.

'Mr Mallen—'

'Hawk, please,' he interjected softly.

'Mr Mallen, I've no idea what was so important that it couldn't wait until normal office hours, but I really don't think this is a good idea,' she said stiffly. 'I tried to contact you this afternoon—'

'You've already said that.' The dark eyebrows rose mockingly.

'But you clearly didn't receive my messages,' she finished a trifle desperately. This was awful; *he* was awful.

'Oh, I did, both of them, but I chose to ignore them,' he said easily, his voice as pleasant as if he were discussing the weather.

'You what?' She couldn't match his calm, her voice high.

'Ignored them.' He smiled maliciously, clearly thoroughly enjoying her open-mouthed discomfiture. 'You suspected that, didn't you?' he added silkily. 'But you expected me to lie to you. I never lie, Joanne. When you know me better you will appreciate that is the truth. However painful, however costly, I never lie.'

Know him better? Over her dead body!

'Now, there is a table booked at the Maltese Inn for nine, so if you're ready?'

The dark face was expressionless, the blue eyes unwavering, and as she gazed into the hard, implacable features she conceded defeat. Okay, she'd go on this wretched evening out, she could hardly do anything else now, but there was no way she was going to be bullied or threatened by this man, whatever his wealth or connections.

'Yes, I'm quite ready.' She looked at him steadily, trying to hide the fact that she felt like a petrified little rabbit in the hypnotising power of a fox, and even managed a tight smile as she said, 'I'm just worried that this evening will be a lamentable waste of your valuable time, Mr Mallen.'

'Why don't you let me worry about that?' he said quietly. 'And I told you, the name's Hawk.'

Hawk. Yes, the name suited him, she thought with a faint touch of hysteria as he took her arm and ushered her out of the flat. She had been mistaken in her analogy of a fox; he was far more like the ruthless, keen-sighted bird of prey he had been named after, and at the moment she had the awful conviction that the quarry in his sights was her!

CHAPTER TWO

THE Maltese Inn was an exclusive little nightclub she had heard about but never had the necessary connections to enter, it being the haunt of the very rich and the very famous. It was chic, select, and its clientele ranged from wealthy film stars and top models to the very élite of England's aristocracy.

Once in Hawk's car, which just had to be a magnificent sporty monster she had never heard of before but which was undoubtedly in the super league—nothing as well known as a Ferrari or Lamborghini for him, she thought nastily—she found herself dumb with nerves.

She glanced at him several times from under her eyelashes, her eyes and senses registering the big lean body clothed in evening dress with a jolt that didn't lessen with the third or fourth glance, before forcing herself to make some sort of conversation. 'This is a beautiful car.' Never had words been so inadequate; never had she *felt* so inadequate. 'What is it?'

'A Cizeta-Moroder V16T.' The piercing eyes flashed over her face for a moment before returning to the windscreen.

'Oh.' She was no nearer and it showed.

'It's an Italian car, designed by Marcello Gandini,' Hawk said easily. 'I like the power, the body style, and it's beautiful and fast. When I drive I like to enjoy the experience, besides which I wanted a car which would take me from A to B in as short a time as possible.'

'And this certainly would.' She glanced round the interior of the two-seater coupé which was as dynamic inside as out.

'I also like unusual things, not necessarily unique but things that haven't been…cheapened by overuse,' he continued softly.

There had been a thread of something in his voice she couldn't quite place, but as she glanced at the dark profile again it gave nothing away, his features relaxed and quite expressionless.

She couldn't believe she was sitting in the sort of car one only saw in the movies, being driven to the most fashionable nightclub in London by a dark, handsome— No, not handsome. She caught her thoughts abruptly, sneaking another glance at him. Handsome was too weak a word somehow for Hawk Mallen; it suggested pretty-boy good looks, traditional appeal, and the lean, hard face, penetrating blue eyes and cruel, sensual mouth were anything but that. She shivered suddenly, in spite of the perfectly regulated temperature within the car.

What on earth was she doing here? She must be mad. Her thoughts did nothing to calm her racing heartbeat. And the Maltese Inn, of all places. It was all Diors and diamonds there, and here was she in her little black dress and off-the-peg jacket… She felt a moment of nausea as her stomach turned right over. She was going to stand out like a sore thumb—

'Look, could you just try and think of me as friend and not foe for an hour or two, at least until the meal is over?' The deep, gravelly voice had amusement at its core; she could hear it curling the edges. 'Good food is life's second greatest pleasure…' The piercing gaze swept over her flushed face for one brief moment but it left her in no doubt as to what he considered the first, and she felt herself blush even more fiercely. 'And I'd prefer to enjoy the meal tonight without indigestion at the end of it.'

'I don't know you, Mr Mallen—Hawk,' she corrected

hastily as he made a growl of annoyance in his throat, 'so how could I possibly regard you as foe?'

'I've been involved with a good few women in my time, Joanne, on a business level and otherwise,' he said quietly, 'and one thing I've learnt along the way is that your sex doesn't need a reason for anything it feels like doing.'

'Well, that's a sexist remark if ever I heard one,' she retorted scathingly, forgetting her nervousness and apprehension as he pressed the fire button. 'You're one of those men who think women are empty-headed little dolls, good for one thing only?'

'Did I say that?' he drawled softly.

'You didn't have to.' She was trying to give the impression of being as controlled and calm as he was, but it was difficult—more than difficult. She might have known he'd be a male chauvinist pig on top of everything else; this was getting worse by the minute.

'You might have been able to read Charles's mind but not mine, Joanne,' he said calmly, 'so please don't make the mistake of thinking you can. And I wasn't insinuating anything about Charles, before further crimes are laid at my feet. I'm quite aware of the platonic relationship between you both—''a father and daughter affection'' were the words used to explain it, I think,' he said easily, 'by none other than his wife.'

'You asked *Clare* about me?' she screeched, her voice reverberating around the car's plush interior and causing the man at the wheel to wince visibly. 'How dare you?'

'Who better to ask?' His sidelong glance took in her scarlet face and he actually chuckled before adding, 'Calm down, Joanne, calm down; it wasn't like that. On the way to pick you up this evening I called by Charles's house with some papers for him to sign, and it was Clare who mentioned you as it happens. They're very fond of you, aren't they?' he said quietly. 'You're quite one of the family.'

She wasn't sure if he was being nasty or not but her temper was still at boiling point and she didn't trust herself to speak anyway. What an impossible man, she thought angrily. If ever she had needed confirmation that her decision to leave Concise Publications had been the right one, she'd just had it. Working as Charles's publishing assistant had been nothing but pleasure, but as Hawk Mallen's...

'Did you enjoy your job, Joanne?' It was as though he had read her mind, and she noted the past tense with a little flutter in her stomach. So, she *was* out on her ear, but then why this dinner tonight? she thought bitterly. So he could gloat, was that it?

'Yes, I did.' In spite of all her efforts to the contrary she couldn't quite keep the thread of antagonism from showing. 'It was interesting, exciting.'

'And from what Charles tells me your input was considerably more than one could normally expect from a publishing assistant; would you say that was fair?' he asked mildly.

She shrugged carefully. 'I've no personal commitments so there was no need to clock-watch if that's what you mean.'

'Not exactly.' The sleek, low beast of a car had just growled reluctantly to a halt at some traffic lights, and he stretched in the leather seat as he waited for amber, the movement bringing powerfully muscled thighs disconcertingly into her consciousness as she glanced his way. Her head shot to the front as though she had been bitten, the colour that had just begun to recede surging into her cheeks again.

What *was* it about him? she asked herself helplessly. Sexual magnetism? The aphrodisiac of wealth and power and authority? Sheer old-fashioned sex appeal? It was all those things and more, and it was devastating. He would have been dynamite on the silver screen, she thought ruefully. Pure twenty-four-carat box-office dynamite.

He didn't speak again as the Cizeta-Moroder sprang away from the lights, but as they travelled along the well-lit London streets her nerve-endings were screaming at her awareness of him, and she had never felt so out of her depth in all her life.

When they drew up outside the refined elegant building of the Maltese Inn he uncoiled his big body from the low-slung car with easy animal grace, moving to the passenger side in a moment and opening her door for her.

'You aren't going to leave it here?' She stared at him in surprise once she was on the pavement, but in the next second a massive uniformed doorman, who looked more like a prize fighter than anything else, was at their side.

'Keys, Bob.' Hawk dropped the keys into the man's outstretched hand with a warm smile along with a folded banknote. 'Look after her.'

'As always, Mr Mallen, as always. Good evening, miss.'

'Good evening.' Joanne smiled into the big ugly face with a naturalness that had been missing in her dealings with Hawk, something the piercing blue eyes noted and filed.

There was another doorman ready to open the gleaming plate-glass door into the entrance lobby, and another who ushered them through that and into the area beyond, where the reception area, powder rooms and cloakrooms were, the nightclub itself being up a flight of wide, graciously curved stairs that would have done credit to any Hollywood movie.

Having divested herself of her jacket, Joanne was

painfully conscious of the plainness of her dress and jewellery as she joined Hawk, the surrounding area seeming full of glittering women, with diamonds on their wrists, throat and ears, and all wearing dresses that must have cost a small fortune.

She was aware of the subdued buzz that Hawk was drawing, especially from the female contingent, as they walked towards the stairs, and it took all her will-power to keep her head high and her face cool and contained as they climbed the marble steps to the nightclub beyond.

That Hawk himself had noticed the covert glances became apparent when, on reaching the top of the stairs, he leant down and whispered in her ear, 'Don't worry, they are the same with everyone; they're trying to work out what us being together means.'

They aren't the only ones, Joanne thought wryly, her nerves as tight as piano wire.

'Too much time and too much money breeds mischief,' Hawk went on cynically, 'as many a damaged reputation has discovered.'

'I wouldn't know.' She glanced back down into the glittering array beneath them as they turned to go through the doors into the dimly lit nightclub, and there was more than one pair of beautifully painted eyes that stared brazenly back at her.

'You don't gossip?'

It was said mockingly but with more than a touch of scepticism, and Joanne paused just inside the room, meeting his sardonic gaze as she said, 'No, I don't. Why? Is that so unbelievable?'

'Yes.' The sensual mouth quirked apologetically. 'I told you I don't lie,' he continued softly, 'and you did ask.'

'You seem to have a very low opinion of the female sex, Mr Mallen,' she said tightly. 'Or am I mistaken?'

It was a direct confrontation, and he smiled slowly, his eyes turning to liquid silver under the muted lighting and his dark skin accentuated by the whiteness of his smile. 'I can't answer that on the grounds that it might incriminate me,' he said lightly.

'I see.' She was about to say more, a lot more, but the appearance of the head waiter, with a smile as wide as London Bridge, put paid to the flood of angry words, and as they were led to what was obviously a superior table, right on the edge of the large dance-floor, she found herself once again overawed by her surroundings.

The champagne cocktails that appeared as though by magic at their elbows the moment they were seated were absolutely delicious; in fact she hadn't tasted anything quite so delicious before, but she noticed that although Hawk ordered a second for her he had nothing more exciting than mineral water.

'I'm driving.' He answered her raised eyebrows with a smile. 'One is enough.'

'How resolute of you,' she answered lightly.

'Not really.' The blue eyes narrowed, his gaze intent as he said, 'My father had three times the permitted level of alcohol in his blood when he went off the road and caused the death of himself and my mother fifteen years ago. He was forty-four, she was just forty; I don't find it hard to say no to alcohol when I'm driving.'

'I'm sorry.' She didn't know what else to say. 'Have you any brothers or sisters?' she asked lamely.

'No.' He didn't elaborate. 'How about you? Do you come from a big family?' he asked quietly.

'No.' She hadn't expected this and it took her completely by surprise, causing her to stammer slightly as she said, 'My...my mother is dead and I never knew my father.'

'No siblings?' The keen eyes had narrowed on her flushed face.

'No, I…I was brought up in foster homes mostly. My mother…she didn't relate too well to children.' She stopped abruptly, appalled at what she had revealed. This man had drawn out of her what it had taken Charles and Clare twelve months to achieve. How could she have told him that about her childhood? she asked herself desperately. It had sounded as though she was asking for sympathy and that was the last thing, the very last thing, she wanted.

The appearance of a waiter at Hawk's elbow in the next moment eased the situation somewhat, and after they had ordered he didn't comment about what had been said before, engaging her in light, easy conversation that taxed neither her brain nor her tongue.

But… And there was a but, she thought silently, even as she laughed at something witty, and faintly cruel, he had just said about a well-known television presenter who had just swept into the nightclub with all the regality of royalty. Yes, there definitely was a but, although she couldn't quite determine what it was.

Possibly the way he was watching her, his blue eyes cynical and probing even as his mouth smiled and made small talk, or perhaps it was the rather remote way he had with him, as though he was surveying everything and everyone from a distance and finding them wanting. Whatever, it was disconcerting, unnerving, and she was immensely glad of the fortifying cocktails to quieten the rampant butterflies in her stomach that had been fluttering crazily since she had first opened the door of the flat to him.

The meal was delicious, but she found each mouthful an effort, mainly because as people finished eating and began to take to the dance-floor she realised the moment Hawk would ask her to dance was imminent.

He seemed in no hurry to explain why he had asked to see her; every time she had tried to broach the matter

he had changed the subject with a firmness that was
daunting, and now dessert was nearly finished and, short
of asking for a second helping, which would only delay
the inevitable, there was no escape. And she didn't want
to dance with him; in fact the thought of him touching
her, however circumspectly, was...disturbing. She finished the last mouthful of chocolate soufflé—it had been
hovering in its dish for minutes and she really couldn't
delay any longer—and almost in the same instant he
stood, bending over her and drawing her to her feet before she could protest.

'You can't come to the Inn and not dance; it really
isn't done,' he said in a deep mocking whisper that told
her he had been fully aware of her thoughts and had
taken what he considered to be the appropriate action.

'Perhaps I don't care about what's done,' she muttered
quietly as she found herself on the dance-floor, stiffening
helplessly as his arms enclosed her.

'Perhaps you don't.' The frighteningly perceptive eyes
ran over her flushed face before he said, his voice low
but alive with wicked amusement, 'Or perhaps it's me?
It's all right, Joanne, my ego can survive—just—if you
confirm my worst fears.'

'Which are?' she asked tightly, her body desperately
aware of the hard male frame close to hers and the un-
deniably delicious masculine fragrance emanating from
the tanned skin.

'That you don't like me?'

'Am I supposed to like you?' she asked shakily.

'Of course.' The arrogance was full of self-mockery
which increased her turmoil. He wasn't supposed to
laugh at himself; that didn't fit the image. 'Every woman
I meet is automatically bowled over by my charm and
pleasing countenance, not to mention my wealth,' he
added darkly.

'You think they are just after your money?' she asked

in amazement. Even the most hardened gold-digger would rock on her heels when confronted by the maleness of Hawk Mallen.

'I think it oils the wheels.' He smiled, but it was a mere twisting of the cruel, sensual mouth and not really a smile at all.

'That's…that's—'

'Realistic.' He cut into her shocked stammering with a lazy drawl, pulling her a little closer as he did so.

'*Awful.*' She stared up at him, her cheeks hot. 'You can't lump the whole female race into one package like that.'

'Can't I?' He considered her for a long quiet moment before smiling again. 'Why not?' he asked softly.

'Because everyone's different; people have different values, different perspectives— Oh, you *know* why not,' she finished tightly, not at all sure if he was teasing her or if he meant what he had said.

'Your personnel file says you are twenty-nine years old, right?' He looked down at her, his dark face unreadable.

She nodded, wondering what was coming next.

'And you have never married.' It was a flat statement. 'Lived with anyone?' he asked quietly.

'That's nothing to do with you.' She struggled slightly in his hold, resenting the personal questioning, but all he did was pull her even closer, settling her against the broad expanse of his chest, his chin nuzzling the red silk of her hair.

'Have you lived with anyone, Joanne?' he asked again, his voice still soft but threaded through with a silky coolness that told her he was determined to have an answer.

'No.' It was useless to fight him but she bitterly resented the interrogation.

'And according to Charles you don't date much—rarely in fact,' he said thoughtfully. 'Very rarely.'

'Did Charles say that?' She was deeply offended and hurt at Charles's betrayal.

'No.' She would have jerked away again but the arms holding her were forged in steel. 'But I'm very adept at reading between the lines and I know the sort of questions to ask that give me the answers I require,' he said easily.

'How clever of you,' she snapped nastily.

'Isn't it?' He moved her slightly from him now, keeping her within the circle of his arms as he looked down at her with hard, narrowed eyes. 'Now I'd say, on a likelihood of ten to one, that you have—how did you put it? Oh, yes—"lumped" the whole male race together fairly successfully.' His tone had lost any amusement, his face absolutely straight as he added, 'Or am I wrong?'

'Quite wrong,' she said cuttingly, her face flaming.

'Oh, Joanne. Joanne, Joanne…' He shook his head sorrowfully, the mockery back. 'And here's me being honest and above board—'

'Are you insinuating I'm not?' she asked hotly.

'Absolutely.' And then he grinned, and all further opposition left her in a big whoosh as she absorbed the difference to his face that his first real smile made. He was devastating, gorgeous, overwhelming… She swallowed hard and prayed for the ground to stop rippling under her feet. He was a man, just a man, and an arrogant, self-satisfied pig of one at that. He'd just lost her her job, hadn't he? She *couldn't* be attracted to him; what was the matter with her, for goodness' sake—?

'But I forgive you.' He had pulled her close again and, mainly because her legs suddenly seemed to have the consistency of melted jelly, she didn't resist.

However, she managed a fairly tart, 'How very gracious of you,' which brought an answering chuckle from above her head, before they continued to dance in silence. It was a slow number—of course it had to be, she thought caustically; even the band was against her—and although she desperately wanted to seem immune to what his body was doing to hers she could feel herself begin to tremble in his arms.

'What's happened in your life to make you so afraid of physical contact?' he murmured after several humiliating minutes when she knew her shaking had made itself obvious. 'I'm not going to hurt you, Joanne. Trust me.'

'Trust you?' She was inexpressibly thankful that he had misread her body's reaction to his, although there was more than a little fear mixed up in the mortifying sexual excitement that had her in its grip. And now, as the music changed, and she saw the waiter approaching their table with the coffee they had ordered, she moved to arm's length, saying, 'That would be rather foolish on so short an acquaintance, don't you think? Look, the coffee's arrived. Shall we…?'

'If you insist.' His tone was dry.

'And then you can tell me the reason for our meeting tonight and then—'

'We can go home?' he finished silkily, his eyes piercingly intuitive. 'Sorry, Joanne, there's the floor show to go yet; you're stuck with me for a little while longer.'

She smiled, a polite social smile as though she thought he was joking, before turning and walking to their table, his hand on the small of her back seeming to burn her skin through the silk of her dress.

How was it that in just a few hours this man seemed to have established an intimacy that even her closest friends didn't enjoy? she asked herself weakly, sinking down on to her chair with a tiny sigh of relief that she had made it without falling to the floor in a quivering heap. The questions he had asked, the things he had suggested! Her racing thoughts were brought to a stunned halt as she felt his lips on the back of her neck, his mouth warm and vibrant against the creamy softness of her skin, before he seated himself with easy composure in his chair.

'Don't...don't do that.'

'What?' Her voice had been a trembling whisper and he surveyed her with brilliantly blue eyes before asking again, 'Don't do what?'

'You know what.' She glared at him, her temper rising as her senses unfroze.

'Kiss you?' he asked softly. 'Is that so hard to say?'

'It wasn't a kiss, it was...' She couldn't find an appropriate word and he let her flounder for a minute before he said, his voice deep and dark and husky, 'Whatever it was to you, Joanne, to me it was a kiss. Do you mean to say that you don't wear your hair like that to tempt more of the same?'

'What?' She was absolutely lost for words.

'The exposure of that soft, fragrant skin, normally hidden by a curtain of silk that keeps the secret place so private—you don't know what a subtle turn-on that is to the average red-blooded male?' he asked softly as she stared at him blankly. 'It's restraint combined with voluptuousness, lasciviousness with suppression—it's ...sexy, every man's dream of the perfect virginal demure beauty who turns into a seductress in the bedroom.'

'You're mad.' Joanne realised she had been holding her breath as the gravelly male voice had woven a sensual spell which had enclosed the two of them in their own little world. 'I just wore my hair up because it looks better with this dress—'

'Oh, don't spoil it.' He wasn't smiling but the devilish eyes were alight with amusement.

'Now, look.' She took a long, deep, hard breath and

forced herself to get control. This was ridiculous; somehow everything had got out of hand and she wasn't at
all sure how it had happened, but one thing she did know
was that Hawk Mallen was playing with her like a cat
with a mouse. She didn't believe for one moment he
was attracted to her—how could a multi-millionaire of
the calibre of this one be interested in a little nobody
like her? It didn't add up—not for one minute, and she
wasn't stupid whatever he thought, and she'd tell him
so right now. 'You assured me this afternoon that we
were meeting for a purpose, that this wasn't a…'

'Date?' he supplied helpfully.

'Yes.' And if he interrupted her again he'd have a cup
of coffee tipped over his head. 'So we've eaten and
danced and done the social chit-chat bit, and now I'd
really like to know why you have brought me here tonight.'

'You don't think it's because I wanted to know you
better, because I'm interested in you?' he asked expressionlessly.

He'd read her mind again, and she had the uneasy
feeling he hadn't found it hard to do. Was she really so
transparent? she asked herself silently. She didn't think
anyone else thought so; in fact, Charles had often praised
what he called her 'poker face', which gave nothing
away whatever the circumstances.

'Mr Mallen—' she couldn't call him Hawk, she just
couldn't '—you could doubtless have your pick of most
of London's finest so the answer to that is no.'

'London's finest.' He nodded thoughtfully. 'I see.'

'So?' She forced a smile. 'If you don't mind?'

He stared at her for a good thirty seconds, his blue
eyes shadowed and intent as they searched her face, and
then he settled back in his seat, stretching slightly before
he said, 'Right, down to business. I don't need you at
Concise Publications, Joanne—' her heart gave a big

leap and then thudded loudly '—but from all I've heard and read and seen I think you would be an asset to the Mallen Corporation. I intend to bring in a new managing director for Concise Publications; I've already approached the man and he's accepted my offer and he'll bring his own publishing assistant with him; they've worked together for years.'

She nodded slowly. So he had never intended to take on the job permanently? She should have guessed, really; Concise Publications was just a tiny little cog in the vast machine of the Mallen empire.

'Are you interested enough for me to continue?' His voice was cool and flat; suddenly he was one hundred per cent remote tycoon and businessman, the wickedly mocking, charming dinner companion having evaporated like the morning mist.

Was she? She stared at him hard, and then nodded again. 'Yes, please,' she said quietly.

The blue eyes flickered, just once, and she would have given the world to know what was going on in that rapier-sharp, ruthless mind.

'Six months ago the Mallen Corporation acquired a publishing house in France, part of Mallen Books; were you aware of this?' She shook her head quickly. 'The undertaking was unusual in that my grandfather had decided to bale the owner out, and if you knew my grandfather you would understand why I say that. He is first and foremost a businessman and age has not mellowed him one iota.'

She caught the thread of affection in his voice which he was trying to hide and looked at him intently.

'The owner was the son of my grandfather's best friend who died some years ago; he actually helped my grandfather financially when they were young, something my grandfather's never forgotten. However, the son has lost thousands, if not tens of thousands, over the last decade through mismanagement and so on, and the firm is a shambles.' The cool voice was scathing. 'My grandfather wanted the family name to continue in honour to his friend; he also decided to keep the son at the helm... Bad mistake.'

He glanced at her now and the blue eyes were as hard as glass. 'The kindest thing you could say about this guy is that he's a Jonah, and that's the information I've relayed to my grandfather. The truth of the matter is that he's been on the take for years; he's the very antithesis of his father. My grandfather is very ill—' Her eyes widened and he nodded slowly. 'Terminal, but I'd appreciate you keeping that to yourself. He doesn't need this bag of worms dumping in his lap, and for some reason his normally acute judgement is faulty where this guy is concerned. He *wants* to believe the best of him; he's all that's left of his old friend.'

'What are you going to do?' she asked quietly. He loved his grandfather very much; try as he might, the cold, clipped voice and expressionless face couldn't hide the look in his eyes, and it touched her. She didn't want it to, but it did.

'I've done it,' he said flatly. 'Pierre is boss in name only now; he's been paid off, and handsomely, and he's quite happy with that. He's got a string of mistresses to support apart from his family and expensive habits; the firm was just an inconvenience to him. But now I want to pull it round, for my grandfather and also his old friend, who was an honourable man. That's where you would come in.'

'Me?' She couldn't think where.

'You've been in publishing since you left university, you have no personal commitments or distractions, and you don't mind working until the job is done. Added to that, Charles tells me your contribution, certainly over the last three or four years, was the one that brought the money in. He'd lost it—the insight, the business intuition—'

'No!' she protested hotly.

'That's what he told me, Joanne,' Hawk said steadily. 'Now, your personnel file tells me you speak French, right?'

'I do, but…well, I'm rusty and—'

'That's no problem.' He dismissed her stumbling voice with an irritable wave of his hand. 'You can easily brush up on that.'

'What exactly are you offering me?' she asked dazedly. In all her wildest dreams—or nightmares—she hadn't expected this. 'Who would I be publishing assistant to?' She knew it was him but she had to ask anyway, and that would be the end of what sounded like the offer of a lifetime in an industry that was known for its dog-eat-dog ruthlessness.

'Publishing assistant?' He stared at her, and then shook his black head slowly, his eyes piercing her through with clear light. 'I'm not offering you a publishing assistant's job, Joanne. I want you to manage the firm for me, turn it around, make it work.'

'Me?' She knew she was repeating herself but this was just not possible; he had to be teasing her in the most cruel way imaginable.

'It would mean giving up your flat and moving to France,' he said quietly, 'and of necessity the position would be on a six-month trial basis. All your expenses would be paid, of course, and you'd have the same salary Pierre did.' He mentioned a figure that made her mouth fall open. 'The firm is already part of Mallen Books and so you wouldn't be completely out on a limb; you'd have a ready-made avenue of contacts and back-up—a security blanket so to speak. But…' He leant forward in his seat, his dark face cold. 'You would have your work cut out to turn the thing round, especially in the present climate. Still interested enough to think about it?'

Joanne looked at him in a daze. She couldn't say a word; she just couldn't.

'If you *are* interested, we can throw a few facts and figures your way and start the ball rolling. I'd like the new manager installed within weeks and as you are as free as a bird there won't be any messy working-of-notice delay. If you're not...' the piercing eyes were holding hers as though in a vice '...then you will be paid twelve months' salary as a gesture of appreciation for all you've done for Charles's firm in the past, and that's the end of it. Well?'

He relaxed back in his seat and grinned, the same devastating, knee-trembling grin as before, his blue gaze washing over her stunned countenance. 'What's it to be, Joanne?'

CHAPTER THREE

'AND he wants your answer tomorrow morning, is that right?' Charles's voice had been sleepy when he'd answered the phone—it was past midnight after all—but once Joanne had begun to talk the telephone had fairly crackled with excitement.

'He wants to know if I'm interested enough to go on to the next phase,' Joanne answered quietly, 'and if I am he'll put me more fully in the picture.'

'And are you?' Charles asked evenly.

'I suppose so, but if I don't make a go of it and I'm left with egg on my face...'

'And if you do make a go of it the world's your oyster,' Charles said steadily. 'Think of it, Joanne; it's a dream of a career move, and frankly it sounds like he's only asking you to do what you've been doing for me for five years. We've worked so closely together there isn't a thing you don't know about managing a publishing house.'

'But this one is so much bigger.' That sounded rude and she added quickly, 'Well, a bit bigger, and it's in France and—'

'You could do it and Hawk Mallen knows it or else he wouldn't have offered you the job.'

'Charles, I'm sorry I phoned you at this time of night, but I don't feel I know enough about the Mallen Corporation and...and Hawk Mallen to make a decision. Would you mind filling me in on what you know?'

'On Hawk or the Mallen empire?' Charles's voice was very dry.

'Both.'

By the time they finished the call, fifteen minutes later, Joanne knew the Mallen Corporation had been founded by Hawk's American/French grandfather over fifty years ago, beginning with a textile warehouse shop that quickly grew into a string of the same and then diversified into more avenues than even Charles was sure of. The old man had had one son, Hawk's father, who, as Hawk had already mentioned, had been killed in an automobile accident, thereupon making Hawk a millionaire several times over at the tender age of twenty.

Charles had said more, much more, but Joanne had found her attention wandering more than once as a pair of very blue, piercingly intent eyes kept swimming into her consciousness. Hawk Mallen was a mesmerising man to be with and the compelling weight of his personality stayed long after the man himself had gone. He exuded energy and power and vigour, and those moments in his arms on the dance-floor... She shut her eyes as her senses swam. If she took this job—*if*—she would make sure she never put herself in such a vulnerable position again.

Her thoughts continued along this same path once the call had ended and she had showered and slipped into bed.

Other women, more worldly, experienced women, might be able to handle a man like Hawk and enjoy the challenge, but he frightened her half to death. She shut her eyes tightly in the warm darkness, her toes curling into the linen covers.

Not that he had behaved as anything but the perfect gentleman on their ride home, seeing her to her door with a polite handshake and almost distant smile that would have sat well on a maiden aunt. In fact from the moment he had explained about the job one could almost have called his attitude cool, certainly formal... She refused to recognise even a shred of pique at his lack of interest. It suited her—the fact that he was concerned only with her ability to do the job he had in mind. *It did.* She knew only too well how the man-woman relationship, with all its complications, could prove a time bomb that ruined the lives of everyone within a mile radius.

As though it were yesterday her mother's face was there, pretty, irritated, as she had handed her over to the social worker at the home. 'It will only be for a little while, Joanne.' Her mother had clearly wished she were anywhere but in the neat, orderly office with officialdom present. 'Just until Mummy gets a nice house to live in.'

The 'nice house' had taken three years to achieve, three years in which she was moved from foster home to foster home, until, at the age of seven, her mother had married. Not again—she had never been married to Joanne's father who had deserted his pregnant girlfriend once the good news was imparted—but for the first time. That marriage had lasted nine months, and by the time she was eight she was back in a foster home again, with the knowledge that her mother could barely wait to see the back of her.

When she was nine her mother had married Bob, and it had been at his insistence that she was once again placed in her mother's care.

She had never wanted to be alone with Bob; she hadn't been able to put it into words at the time—the strange feeling she experienced when his pale, almost opaque eyes slid over her slim, childish body—but when the marriage had been two months old, and the police had arrived on the doorstep one morning, she had known then, young as she was, that she had been right to withstand his overtures of friendship. He had been convicted of several cases of child abuse, a paedophile of the worst kind, and strangely her mother had seemed to blame her for the break-up of her second marriage, screaming at her that she should never have had her back to stay, that if Bob hadn't known about Joanne he wouldn't have asked her to marry him and she would have been spared all the resulting humiliation.

She had been dispatched to the children's home the day after the court case, and had known then that she would never live with her mother again. Her mother had visited her now and again over the next few years, usually with a different 'uncle' in tow each time, some jovial and loud, some not so jolly, but had always managed to make her feel the visit was on sufferance.

The caustic memories of a thousand little rejections which added up to a gigantic whole had burnt so painfully deep within her psyche that even now they made her screw up her eyes and curl into a tight little embryonic ball under the covers.

Commitment, marriage, men—it all meant disappointment and betrayal; she had learnt the fact first-hand, watching her mother's desperate search for love. And children—the biological fruit of that sexual urge which drove men into pretending they were what they weren't, and foolish women into believing it—were the innocent casualties that suffered the most.

She had vowed many times during her tear-filled adolescence that she would never allow herself to be subjugated like her mother; she didn't want or need a man in her life—they meant trouble and pain and ultimately disappointment. Her mother had grown bitter in time— in the last conversation they had had before she died, she had told Joanne over and over again that it wasn't in a man's nature to be monogamous, that marriage and fidelity were the world's biggest lie.

Did she, Joanne, really believe that? she asked herself now, her eyes still tightly shut. She wasn't sure, not deep inside, but she was sure that she would never dare to take the risk, and also that casual relationships, of the sort her mother had eventually subscribed to, were not for her. And whenever the longing to have someone—one man, to come home to, to love—overwhelmed her—as it did more and more as each year ticked by—she drew on the memories and the agony of the past and it fled.

She had her work, her home and her friends—it was safe, controlled, she was in charge and no one could hurt her. It wasn't ideal, but it would have to do.

Charles and Clare had helped her erase some of the pain of the past, as much by the way they lived, their devotion to each other and their children, as their actual friendship. For the first time she had found it within herself to acknowledge that some folk—the lucky ones—could find that elusive element called true love and hang on to it despite all the trials and heartache. But not her. Definitely not her. She just didn't have what it would take. She had made that decision years ago and there was no reason for any doubts now—*none*, not one.

Once Joanne had accepted Hawk Mallen's offer the next day she found herself swept into a kind of whirlwind that had her breathless most of the time. In view of all she had previously decided about the need for a change, for fresh fields and new horizons, the offer was too good to turn down, but she had thought one of his countless minions would deal with her from that point and it was disconcerting to find that Hawk himself intended to oversee each detail. He was the sort of man who generated excitement and flurry and sheer atmosphere wherever he was, and the following weeks sped by in ever increasing velocity.

Of course she could appreciate Bergique & Son's future was close to his heart, or his grandfather's, to be more precise, and he needed to keep a tight hold of the reins, but the apprehension and unease she had felt that

first night was always there, at the back of her mind.
And she couldn't quite work out why. He was businesslike, cool, remote, but not unhelpful—very much the
austere, detached tycoon, but always ready to listen to
her ideas or opinions. And yet… 'Oh, stop imagining
things.' She leant against the wall of the lift which was
whisking her up to the meeting with Hawk that morning.

Just because she had caught him looking at
her…oddly once or twice, it didn't mean he was regretting his decision to appoint her manageress of the failing
firm, or that he was going to tell her he had changed his
mind, or any of the other scenarios she had gone through
each night in the quiet of her bed.

He was just a disturbing man, that was all it was, and
in a few more days she would be over the Channel in
France and he would be here in England, or dashing off
to America or any one of a dozen countries he seemed
to visit frequently. She just had to be cool, calm and
collected, serene even, in the five days that were left.
That wasn't beyond her, surely?

It shouldn't have been. It probably *wouldn't* have
been, if poor Maggie, who had been totally overawed
by Hawk's commanding presence from day one, hadn't
tripped over her own feet and deposited most of their
morning coffee right over her illustrious boss's immac-
ulate silk-covered chest.

As the burning liquid hit his torso Hawk swore—once
but very thoroughly—leaping up from his chair like a
scalded cat—and scalded he certainly was. The bedlam
was immediate, Maggie's horrified apology cut short as
she burst into tears, several people from the outer office
cannoning into the room at the sound of Hawk's yell,
the telephone choosing that moment to begin ringing and
all the papers on Hawk's desk tumbling to the floor as
Joanne jumped up to help and knocked them with
her arm.

'*Quiet!*' The thirty-second mayhem stopped as suddenly as it had begun as Hawk roared the order into the chaos, the only sound breaking the dead silence that followed being Maggie's muted wailing and the continuing ring of the telephone. 'Please, I'm fine, no harm done—get Maggie a cup of tea or whatever else you keep out there for emergencies,' Hawk fired in a staccato burst that told Joanne he was very definitely not all right. 'And someone answer that damn phone!'

As the others filed out, taking the weeping Maggie with them, Hawk shut the door behind them, wincing slightly as he did so, before peeling his steaming shirt out of the flat waistband of his trousers, discarding his tie and beginning to undo the buttons.

'What are you doing?' It was a squeak.

'What do you think I'm doing?' He clearly wasn't in the mood for rhetorical questions and she really couldn't blame him, but neither could she quite believe he was going to strip half naked in the office in the middle of a working day. He was, and apparently with a complete disregard for modesty that left her breathless. Only it wasn't just his lack of propriety that was causing the blood to race through every nerve and sinew.

Clothed, Hawk Mallen had the sort of lean, athletic physique that made the female heart beat a little faster; *half* clothed, the dark power radiated from him in tangible waves, impossible to ignore. Not that Joanne made any attempt to ignore it—she looked; she couldn't help it.

'Joanne?'

It was humiliating to realise he had spoken her name twice before it registered on her dazed senses, but the big broad shoulders and hairy, muscled chest had her knees ready to buckle under her. Useless to tell herself she was pathetic, ridiculous—a female voyeur; he was affecting her in a way no other man had ever done before and in a way she wouldn't have dreamed possible even moments before. He was…well, he was… She dragged her eyes up to the piercing blue gaze which was waiting for her.

'I asked you if you would get someone to pop to Harrods and pick up a shirt,' he said softly, his lips quirking with amusement. 'It's nearer than my hotel and I have an account there; they'll know what to send.'

He knew! He knew the thoughts that had shocked her with their lasciviousness and he was laughing at her.

Her head shot up, her honey-brown eyes darkening as the knowledge provided a welcome shot of adrenalin. 'Of course.' Her voice was taut and she kept her eyes strictly on his face, but the tanned expanse beneath them was still there.

'And perhaps you'd dispose of this?' He handed her the damp shirt, the muscles in his chest flexing as he did so. 'I'm going to hose myself down in Charles's washroom; I can feel that damn coffee's still burning my skin.'

She took the shirt as though it were going to bite her, knowing her face was flooded with colour but unable to do anything about it. He'd done this on purpose—oh, not the coffee, she couldn't blame that on him, but this…this *flaunting* of himself, she thought balefully. To embarrass her, to show her he was as unconcerned about her seeing him in a state of undress as…as the office furniture! It was added confirmation, as if she needed any, that she was just a working machine to him, little more than a number—

'Joanne?' The dark voice was patient. 'Harrods?'

'Oh, yes—yes, of course.' She shot out of the office as though the devil himself was after her, and in a way she felt that he was.

How could she have ogled him like that? she thought miserably after she'd sent one of the office staff darting off to Harrods. She'd all but licked her lips! What must he have thought? That she was attracted to him? Worse, that she was letting him *know* that she was attracted to him? She'd die if he'd thought that—she would; she'd just die—

'Joanne?' Maggie's woebegone voice cut into her painful introspection. 'How mad is he—Mr Mallen? I can't believe I did that.'

You and me both, Joanne thought as the mortification burnt deep. 'He's all right; don't worry.' She forced her voice to sound bright and matter-of-fact. 'Worse things happen at sea and all that.'

'I wish I was at sea; I wish I was anywhere but here,' Maggie said flatly. 'I don't know what it is about him but he makes me all fingers and thumbs; do you know what I mean?'

I do; oh, I do. 'He's only here for another three weeks—' Joanne smiled briskly into Maggie's puppy-dog eyes '—and then Mr Brigmore's replacement will be at the helm. Just…just treat him like you would Mr Brigmore till then, Maggie.'

'Just treat him like you would Mr Brigmore'. The absurdity of the statement hit her full between the eyes a little while later when she took the neatly packaged silk shirt in to Hawk. She hadn't ventured back into his office in the meantime—she knew her limitations and sitting opposite a half-naked Hawk Mallen discussing business matters was one of them—and her knock at his door was tentative in the extreme.

He was sitting at his desk as she entered, apparently engrossed in the papers in front of him, but as he raised an expressionless face to her, his startling blue eyes hooded and cool, she knew, she just *knew*, he was fully aware of the impact his raw, vigorous brand of masculinity had on the opposite sex.

'Your shirt.' She wanted to fling the thing on his desk

and run but she forced herself to smile politely and hand it to him without undue haste.

'Thanks.' He smiled, and her heart jerked and then flew round her chest like a caged bird. 'I presume poor Maggie is still covered with confusion?' he said quietly as he undid the Cellophane, shaking the beautiful grey silk shirt free of creases. 'Was she like that with Charles? So jumpy all the time?'

With Charles? Was he joking? She looked straight into the tanned face and saw he was perfectly serious.

'No, not really,' she said carefully.

'But I make her nervous.' His eyes were intent on hers as he pulled the silk over muscled skin and she forced herself not to swallow, although agitation had created a lump in her throat the size of a golf ball. 'Why is that? Is she worried she might lose her job?'

Oh, get a move on, for goodness' sake. He had stood up to pull on the shirt and now he moved round in front of his desk, perching on the edge of it as he began to fasten the buttons from the bottom up. There was something so intimate, so ridiculously intimate in the action that funny little sensations seemed to be going off in every part of her body, her skin hot and flushed and her mouth dry.

'Her job?' Her voice sounded vague even to herself and she forced it down a decibel as she said, 'No, I don't think so; she just isn't very good with new people at first.'

'I see.' The blue eyes narrowed and he leant forward, the last three or four buttons still undone and revealing far more dark curling body hair than was good for her pulse rate. 'And you?' he asked softly. 'What about you?'

'Me?' The squeak was back.

'Have I won you over by my decorous behaviour over the last few weeks?' he asked with wicked ease, his eyes almost silver as they moved over the rich curtain of silky red hair and down to her eyes again. 'Or am I still the monster from hell bent on destruction and ruination?'

'I didn't say that,' she protested quickly.

'You didn't have to.' The deep husky voice with its unusual gravelly texture was self-deprecating. 'I've seen dislike and fear in eyes far more adept at hiding it than yours. Besides—' he leant back again, the movement bringing hard-muscled thighs into play '—I seem to remember you accused me of throwing poor Charles out on his ear? And "poor Charles" was your terminology, not mine, incidentally,' he added drily.

'I've said I was sorry about that.' She looked at him steadily.

'And it's very bad manners to bring it up again?' He added the bit she hadn't dared to say. 'But then I'm not a true-blue Englishman, am I, Joanne?' he said silkily. 'My paternal grandparents were of American and French extraction, and my father married a beautiful Italian countess, so that makes me a…mongrel?'

A mongrel? There was no mongrel ever born who looked like Hawk Mallen. But the Italian bit explained his dark good looks, she thought silently, and the jet-black hair that was such a devastating contrast to the brilliant blue eyes. The eyes must be from his father's side… She checked her thoughts and said hastily, 'I hardly think a mongrel.'

'No?' He grinned at her, his teeth white in the tanned skin of his face. 'Well, perhaps not,' he conceded sardonically. 'I would certainly kill any man who suggested so.'

'I don't doubt it.' And she meant it.

'But you haven't answered my question, tactful Joanne,' he drawled mockingly.

'What question?' She wanted to whirl round and run, turn the clock back an hour to the state of play that had existed before the wretched coffee, before this broodingly dangerous being had emerged from the tycoon's skin; but it was too late.

'Have I persuaded you that I am a normal nice man?' he asked drily. 'Or is this outside the realms of possibility?'

'I don't know what you want me to say.' She stared at him, her golden eyes enormous. 'I work for you—'

'Forget the working for me.' It was sharp, too sharp, and as he saw her flinch he moderated his tone, his eyes continuing to gleam like molten silver as he said, 'Tell me the truth, Joanne, that's all I ask.'

That was never all a man like him asked, she thought faintly, but if he wanted the truth then he could have it, job or no job.

'I don't think "normal" and the name Mallen are compatible,' she said quietly. 'From what I've heard about your grandfather he is out of the ordinary too. As for nice—well, I don't know you, do I?' she prevaricated uneasily. 'You might be.'

'But you doubt it.'

She had expected him to be angry but the hard mouth was twitching with amusement.

'You are right about my grandfather, Joanne,' he said thoughtfully after a few moments of holding her with the mesmerising power of his eyes. 'He is a character, quite a character. Ruthless, irascible, probably the most impatient man I've ever met—'

'But with a heart of gold?' she put in daringly before she could stop herself.

The quirk to his lips acknowledged her bravery. 'No, he is as hard as iron.' All amusement fled as he added, 'He's had to be; if you knew his life story you would understand that. He was born poor, dirt-poor, and when he first met my grandmother he told her he wouldn't marry her until he had made his first million. She was

from a rich French family, you see, and people said...
Well, you can imagine what they said,' he added flatly.

'She waited ten years for him and they had two years
together, as man and wife, before my father was born.
She died having him.' Her shock was evident and he
shook his head slowly as he said, 'He never looked at
another woman after she died and he's had offers—
plenty. My father was the image of her, apparently, but
strangely they never got on. It caused the old man a lot
of grief, especially after my parents were killed, although
he's never discussed it.'

'But he has you, his grandson.'

'Yes, he has me,' he agreed softly.

'And that's more family than some people have.' She
hadn't meant to vocalise that thought, it had just popped
out of its own volition, and now she flushed scarlet as
she lowered her eyes and aimed to bring the conversation back on a more mundane level. 'That financial statement you had from Pierre—I think—'

'Why are you so frightened of me, Joanne?' he asked
quietly.

'What?'

As she raised her eyes again he levered himself off
the desk, bringing his lean, lithe body to within inches
of her own and noting the little backward step that she
made before checking herself with a tightening of his
mouth.

'You find me threatening, is that it?' He moved an
inch or so closer and this time she forced herself to stand
absolutely still, her small chin rising a notch as she
stared steadily into the glittering eyes. 'An alien in the
safe little world you have created for yourself?'

It was so near the mark that her breath caught in her
throat for a moment, his subtle menace more pronounced
as he came close enough for the wickedly blended, sensual aftershave he wore to stroke her senses, heightening

her awareness of him so it became painful. She had to stop this, had to defuse things...

'I work for you, that's all—'

'Perhaps I don't want that to be all,' he said silkily.

Her eyes were locked with his, her limbs frozen, even as her brain was telling her to get out, to remove herself from the line of fire. His height was forcing her head to tilt back as she stared up at him and she was vitally aware of the muscled breadth of him, of the power of that magnificent chest cage she had so recently seen in all its splendour.

'What about you, Joanne?' His voice was warm and deep, caressing her as expertly as though he were touching her. 'What do you want?'

She wanted to tell him she wasn't interested, that he had to leave her alone, that he was the last man, the very last man, she would get involved with, but somehow all she could do was stare at him, quite unable to move or speak.

'You are...tantalising, do you know that?' he asked huskily. 'A delicious blend of grown-up woman and young girl contained in a creamy soft skin that makes me want to bite it—gently of course,' he added softly as her eyes widened. 'And that dusting of freckles across your nose—I didn't know women still had freckles. Come out with me tonight, to a show or something.'

'What?' The last bit was so abrupt she didn't know if she had heard right.

'A show. With me. Tonight.' It was said mockingly, but there was a note in the dark voice that made her toes curl, and it was this, more than anything, that flashed a red warning light in front of her vision.

'I don't think so.' She tried for cool firmness and failed miserably. 'I've always held the belief that work and play should be quite separate,' she said primly, avoiding his eyes.

'So have I,' he agreed immediately.

'Well, then.'

'But there always has to be one exception to the rule, besides which within days you won't be around for it to matter much, one way or the other,' he said smoothly.

So this was going to be a wham, bam, thank-you-ma'am kind of evening? she thought numbly. What was he expecting? Payment in kind for the marvellous job offer? Was that it? And then she could scoot off across the Channel, no doubt forgotten the moment her bag was packed?

'Joanne?' He took her shoulders in his hands, his touch jerking her head—which had been drooping forward—up to meet the ice-blue gaze. 'I'm suggesting an evening out, just that, okay? I have never yet used my position to blackmail a woman into my bed and I have no intention of starting with you.'

He'd done it again—read her mind, she thought frantically.

'And while we're on the subject you got the job on merit, pure and simple, just in case that fertile little imagination of yours has decided otherwise.' He was mad; that much was obvious from the frosty countenance surveying her.

'I didn't think—'

'And don't lie to me.' The black brows frowned at her. 'I told you before, I expect the truth.'

He was still holding her, her eyes on a level with his tanned throat, and whether it was the fact that her heart was pounding like a sledgehammer, which was humiliating in itself, or that whatever the situation he always seemed to put *her* in the wrong, she didn't know, but suddenly she found herself saying, 'All right, I did think you were proposing more than a show if you want to know, and frankly that wouldn't be too unusual in this day and age with most of the men I know,' she finished caustically.

'Then perhaps it's time to get to know a different sort of man,' he said silkily. 'One that can think with his brain rather than a lower part of his anatomy.'

'Like you, you mean?' she flashed back hotly.

'Why all this anger and resentment?' He had changed. In an instant the derisive cutting element had gone and the sensuously persuasive and much more dangerous Hawk was back, his eyes almost stroking her hot skin as they wandered over her flushed face. 'Is it such a crime to want to spend an evening in your company, Joanne? In spite of all the formidable keep-off signs you must have the occasional brave man dare to make such a suggestion?'

She shrugged, moving away from him as she did so, and he made no effort to stop her. 'I don't have much time for socialising,' she said briefly, feeling a little better when there were a few feet of air between them.

'So your idea of keeping work and play separate boils down to all work and no play?' he asked mockingly. 'What an industrious little worker I have in my midst.'

'I would have thought you'd be pleased,' she said tightly, refusing to be drawn.

'So would I.' He stared at her for a moment, his voice thoughtful. 'Yes, so would I. My loss of a theatre companion is Bergique & Son's gain after all. Well, it will have to be lunch, then—nice tame lunch in a busy crowded restaurant where you will be quite safe from my wicked intentions.'

She glared at him, she couldn't help it, but he seemed oblivious to her fury, turning to pick up the tie which had arrived with the shirt and walking round to the other side of the desk again as he said, 'Be ready at twelve.'

'But—'

'And order some more coffee, would you? Preferably

delivered by anyone other than Maggie,' he added drily, his eyes on his desk.

Immediately it was all business mode again, the rapier, sharp mind she had come to respect and admire over the last few weeks homed in on the financial report from Pierre Bergique they had been about to discuss when Maggie had committed her prize *faux pas*.

She had never met anyone who could metamorphose so completely, she thought testily, passing on the request for coffee before reseating herself opposite the big dark figure behind the desk. He couldn't have any real feelings at all; it seemed as though he was made of granite, hard, unyielding granite, with just a covering of flesh and skin on the outside. But what an outside…

The brilliant blue eyes suddenly rose and focused on her face and she felt their impact like a bolt of lightning. 'Relax, Joanne,' he said easily. 'You're no good to me all tensed up and ready to strike; I want your full attention on this report.'

'I beg your pardon—?'

'You were thinking of excuses to get out of lunch.' The cool voice was irritatingly sure of itself but she didn't dissuade him; she would far rather he think her lack of concentration was due to what he had suggested rather than her musing on his magnificent body. 'Rest assured there isn't one, so let's press on with the matter in hand.'

'I'm more than ready to do what you want.' It was an unfortunate choice of words, and the haughty expression with which she had spoken the clipped declaration faltered as his black eyebrows rose.

'I wish.' Two words, and his head had already lowered to the papers in front of him, but the shivers of sensation continued to flow up and down her spine for a few minutes more, making the full attention he had requested impossible.

*   *   *

The sky was overcast and there was a slight drizzle in the air as they walked out of the building at three minutes past twelve, the cold October day making the warmth of summer a distant memory. Hawk's car was crouching in its reserved space next to her little red Fiesta, and never had 'his' and 'hers' been so markedly different.

The thought brought a little smile to her lips as Hawk opened the passenger door for her and she slid inside the luxuriously plush interior, and he paused before moving round the car, peering in the open door as he said, 'What?'

'What?' She arched her brows at him although she knew exactly what he had meant.

'Why the smile? You don't often smile in my company,' he added sardonically.

'It was nothing, just the cars. It just struck me yours looks as though it could eat mine for breakfast,' she said lightly.

'If you work the miracle with Bergique & Son you'll be able to treat yourself to anything you fancy.' There was a note to his voice she couldn't quite place.

'I'm quite content with my little Fiesta,' she said quietly.

'Are you, Joanne? Quite content, that is?'

They both knew he wasn't referring to her choice of car, and she stared up into the dark, handsome face above her, forcing her eyes not to fall from his and her features to betray none of her inner turmoil as she said, 'Perfectly. It's never let me down yet, besides which I wouldn't feel comfortable driving anything too flash.'

'Flash?'

She had nettled him and it felt wonderfully good. 'My Fiesta is ideal for nipping in and out of London traffic,' she continued sweetly, 'and I can park it almost anywhere.'

He eyed her darkly for one moment before shutting the passenger door very quietly, and as he slid into the driving seat a few seconds later she had the brief satisfaction of knowing she had held her own for once.

There were several good restaurants within easy reach but after they had been driving for some fifteen minutes, the powerful car growling with impatience at the lunchtime traffic, she asked the question that had been hovering on her lips for the last few miles. 'Where are we going?'

'I've an appointment before we eat; you don't mind?' he said absently, his eyes on the road ahead. 'It won't take long.'

'No, of course not.'

He didn't elaborate further and she didn't like to ask, but when, nearly half an hour later, they still hadn't arrived and the concrete jungle had given way to an altogether more pleasant residential aspect, she was just on the verge of nerving herself to enquire as to the exact location of their destination when Hawk drew off the wide, tree-lined street and on to what was virtually a private road. 'Hawk? Where—?'

'Hang on a moment.' As she'd spoken a pair of massive wooden gates, which wouldn't have been out of place in a bank, had appeared in front of them, set in an eight-foot-high brick wall that was formidable. As the driver's window wound down he inserted a small key into a little box and immediately the gates glided open, revealing a long winding drive threading through beautifully landscaped grounds.

'Who lives here?' she asked nervously, her eyes turning to the hard dark profile as the powerful car moved smoothly forward.

'A business colleague.' If he heard the note of panic in her voice he didn't comment. 'He's emigrating to Canada shortly and has given me first option on the house before he puts it on the open market. He's taken his family to Bermuda for a few days so suggested I might like to browse round and make up my mind for when he returns. He's due back tomorrow but it's been one hell of a week and this is the first opportunity I've had to call by.'

'You're thinking of buying a house in England?' she asked faintly. She knew he had a mansion of a place in the States, Beverly Hills, no less, as well as a bachelor pad in New York—the office grapevine had been full of it—but why England? He had told her he had no intention of overseeing Concise Publications any longer than it took for Charles's replacement to settle in, but then, the Mallen Corporation was huge. Obviously they had far bigger fish to fry in London than Charles's operation, so why not a home here? She knew he hated the anonymity of hotels; he had been nothing if not vocal about the subject for weeks.

'Maybe.' The blue gaze flashed over her worried face and shining red hair before returning to the windscreen. 'Maybe not. I loathe hotels, that much is common knowledge, but in the States and Italy I've got my own places—' the office gossip missed the one in Italy, Joanne thought wryly '—and I usually stay with a friend when I'm in Germany. Other countries normally only necessitate a brief visit.'

Friend of the female gender? She was surprised at how much the thought hurt. No, not hurt, she corrected quickly in her mind, her face flaming as though she had voiced it. Irritated, annoyed, that was all, and only then because she hated the thought of any man clicking his fingers and women falling into line, be they Germans, Italians, or little pink Martians with blue spots.

'Hmm, impressive.'

His voice focused her eyes on the imposing residence at the end of the drive, and she had to agree with him—

it was impressive all right. The house was three storeys tall, liberally covered in red and green ivy with myriad windows and the sort of front door that would grace any stately home. It was huge, splendid, the sort of place that would take a small army to run and maintain it, and Joanne hated it on sight.

It didn't improve on further acquaintance. The interior was larger than life, the last word in elegance, but Joanne couldn't believe that real flesh-and-blood people lived in such a dignified, coldly perfect mausoleum of a place—especially children.

She said little as they were shown round by a young attractive housekeeper who looked as though she did modelling in her spare time, but then neither did Hawk, beyond refusing refreshments at the end of the tour and ushering her out to the car with the minimum of good-byes.

'Well?' They stood at the bottom of the curved stone steps, looking out across the vast expanse of bowling-green-smooth lawn surrounded by massive oaks. 'What did you think?' he asked expressionlessly. 'Some kind of edifice, eh?' His American accent was suddenly much stronger—she normally barely noticed it—and she paused for a moment before answering.

Should she prevaricate, humour him? she thought flatly. All Americans loved stately homes—it was an appreciation given to them along with their mother's milk—and this home was certainly stately. If he intended to buy it, and she told him what she really thought, he wasn't going to be very pleased. But he *had* asked. And he had a mania for the truth…

'It's certainly that.' She paused again. 'But…'

'But?' he asked coolly.

'I'm sorry, it's beautiful, but as a home it just wouldn't be my cup of tea,' she said colloquially.

'There's no warmth, no real feel about it. I'm sorry,' she added again when he still didn't speak.

'You're a roses round the door girl?' The tone was cynical in the extreme, and immediately her hackles rose.

'Probably.' And she was damned if she was going to apologise for the fact to him.

'A cottage in the country, with resident cat, dog and pigeons, not to mention a couple of fat healthy babies thrown in?' he continued derisively.

She felt her temper rise but didn't even try to hold on to it. 'If I ever got married, and frankly that's not on my agenda, I'd much prefer what you've just described than that…that so-called edifice,' she bit back heatedly. 'And if you're insinuating that makes me naive, so be it. Money isn't everything, you know. Just because you've been born with a silver cutlery set, let alone a spoon, it doesn't make you an authority on what other people should like.'

'Indeed it doesn't,' he said gravely.

'And considering you're always belly-aching about the truth you shouldn't object when you get just that,' she continued hotly.

'Belly-aching?'

'Added to which I didn't ask to come and look at your wretched house; in fact I didn't have any say in the matter—something which is not unusual with you!'

'Joanne, I don't *like* the house—'

'And you might be a multi-millionaire with the power to scare people half to death, like poor Maggie, but you function just the same as everyone else, Hawk Mallen, at root level—the same bodily needs, the same requirement to bathe, to eat, to go to the loo—'

'Please, don't go on; delicacy forbids it.'

'And don't *laugh* at me!'

When, in the next moment, she was pulled into his

arms and his mouth descended in a kiss that was all fire and sensation, she never even thought about struggling. As her head began to spin she felt herself folded even more securely against the hard bulk of him, the kiss becoming warm, sensuous, coaxing, turning her legs to jelly and her limbs fluid. That delicious fragrance, peculiar to him, was all about her, fuelling the need, adding another dimension to the sexual fever that had flared so suddenly she couldn't fight it.

His mouth was experienced, his tongue exploring, and the ripples of desire that were flooding every part of her body far too sweet to deny.

The cold October afternoon, all the warnings she had given herself for weeks, the fact that this was Hawk Mallen—*Hawk Mallen*—weren't real any more. All that was real was this world of light and pleasure and sheer sensation behind her closed eyelids, a world she hadn't known existed, hadn't imagined in her wildest dreams.

And then it stopped. His head lifted from hers, his arms released her, and his voice, controlled, tight even, spoke as matter-of-factly as though they had been discussing the weather. 'Lunch, I think?'

CHAPTER FOUR

SHE must have been mad, quite, quite mad. Oh, *Joanne*... She ground her teeth in frustration, twisting violently in the bed, which was already a heap of tangled covers, before flinging herself jerkily to the edge and sitting up in one irritable, furious movement. How could she, how *could* she have let Hawk Mallen dominate her senses so completely earlier that day, after all the warnings she had given herself for weeks?

That first evening, back in September, she had made a cast-iron resolution never to become vulnerable around him, never to let her defences down, to maintain a distance at all costs. And she had kept it through all the following weeks of working together; she had been calm, efficient, in control. Or, at least, she had *thought* she was in control.

The notion that Hawk had allowed her to think that way while he had been quietly biding his time had her eyes narrowing in a face that was already flushed and cross. It hadn't been difficult to maintain a distance over the last few weeks, if she thought about it, because Hawk himself had been the same. What had been his idea? Lulling her into a false sense of security before he struck?

She shook her head bewilderedly as she rose from the bed, slipping her thick, cosy towelling robe over her nightie before wandering over to the window and gazing out over the sleeping night, the darkness dotted here and there by the odd light, which showed there were other night owls who couldn't sleep.

She had to be careful not to let her imagination run

away with her here. Okay, he had let her know he found
her interesting enough to suggest an evening out at the
theatre, but he had known, like her, that if she accepted
it would of necessity be a one-off before she left for
France, and very probably he had been at a loose end
and had thought she would fill a convenient slot. And
the kiss at lunchtime? Well, he'd made it very clear how
he'd considered that! Her cheeks burnt and she yanked
the belt of the robe more tightly round her slim waist.

It hadn't touched him at all; in fact once he had released her he had dismissed the moments when she had
been in his arms without so much as a word, walking
over to the car and opening the passenger door with an
air of— What? she asked herself wearily. Coldness?
Indifference? Self-assuredness? And she had noticed that
all through lunch and the rest of the afternoon back at
the office he had been very careful not to have any physical contact of even the most platonic kind.

'Not that I wanted any.' She spoke the words out loud
with a kind of defiance, her arms crossed over her middle and her hands clutching her waist. 'I can do without
any come-on from Hawk Mallen; in fact that's the *last*
thing I want.'

The realisation that she was talking to herself dawned
as she heard the hollow note in her words, and she shut
her eyes tight for an infinitesimal moment before stalk-
ing into the kitchen and fixing herself a cup of hot milk,
intensely irritated with both herself and Hawk. She
didn't need this, she really didn't—post-mortems on past
conversations were bad enough at the best of times and
two o'clock in the morning was most definitely *not* the
best of times, not with a busy day looming in front of
her and a desk full of urgent correspondence.

No doubt Hawk was fast asleep. She gulped a mouthful of hot milk so fast it burnt her throat. Oh, blow him,

blow Mallen Books, France, Bergique & Son...
everything.

She finished the milk, snuggled down in bed, blanking
her mind of everything but the warm comfort of the
electric blanket without and the hot sweet milk within.
It was a trick she'd learnt in the blackest days of her
childhood, and although it was harder than normal tonight to prevent thoughts from intruding she managed
it—just—slipping into a troubled slumber populated by
cloudy dreams as soon as she pulled the covers up round
her ears and shut her eyes.

'All ready for tomorrow?'

'I think so.' Joanne tried to keep all trace of nervousness out of her voice as she answered Hawk's expressionless enquiry. 'I was going to ask you for the tickets
and so on, actually; I've been meaning to for days but
it's been so hectic...' The last few days since their
lunchtime date had passed in a whirl.

'Don't worry, it's all in hand. I'll bring them along
tomorrow morning when I pick you up.' He had raised
his head from the papers on his desk as he had spoken,
his voice steady, and as the piercing eyes met hers she
knew he knew how she would react to his words.

'There's no need for you to pick me up.' In spite of
the knowledge she was confirming his expectations she
couldn't say anything else. 'I've already ordered a taxi,'
she continued uncomfortably, 'but thanks for the offer
anyway.'

'Cancel it.' His eyes returned to the file at his fingers
as though the matter was finished.

'I don't think—'

'Cancel it, Joanne.' It was said in the tone he used
when he considered she was being tiresome, and it never
failed to grate unbearably. 'It makes far more sense for

us to travel together with our destination being the same.' His eyes met hers again.

'You're flying somewhere tomorrow?' she asked in surprise, and then, as the level gaze continued to hold hers and an awful suspicion washed over her, she added weakly, 'Where to?'

'You didn't really think I would throw you in the deep end without a float, did you?' he asked quietly, the dark, husky voice sending tiny little shivers down her spine. 'I'm coming over with you to introduce you to the staff and get things off on the right foot. I shall stay the night, maybe two. Is that all right?' he added with a touch of sardonic wryness that told her her face was speaking her mind.

'There's no need, really,' she said firmly.

'There's every need.'

She looked hard into the enigmatic face in front of her, wondering exactly what was going on in that ruthless mind. 'I'm not overawed by any of this, Hawk,' she said tightly.

'Whether you are or whether you aren't is of no account; I want the French workforce to know that I'm backing the new management one hundred per cent and that they'll toe the line or else.' There was a touch of grimness to the cool voice now. 'People are people the world over, Joanne, and from what I can make out Pierre let his staff get away with murder, simply because he wasn't bothered one way or the other beyond feathering his own nest. You'll meet opposition, covert maybe and perhaps not so covert, but I want to minimise it as far as I can.'

'I can deal with it—'

'Trust me, Joanne.' Blue eyes held honey-brown with a power that was unbreakable. 'I know what I'm talking about.'

'I don't doubt that,' she said primly.

'Yes, you do.' He smiled, his lips twisting wryly. 'You were trying to determine if I had an ulterior motive for accompanying you across the Channel, weren't you?'

It was a challenge, and if she had learnt one thing with this fierce, strange individual it was that you didn't duck and dive.

'Yes.' She stared straight at him, her smooth skin flushing slightly. 'I was. *Have* you?'

'That's what makes you so good at your job, Joanne,' he murmured drily. 'You have no hesitation in going straight for the jugular if you feel right is on your side.'

'You haven't answered my question,' she said steadily.

'That's right, I haven't.' He smiled again, and his eyes were burning into hers.

'And you don't intend to?'

'Right again.' As she opened her mouth to protest he stood up, moving round the desk and to her side with cat-like swiftness. 'You are such a mass of contradictions, aren't you?' he said with a softness that took her fury away and reduced her to a quivering jelly inside. 'So fierce, so straight, at times, and other times as nervous as a little fawn.'

'I hardly think so.' She tried for a sophisticated coolness and failed miserably.

'Your eyes are the colour of a baby deer in its first year, do you know that?' he continued huskily. 'A sun-kissed golden-brown and velvety soft—eyes a man could drown in.'

'And yours have the sharpness of the sea under an icy winter sky, crystal-clear and bitingly cold.' It wasn't meant to be complimentary but he considered her words with his head slightly tilted, those same eyes of which she had spoken laughing at her.

'I quite like that analogy,' he murmured softly. 'It

wouldn't do for an individual bearing the Mallen name to have puppy-dog eyes.'

Don't let it happen again, Joanne; be strong, be strong. The voice in her head was savage. Look how you felt last time when he was soft persuasion one minute and as distant as the man in the moon the next.

She didn't want her confusion to show, but her surreptitious nip on her bottom lip was caught by the blue gaze, and after one second more he turned from her, his eyes hooded.

'I will pick you up at nine in the morning, Joanne.' His voice was reasonable, even, the sort of voice one used when discussing somewhat boring arrangements. 'On the dot.'

'All right...thank you.' The gratitude was grudging but she couldn't help it. She had been nervous enough about the following day before she knew Hawk was going to accompany her, but now... She forced the panic which was gripping her throat to subside with sheer willpower. Everything he had said was reasonable, practical; she knew that if she considered it rationally. His approving presence would give her an edge with the staff she could well do with in the circumstances; it was just that... Rationality didn't seem to have any place in her feelings about Hawk Mallen.

She glanced at him now as he sat down in the enormous leather chair which had always seemed to swallow Charles but fitted Hawk's powerful body perfectly. A shaft of sunlight from the cold but sunny October day outside was glancing through the window on to his cropped head, turning the short hair blue-black, and somehow the bent head was terribly appealing. She wanted to run her fingers through that springy, virile hair, just once, to see what it felt like; she wanted—

She caught her thoughts with something akin to horror, desperately relieved he hadn't looked up as she had stared at him. The sooner she got to France, settled in, and Hawk left, the better.

Joanne was painfully touched, later that afternoon, by the serious and emotional send-off she received from the office staff. Along with a host of cards, an expensive set of brand-new luggage and copious hugs and kisses, Maggie took her to one side and presented her with an exquisite little crystal clock, tiny but beautifully made. 'It's from me, just me,' the young junior said earnestly, her brown eyes liquid with tears. 'You've been so good to me, Joanne, especially when I first started and was so petrified; I can never thank you enough. I shall miss you like anything.'

'Oh, Maggie.' It was too much, and as Joanne began to cry Maggie joined her, and as the two of them hugged Joanne felt a moment of utter desolation.

'Here.' When she was firmly, but kindly, parted from Maggie, and a balloon glass with a hefty measure of brandy was put in her hand, she recognised Hawk's voice but was unable to see him through the streaming tears. 'Drink it, all of it, and then we'll open the champagne,' he murmured quietly in her ear, before raising his voice to the assembled staff and saying, 'Champagne, everyone, to celebrate Joanne's departure to brighter and better things. And there's a cold buffet laid on; the caterers are on their way up, so clear some tables, okay?'

The resulting bustle and chatter gave Joanne a much needed chance to compose herself, although when she saw the sumptuous spread which Hawk had laid on, along with the bottles of very good vintage champagne, she nearly succumbed to the flood of emotion again. 'You...you shouldn't have gone to so much trouble,' she said weakly after all the appropriate toasts had been made and everyone was in little groups, plates and glasses in hand, talking animatedly. 'I didn't expect anything...'

'Perhaps that's why I did it,' Hawk said softly. They were standing slightly apart from the merry throng, Hawk having insisted on filling her plate for her and standing over her while she tried to force some food past the huge lump in her throat. 'Besides which, everyone thinks one hell of a lot of you, Joanne. I might have had a mutiny on my hands if we hadn't lashed out a bit.'

She glanced up at him, her gaze still luminous with the tears she was holding at bay, and as he stared down into the huge honey-brown orbs the wry smile on his face faded, and their eyes locked and held for endless moments.

'Joanne—?' He stopped abruptly, and his voice was husky as he continued, 'You know they don't want you to go?'

'Don't they?' She wasn't sure if he was talking about the office staff or if his words held a deeper meaning, and she was terrified of the possibility of the latter even as she longed for it with an intensity that shocked her.

'They'll miss you; things won't be the same...' His voice was deep and gravelly, the words seeming to be dragged up from the depths of him, and almost in the same instant he turned from her with a savage movement that spoke of escape and said, 'More champagne?'

She stood quite still as she watched him cross the room and pour a stream of the golden sparkly liquid into one of the large fluted glasses, her senses reeling. She hadn't imagined the raging desire in his eyes when he had looked at her—she hadn't—but there had been something else too, something...dark. She shivered suddenly, in spite of the perfectly regulated temperature within the building. What on earth had happened in his life to make him look like that? she asked herself weakly, but in the next second she was surrounded by a loud, laughing group who drew her into their midst, forcing her to push her agitation to the back of her mind.

When Hawk joined them, just a moment or two later, he handed her the glass of champagne with a smile and a nod, his face cool and distant and the big body slightly aloof. The brief baring of his soul had gone, to be replaced by the ice man who was in perfect control of himself and those about him—benevolent host, gracious conversationalist, but definitely, overwhelmingly untouchable.

CHAPTER FIVE

THE combination of a glass of brandy, two of champagne, and a long day full of emotional turmoil, added to the fact that Joanne had slept badly for the last few nights, ensured that she was asleep as soon as her head touched the pillow that night.

When her neat little bedside alarm woke her at seven the next morning, it was to the realisation that she had completed none of the last-minute preparations she had planned to do on her last evening in England, and that once the taxi had deposited her home the day before she had managed to get up the stairs, into her flat and into bed, and that was all, such had been her exhaustion.

Consequently, the two hours before Hawk arrived were spent in a mad dash that left no room for apprehension or doubts, and when the doorbell rang, spot on nine o'clock, she was just ready.

'Hi.' He was lounging against the outer wall when she opened the door, big and dark in a long charcoal overcoat which was open over a grey business suit and pale blue shirt. His cool self-assurance was staggering.

'You haven't changed your mind, then?' He nodded to her suitcase, placed in readiness at the side of the door, as he spoke, and she forced an answering smile that nearly cracked her face.

'Hardly.'

'It's been done before.' The handsome face was cynical.

'Not by me,' she said carefully. 'If I agree to something I carry it through, difficult though you may find that to believe.'

'I don't find it difficult.' His eyes narrowed to blue slits as he spoke, the intensity of the piercing gaze unnerving, and she had the strange unaccountable impression he was on tenterhooks about something and endeavouring to conceal it—although what she couldn't begin to imagine.

He picked up the lightest of the three cases, tucking it under one arm before lifting the other two, which weighed a ton, with an ease that told her the powerful body was as finely honed as she had suspected.

'Any last-minute goodbyes?' he asked quietly as she joined him on the landing after closing the front door.

'No, just the key to pop through the letterbox of the flat below.' Now the moment had come she had none of the turmoil of the day before, merely a sense of inevitability. 'I said all my farewells yesterday.'

'Except one.' Dark eyebrows rose quizzically.

'Who?' She stared at him in surprise.

'Me,' he said softly.

'But I haven't left you,' she replied quickly. 'You're coming with me.'

'Ah, yes.' He smiled slowly and her skin began to tingle as the dark, alien side of him took over her senses. 'So our goodbyes are yet to be said?' It was said in a slightly amused voice but again the feeling that there was more below the surface had her staring at him with a straight face, her eyes big and golden in the cream of her skin and her hair framing her face like shimmering fire.

Once in the taxi he chatted easily about this and that, his manner relaxed and informal, but she had her work cut out to appear normal, the proximity of the big muscled body so close to hers sending little shock waves through every nerve and sinew with each tiny movement he made.

'Relax, Joanne.'

'What?' One moment he had been relating an amusing story about a business colleague they both knew, the next the hard blue gaze had fastened on her face and his hand had covered hers, his flesh warm and firm.

'You're nervous, on edge, and there's no need to be,' he said softly.

There's every need. 'I...I know that; I'm fine.'

'Little liar.' It was said quietly, his eyes skimming her face before coming to rest on her mouth, their touch like a warm caress. 'Is it just the unknown that puts that touch of fear in your eyes, Joanne?' he murmured. 'Or are you frightened of me too, of how it could be if you let it happen?'

'What?'

'Don't tell me you haven't felt it because I won't believe it; I've seen the reflection of what I feel in your eyes,' he said huskily. 'You wonder what it would feel like to be close to me, really close, for me to make love to you. You want me, Joanne; you can't deny it. You want me every bit as much as I want you.'

'You're mad.' She stared at him shakily, the fear of which he had spoken turning her eyes dark.

'No, merely honest. It's the most natural thing in the world for a man and woman to be attracted to each other; there's nothing wrong in it, and our physical chemistry is so hot it's sizzling.'

'You're talking about an affair.' She couldn't believe this conversation was taking place, but at the same time it was almost as though she had been waiting for just this from the first moment she had laid eyes on him.

'I'm talking about enjoyment, the giving and receiving of pleasure,' he said softly. 'I want you, Joanne, I admit it; I haven't felt like this in a long, long time. We could be good together; I could make you want me in a way you've never wanted a man before.'

'Hawk—'

'What was his name, Joanne, the man who made you retreat into this formidable glass tower you inhabit?' he asked with a sudden intensity. 'Whatever he meant to you, whatever it was like, with me it will be better. I would always be totally honest, there would be no guessing games, no cruelty. When it was over, whoever ended it, it would be quick and final—'

'I don't want a relationship with you.' He was propositioning her on the one hand and telling her he would finish it cleanly on the other? she thought dazedly, anger providing a welcome shot of adrenalin that went some way to quelling the hurt. How dared he? How *dared* he assume she was just waiting to fall into his arms like an overripe peach? And what about him anyway? If anyone retreated into towers it was him, although his were made of inches-thick steel.

'Yes, you do, although you can't bring yourself to admit it,' he said with an assuredness that hit her on the raw.

She stared at him icily, and something of her utter outrage must have got through because he took his hand from over hers, leaning back in his corner of the cab as he surveyed her with narrowed blue eyes.

'Does my taking the job in France have anything to do with this conversation?' she snapped tightly. 'And I want this wonderful truth that you're always going on about, mind.'

'I offered you the position at Bergique & Son because I feel you would be an asset to the Mallen Corporation,' Hawk said coolly. 'Any personal liaison with me is something quite separate.'

'But it wouldn't go amiss to have a nice warm bed waiting for you when you visit?' she asked tartly. And any emotional involvement would mean he was completely sure of her loyalty to the Mallen empire. That, probably, was what all this was about; he was certainly cold-blooded enough to think that way. Oh, he was just a cynical brute of a man. And to think she had actually been *grateful* for all his apparent thoughtfulness yesterday, for the way he had steered her through the last difficult goodbyes, for his generosity over the leaving party, for his accompanying her to France to ease the way for her. *Ease the way!* Fury combined with humiliation at her naivety. It had all been about trying to manipulate her to his will, and in such a way that Hawk, and the Mallen empire, couldn't lose.

'I take it that's a no to my suggestion we get to know each other better?' he asked drily.

'Dead right.' It was scathing.

'Pity. Patience is not normally one of my virtues but it looks as though I'll have to draw on hitherto unused resources,' he drawled slowly. 'But I can wait, Joanne, when I have to. And something tells me you are well worth waiting for.'

'Do you expect me to thank you for that observation?' she asked cuttingly, praying that the trembling in her stomach wouldn't reveal itself to the rapier-sharp gaze.

'It would be nice.'

The dark amusement was the last straw. 'Hawk, whatever impression I might have given you I don't go in for tawdry little affairs,' she said tightly, her voice quivering with the force of her emotion. 'When I give myself to a man it will be because I love him, all of him, not just his body or the cheap thrill of a few weeks or months of sexual gymnastics—'

'Wait there a moment.' He cut into her fury with a raised hand as he straightened in his seat. 'What are you saying here? You aren't asking me to believe that you haven't...' His voice trailed away and hot colour washed over her in a burning flood as it dawned on her what she had revealed. 'I don't believe it...'

'I'm not asking you to *believe* anything,' she said with

as much dignity as she could muster in the circumstances, 'and whatever interpretation you put on my
words is your own; I have no intention of explaining
anything to you.'

'Joanne—'

'I just value myself as something more than a body
on two legs, all right?' Or as a useful little tool for the
Mallen empire, she thought hotly as the humiliation and
embarrassment became almost more than she could bear.
Oh, why hadn't she kept *quiet*?

Hawk was used to shrewd businesswomen, or rich
young females who flitted from one affair to another like
graceful, bored butterflies, or—oh, a million and one
other connotations on the theme. One thing he wasn't
used to were twenty-nine-year-old virgins who acted like
outraged paragons when he suggested they might get to
know each other better—albeit very much better, she
thought weakly.

Not that she was ashamed of what and who she was—
she wasn't; she just hadn't meant to broadcast it to the
one person, above all others, who would be sure to treat
the news with contempt.

Not that Hawk Mallen looked contemptuous—stunned
would have been a better description, she thought flatly.
No doubt he was already regretting the waste of a couple
of days when he could have been frying other, more
obliging fish. The thought prompted her to say, but not
with as much tartness as she would have liked, 'I think
it better that I go to France alone in the circumstances.'

'What circumstances are you referring to? I wasn't
aware anything had altered.' He met her eyes as he
spoke, and Joanne wasn't to know it was the finest piece
of bluffing Hawk Mallen had ever indulged in—and that
in the dog-eat-dog world of high business where a poker
face and an expressionless voice could mean the gain or
loss of millions.

The flight to France, and journey to Bergique & Son which was situated in the heart of Paris, was conducted in a tense, screaming silence that had Joanne's nerves stretched as tightly as piano wire by the time they arrived at the pleasant, stone-clad building close to the Seine.

Hawk had said very little since their conversation in the taxi in England. Beyond pointing out one or two of the sights to her once they were in the car on the other side of the Channel he had only spoken to enquire if she was comfortable on the plane, if she would like a drink, and other such social niceties. Joanne had answered him in monosyllables, not because she was trying to be awkward but because she could only manage to force one or two words past the constriction in her throat.

It didn't help that the elegantly attractive stewardesses hadn't been able to keep their eyes off him either—she was sure that given the least bit of encouragement he would have had two telephone numbers pressed on him, and in spite of her earlier rejection of his advances it had rankled—painfully. He was a free agent, all the model-type beauties in the world could come on to him and she wouldn't have the slightest right to object, but…it still rankled.

She had found herself watching him from under her eyelashes, seeing how he responded to the subtle—and once or twice not so subtle—overtures by the two glamorous women, but he hadn't even appeared to notice them. Not that that meant anything, she told herself tetchily. With all the women who no doubt threw themselves at him every day of the week he could afford to be choosy. And that brought her back to the unescapable conclusion she had been forced to earlier, which was hurting more and more despite her telling herself, every minute, every second, that she was a complete and utter fool to care.

Hawk Mallen had a whole host of adoring females

who would be only too pleased to be at his beck and call; he needed another one like a hole in the head. So why had he propositioned her? Partly because he was attracted to her, yes, she had to give him that, but also because it would be very useful for him to have a nice devoted mistress installed at Bergique & Son to keep an eye on things for him, and also oblige with a warm bed when he deigned to visit France. Two birds with one stone. Clever.

'Bergique & Son. We've arrived.' They had just drawn up outside the three-storeyed, endlessly long structure, set in one of the great boulevards that had Paris's unmistakable stamp about it, and as Joanne gazed through the car window she felt a little shiver slither down her spine.

This apparently innocuous building was where she was going to prove herself over the next few months, or fail miserably, and after all that had happened earlier that day it was suddenly a matter of life or death that it was the former prospect.

She had to prove she wasn't a naive, ingenuous type of individual, but an intelligent career woman who was as much in charge of her private life as her career, that she knew exactly where she was going and how to get there. Because Hawk Mallen would be looking on, for sure, albeit from a distance, assessing, judging, probing. He was…formidable.

'Joanne?' Her head shot round to meet his; there had been that certain note in his voice she had heard just a few times before—soft, caressing. 'I want you to succeed here; I'm not your enemy.'

'I…I know.' She tried to sound convincing.

'No, I don't think you do.' His blue eyes had turned to glittering silver in the sunlight streaming through the car window and his mouth was rueful, sensuous, turning her limbs liquid and sending the blood racing through her veins. 'I want you, I have no intention of pretending otherwise, but that doesn't mean I'll behave like a sulky little boy if you don't want to share the warmth of my bed. You can rely on my backing, one hundred per cent, for anything you see fit to do within Bergique & Son.'

'Thank you,' she murmured quietly. She didn't know what to think; did anyone know what to think around Hawk Mallen? 'You must see it's better we keep our relationship on a business footing?'

'Must I?' He was watching her intently, his narrowed eyes roaming over her flushed face as her gaze fell from his. 'Why?'

'Because it wouldn't work; I'm different to you,' she said firmly.

'It's the difference that has me up at two in the morning having cold showers,' he said huskily.

The confession was unexpected and as her gaze met his again she saw raw hunger in the dark male face.

'Hawk, I'm going to be based in France, and you…you're all round the world. You just want an affair, some fun when you visit—'

'No, you are wrong; I want more than that,' he said softly. 'You have got into my head, my bones, my blood; I have never trodden so carefully with a woman before, Joanne.' She stared at him, knowing that the punchline was going to follow, and it did.

'But I have to be honest too,' he said with a curious flatness. 'Women always complicate things by talking about love, when what they really mean is passion, desire, and I have learnt it is kinder from the outset to lay down the rules of play.'

He meant it; he really thought he was being fair, ethical in his cold-bloodedness, she thought faintly. She paused a moment, and then took a deep breath before she said, 'You don't believe two people can fall in love and live happily ever after?'

The driver of the firm's car, a long black limousine with lusciously soft leather upholstery, had been waiting outside to open Hawk's door for the last few moments, and now Hawk wound down his window and told him to carry the cases into the building, before rewinding it and turning to Joanne.

'I don't believe in happy ever after, no,' he said quietly, the devastatingly attractive face deadly serious. 'Look at the statistics, for crying out loud. I can believe in the power of obsession, sexual or otherwise, and I know desire and passion are real, but the notion of two people promising to stay together for the rest of their lives is pure folly, Joanne. Men and women can have good strong relationships, but inevitably that first sexual thrill dies and then, if they are locked into a marriage contract, one or the other of them will cause misery by sleeping with someone else.'

He stared at her unflinchingly, his sapphire gaze hard. 'The best relationships are the ones unclouded by any messy emotion,' he said evenly, 'where both partners have their eyes wide open.'

The basic idea behind Hawk's words—that love was an elusive dream without real form or credibility—was so near everything she had told herself in her youth and miserable teenage years that for a moment the past was more real than the present, and she felt the shock of it jolt her heart violently; but then an inner voice made itself heard.

She might have been sceptical, wary of love and the promises that went with it, but that time was past. Something had happened and she knew what she believed now—that there was something finer, more noble, more lasting than mere sexual involvement and an agreement of minds, or cold-blooded business arrangements where men and women slept together to further their careers.

Something of what she was feeling must have shown in her face because Hawk turned to look straight ahead, and now his profile was cold. 'It's dangerous to let yourself be fooled, Joanne,' he said flatly.

'I can't agree—'

'When my parents died so unexpectedly I had to go through their papers, personal and otherwise,' he said levelly, interrupting her as though she hadn't spoken. 'I found my mother's diaries...' There was a pause and then he said, 'They were a catalogue of despair and heartache and bitter grief. It would seem my father had had affairs from their fourth or fifth year of marriage, and they had broken my mother's heart, destroyed her self-esteem and turned her into someone she clearly didn't like.'

She didn't dare make any sound or movement; besides, she wouldn't have known what to say.

'The diaries acknowledged he still cared for her in his own way, as a friend, companion, but she wasn't enough for him; that was the truth of the matter however he tried to explain the other women away. My grandfather knew what was happening; in fact it had caused a final wedge between him and my father that was insurmountable and was a further complication between my parents.'

'But your grandfather didn't agree because he had loved his own wife so much,' Joanne said gently. 'Surely that must tell you that love is a real emotion?'

'They only had two years together before she died,' Hawk said quietly. 'Who knows what would have happened if my grandmother had lived?'

'Do you believe that—*really* believe it?' she asked huskily.

He turned his head and met the honey-brown gaze, and for a long moment, as he looked into the velvet orbs, he said nothing.

'Do you?' she persisted.

There was a flicker in the silver-blue eyes, a veiling of his thoughts, and then he said, 'Yes, I do. But I have been very remiss—this is neither the time nor the place for such a conversation, and you must be anxious to meet everyone now you are here.'

'It's all right—'

'No, it isn't. Forgive me.' He had retreated again, and so completely it was like a slap in the face.

The next two hours sped by in a whirl of introductions, numerous offices, social pleasantries and different faces, and over it all, every minute, every second, Joanne was aware of Hawk's dark, brooding presence on the perimeter of her gaze.

There was a subdued furore everywhere they went— less to do with her appearance than with Hawk's, Joanne reflected wryly—and plenty of sycophantic chit-chat that indicated everyone was well aware of the precarious state of the firm and why new blood had been brought in. Pierre was conspicuous by his absence and his sylph-like secretary, Antoinette, a slender, graceful nineteen-year-old who stared at Joanne with great dark eyes and a carefully blank face, made his apologies in a neutral voice that gave nothing away.

Nevertheless, Joanne was aware the French girl didn't like her, and the knowledge was a little disconcerting, considering they would be working closely together in the future.

She would perhaps have been a little more concerned about Antoinette, the somewhat slipshod air of the firm in general, and her growing certainty that the job was going to be even harder than she had expected, if a large segment of her mind hadn't been taken up with Hawk's amazing revelation about his parents. His father's betrayal and his mother's anguish had affected him deeply, that much was obvious, but she couldn't rid herself of

the impression that there was something more he hadn't
told her, another complication that had driven the deep
lines of cynicism into the sides of that sensuous mouth.

But he wouldn't tell her if there was. She glanced
across at him now as he stood talking to Antoinette on
the other side of the room, the beautiful French girl
clearly hanging on his every word. Intuition told her he
regretted revealing as much as he had already, and he
wouldn't thank her for the impulse which had prompted
it. He was a loner, the original wolf who walked alone,
and to get mixed up with a man like him would be emotional suicide, even if she didn't love him.

Love him? The shock of the thought caused her to
stare glassy-eyed at the young man who was trying to
engage her in conversation, and she must have gone
white because he immediately suggested she sit down,
that he fetch her a glass of water, or perhaps she needed
some fresh air? 'It has been a long day for you.' The
French voice with its sexy accent was ingratiatingly concerned. 'Yes?'

'Yes.' She aimed for a lightness she was far from
feeling. 'But productive.' Act normally, put this to the
back of your mind till later, talk, *smile*…

It was another half an hour before Hawk suggested he
take her to the apartment which had been rented for her
as part of the job package, and every single muscle in
her face and body was so tense she felt like one giant
ache. She couldn't risk the luxury of thinking; she was
working on automatic and dealing purely with the absolute present—what she could see and hear and feel. If
she started to think she would become petrified, or burst
into tears, or shout and scream, and none of the options
were attractive.

'You handled that just fine.' The American drawl was
more obvious than normal as they walked out of the

building and over to the car which had just been brought round to the front. 'I'm impressed.'

'Are they, though?' She smiled as she said it but he caught the underlying tension that made her voice over-bright.

'I think so.' He opened the car door for her and the piercing blue gaze watched her as she slid into the back of the car. 'And if they're not they soon will be.' He was leaning on the top of the door as he spoke and for a moment their eyes caught and held before he straightened, shutting the door with a soft slam.

Why did he have to do that—be so...nice? she asked herself savagely as he walked round the back of the car and slid into the seat beside her, tapping the glass divide once he was seated and indicating for the driver to pull away. Solicitude and tact didn't come naturally with Hawk Mallen—she had observed him in action for weeks and a barracuda couldn't be more ruthless—and it made the gentleness he had just displayed terribly seductive.

The late afternoon sky had darkened in the last hour, black storm clouds looming threateningly in the October twilight, but Joanne could see the slender spire of the Notre Dame, the Grande Dame of Paris, against the grey sky as the first drops of rain began to splatter against the car windows.

'We're in for a storm.' Hawk glanced at her, his male bulk big and alien in the car's interior. 'I was going to suggest we tour round for a while, see some of the sights and have a meal, but perhaps you'd rather go straight to the apartment?'

'Yes, please.' In spite of the spaciousness within the limousine his nearness was making her breathless.

'Your alacrity is a little dampening,' he said drily, his sapphire eyes glittering in the darkness of his face. 'Is my company really so hard to take?'

'I didn't mean it like that,' she protested weakly.

'No?' He smiled, that wonderfully elusive sexy smile that he used so rarely but with such devastating effect. 'Then I might get a cup of coffee in your new home?'

'But what about him?' She gestured agitatedly at the driver.

'Three's a crowd if that's what you mean, but don't worry, I have no intention of making the poor guy hang about waiting for me,' Hawk said easily. 'I'll get a cab from your place to my hotel, okay?'

Her place. She stared at him, her brain refusing to function. 'But...' He wasn't going to take no for an answer; she could see it in the sudden narrowing of his eyes. 'I haven't anything in; I haven't even *seen* the apartment yet—'

'No problem.' His gaze traced the outline of her lips, making her flesh tingle. 'I had the concierge take care of that.'

'Oh.' That was that, then; Hawk Mallen had spoken and the rest of the world could only obey—

'I know I should wait until I am asked, but I have the nasty feeling I would wait a long time, Joanne.' His voice was suspiciously humble now as though he had read her thoughts—which he had—but in spite of the knowledge she was being duped she just couldn't resist the little-boy charm.

'Well, if you've the time...' she said helplessly, the anger that had risen at his arrogance magically gone.

'That I have.' He grinned suddenly, his eyes wicked. 'The pleasure of a few minutes in your company is worth any sacrifice—'

'Oh, *please*...' Her voice was sarcastic but she couldn't help smiling back, even as the warning bells began to ring loud and hard. He was dangerous, so, so dangerous, and never more than now, when he was wielding that powerful magnetism for his own purposes, his eyes merciless as they took in her flushed confusion. She ought to tell him she was tired, that it had been one hell of a day, that she needed time alone to sort out the muddle of her thoughts, all of which would be true.

But she wasn't going to—her eyes darkened at her stupidity—because she wanted to be with him for a few minutes more. She wanted to have him to herself, to know that he was concentrating on her and her alone. He didn't love her, she knew that, but she had spelt out the rules of play loud and clear that morning, and if he still wanted to spend time in her company, knowing how she felt, surely that was all right? She was trying to justify herself against the accusing voice in her head telling her she was playing with fire, even as she acknowledged she had no defence.

Hawk slid aside the glass partition separating them from the driver, giving the address of her apartment before explaining their change of plan and then settling back comfortably in his seat.

She was vaguely aware of the street cafés, elegant architecture and unmistakable ambience which was Paris as the car bowled along wide boulevards, but the excitement, the magic, was all enclosed within the car for Joanne.

It was utter madness, the worst sort of foolishness, to fall for a man like Hawk Mallen, she acknowledged desperately, her heart thudding a tattoo as the electricity within the car became frightening; but if he didn't *know*, surely she was safe? He thought she was merely attracted to him on a physical level, he'd made that plain, so all she had to do was maintain the principles she'd set that morning. Simple really...

The apartment was situated in the north of Paris, in Montmartre, which seemed to Joanne very much a little village in its own right. Although the bustling centre was a hive of activity, the area in the north-east where her modern apartment block stood, shaded by large trees, was more quiet, with an abundance of green parkland and sleepy museums.

'I thought you would prefer something restful to come home to after a hard day's work,' Hawk said quietly as the driver unloaded her luggage and Hawk's overnight bag from the limousine, 'and La Villette is one of the gentler spots in Paris.'

'It's lovely.' Joanne managed a smile as Hawk sent the driver on his way and picked up all the luggage, a bag under each arm and suitcases in either hand, before leading the way through the paved garden with fountain and up the five broad steps to the front door.

The concierge was there immediately they stepped into the elegant foyer, a small dapper man who was all smiles and teeth. 'Monsieur Mallen, Mademoiselle Crawford, welcome, welcome.' The high, excited voice matched his appearance, and he barely paused for breath before saying, 'Everything is ready as you requested, Monsieur Mallen; I am sure Mademoiselle Crawford will be most comfortable, but if there is anything I can do, anything at all…'

'Merci.' Hawk was polite but firm. 'I'm sure Mademoiselle Crawford will call if she needs you, Gérard. There is no need to accompany us; I have the key.'

'But the cases, Monsieur—'

'No problem.' Hawk cut short the anguished protest by the simple expedient of pushing a folded note in the little man's hand before striding purposefully to the lift, Joanne following in his wake.

'Merci, Monsieur Mallen, merci beaucoup.'

It had clearly been a generous tip, Joanne reflected wryly as the concierge continued to beam rapturously while Hawk placed their luggage in the lift and drew Joanne in beside him, the little man only turning to prance away as the lift doors began to close. And then a sudden thought struck her. 'You seem to know your way around,' she said suspiciously. 'Have you been here before?'

'Of course.' The vivid blue eyes with their thick black lashes looked straight at her as he said, 'You didn't think I would take an apartment for you without checking it out first?'

'You?' She realised her mouth was open and shut it with a little snap.

'Yes, me.' He smiled lazily. 'I had Antoinette do the donkey work and narrow it down to three suitable places from which I chose this one.'

'I see.' And she did. This, then, was to be his love-nest in France, and no doubt there were others in different parts of the world, perhaps with other 'manager-esses' keeping them warm? 'Why?'

'Because it was the most suitable.' He knew that wasn't what she had meant—she could tell so from the sardonic gleam in his eyes—but short of asking him out-right if he had an ulterior motive in looking over her new home she couldn't say much more. But she didn't like this; she didn't like it at all, she thought silently.

'Gérard lives on the ground floor just off the foyer,' Hawk continued evenly, 'and nothing much gets past him. I like that.' The lift slid to a halt and he bent to pick up the cases again as he added, 'You can't be too careful in this day and age.'

Indeed you can't, she thought tightly as she glanced at the black head, the short, springy hair shining with virile health. But her concern was less in the nature of a possible intruder than the man a foot or so away from her, who had turned her life upside down and inside out over the last few weeks.

'Stop frowning and come and see your new abode.'

She opened her mouth to say she wasn't frowning as

he straightened, but then realised she was and hastily smoothed her features as the piercing gaze came her way again.

They stepped from the lift into ankle-deep carpeting, and as Hawk moved across the small cream-coloured square of space to the front door, setting down the cases and inserting a key in the lock, she stared about her bewilderedly. 'Where are all the other apartments?'

'There is one on each floor, five in all,' Hawk said easily. 'This is the top one to give you more of a view.'

'Hawk—'

But he had already stepped into the apartment and she had no choice but to follow him in. It was the last word in luxury, and immediately the concierge's fawning behaviour became clear. This wasn't the sort of place normal people, like her, lived in, she thought helplessly. This was way out of her league, job or no job. She could never afford this—

'Do you like it?' He was watching her face very carefully although in her shock she wasn't aware of it.

'Like it?' The room they had entered was an elegant drawing room in pale blue and yellow which seemed to stretch endlessly—impressive, beautiful, with dark wood furniture and a beautiful suite, TV, hi-fi, bar... 'I can't afford this, Hawk, you know that,' she said tightly, anger curling through her stomach.

'It's part of the package,' he said expressionlessly. 'I thought you realised that.'

Keep calm; match him for coolness. Her brain was giving orders she obeyed automatically. 'This is not a normal apartment,' she said evenly, 'and you know it.'

'Normality is relative.' He walked across the room to the fireplace where a living-flame fire was flickering red and gold. 'I had this put in to make it more homely,' he said coolly.

'Hawk, this is ridiculous—'

'Come and see the view,' he interrupted authoritatively.

She joined him at the huge patio windows which opened on to a large balcony, beyond which it seemed as though all Paris was stretched out before her, taking great steadying breaths as she did so.

'Do you want to go outside?' he asked quietly.

'No, I do not.' It was clipped and terse.

'Come and see the rest of it, then,' he said calmly.

He wasn't giving her time to think, let alone talk; that much registered. He was bulldozing her along as though this were all *fait accompli*, and it wasn't. She couldn't *let* it be. What would people say? What obvious conclusion would they come to if she allowed him to install her in a place like this?

The rest of the apartment was equally superb—the separate dining room in pale gold, the massive fitted kitchen and breakfast area, the *en suite* bathroom, a splendid marbled construction in cream and honey-brown, and the bedroom with its huge four-poster bed and silk hangings. It was all incredible, larger than life—very much like Hawk Mallen, Joanne thought as the anger began to take over, flushing her cheeks scarlet.

'You must see I can't live here, Hawk.' She faced him after the tour in the same spot they had started in, just inside the front door. 'It would make my position at Bergique & Son impossible from the start.'

'Why?' The huge, high-ceilinged room suited him perfectly; he had perfect domination over his surroundings as he stood watching her silently, his hands thrust in his pockets and his blue eyes narrowed like lasers on her hot face.

'You don't need to ask that, surely, not a man of the world like you?' she said cuttingly. 'Everyone would assume I was your mistress; you know they would.'

'I would have thought that could only strengthen your

position,' he said with outrageous arrogance. 'Give you the sort of edge you need.'

'I don't need an edge from you.' She drew herself up straight, her face fiery. 'I'll sink or swim by my own efforts, thank you—'

'Don't be so childish.' The complete lack of emotion in his voice and face made her even madder.

'Childish?' Her voice was far too shrill but she didn't care. 'I'm not so childish that I don't know why you've rented this place, Hawk Mallen. And that little man downstairs knew too, didn't he? In fact the whole world and his wife probably know.'

'Perhaps you'd like to be more specific?' he said softly.

'Do I have to spell it out?' she hissed furiously, his composure all the more irritating when she was so up-tight she could barely speak.

'Humour me.' There was a thread of steel in the grav-elly voice now but for once it didn't intimidate her. Whatever he said, however he explained it away, she just *knew* he had originally set this place up thinking she would become his mistress. How dared he? *How dare he* assume so much?!

'You thought I would allow myself to be bought, didn't you?' she accused grimly, watching him with an-gry eyes as he crossed the room to stand just in front of her, his big body formidable. 'You arranged all this, the apartment, everything, thinking I would agree to sleep with you. I know it's the truth, Hawk, whether you admit it or not.'

'I wouldn't insult your intelligence by pretending any-thing else.'

It was said coolly, and without the slightest shred of embarrassment, and for a moment she was so taken aback she just stared at him before her hand lashed out and connected with the tanned skin of his face in a ringing slap.

'You...you—'

'Now just hold on there.' He caught one hand, and then the other, as she attempted to hit him again, and she saw, with a measure of satisfaction despite the circumstances, that his cool had quite gone. 'Hold on a damn minute, will you, woman? I admit I'd hoped we might get together when I looked at this place, but that wasn't the sole reason for buying it. I wanted to know you were safe, in a good environment and with some protection—'

'You liar—'

'I never lie, Joanne,' he said grimly. 'If you had agreed to start a relationship with me that would have been the icing on the cake, of course it would, I admit it, damn it, but there was never any question of *buying* you. I know enough about you to realise you can't be bought.'

'Do you? Do you indeed?' she shot back furiously. 'Then tell me, if the new manager were old and ugly, or married, would you have got this particular apartment? Is this the normal sort of package you give to new employees you aren't worried about impressing?'

He stared at her for a good thirty seconds, his face working, and she knew he wanted to deny it but also that he couldn't, the devastating honesty that was an integral part of him blocking the words, and then he pulled her against him, so violently she almost lost her breath before his mouth swooped down on hers in a kiss that was all fire and fury.

'No!'

She fought him—afterwards she reminded herself over and over that she had fought him—but it had been too late the moment his lips had touched hers. That very second she had begun to drown in a multitude of sensations that had no rhyme or reason to them, her love for him taking over so completely that what was all wrong felt terrifyingly right.

He had moulded her into his frame from that first moment, his male body encompassing hers in a manner as old as time, the perfect jigsaw, and she was left in no doubt as to the state of his arousal.

And he knew. He *knew* her resistance was paper-thin, because after the first few minutes his hold on her slackened, just enough to prove she was in his arms because she wanted to be.

She moaned, she couldn't help it, as he began to nip and taste and savour her mouth, exciting her so seductively, so expertly that she was quivering and moist in his arms when the kiss was no longer light and teasing, but a declaration of intent.

Joanne shivered helplessly as the sensuous mouth played with her shell-like ears before moving to the sensitive skin of her throat, seeking the slight swell of her cleavage just visible under her businesslike blouse. He was good, he was so, so good, and although she knew he didn't feel the same, that he had stated exactly what she could expect from him, her heightened emotions were quelling all lucid thought.

There was electricity flowing through her veins instead of blood; she could feel it in every nerve and sinew as it created an ache that was unbearable.

His body heat released the faint trace of expensive aftershave that was still on his skin, and she couldn't believe what the erotic fragrance did to her senses, entwined as she was in his arms.

He thrust his tongue into her mouth, in the same way he wanted to thrust into the warm, pliable female body that was so soft and fluid against his strong male frame, and as he felt her answering response sensation exploded through him like raw fire, causing him to become rock-hard.

'Joanne, Joanne…' His breathing was ragged as the palms of his hands slid over the smooth silky skin of her stomach, the warmth of her, the slight moisture on her flesh, creating a pleasure-pain that was overwhelming.

All that had happened earlier that day—the knowledge that he was manipulating her, the whole situation, to his and the Mallen Corporation's advantage—just didn't seem to bear any weight when she was in his arms. Joanne knew it—a tiny rational part of her mind was shouting the warning with all its might—but it was ineffective against the bewilderingly new sensations she was experiencing for the first time.

His hands were in the glowing red silk of her hair, pulling her head gently back to tilt her mouth for greater invasion.

Was this how her mother had felt with the man who had given her her one and only child? Joanne asked herself helplessly. She had always sensed her mother had felt something special for her father—not that she had ever admitted it, but despite her bitterness and resentment that Joanne looked like him there had always been a longing in her eyes when she had spoken his name that hadn't been there with all the others.

Perhaps she *had* felt like this; perhaps you only felt like this once in a lifetime and that was why her mother had wasted the rest of her life trying to find that elusive feeling again?

Her body was boneless now, her legs trembling so much it was only Hawk's arms holding her against him which were keeping her upright, and she could hear herself murmuring his name, *moaning* his name, as he ravished her throat in an agony of desire.

And then, shockingly, unbelievably, just when she thought he was going to draw her down on to the thick deep carpet and she would have to find some strength to fight him, if she could, he moved her out of his arms and walked to the door.

His voice told her—its deep tones penetrating the fog of desire that still held her in its seductive grip—that she should get a good night's sleep, that she was tired, and, lastly, that he would see her in the morning.

CHAPTER SIX

TWICE. It had happened twice, and she was going to make darn sure there wouldn't be a third time.

Joanne had sunk down on to the carpet as Hawk had left, her shaking legs unable to hold her a moment longer, and had remained there for long minutes with tears streaming down her face. How could she have been so weak as to let him walk all over her like that? she'd asked herself over and over again through the tearing pain, before forcing herself to rise and walk slowly into the bathroom, where she had washed her tear-stained face with trembling hands.

She stared at herself now in the mirror, her eyes still liquid with the tears she was holding back by sheer will-power and her nose red and shiny.

What had it all been? An exercise in subjecting her to his will? A demonstration of his power and authority? The cruellest sort of proof that he could take or leave her despite all her brave words? Probably a mixture of all of those things, she thought bleakly, brushing a strand of damp hair off her face and shutting her eyes tight for a moment. If he had continued the lovemaking she would have found it difficult to resist full intimacy, and she would have hated herself afterwards, and him too. But she would still have loved him and that was more scary.

So... She opened her eyes and narrowed her gaze on the blotchy face in the mirror. Pull yourself together, girl. Nothing has happened, not really, even if it was more by luck than judgement. She wasn't sure why he hadn't followed through on his advantage; probably he thought he was softening her up for the kill? Or maybe once she was in his arms her inexperience had turned him off? Or perhaps—

'Stop it, stop it, stop it.' She spoke the words out loud through clenched teeth, as angry with herself as she was with him. The whys and wherefores didn't matter, not really. Whatever his motives she was taking this as a warning that one little moth had got terribly near the flames that could easily consume it, and it wasn't going to happen again. She shook her head savagely. No way.

'What the hell are you talking about?' Hawk asked tightly.

'I'm moving out this morning; I mean it.'

'*Joanne.*'

'You can ''Joanne'' me all you like, Hawk, but I *mean* it.' He had just arrived at the apartment to inform her the firm's car was waiting downstairs, his eyes immediately narrowing on her suitcases and bag near the front door, but she had faced him bravely in spite of the fact that her insides were melted jelly. She couldn't remember ever feeling such humiliation and embarrassment before, but she would rather die than let him know, she thought grimly, staring resolutely into his angry face.

'Joanne, I haven't the time or the patience for this,' he said coldly.

'Tough.' It wasn't quite the way to talk to one's employer, she thought with a touch of hysteria, but then Hawk Mallen wasn't the average boss. 'I'm bringing my bags with me and I'll move into a hotel until I find something within my price range; we can sort out a reasonable allowance for accommodation later.'

'I don't believe this is happening.'

He didn't look as though he did either, she thought weakly, and he had never looked more gorgeous, which she really didn't need.

'You are seriously telling me you won't stay here?' he said, after a good thirty seconds when they had stared at each other like two gladiators in mortal combat. His voice held a touch of bemused incredulity and it made her want to laugh—something she had thought last night would never happen again. 'The place has a lease for six months.'

'That's not my problem.' She could see he was freshly shaved, the tanned skin begging to be touched— She cut the thought firmly and returned to the attack. 'I am not prepared to be talked about, Hawk, and neither do I want to stay on here under false pretences. You clearly had something other than a work relationship in mind when you took this apartment, and as I have no intention of fulfilling that requirement—' if he mentioned last night she would kill him, on the spot '—I wouldn't be comfortable continuing here.'

'You really *are* serious.' How could someone so soft and small and kitten-like be so *unreasonable*? Hawk asked himself furiously. 'Joanne, this is crazy.'

'I don't think so; it would be crazy to stay here, though.' She could see she had totally thrown him and it felt so good, so wonderfully good, after the miserable night she'd had when she'd walked the beautiful apartment till dawn. She wanted to hate him, all through the long dark night hours she had tried to hate him, but although her head was in agreement her heart just wouldn't fall into line. He was the epitome of the love-'em-and-leave-'em types her mother had fallen for, she'd told herself angrily—only after one thing, shallow, heartless—but still, as the first pink rays had crept over the balcony floor, her heart had wept for what might have been.

'That's your last word on the matter?' he asked grimly.

'Yes.' She stared at him a little nervously now, wondering what he was going to do.

'Right.' He walked across to the telephone and picked it up, tapping in the number in a manner that could only be termed vicious. 'Antoinette?' His voice was icy. 'Miss Crawford and myself won't be in the office till this afternoon, and cancel the lease on Miss Crawford's apartment, would you? It isn't suitable.'

The French girl must have been as surprised as Hawk had been, because he next said, the words bitten out through clenched teeth, 'For a number of reasons,' and then, 'I don't care about that; pay the damn thing in full,' before slamming down the receiver so hard it jumped up again.

'Right, we flat-hunt.' He glared at her, his eyes blue ice. 'Satisfied?'

'You don't have to do that; I can find something later and stay in a hotel for now—'

'I am not leaving France until I see you settled in suitable accommodation that I have personally inspected, right?' The glare intensified. 'You don't know Paris, the safe and not so safe areas, and frankly you are a con-man's dream.'

'I am not!' she protested hotly, her cheeks burning scarlet.

'Yes, you are,' he countered, his voice deep now, too deep, its texture making shivers dance down her spine as he eyed her grimly. 'How you've got to the age of twenty-nine without being snared by some man a little bolder than the rest I don't know,' he said darkly. 'Perhaps it's because you're just too good to be true.'

She didn't know if he was being nasty now, especially in view of her abandonment last night, but she couldn't think of anything to say anyway, just staring at him with big, wary honey-brown eyes as she forced herself not to wilt.

'Come on.' He turned to the door, his voice suddenly brisk. 'I had planned to leave France this afternoon; my work schedule is hellish and I haven't got time to waste. I know the agents Antoinette used to find this place; we'll give them a visit.'

'I don't want anything like this—'

'Trust me.' It was said tongue-in-cheek but his eyes weren't angry now, and she had to fight against the flood of relief and joy filling her body. He wanted to find her somewhere where she would be safe; he cared enough for that? Don't be stupid! The voice in her head answered the spurt of hope immediately. You're here to do a job for him and he wants you one hundred per cent the capable machine he expects. If there were difficulties it would affect your work; that is all he is thinking of.

Hawk didn't leave France that afternoon. It was four o'clock before they found her an apartment, after visiting several others scattered all over the city, but immediately she saw it she knew it was the one.

She had insisted on speaking to the agents herself, Hawk's idea of price range being in the super league, and had liked the sound of the converted house, three storeys high with the apartment occupying the top floor, in a quiet square close to the Latin Quarter.

The rain and wind of the night before had given way to weak sunshine when they reached the old cobbled square dotted with gnarled trees, benches complete with old men in berets and young grandchildren about their knees, and a general air of bygone tranquillity that sat well on the stately houses trying to maintain a semblance of dignity despite crumbling balconies and flaking paint. Joanne thought it was charming.

'Right, I've seen enough; on to the next one,' Hawk said abruptly as their long-suffering driver parked on the road opposite, and Hawk's gaze followed hers across to the sleepy square.

'Hang on a minute; I haven't seen the apartment yet,' Joanne protested quickly.

'You don't need to, surely?' Hawk said disparagingly.

'Of course I do.' She turned to him, a ray of autumn sunshine turning her smooth bob to red fire. 'It looks lovely.'

'Lovely?' The bemused incredulity was back. '*Lovely?* What, exactly, are you looking at, Joanne?'

'I'm looking at happy children with people who love them, who have got time to *care*, at a quiet little haven in the midst of all the busyness, at those wonderful old cobbles and ancient trees, at—' She stopped suddenly. 'Why? What are you looking at?'

The blue eyes stared back at her, moving over her creamy skin, fine eyebrows, small straight nose and generously full mouth, before returning to capture her gaze again.

'Hawk?' She knew she was blushing at the quiet scrutiny but she couldn't help it. 'What did you see?'

He turned his eyes to the square again, and this time his voice was without expression as he said, 'I saw old trees, a square that needs cleaning up and terraced houses that look like a good wind would blow them down.'

'That's what you see?' She shook her head slowly, the movement causing her hair to shimmer like liquid silk. 'Then I'm sorry for you, Hawk.'

'Don't be.' The reserve was back, stronger than ever, and his voice was frosty as he said, 'You intend to inspect this one, I gather?'

'Yes, I do.' He didn't like it but she couldn't help that, she thought silently.

'And you'll take it whatever now, yes?' he suggested grimly.

'You mean to spite you?'

'Exactly.'

'Is that what you think of me?' She was angry and she was glad of it; it helped to keep the hurt at bay. 'Then you won't want to come and see yourself, will you?' she challenged stiffly.

He didn't answer, giving her a long level look that was quite unreadable, before opening his door and walking round to hers and helping her alight, still without saying a word.

The plump, motherly landlady whose house it was occupied the ground floor, and, she told Joanne in French, the young couple who occupied the second floor were very friendly and very happy. 'Just married, you know?' she added with a beaming smile, her eyes narrowing slightly on Hawk.

'How nice.' Joanne managed a fairly normal smile but made sure within the next few moments that she made her working relationship to Hawk quite clear—there had been a definite matchmaking gleam in the Frenchwoman's eyes.

She didn't know exactly what to expect as she climbed the polished wood stairs—no executive lift here, she thought wryly—but when she reached the top floor and opened the door to the flat her first impression was the enormous capacity for light within the sitting room that faced her. The walls were painted cream, and a honey-fawn carpet and curtains emphasised the rays of mild golden sunshine streaming through the two floor-to-ceiling windows. There was no door to divide the sitting room from the kitchen and dining area, but the clever arrangement of the furniture made each section feel remarkably self-contained.

The pale colour scheme was carried through into the small bedroom and tiny bathroom, and although the square footage of the apartment was small—in fact the whole would probably have fitted with room to spare into the drawing room of the grand apartment she had left that morning—the general effect was one of space and light.

'I love it.' Joanne walked across to the minute balcony which led off one of the French windows, and was only large enough to accommodate two cane chairs and a small eighteen-inch table, and looked at the view across the square. 'And I'm not saying that to be awkward, incidentally,' she added, 'whatever you think.'

'It's small,' Hawk stated flatly.

'It's compact,' she countered quickly.

'And the area isn't the best you could do.'

'Hawk, I never have lived in the "best" areas,' Joanne said tightly, memories of the children's home, where she had spent the last few years of her childhood after her mother's second marriage had ended so disastrously, burning vividly on the screen of her mind. 'And, as you said yesterday, everything is relative.'

'That's not quite what I said.' He eyed her grimly for a moment, Madame Lemoine hovering in the doorway behind them. 'You're quite sure you won't reconsider the apartment in Montmartre?'

'Quite sure,' she stated firmly.

'And if we look at further apartments you'll come back to this one, won't you?' It was said with such an air of resignation that she wanted to smile, despite the bittersweet pain being with him induced.

She nodded slowly. 'It's friendly, Hawk, and...me somehow. I like it.'

'So be it.' He shot her one exasperated look before walking past and conferring with the little Frenchwoman, Joanne in the meantime wandering round inspecting cupboards and drawer space.

'You can move in tonight.' He came up behind her as she stood looking down into the square again to where an old man and two small children were feeding a noisy squad of jostling birds. 'If you want to, that is.' Madame Lemoine had bustled happily away.

'Yes, I do…thank you,' she murmured awkwardly. 'I…I'm sorry I've delayed you—'

She turned as she spoke, and when her eyes met his felt that little jolt of electricity she always experienced when the full power of the piercing blue gaze took hers.

'My choice.' The words were brief, concise; he was a man who rarely elaborated on the essential, which made it all the more remarkable when he added, 'The sunshine is turning your hair to living flame, do you know that? And your eyes are as dark as a night sky, although sometimes they're the shade of warm honey. Who do you get your colouring from—your mother or your father?' he asked softly.

The question hit her in the solar plexus but she didn't duck it. 'My mother was a natural blonde,' she said stiffly, 'but my father had red hair and brown eyes, according to her. She…she didn't like it, that I took after him.'

'One of the reasons for the foster homes?' he asked quietly.

He hadn't referred to their conversation on that first evening over the last few weeks, and she had convinced herself he had forgotten it, dismissed it as unimportant, although she realised now that was silly. Hawk Mallen forgot nothing about anyone—it was all noted and filed away in that computer-type brain in case it was useful for the future.

'Possibly.' She shrugged, lowering her head and aiming to sidle past him but he caught her shoulders in his large hands and held her fast.

'Was it rough?' he murmured gently. 'Your childhood? Is that why you hold the world in such distrust?'

'I don't.' The suggestion shocked her.

'Joanne, when someone who looks like you do has never formed a close relationship, there's something badly wrong.' His voice was steady and firm and it was clear he wasn't going to let go of either her or the conversation.

'I could say the same about you,' she shot back quickly.

'Yes, you could, but it wouldn't be true,' he said softly, and for a moment the import of his words didn't hit her. Then, as her eyes widened with the knowledge of what he had just admitted, and the pain and searing jealousy attacked in the same instant, he continued, 'But it was a long, long time ago, and anyway, we aren't discussing me.'

'We aren't discussing me either,' she snapped testily, wrenching herself out of his grasp. 'I work for you, Hawk, that's all, and my life is my own, past and present.'

'When do you have fun, Joanne?' He ignored her former words as though she hadn't spoken and it was terribly irritating. 'Or is that a three-letter word that doesn't feature in your vocabulary?' he continued silkily.

'I'm in no doubt it features in yours,' she said tartly, 'although it's spelt S-E-X, right?'

'Ouch.' He smiled, a lazy, sexy smile, before saying, 'I rather walked into that one, didn't I? You don't trust me an inch, do you, my fiery little puritan?'

She didn't like the 'puritan' bit; she wasn't sure if she liked the 'fiery' bit either if it came to it—it suggested a lack of control, and that wasn't at all the image she wanted to present to him. She took a long, silent pull of air, counted to ten, and then said sweetly, 'I'm sure you're an absolutely trustworthy employer, Mr Mallen,' before walking smartly to the door. 'Shall we bring up my things?'

He was grinning as he followed her out of the flat and

down the stairs, and as she caught sight of his face she
tried, desperately, to hang on to the anger and hurt—it
was all the protection she had—but it was difficult. He
was so seductive when he was like this, and although
she knew he was a virtuoso in the seduction techniques
it was head knowledge, not heart, and didn't help at all
against that magnetic pull he exerted as naturally as
breathing.

'I'll take your cases up and leave you to get settled
in,' Hawk said as they reached the car. 'There's a few
phone calls I need to make.'

'Oh, but I thought we were going into the office?' She
was flustered and it showed. 'I can just leave my
things—'

'The day's over.' It was; dusk was already falling rapidly into the square, tingeing it with a bluey-grey softness, and there was the bite of frost in the air. 'I'm going
to call in and inform Antoinette of the new arrangements, make those calls, and then pick up some bare
essentials for you on my way back to my hotel. Okay?
One day is going to make no difference one way or the
other, Joanne. Go up, unpack, have a bath and relax until
you hear my knock.'

'Hawk, there's no need; I can pop out myself—'

'Just do it, Joanne, will you?' he said with pointed
weariness. 'You won the major battle today; *you've* chosen your accommodation and established you are an independent, tenacious free spirit and I am suitably hum-
bled. Rest on your laurels.'

He didn't look humble—in fact the word was ludicrous when applied to Hawk Mallen, Joanne thought
wryly—but he had made his point and she nodded quietly. 'All right. Thank you.'

She saw the dark eyebrows rise sardonically at her
meekness and fought against smiling. She couldn't afford to soften in any way, shape or form; this was a

battle, and she was fighting as much against herself and her weakening emotions where this man was concerned as against Hawk himself. He was just so dangerous, fascinatingly, hypnotically dangerous, and utterly ruthless in his desire to conquer, and if he ever had an inkling of the true state of her feelings for him... The thought propelled her into the house ahead of him and up the stairs as though the devil himself were after her.

Once alone amid her strewn possessions, Joanne stopped for a moment in her unpacking as she caught sight of herself in the bedroom mirror, noting the tension frown that marred her forehead.

Hawk was right; once she finished unpacking the first thing on the agenda was a hot bath, and she could wash her hair, change, spoil herself a little. He wouldn't be back for at least a couple of hours and the headache that was beginning to drum at the back of her eyelids needed soaking away. She nodded at the serious-faced girl in the mirror.

And once Hawk had dropped a few provisions off she'd fix something light to eat with a hot drink, and probably take it to bed with one of the books she'd brought with her from England. A nice relaxing night in her new home... She glanced round the pretty room in varying shades of lemon and ivory before leaving the suitcases and walking through to the sitting room again. She had been right to insist on moving from that first apartment, she told herself with a feeling of deep relief. She could be herself here, in this little oasis from the pressures that would undoubtedly come her way as Bergique & Son's new manageress. In fact she could have been happy—if only a certain tall, blue-eyed individual hadn't blazed on her horizon like a threatening black meteor.

*   *   *

The threatening black meteor was back at just gone seven, his arms full of groceries and his face—although she didn't like the tender pang that accompanied the thought—grey with tiredness.

Joanne, on the other hand, had bathed, washed her hair and spent a contented hour or two arranging her belongings before crashing out in front of the TV. The resulting feeling of guilt was overpowering, and when he placed the bags in the kitchen, remarking as he did so, 'There's a couple of bottles of good wine in that lot, and steaks and so on,' her following words were inevitable.

'Would...would you like to stay for a meal?' she asked hesitantly.

'Great.' It was immediate and satisfied, and although she knew he had set the whole thing up she couldn't be angry. He *did* look exhausted, and if she had accepted the first apartment he would be back in England now, so it was all her fault...in a way. 'I'll open the wine, shall I?' he asked with suspicious meekness that only confirmed the whole exercise had been planned.

'What about the car, the driver?' She gestured at the window to the square outside. 'Aren't you going to tell him?'

'I came by taxi.' His eyes glinted wickedly.

'And you didn't think to ask it to wait?' she murmured sarcastically. 'How fortunate I suggested you stay.'

'I had faith in your compassion.' He smiled slowly. 'Where's the corkscrew?'

She gave up. He couldn't be shamed; she should have known—he was impossible!

'Here.' She opened a drawer and gave him the cork-screw. 'But it's just dinner, okay? I'm as tired as you are and I need my bed.'

'I need your bed, Joanne,' he said, with a ridiculously lewd expression that was supposed to make her laugh.

It did, but it also sent her heart thudding as a cold clear warning hit her brain. Don't forget, he's never more dangerous than when he's amusing and charming, like now. You've no defence against this man but he doesn't know that, so play it cool and keep things easy.

The red wine was mellow and fruity, the sort that tasted of a thousand summer days and must have cost a small fortune. With Hawk perched on a breakfast stool watching her while she worked, preparing a salad to go with the steaks, Joanne consumed two glasses without even being aware of it, until her head became a little muzzy and she found herself giggling at something he said.

'I think I need some food.' She took a couple of raw mushrooms and popped them into her mouth, one by one. 'What on earth's in that wine anyway?'

'Just grapes and sugar and—'

'You know what I mean,' she admonished gravely. 'You aren't trying to get me tipsy, are you?'

'Would I?' The sapphire-blue eyes were laughing at her and it should have mattered—but it didn't.

She nodded solemnly, but then, in the next moment, he had taken the salad bowl and set it to one side, folding her into his body without saying a word.

Joanne's mistake was in opening her mouth to protest, because he simply seized the chance to plunder it, his tongue sending tremors of desire into every nerve and sinew.

He had already taken off his jacket and tie, his shirt open at the neck, and as her palms pressed against his chest she could feel the prickle of dark body hair under the silk and the combination was unbearably erotic.

'You're beautiful, Joanne, just beautiful,' he whispered softly as his mouth nibbled at her lower lip. 'You've no idea what you do to me.'

She had, oh, she had, if it was just a fraction of what he did to her, she thought helplessly.

'I could eat you alive, do you know that?' His mouth moved to her earlobe and she thought she would die. 'Every single inch of you.' His hand covered her breast, caressing it slowly through the thin cotton of the T-shirt she had changed into, and immediately the tip flowered beneath his expert fingers, aching and ripe.

She arched against him, her hands going up to his shoulders as she pressed herself against the hardness of his body, and then, as a sizzle and a splutter from the grill touched her senses, she jerked away, her voice agitated. 'The steaks! I can't burn the steaks on my first night here; what would Madame Lemoine think?'

'Damn Madame Lemoine.' But he let her move away and rescue the food, settling himself back on his stool as he purposefully poured them both another glass of wine, although Joanne determined not to have another drop until she had eaten.

They ate at the tiny dining-room table that was barely big enough for two, and Joanne made sure the third glass of wine lasted until dessert, a wonderful chocolate mousse piped with thick fresh cream that tasted divine.

'That was absolutely gorgeous.' She was licking her spoon clear of even the faintest trace of chocolate as she spoke and raised her eyes to see Hawk's narrowed gaze resting slumberously on her face.

'You look like a contented little cat,' he said huskily. 'I can almost hear you purr.'

'I love chocolate mousse,' she admitted with a faintly embarrassed smile. 'It's so decadent.'

'What else do you love, Joanne?' he asked softly. 'Do you realise I don't know the first thing about you besides the black and white information in your personnel folder? What music do you like? What books do you read? *Talk* to me.'

Talking was safer than not talking, and so she talked, guardedly at first, and then more freely after Hawk opened the second bottle of wine. And he responded in kind, telling her about his childhood, his youth, and then his desire to carve out a name for himself beyond that of Jed Mallen's grandson. The room was intimate and shadowed, lit only by the glow of the standard lamp in one corner, Hawk having turned the main light off before they ate, and Joanne was just thinking things were a sight too cosy for her peace of mind when Hawk said, 'Time I was making tracks.'

'What?'

His voice had been easy, cool, and she didn't feel like that; in fact she felt far from it. He had been leaning back in his seat for the last half an hour, his arms crossed over the broad expanse of his big muscled chest, and the open shirt collar displaying a hard tanned throat and the beginnings of black curling body hair. The silky material of his shirt seemed to emphasise rather than diminish his magnetic masculinity, and, try as she might, she had been struggling to dispel the thought of what he would look like without it for the last little while—and failing miserably. He looked darkly brooding, his Italian genes very much to the fore, and tough, and sexy, and...

'It's been a long day and you said you were tired,' he said softly.

She stared at him, trying to hide her irritation and ashamed of the resentment that had flared, hot and strong, at his offer to leave. He didn't want to kiss her. Well, that was fine, fine, she told herself silently; she would only have had to put him in his place if he had tried—whatever Hawk's place was. 'I am tired,' she agreed stiffly. 'Thank you for all the provisions you brought in; I really must pay you—'

'Don't be silly.' He interrupted her lazily, standing up and stretching like a powerful black beast of the forest, his piercing blue gaze never leaving her unknowingly vulnerable face that betrayed her confusion and hurt all too clearly. 'Look on it as a house-warming present if that makes you feel better. I only bought the bare essentials, by the way; the bulk of the order will be delivered some time after six tomorrow so make sure you're back by then.'

'Yes, I will, thank you…' He really *was* going to go, she thought numbly as she watched him reach for his jacket and shrug it over his broad shoulders, slipping his tie into one of the pockets as he did so. Whatever she had expected it wasn't this.

Hawk knew that, and his voice was an easy drawl as she walked with him to the front door. Tonight was not the night, much as his aching loins tried to persuade him differently. She had opened up more than he had expected, but she was still like a nervous doe, ready to bolt before the hunter.

When he took her—and he *would* take her—it would be with her full capitulation, mental and physical, and she would want him as much as he wanted her. He didn't question why her absolute surrender was so important to him, and his goodnight kiss was long and unhurried, his hand tender as it cupped her jaw and the gentle eroticism of his mouth controlled and determined.

'Goodnight, Joanne.' When he lifted his head she was trembling. 'The car will pick you up at eight in the morning.' And then he was gone.

CHAPTER SEVEN

JOANNE didn't know whether to be relieved or disappointed nine hours later when Hawk phoned, at seven in the morning, to say he was on his way to the States to deal with an emergency that had arisen in one of the Mallen subsidiaries. He wished her well in the new job, told her he would be in touch at some point to discuss how things were going, and that was that.

She put down the phone with a feeling of disbelief. So... Her restless night, the agitation at the prospect of seeing him that morning which had had her up and eating breakfast before six, had all been for nothing. He had happily upped and gone.

She sat down suddenly on one of the chairs and gave herself a thorough talking-to. Why shouldn't he just go? He was her employer, that was all, and he had done what was necessary and introduced her to her new staff. There was no reason for him to stay another hour in France— *not one*—and the last person he was answerable to was her. She was just glad—fiercely, overwhelmingly glad— that nothing of any significance had happened last night. His actions this morning only proved, beyond doubt, that all her misgivings were spot-on, she told herself miserably.

She was ready and waiting for the car at eight, and the flow of angry adrenalin that had begun with Hawk's cool voice that morning continued to flow all day, working to her advantage as she consumed vast quantities of data and had Antoinette, and the rest of the somewhat lethargic office staff, scurrying about like headless chickens. It was clear that the lackadaisical listlessness that

Pierre had allowed to take hold had permeated the entire firm, and also that certain members of the staff didn't appreciate having their cosy little world shaken to its foundations, Antoinette for one.

She was just considering taking the sulky French girl to task in spite of it being their first day together, having asked, three times in quick succession, for a folder which still wasn't forthcoming, when she looked up from her desk to see a tall, heavily built, floridly handsome man in the open doorway, his dark eyes fixed on her face.

'You must be Joanne Crawford?' He spoke before she had the chance to open her mouth, his English almost perfect and accentless. 'I am Pierre Bergique, Miss Crawford, and I must beg your forgiveness for not being here to introduce you to my staff personally yesterday.' He smiled, a wide crocodile kind of smile which didn't reach the hard, calculating black eyes. 'I trust Antoinette is looking after you in my absence?' he asked smoothly.

'Good morning, Pierre.' Hawk had warned her to start exactly as she meant to carry on with this man, and she saw the advice was apt as the toothy smile dimmed a little at her cool response. She couldn't allow him to relegate her to an underling—as his carefully worded greeting had aimed to do—neither could she acquiesce to the notion that he had authority over the staff any more. Pierre knew his position full well, and he was damned lucky not to be in a prison cell at this very moment, she thought tightly.

She rose with measured aplomb, walking round the desk and across the room before she held out her hand and said, 'How nice to meet you...at last. I'm sure things are going to work out splendidly, and rest assured I shan't hesitate to call on your services if I need to.'

Cold black eyes held determined honey-brown ones for a long—a very long—moment, and then Pierre took her hand, raising it to his lips and lightly kissing it before saying, his voice oily now, 'Charmed, charmed, my dear. I had no idea our intrepid new leader would prove to be quite so young and beautiful. Hawk must have been very impressed by your...capabilities.'

'Thank you.' It was all she could do not to whip her hand from his and rub the back of it to erase the feel of his fleshy lips, but she forced herself to smile and wait for a few seconds, ignoring the veiled innuendo in the barbed words, before turning away.

'I understand you will be working from home now, Pierre,' she said calmly as she re-seated herself, hoping the thudding of her heart wasn't making itself known. 'I would prefer that you check with me in the future before you call by so that I can make sure I'm available for you, and avoid wasting your time.'

Hawk had made it clear to Pierre that the offices were out of bounds beyond the occasional visit expected of a figurehead, and the clearing of his debts and the generous salary he was receiving each month for doing nothing were conditional.

'Of course.' It was too quick and too congenial. 'Anything you say.'

She didn't trust him an inch. 'Good.' She forced another smile but her flesh was creeping. This was one ugly customer, Joanne thought grimly, despite the façade of expensive clothes, well-groomed exterior and handsome, smiling countenance. This man could be nasty—she had seen too many like him in her working life to doubt her gut feeling—and she could understand Hawk's insistence that Pierre was virtually barred from crossing the firm's threshold now, although she had thought him a trifle hard when he had first told her.

'Perhaps you would allow me the pleasure of taking you to lunch one day?' The charm was out in full force, but it was too late; she had seen the man behind the mask and they both knew it.

'Thank you but I'm going to be busy for the next little while getting everything together,' Joanne said politely. 'Maybe after then?' Again they both knew there would be no lunch.

'Of course; just let me know when it will be convenient,' Pierre murmured with silky synthetic civility. 'And now you really must excuse me—a previous appointment...

Joanne breathed a sigh of relief when the door closed behind him, her body deflating in the chair like a punctured balloon. What a creep, but a crafty, astute creep, which also made him dangerous, and that was what she had to remember. He had been fooling people for years until Hawk had come on the scene and spoilt his little games; she had to be on her guard and take nothing for granted.

The next few weeks were challenging, frustrating, exhausting, at times stimulating and other times disappointing, but despite the hard, grinding work, long hours and mental and physical tiredness Joanne welcomed the pace. It made her so numb, so exhausted by the end of the day that all she could do was fall into bed and slip into a deep, dreamless sleep, sometimes without even having eaten her evening meal. But she could keep her thoughts away from Hawk and that was the main thing.

Sometimes she awoke, at the shrill command of her militant alarm clock, with his name on her lips and the faint recollection of shadowed memories buried deep in her subconscious, but mostly she could steel herself to deal solely with the job in hand, and she was glad of it.

He had rung two or three times a week since she had been in France, and she always came off the phone a quivering heap and desperately thankful he couldn't see how the sound of his deep, husky, totally male voice affected her.

Useless to tell herself he was ringing purely to see
how the Mallen investment was progressing, that she
meant nothing to him, that she was one of dozens, *hundreds*, of women whom he would invite to share his bed
if he felt so inclined. She heard his voice and she melted;
it was as simple—and as humiliating—as that.

So in the middle of November, on a particularly foul
Friday when the rain was slashing at the windows of her
office and nothing had gone right, she viewed the ap-
parition in her office doorway as a figment of her fevered
imagination and nothing else. Until it spoke, that was.

'Busy?'

Busy? She stared at Hawk as her brain struggled to
respond. He was lounging against the open door, big and
dark in a heavy leather jacket and black jeans, which
were as different from the designer business suits he normally wore as chalk from cheese. The sight of him
stopped her breath.

She forced herself to talk, to say *something*. 'I didn't
know you were coming.'

'Neither did I until this morning.' He didn't move or
smile.

She waited for him to elaborate, and, when he didn't,
rose quietly from behind her desk, setting her face in a
polite smile of welcome befitting a humble employee
greeting the illustrious head of the Mallen Corporation.
'It's nice to see you again; is there anything specific you
want to see me about?' she asked quietly.

'Don't tempt me, Joanne.' The look in his eyes was
so blatant, and so sexual, that she blushed hotly as she
held out one small hand for him to shake, and when he
simply took her fingers in his and drew her close for a
moment, his eyes roaming over her face before he kissed
her lips in a light stroking movement that was over as
soon as it had begun, she was still too stunned at his
sudden appearance to offer any resistance.

'So...' He stepped back a pace, watching her with glittering eyes. 'Have you missed me?' he asked with the Mallen arrogance.

'Missed you?' How could he get so instantly under her skin? she asked herself angrily. 'Of course not.'

'Liar.' It was said matter-of-factly but still grated unbearably, tightening her mouth and narrowing her eyes.

'Hawk, I'm here to work and work I have,' she declared firmly. 'What on earth makes you think I've missed *you*?'

'Because it's impossible for me to have been feeling the way I have without you feeling something similar.' It was so surprising, and so unexpected, revealing as it did the man beneath the cool, arrogant exterior, that she just stared at him without saying anything. 'I've been sleeping you, eating you, tasting you,' he said softly. 'It's driving me nuts, Joanne. Every time I shut my eyes at night there's a slender titian beauty there, with honey-gold eyes and the sort of figure that makes a man ache.'

'Hawk—'

'It makes *me* ache—hell, how it makes me ache,' he murmured huskily. 'I'm in and out of that damn shower all night.'

'You're talking about sexual attraction—'

'I know; believe me, I know,' he agreed with a sardonic lift of his eyebrows.

'And I'm sure a man of your considerable experience could easily find a number from his little black book to take care of things,' she continued firmly, as though he hadn't interrupted. She was *not* going to be swept back into his orbit and then discarded so abruptly again; she just wasn't.

'Perhaps I haven't got a little black book?' he suggested softly.

'And perhaps pigs fly?' Joanne said sweetly, desperately glad the trembling in her stomach hadn't communicated itself to her voice.

'You think I'm the worst sort of philanderer, don't you?' It was a statement, not a question. 'And after I've been so restrained too,' he added sadly.

'Huh.' She had seen the wickedly amused glitter in the sapphire eyes and she wasn't fooled.

'Enough of this sparkling repartee.' He grabbed her suddenly, lifting her up and swinging her round as he kicked the door shut. 'You're going to spend the weekend with me.' It was another statement rather than an invitation.

'*I am not.*' It was hard to think while held close to his big masculine body, but the answer was instinctive anyway. He looked so good, he smelt so good, she wouldn't *dare* spend time with him.

'Reconsider.' He kissed her again, but this time it was no brief salutation but a long, deep, hard invasion that sent every nerve and sinew into overdrive. She found her arms snaking up to his broad shoulders and had to clench her fingers to restrain them, determined not to give in to the quivering hot excitement. 'Please?' he added softly as he lifted his head.

'No, I'm here to work—'

'Not at the weekends; even the wicked slave-driver Hawk Mallen doesn't expect that. Besides, you've been working too hard,' he said with sudden seriousness. 'You've lost weight, you look drawn.'

'Oh, thank you so much,' she muttered sarcastically, trying to pull away but knowing she wouldn't have any effect on the steel-hard arms. So he didn't like the way she looked now?

'But even more beautiful,' he added gently, his mouth twisting with amusement at her reaction. 'You have an ethereal quality now, as though a breath of wind would blow you away.'

'Hawk, let *go* of me.' She turned her head towards the door, worried Antoinette and the rest of the office staff would wonder why the door was shut, or, worse still, knock and walk straight in. Antoinette would make a meal of such a tasty titbit.

'Not till you agree to spend the weekend with me,' he said firmly. 'I can stay like this all afternoon; I'm enjoying it.' There was swollen evidence to prove he meant what he said, his hard body stirring against the soft swell of her stomach even as he spoke, and making her legs feel weak at his alien masculinity.

'What…what do you mean by ''spend the weekend''?' she asked breathlessly, fighting against the urge to arch against his maleness, and then betraying her arousal helplessly with a tiny moan as one large hand stroked a sensual path from her throat to her waist, lingering possessively on the swell of one ripe breast.

'I want to show you France, my suspicious little siren.' He moved her slightly from him in order to look down into her flushed face. 'Although I can be persuaded otherwise,' he added softly. 'My hotel room has the biggest double bed you've ever seen—'

'*Hawk.*'

'Okay, okay.' His eyes crinkled as he gave the devastating smile he used so rarely, and she felt the impact right down to her toes. 'I promise I'll behave; how about that? No petting, no lovemaking—just a weekend spent in each other's company. I'm leaving for the States again first thing Monday morning and I know the next couple of weeks are going to be the very devil. I just wanted to be with you, Joanne; that's the top and bottom of it.'

It might have been calculated, he might be being manipulative again, but she couldn't struggle against the overwhelming desire to be with him when he looked at her like that. And he *had* promised…

'All right.' She felt such a burst of happiness that she

wanted to press herself into him and pull his head down to hers, and to fight that impulse she quickly stepped back a pace, purposely forcing his hands to drop to his sides. 'But a promise is a promise,' she warned shakily. 'And you've promised no lovemaking.'

'And you'll keep me to mine, no doubt,' he drawled wryly. 'I always thought women were the weaker sex, but since meeting you I've had to change my mind. I certainly chose well in Bergique & Son's new manager; if you deal with Pierre half as sternly as you deal with me, the poor guy won't know what's hit him.'

It was said mockingly, his eyes laughing at her, but a little chill crept into her heart as she turned away towards her desk. She wanted to be with him because she loved him; it might be foolish, crazy, but that was how it was. But Hawk? Hawk didn't know the meaning of the word love, and she forgot that at her peril. He wanted her body, he perhaps wanted an agent in the nest of vipers he had uncovered too, but anything permanent, with any sort of future? No chance.

The weekend began on the Friday night with a wonderful wander through the colourful streets, boulevards and cobblestone lanes, under a dark moonlit sky that had banished even the smallest rain cloud. The beautiful city, with its hundreds of statues, museums, countless churches, fountains and squares, narrowed down to one tall, dark, handsome man for Joanne, and a pair of piercingly blue, riveting eyes. Everything else faded into oblivion.

They ate at one of the many restaurants dotted around the streets of the gourmet capital, where taste, like the other senses, was taken so seriously. The restaurant was small and nondescript from the outside, and the interior wasn't much better, but the food was out of this world. They feasted on *crudités variées*, a mixture of raw vegetables with oil and vinegar, followed by steak *au poivre* which melted in the mouth, and was ably enhanced by the excellent champagne Hawk had ordered. The dessert—*un mystère*, which turned out to be vanilla ice-cream with meringue in the middle and chopped nuts on the outside—was perfect to follow the steak, and when Joanne accepted a second helping Hawk couldn't hide his surprise at her appetite.

'You said I was too thin,' she reminded him drily as she lifted her spoon and prepared to attack the delicious concoction. 'You ought to be pleased.'

'I am, oh, I am,' he assured her gravely, 'but I did not say you were too thin. You looked weary, that was all.'

Weary? Heart-sore, bone-achingly sad, perhaps, she thought painfully. 'I'm fine.' She beamed at him, determined to give nothing away. 'It's just been hectic, that's all, and I've needed to be fully alert at all times.' But never so much as now. 'There are one or two things I need to discuss with you, incidentally; we are going to have to reschedule—'

'Not now.' He interrupted her with a lazily raised hand that was none the less authoritative. 'The weekend is ours; Monday morning is soon enough for you to once again become the super-efficient career woman Bergique & Son know and love.'

'I don't know about the love,' she said wryly. Over the last few weeks she had been pleased to discover she was being treated with respect—grudging respect in some quarters—by her staff, and there were several now whom she liked, and who she felt liked her, but it had been an uphill struggle.

Since the incident with Pierre in her office, Antoinette had fallen into line, the sulkiness disappearing as though by magic and the girl appearing, to all intents and purposes, to be fully committed to her new boss. But... And there was a big 'but', Joanne thought pensively. She didn't trust the beautiful French girl, not one little bit. The turn-around had been too quick and too complete—something smelt fishy.

'I said Monday morning is soon enough to think of work.' Hawk's voice was a little put out and Joanne suddenly realised she was staring into space, and that it was highly likely Hawk didn't have too many women do that in his presence. She was surprised she had, to be honest, but the creepy, goose-pimply unease she had been feeling for days, if not weeks, had momentarily intruded into the evening and absorbed her in its shadow.

'Sorry.' In view of all the humiliation and pain she had suffered through him she couldn't resist adding, 'I was daydreaming,' as she gave him a cheerfully innocent smile.

'Charming.' The sapphire gaze was penetrating, but he smiled back. 'You believe in keeping your men humble, is that it?'

Humble? *Hawk Mallen?* The raw sexuality and powerful aura didn't lend themselves to humbleness, she thought breathlessly as the devastating smile did its usual damage to her equilibrium. In fact you might as well have asked the fierce bird of prey from whom he had taken his name to be humble, as the big dark man watching her so closely.

'I don't have men in the plural,' she prevaricated sweetly, knowing her colour was high. 'As you well know.'

'And heartily approve of,' he said solemnly. 'I think one man is more than enough for you, and, funnily enough, I know just the man...'

That evening was the beginning of the most wildly happy two days she had ever known, and, amazingly,

Hawk kept his promise—apart from the odd lingering kiss he assured her didn't count.

He picked her up from her apartment on Saturday morning very early, but already the November day was promising that the rain of the last week was a thing of the past, as it allowed a cold but bright sunshine to bathe everything in its light.

The sports car Hawk had hired for the weekend was lean and low and fairly ate up the miles as it headed towards the medieval majesty of Burgundy, passing Cistercian abbeys, dignified towns of stone, fortified hill-top villages and wonderful roaming countryside, on its way to Dijon.

They ate lunch at a charming little *hostellerie*, and the toasted ham and cheese sandwiches, followed by bar-quettes au marron—pastry boats loaded with almond paste, chestnut cream, and sealed in with milk chocolate on one side and coffee icing on the other—were sublime. But anything would have tasted sublime—because she was with Hawk. And it frightened her. Frightened, ex-hilarated, excited, but mostly frightened. Because it would end. It had to.

They reached Dijon just after one in the afternoon— Joanne having insisted they stop and wander round one of the towns on their way—and the once-capital of the Flemish-Burgundian state was at its regal best in the bright sunshine.

'An afternoon of improving your mind?' Hawk asked lazily, after they had parked at the edge of a delightfully ancient little market-place, where Hawk bought them both the most enormous ice-creams. 'We can visit the Musée des Beaux-Arts, and perhaps you would like to see the Well of Moses? It is a very powerful sculpture, very moving.'

'Is it?' She licked a blob of strawberry ice-cream from the corner of her mouth, and Hawk's eyes followed her

pink tongue, his gaze slumberous and hot. She was looking at a real flesh-and-blood sculpture that would knock
the Well of Moses into a cocked hat, Joanne thought
silently, with an irreverence that would have made Claus
Sluter turn in his grave. 'I don't mind what we do.'

'A submissive *and* beautiful woman… My cup run-
neth over,' Hawk drawled mockingly.

Later that evening, after they had dined at the elegant
and luxurious hotel where Hawk had reserved rooms—
'Two singles,' he had emphasised sadly as they had
sipped their pre-dinner cocktails. 'Now, I deserve some
credit for that at least, Joanne—' He suggested a walk
in the beautifully landscaped gardens that were lit as
brightly as day with hundreds upon hundreds of tiny
swinging lanterns.

She stared at him warily. From what she had seen of
the gardens earlier that evening as they had watched a
sunset that was all vermilion, glowing mauve and deepest rose-gold, they were the epitome of a romantic stroll
for two—complete with hidden bowers, tiny fountains
and the inevitable love-seats dotted about the most intimate corners.

'I don't know…' The mellow, incomparable wines of
the region, two of which she had imbibed pretty freely
at dinner, were not conducive to good control.

'Well, I do.' He solved her dilemma by taking her
hand and drawing her up from her seat, and again she
found herself relishing the power, the authority, the sheer
masculinity in his lean, strong frame, which had drawn
the eyes of more than one predatory female during their
meal.

And she knew what most of them were thinking. Why,
why, is he with her? But he was, and it was her he had
asked to walk with him…

This intoxicating thought carried her out into the gardens in something of a smug daze, but as the cool night air stroked her face, its warning caress carrying the scent of starry, frost-touched nights, cold reason asserted itself.

Her mother had been the sort of woman who had allowed men to use her, time after time after time, and then walk away when they had had enough. She didn't know if her mother had loved these men—she had certainly felt more for them than she had her own flesh and blood, that was for sure—but there had been something, some elemental driving desire to be loved, that had proved weakening and dangerous. Could those sorts of things be passed on in the genes?

As Hawk tucked one of her arms in his, the strength and bulk and smell of him overwhelmingly intoxicating, her mind raced on.

She *knew* he couldn't—or wouldn't—accept the concept of a monogamous lifestyle, that he didn't want to even try. She was a passing whim with him, perhaps a challenge that had stirred his jaded appetite for a while, added to which her usefulness at Bergique & Son couldn't be ignored. In fact—and here her mind balked a little as she made herself face the truth—he was a loner, a man who answered to no one, kept his own counsel and liked it that way. He would never settle down, he just wasn't the type, and that was exactly—*exactly*—the sort of man her mother had been inexplicably drawn to, despite all rhyme and reason, in the same way a moth was drawn to the bright light that would ultimately spell its destruction.

'What are you thinking about?'

His voice was soft and deep, and its very gentleness made her speak before she considered her words. 'My mother, actually,' she said quietly.

'Do you miss her?' There was no shred of surprise in

the calm voice, although it couldn't have been the answer he was expecting.

'Not in the way you mean; she wasn't that sort of
mother,' Joanne said with painful honesty.

They had walked into a part of the garden that was
almost Victorian in its layout, very sheltered and pretty,
and now, as he drew her down on to a lacy wooden seat,
it felt as though they were the only two people alive in
all the world. The night was breathtakingly still, not a
sound from the hotel in the distance disturbing the tranquillity, and when Hawk said, 'Tell me about her, about
you, about your childhood,' the strange, almost dream-
like quality of the night loosened her tongue.

He was a good listener—too good—and when she fell
quiet, some twenty minutes later, it was with the realisation she had said far more than she intended.

'I'm sorry, Joanne.' And he was, and also murder-
ously angry with the woman who had borne her and then
cast her aside at such a young, vulnerable age. The anger
he was trying to hide made his voice grim, hard even,
and she cast a quick troubled glance at him before looking straight ahead again.

'It's all right,' she said stiffly. He was annoyed with
her for going on the way she had, she thought wildly.
She shouldn't have said all that—she couldn't believe
she had; he had probably just wanted a few light facts
about her early life, not an in-depth year-by-year account. He must think she was pathetic—

'No, no, it isn't,' he said flatly, still in the same forbidding voice. 'Every child should know it's loved and
wanted.'

'Were you?' She wouldn't have dared to ask normally, but here it seemed right, and she wanted to turn
the conversation from her.

'Loved and wanted? Very much,' he said quietly. 'My
mother…my mother was the sort of person who lived to

make others happy, and her whole life revolved around my father and me, and her friends. You could say she was her own worst enemy.'

'By loving her family?' Joanne protested.

'By caring too much—for my father at least.' He raked a hand through his short black hair. 'She never revealed, by one word or action, the misery he inflicted upon her. She simply fought through every day of her life trying to make things right that could never be right. I can't accept that sort of emotion can be called love—it is obsession, the most damaging sort of obsession.'

'You're saying that simply because you can't handle the fact that love exists,' Joanne said quietly. 'Perhaps she considered that the good times she had with him were worth all the pain and anguish.'

'Then she was a fool.' The words were dragged out of the depths of him, his voice harsh and jagged. 'Just as your mother was a fool. And I still think that what my mother felt for my father, and your mother felt for her husbands and lovers, was obsession, not love. I can't accept—' He stopped abruptly, a muscle clenching at the side of his jaw, before he said, 'What the hell? None of it matters in the long run.'

'Hawk—'

'I'll show you what's real one day, Joanne.' His voice was savage and cold, and made his following words all the more chilling. 'I'll make love to you until nothing and no one exists, until the earth melts away and all you can see and hear and touch is me. I shall kiss every inch of your body, see you mindless beneath me, begging for what only I can give you. And you'll want me—you'll want me so badly you'll be on fire—but we'll both know exactly what we are doing.'

'And it won't mean anything?' she asked faintly, caught up in his blackness.

'Of course it will mean something.' He caught her

face in his hands, his eyes urgent now and the terrible anger fading. 'It will mean one hell of a lot but we won't be fooling ourselves, don't you see? You are a casualty of your mother's obsession with this fantasy called love—'

'No, I don't want to hear this.' She jerked away from him, her voice shaking. This was all wrong; he had twisted everything to make it all wrong but she couldn't find the words to tell him...

'Shh. Shh, now.' Suddenly he was tender, frighteningly tender, folding her into his big hard frame and holding her close to his heart for a long moment, before lowering his head and taking her trembling mouth in a kiss that was pure enchantment. 'So fierce and so brave, so beautiful...' His voice was a soft caress against her lips and she couldn't fight it—or him.

One moment he was fire and brimstone, the next fiercely tender, and the effect was hypnotic. She didn't understand him—she didn't have a clue what went on in that ruthless male mind, and perhaps it didn't matter anyway, so long as he didn't guess the state of her true feelings towards him. Because one day soon his desire for her would wane, when someone else more suitable caught his fancy, and that would be that. He would give up the chase, retire gracefully, and no doubt allow the new lady the pleasure of licking his wounds.

He explored her mouth slowly, taking his time, and her bones dissolved into a warm, aching throb before he raised his head again.

'You're still holding me to that promise?' His voice was dry, very dry, and she just knew he knew she wanted to say no.

She nodded. The tumult of sensuous pleasure his lips had induced was not conducive to clear speech, and she didn't intend to give him the satisfaction of hearing her shaky whisper.

'Pity.' He bent and kissed the tip of her nose before pulling her to her feet. 'Great pity...' he drawled easily, his mouth drawn to hers again in a searching, lingering kiss that sent waves of pleasure right down to her toes, before he lifted his head and slipped an arm round her waist as they began to walk down the secluded little path again.

He could kiss, he could *really*, *really* kiss, she thought fretfully, desperately hoping her trembling hadn't been noticed by that wicked narrowed gaze. But then, he'd had plenty of practice, hadn't he? It was easy for him to remain controlled, cold even.

And why, *why* had she told him all that about her childhood, let him in like that, when she knew he wasn't really interested and would view it exactly as he had, with barely concealed contempt?

'Is that the first time you've shared with anyone about your mother?' The deep gravelly voice was quite expressionless, and, tucked into his side as she was, she couldn't see the look on his face to gauge how best to reply, and simply decided to go for the truth.

'Yes.' She paused a moment before continuing quickly, 'It simply hasn't cropped up before—'

'Now don't spoil it with a lie.'

'How dare you—?'

'I'm honoured you trusted me enough to tell me, Joanne.' He stopped, moving her round to face him as he held her within the circle of his arms, his face deadly serious and stopping all coherent thought in her head. 'I'm glad she's not around any more because I would have had a hard job to keep my hands off her, but...I'm glad you told me.'

No, don't; don't do this to me. She stared up at him, her honey-brown eyes wide and swimming with emotion. The fire and brimstone she could cope with, the ardent lover...possibly—certainly the ruthless, hard businessman was a cinch—but this tender, quiet side of him that she had seen over the last twenty-four hours was something else. Something…devastating.

'Come on.' He moved them on again, and now there was a wry quirk at the corner of the hard, firm mouth. 'Keep moving, my nervous little fawn, because when you look at me like that I'm very tempted to do something I've never done before in my life.'

'What?' she asked nervously.

'Break a promise.'

Joanne awoke the next morning with her heart singing and her pulse racing at the thought of another whole day with Hawk. She gave herself a stern talking-to in the shower, and again when she was drying her hair and getting dressed in black leggings, high black boots and a long baggy cream jumper, but the singing remained.

She loved him. Utterly, completely—against all the odds and every grain of common sense, she loved him. And she was going to take this last day of the magical weekend—which would probably never be repeated— and *enjoy* it.

They left Dijon after breakfast to travel southwards towards the time-mellowed villages of Provence, the delightful contrasts of southern France adding to the enchantment of the day. Hawk made for Cassis, a picturesque fishing village on the coast, where they enjoyed a delicious alfresco lunch of freshly caught crab sitting on the verandah of a seafood restaurant, with the weak November sun warming their heads while they ate.

The afternoon was spent strolling round the capital of Provence, Aix-en-Provence, and visiting the fine cathedral, although Joanne noticed very little beyond the tall, dark man at her side. She was falling more and more in love with him—she couldn't help it—and it scared her half to death, making the time bittersweet.

It was late afternoon and they were walking along a road bordering a gracious square, when Joanne noticed two small children with their noses pressed against a shop window, watching a clockwork Santa Claus filling his sledge with toys. The laughing little tots were enraptured, their mother standing indulgently to one side as she smiled at their rosy faces, and as they passed she nodded at them and they nodded back, although Joanne felt her face had frozen.

'What is it?'

She hadn't thought Hawk had noticed, and now she tried to prevaricate as she said, her voice bright, 'I'm sorry?'

'Something in that little scene back there upset you. Why?' He stopped dead, turning her round to face him and looking down into her eyes, his gaze piercingly intent as he repeated, 'Why, Joanne?'

'I don't know what you mean.' *Enough.* Enough soul-baring for one weekend, she thought desperately as she stared back up at him, so big and dark and handsome in his black leather jacket and black jeans. Tomorrow morning, or the next day, he would be gone—probably for weeks, maybe for months—and she wanted to get through this weekend with nothing but pleasant memories to look back on.

Whenever they parted, whatever the circumstances, she was always left feeling vulnerable and broken, and she didn't want that this time. She had to master this overwhelming longing to draw close to him, to lower her defences and let him in, because it wouldn't mean to Hawk what it meant to her. He didn't *understand* what this exposure of her innermost self was costing her.

'Yes, you do.' He wasn't going to let it go; she could read his determination in the set of his mouth and narrowing of his eyes. 'Was it the children? Was that it? Or—'

'No, it wasn't the children,' she said quietly, horrified at the possibility he might think she was neurotic about children and families after her revelations the night before. 'They were sweet and their mother looked nice.'

'What, then?' he persisted softly. 'Tell me; I want to know.'

'I just don't like Christmas, that's all.'

She made to walk on but he caught her arm as she moved out of the circle of his arms, swinging her back to face him, his brow furrowed with enquiry. 'When I say tell me, I mean *tell* me,' he said firmly. 'That wasn't an answer. Explain.'

'Hawk, I'm sorry, I don't mean to be rude, but why should I?' she said tightly, trying to hide the panic his insistence was causing. 'If I don't like Christmas it's no big deal, is it? Lots of people the world over find it one big headache—it's so commercial.'

'You're not lots of people,' he said softly. 'You're thatched country cottages with roses round the door and big fat tabby cats, you're roasting chestnuts and log fires, you're snowmen, and frosted spider webs and a hundred and one other things I could think of, so...' He paused, his eyes blue light. 'Why don't you like Christmas, Joanne? And don't give me the ''commercial'' garbage either.'

She stared at him helplessly, suddenly overwhelmed by the most awful feeling that she wanted to cry. She couldn't, she *couldn't*, she told herself fiercely. It would embarrass them both and there was no logical reason for it anyway; just because he'd said something nice... If it *was* nice—perhaps he meant she was predictable and boring? But he hadn't said it that way...

'Well?'

His voice was very gentle, and to combat the emotion that was causing a physical pain in her chest her own was almost harsh as she said, 'Christmas was always a difficult time when I was a child, that's all. The home…the home did its best, but it wasn't like family.'

From the age of nine, after her mother's disastrous second marriage had ended so abruptly, she had resided permanently in the children's Home with no more placements with foster parents, and it had been then that the full significance of her isolation had washed over her.

She had been dispatched back just two weeks before Christmas, confused and heartbroken at her mother's rage towards her, and had cried herself to sleep for the next few nights, longing for even a glimpse of her mother's face.

And then Christmas Eve had come, its mystery and wonder taking hold of her even through the turmoil and pain, and she had been sure, so sure, her mother would visit her. Why she had been so adamant she didn't know, even now, but only her mother could make everything all right, and how could she not come at Christmas? And so she had waited, and waited… And the long day had eventually drawn to a close, and still she had sat at one of the windows looking out into the snow-filled darkness, until one of the home's helpers had persuaded her to go to bed. It had been March before she saw her mother again…

'Don't look like that.' His voice was strained, and it brought her out of the black reverie with a peculiar little jolt, her eyes focusing on his face instead of the small, lost child in her mind.

'Like what?' she asked shakily, her face very pale.

'Crushed, defeated,' he said with a painful grimness. 'We will forget this conversation; I will not allow it to spoil what little we have left of the weekend.'

The tone of his voice stunned her even as she found it impossible to determine exactly how he was feeling, and the next moment he had swept her along the street, his arm about her waist, as they made for the car.

'We are going to have a wonderful meal—I know the very place—and then I am going to fly you back to your apartment in time for you to be tucked up with your cocoa and hot-water bottle before midnight.'

His voice was mocking and light, but as her feet were hardly touching the floor it was some moments before she could gasp, 'Fly? In the air, you mean?'

'Is there another way?'

'But how?' They reached the car and she leant against the smooth bonnet as she repeated, 'How, Hawk? I mean—'

'A friend of mine has a private airfield near here, and I told him we'd be along this evening,' Hawk said calmly, as though he were suggesting they call by and have coffee with someone. 'I do have a pilot's licence if that's what's worrying you.' He raised his eyebrows sardonically, thoroughly enjoying her open-mouthed surprise.

'But what about the car?' she asked weakly.

'It will be collected.'

How the other half lived. She stared at him with wide eyes, not sure of what to think. He clicked his fingers and the world snapped smartly to attention, doffing its cap as it did so. How could she imagine, even in her wildest dreams—and there had been a few of those since she had fallen in love with Hawk—that she could ever mean anything more to him than a passing pleasure?

As he opened the car door she slid inside with a careful smile, even as the pain in her heart caught her breath. The weekend was over. Reality was back.

CHAPTER EIGHT

DURING the next few weeks Joanne worked very hard, even harder than she had done before Hawk's flying visit. She arrived at the office long before the rest of the staff and was still there for hours after they had vanished into the chill of the winter evenings, often leaving well after nine o'clock when the nights were cold and dark and the moon sailed brightly in a lonely sky.

She welcomed the hard, grinding slog; it was a very necessary opiate against the agony of soul that gripped her if she allowed herself to think of Hawk—in fact she didn't think she could have got through those few weeks leading up to Christmas without it.

He had dropped her at her apartment on the Sunday evening of their weekend together with nothing more adventurous than a brief, but passionate, embrace, and a long, lingering kiss that had brought fire to her cheeks and pain to her heart.

The next morning at the office he had very definitely stepped into business mode, his manner cool and remote and the ruthless side of him to the fore as he had caused a miniature whirlwind of panic and confusion among the rest of the staff, who had spent the day running hither and thither in ever decreasing circles.

Everyone—including Joanne—had breathed a deep sigh of relief when he had flown back to England that same night, although the next day the office had seemed strangely dull and empty, and the hours endless. His phone calls since then had been spasmodic and often terse, and in the last few days approaching the holiday period her heart had finally accepted what her head had been trying to tell her for weeks—the celibate weekend had convinced him to leave her alone. And instead of the relief that would have been logical in the circumstances there was only a deep, dark, consuming blackness that ate away at her appetite, her sleep, everything that made up life.

She had to get the victory over this. As the taxi-cab whisked her home that night, three days before Christmas, Joanne looked at her wan reflection in the window and sighed heavily. She had enough on her plate as it was—the more she delved into the workings of Bergique & Son, the more she discovered just what a crook Pierre Bergique was and how many dubious deals he'd had going for him—and she just couldn't afford to be distracted by any sort of personal life.

Personal life? The phrase mocked her. Some personal life she had—on a par with the average nun, although if she had to put them side by side the nun would have her vote.

She sighed again, the icy drizzle outside the warmth of the cab clothing everything in a grey gloom that perfectly matched her mood. She wished she'd never stepped foot in France and taken on the daunting task of turning Bergique & Son round, she wished she'd followed her instinct and branched out into pastures new, without any threads from the past still clinging on to her; but most of all, *most of all*, she wished she'd never heard of Hawk Mallen.

She paid the driver and walked into the house with her head down and her mind a million miles away, and as she bumped into someone in the hall she was just going to apologise when her eyes met the piercing blue gaze that had haunted her for weeks.

'What time do you call this?' He sounded angry and irritated, and from one blinding moment of wild delight she plummeted into raw pain and hurt that he could care so little when she cared so much.

'Nearly ten o'clock,' she said crisply. 'What time do you call it?'

'Too damn late, that's what.' He glared at her, the sapphire eyes as cold as glass. 'I've got better things to do than sit here twiddling my thumbs while you gad about on a date.'

'A date?' Her senses were registering he looked gorgeous, totally drop-dead gorgeous, her fingers were itching to give him a good slap. 'What on earth are you talking about?'

'I'm talking about the reason you are so late home,' he said icily. 'Your hours are nine to four forty-five, and it is now—'

'I know what the darn time is,' she hissed furiously, longing to scream at him but knowing it would fetch Madame Lemoine out of her burrow like a bullet out of a gun. 'And not that it's any of your business, but I've been working, *working*, like I have done every other night I've been in this damn country. How do you think I've been getting the sort of results I have if I'd limited myself to a nine-to-five mentality? Answer me that! Or do you think I'm one of those females that sits about chatting on the phone all day and painting her toenails—?'

'Don't you mean fingernails?' he interjected with sudden and suspicious meekness.

'Fingernails, toenails—the thought's the same,' she bit back angrily. 'Besides which you've got no right to object one way or the other. You didn't tell me you were visiting France—'

'I had a fax sent this morning.'

'Well, I didn't receive it,' Joanne snapped tightly, 'and even if I had, and I'd made previous arrangements of some sort or other, I wouldn't have changed them.

You own my work time, Hawk, not the rest of me, so let's get that quite clear.'

'Clear it is.' The coldness had evaporated like the morning mist and pure Mallen charm had taken its place. 'Have you eaten?'

'Eaten?' The sudden switch in mood and conversation had lost her.

'Because if not I would suggest you do so and then get an early night. We're flying to the States tomorrow morning, and no doubt you'll want to be up with the lark.'

She nearly said, The States? in the same tone of voice she'd said, 'Eaten?' and stopped herself just in time, taking a deep calming breath before she spoke with a quietness she was proud of considering the circumstances. 'I have no more intention of flying to America in the morning than I have of allowing you to dictate what time I go to bed,' she said firmly. 'I don't know why you're here or what's wrong, but you're not bullying me like you do everyone else, Hawk.'

'My grandfather is worse.' The blue eyes were steady as they held her honey-brown gaze and watched it widen with shock and concern. 'He's expressed a wish to see you.'

'Me?' She stared at him in astonishment.

'You are now in charge of his old friend's pride and joy, Joanne,' Hawk said quietly. 'I would have thought it only natural he wants to see you for himself.'

'Oh, I see.' She didn't, not really; in fact it seemed crazy to request her presence in America when Jed Mallen could have all the relevant facts and figures as to how she was doing in a few moments of time thanks to modern technology. 'But I can't leave tomorrow. I'm sorry, but I just can't. I've things to do, people to see—'

'I thought you said you weren't involved with anyone here,' he said softly, his voice cold again.

'Business people, Hawk.' She glared at him before remembering he must be worried sick about his grandfather, and, making a conscious effort to moderate her tone, she continued, 'There's the matter of Netta Productions for a start. I'm supposed to meet the son of the ex-managing director tomorrow and I need to hear what he wants to say; he's sure his father was bankrupted deliberately—'

'Delegate.'

If he was trying to wind her up he was certainly succeeding, Joanne thought tightly as she struggled to keep any irritation from showing. Delegate indeed! 'It's not as simple as that, as well you know,' she said flatly. 'Surely your grandfather wouldn't mind if I saw him at the end of the month?'

'And what will you do over Christmas—work?' he asked with a curious lack of expression. 'Is that the way you take care of your particular ghosts, Joanne—by pretending they don't exist? Well, I'm sorry, we're flying tomorrow, and the return ticket is for December the twenty-ninth.'

'You mean stay over Christmas?' she asked weakly. 'Is that what you mean?'

'That's what I mean, Joanne,' he drawled mockingly, temper and aplomb apparently quite restored. 'Bergique & Son won't grind to a halt because you leave the helm briefly. If there's one thing I've learnt in life it's that no one is indispensable, however much they like to imagine they are.'

'I don't imagine anything—'

'I do.' Suddenly his eyes were blue fire, hot and sensuous. 'Hell, you wouldn't believe what I imagine...' He pulled her into his arms almost roughly. 'You're in my head, do you know that? Locked in there, all long legs and creamy smooth skin... You drive me crazy.'

He bent his head and his mouth was hungry on hers,

so hungry it lit an immediate flame in the core of her. She didn't want to respond to him; it wasn't *fair* that he could move in and out of her life like this, taking her up and then dropping her at will, but she might as well have tried to stop the rhythm of the tides as withstand him.

'I've thought about you every moment,' he whispered against her lips. 'Shy, beautiful Joanne. What is it about you that I can't get out of my mind?'

She opened her mouth to answer, to tell him that he couldn't fool her with all his sweet talk, but he took the words before they were uttered, his lips and his tongue probing as he folded her more deeply into him, wrapping his big dark overcoat round her as he enclosed them in a blanket of warmth.

'Say you'll come with me, Joanne.' She was utterly captivated by the time he raised his head again, lost in the flowing river of sensation that had turned her fluid. 'I want to spend some time with you, to show you my home, my friends. Say you'll come?'

This was a planned assault, an orchestrated campaign to get what he wanted, but even as the warning flashed through her mind she knew she was going to say yes. It was the gentleness that had done it, the languorous tenderness he had displayed that was so very un-Hawk-like and consequently terribly seductive.

'Well?' His voice was husky and deep. 'You'll say yes?'

'Would it make any difference if I said no?' she asked shakily, that tiny instinct in the back of her mind forbidding the total capitulation she longed to give. 'Would you take any notice?'

'You know I wouldn't.' He smiled, a wry little smile that crinkled the corners of his eyes. 'But it would be good for my ego to have you there with me instead of fighting every inch of the way.'

'Your ego needs help?' she asked disbelievingly, pulling away an inch or two to look more closely into the devastatingly attractive face.

'Around you, yes.' She couldn't read anything in his deadpan expression, the mask he was so good at adopting suddenly very firmly in place. 'But I'm a big boy now; I can take it,' he added with mocking dryness, before turning and walking with her still held within the circle of one arm to the stairs. 'I'll see you to your door.'

'There's no need.' She was trembling but she couldn't help it. Here, in the hall, with the possibility of Madame Lemoine or the other flat-dwellers liable to appear at any moment, she had had some protection. But upstairs...

'Joanne, I've been waiting for over four hours to see you; I'm tired, I'm hungry, and I was cold...until I held you in my arms, that is,' he said with wry self-derision at his all too obvious arousal, the alien power of which she had felt as he had held her close. 'I'm going to see you to your door, and then leave you to your chaste little bed, okay? I'm bushed too.'

She couldn't answer so she just nodded, the confession that the great Hawk Mallen, the powerful and authoritative figure who had the world at his fingertips and a reputation for ruthlessness that was second to none, had been waiting for four hours in the hall of a little French house to see *her* rendering her dumb.

'Goodnight, little fawn.' They had stopped outside her front door and he cupped her face gently, his eyes piercingly blue as they looked into hers. 'Hell, you're lovely...' This time the kiss was fierce and burningly hot as he slipped his hands beneath her open coat and under the soft wool of her waist-length jumper, his fingers encircling the soft swell of her breasts and branding her skin with heat. She could feel him shaking as his tongue penetrated the sweetness of her mouth, his body rock-hard against hers, and his heart slamming against his chest like a sledgehammer.

Her love for him, stimulated by the need he couldn't hide, was sending her up in flames and she found she was breathing his name as she kissed him back with ever increasing passion, her head swimming and a wild clamouring in her senses that caused her to press deeper and deeper into the powerfully muscled body against hers.

'Damn it, Joanne, another minute and I shan't be able to stop.' His voice was a low growl of frustration and need, and as he unwound her arms from round his neck she saw his control was paper-thin. 'And that would really blot my copy-book, wouldn't it?' he stated with grim amusement. 'Your body might be willing but there's still that hesitation in your eyes that tells me you don't trust me yet.'

'It's important that I trust you?' she asked shakily. Trust him? She'd die for him.

'Strangely, yes.' He stood looking down at her, his face shadowed and dark and his big body taut and still. 'Yes, it is. Get some sleep, Joanne, and I'll see you in the morning.' His voice was suddenly cool, almost remote, and he had turned on his heel and begun to walk down the stairs before she could reply.

Los Angeles was everything Joanne had expected and more, but the shock of Hawk's sudden appearance, added to the long plane journey and electric tension that was gripping every nerve and sinew, rendered her almost deaf, dumb and blind on their arrival on the balmy West Coast. She was aware of the pleasant temperature—after the icy drizzle they had left behind in Paris the warm soft air that resembled a mild spring day in England was wonderfully relaxing—but little else registered on the drive from the airport to Hawk's home in Beverly Hills, the mental and physical exhaustion that had been steadily building for the last few weeks paramount.

Hawk seemed to understand perfectly, taking care of her in the same way he did everything else—calmly, firmly and with absolute authority, so that she was whisked effortlessly from pillar to post almost without being aware of it.

As they drew up outside Hawk's mansion, Joanne's impression of high, impenetrable walls—the perimeter surround being ten feet high—was overtaken by one of light and colour and life as they left the car and walked to the open door, where a pretty little maid was waiting for them.

The hall was vast and dominated by the biggest Christmas tree Joanne had ever seen, a vision of gold and red, with antique golden baubles, stars and ribbons, tiny flickering red candles and gold-berried ivy, all of which matched the deep red sofas scattered about the lushly carpeted expanse. Several piles of ravishing gifts were stacked under the tree, wrapped up in shiny gold paper and tied with green and pistachio ribbons.

'It's beautiful.' Joanne's voice was a soft murmur but Hawk heard it, and also recognised the dazed, vacant note as being indicative of near collapse.

'And it will still be here tomorrow,' he said quietly, 'along with the rest of the house. For now it's bed for you.'

'What?' Even in her tired state the word 'bed', when spoken by Hawk Mallen, was not to be ignored. She hadn't quite summoned up the nerve to ask him what the sleeping arrangements for this little holiday extravaganza would be, and she still couldn't find the words, but it didn't matter. He had read her mind. As always.

'I'm sorry, Joanne, but you can't get your itchy little fingers on my body tonight,' he said sardonically, with a cool disregard for the listening maid that brought mortifying colour flooding into Joanne's pale face. 'You'll have your own suite while you are my guest; kindly see that you stay in it without any midnight ramblings.'

'Hawk, that's not funny—'

'You're suffering from a combination of jet lag and overwork,' he continued as though she hadn't spoken. 'Tomorrow you have the morning in bed, okay? And Conchita will bring you a dinner tray once you've bathed and slipped into bed tonight.'

'I'm not a child,' she protested quickly.

'Tell me about it.' He gave a theatrically leering smile, his eyes laughing at her, and in spite of herself she smiled back. He was impossible. Quite, quite impossible, and she loved him so much it scared her to death.

Her suite was like something out of a Hollywood movie, and made the first apartment that Hawk had chosen in France seem positively modest.

'Conchita will run you a long hot bath.' Hawk signalled to the maid as he spoke, who immediately disappeared into the huge blue marble bathroom which boasted a bath that would easily have accommodated a team of rugby players. 'And while you're soaking she'll unpack your things and turn the bed down. Ring when you're ready for your meal; there's a bell-push over the bed.'

'Right…thank you.' She was too exhausted to hide the fact that she was completely overawed, her stance very much like that of a tired and nervous child as she stood just inside the luxurious blue sitting room after her quick tour of the suite, unconsciously nipping at her lower lip, her eyes shadowed with fatigue and apprehension.

'Come here.' His voice was very quiet, and as he beckoned her to him in the middle of the room she moved slowly to his side. 'It will all fall into place in the morning, Joanne,' he said softly. 'Trust me in that if nothing else.' His arms were comforting as he pulled her against his broad chest, but the deliciously male smell of him, added to the muscled power of the big body, brought the quivery feeling snaking through her limbs, and after he had kissed her—lightly, as though she were a kid sister or maiden aunt, she thought testily—she stood quite still in the middle of the room as he left, not trusting her legs.

She cried in the bath once she was alone. How could she even begin to compete with the beautiful, sophisticated women he was used to? she asked herself miserably, lying back in the warm, scented water with her eyes shut as hot tears burnt a path down her cheeks. They would take this house in their stride, revel in it, live up to it, whereas she... She had never felt so like a fish out of water in her life—the outsider looking in. Even the worst times in the home couldn't compare to the misery that was swamping her right now.

It wasn't as though he had *chosen* for her to come here even. His grandfather had wanted to meet her and so she had been brought over like...like a package, a parcel, she thought desperately. That was all she represented to him—a commodity, a useful piece of equipment, a loyal employee— *Oh, stop it! Enough!* The words were caustic in her head as she realised, even in her anguish, she was going too far.

He liked her, he was physically attracted to her—that much she was sure about, whether she was versed in the arts of love or not. He would be only too pleased to have an affair with her; he'd made that plain too. Yes, there was no doubt he was genuine in his desire for her—the trouble was he didn't desire or like her enough for it to be love. And, loving him as she did, that made the whole situation a very definite checkmate. And neither of them won.

She stayed in the bath until the water was tepid, her aching muscles slowly relaxing as the silky warmth did its job, and after washing her hair she climbed out slowly, surprised at how leaden her legs felt. It was all she could do to slip into her nightie and towel-dry her hair, and the thought of drying it with the hairdryer was beyond her, so she left it damp about her neck as she slid into bed and rang for Conchita to bring her meal. Not that she really wanted to eat...

Only it wasn't the little maid who came into the room after a polite knock.

'Hawk!' She shot down in the bed, embarrassingly aware of the transparency of the nightie, her lack of make-up, her scraggy hair... 'What are you doing?'

'Bringing your meal—what else?' He walked across to the bed with casual animal grace, looking even more devastating than usual in charcoal jeans and an ivory silk shirt that made his dark good looks more foreign. 'Sit up and eat it while it's hot,' he added easily.

'I... You... Put it on the bed.'

'Joanne, don't be tiresome.' He sounded irritated and she really couldn't blame him; he must think she was more like a naive schoolgirl than a grown woman, she thought miserably. She dared bet his other women would be only too pleased to display their wares in similar circumstances, but then no doubt they wouldn't be caught looking like drowned rats in off-the-peg nighties. She just hadn't expected *him* to bring the food.

'There are two glasses; I thought we'd share a bottle of champagne while you eat to celebrate the beginning of the Christmas holiday,' he said coolly, watching her with narrowed blue eyes as she struggled up in the vast bed, the sheet wrapped round the top of her like a shroud. 'Are you cold?' he added mildly.

'No... Yes... I'm all right.' This was getting worse by the second.

'I'm not going to leap on you and have my wicked way.' It was said so conversationally it didn't register for a moment, but when it did she blushed scarlet. 'Relax, Joanne; you're making us both nervous.' There was a touch of steel in the coolness now.

It was all right for him, she thought testily. There he was, groomed to perfection as normal, calm, self-assured, perfectly in control, whereas she... The thought opened her mouth before she had time to consider her words. 'I...I look such a mess,' she said painfully. 'I didn't expect you to come.'

'Is that what's wrong?' he asked, the surprise in his voice telling her he hadn't considered such a possibility. 'Joanne, Joanne, Joanne...' He sat down on the bed, placing the tray at his feet before reaching forward and cupping her face in the palms of his hands. 'Don't you realise how beautiful you are, even freshly scrubbed and looking about sixteen?' he asked softly, the tenor of his voice making her shiver.

Freshly scrubbed and looking about sixteen! She gazed at him in frustration. She didn't *want* to look freshly scrubbed, she wanted to look alluring, voluptuous, sexy—like the other women he was used to. She wanted to dazzle him with her wit and sophistication, drive him mad with desire. She wanted—she wanted the impossible.

He bent down and picked up the tray, placing it on her knees before taking the cover from the plate to reveal a light meal of fluffy ham omelette and salad and baby new potatoes.

She stared at it miserably. She shouldn't have come. *She shouldn't have come.*

'Here.' He placed a wine glass in her hand before opening the bottle of champagne he had taken off the tray, its joyous explosion totally at odds with how she was feeling inside. 'Eat, drink and be merry,' he said mockingly, looking intently at her woebegone face. 'You're only stuck with me for a few days, Joanne; it isn't the end of the world.'

'I...I'm very pleased to be here.'

'You look it.' His voice was dark, grim even, as he poured her a glass of the sparkling effervescent liquid, before rising to his feet.

'Aren't you having one?' she asked quickly.

'Joanne, I know the image you have of me is of a womanising blackguard who hasn't got a sensitive bone in his body, but even I have my limits,' he said evenly, his face a study in controlled neutrality. 'We'll take this evening as a washout and try again tomorrow, okay?'

'Hawk—'

'And don't make any excuses; I really couldn't take them tonight.'

He was gone before she could say anything more.

CHAPTER NINE

'So you're the Joanne Crawford I've been hearing so much about?'

It wasn't quite the opening line Joanne had imagined, and she found herself staring at Jed Mallen for a few moments before she collected herself and took the hand he was holding out for her to shake.

'Good afternoon, Mr Mallen,' she said politely, her heart beating a tattoo that was mercifully hidden from the bright blue eyes so like his grandson's, the direct, intent gaze seeming as though it wanted to get inside her head. 'I'm very pleased to meet you.'

'Likewise.' He had risen at her approach into the room, but now sat down again, saying almost irritably, 'Sit down, sit down, young woman; don't stand on ceremony.'

'Thank you.' She did as he bid but was unable to stop the colour from flooding into her cheeks. She hadn't known what to expect on meeting Hawk's grandfather— probably a bent old man who was showing the ravages of the illness he was battling against, if she had thought about it at all—but Jed Mallen was still tall and upright, virile almost, with a shock of springy white hair above a face that was handsome in spite of the lines of pain radiating from the piercingly clear blue eyes. She could see how this man had carved an empire for himself despite all the odds against him; Hawk was definitely a chip off the old block.

'Are you too warm?' Jed Mallen indicated the huge roaring log fire that was crackling in the fireplace of the beautiful, but very masculine, drawing room she had been shown into. 'The treatment I've been undergoing makes me susceptible to the cold, I'm afraid.'

'No, I'm not too warm, Mr Mallen; I'm afraid I'm one of those people who can never be too warm,' Joanne said quickly.

'Hmm, I can see why.' The laser-like eyes burnt up and down for a moment. 'You're too thin—or "slim", as it's supposed to be called these days. You don't live on lettuce leaves and carrots, do you?' he added caustically.

'No, I don't.' Joanne's hackles had risen and she answered smartly and with a marked lack of the ceremony he had spoken of earlier, her face stiffening tightly.

'And it's none of my damned business anyway.' He finished what she had left unsaid with a wry smile that was identical to Hawk's. 'Do you know, I think we'll get along just fine, Miss...? Can I call you Joanne?' he asked abruptly.

'Yes, of course,' she answered a little weakly.

'Thank you.' He sat back in the large winged leather armchair as he said, 'And my name is Jed, but of course you know that. Hawk isn't with you, is he?'

'No, there was an emergency in the San Francisco office this morning—'

'Yes, yes, I know; I arranged it,' he said briskly, with the touch of brusqueness she suspected was habitual with him, and then, as he caught sight of her look of surprise, added, 'You don't approve? He'll be back tonight, never fear—he is used to taking a plane here and there at a moment's notice—but I wanted to meet you for the first time without him around. Did you have a good flight?'

It was as though he had suddenly remembered his manners, and Joanne had to hide a smile as she replied, 'Very good, thank you.'

'Do you like my grandson, Joanne?'

'What?' She forgot this was the head of the Mallen

empire, a powerful, ruthless and, if half the stories about him were true, cruel multi-millionaire, and reared up in her seat as though she had been stung. What on earth had her liking Hawk to do with anything? she asked herself angrily. She was here as the manageress of Bergique & Son, wasn't she? And if he was doubting her ability to do the job—if he thought she had been sleeping with his grandson in order to get the position—

'I said, do you like my grandson?' The tone was flat, expressionless, and his face was perfect for playing poker. 'A simple yes or no will suffice.'

She stared into the hard, handsome face for a moment, the crackling of the fire, the subdued glow from the discreet lighting in the huge, sombre room, the absolute quiet beyond the walls all adding to the unreality of the moment. 'Yes, Mr Mallen, I like your grandson,' she answered quietly, in a tone as flat and even as he had used. 'He is a very fair employer.'

The formidably intelligent gaze roamed over her for a full minute—during which time she sat still and stiff with dignity—before he smiled, nodding to himself as he said, 'Yes, I understand now. You *are* different.'

'Different?' This extraordinary conversation was fast leaving the realms of reason. 'I'm sorry, Mr Mallen, but I don't understand—'

'Jed, my dear.' He adjusted his position in the chair, and she noticed the wince of pain he tried to hide with a rush of guilt and compassion. This was Hawk's grandfather and he was dying; she really shouldn't have got on her high horse—

'Would you take afternoon tea with me, Joanne?' He interrupted her racing thoughts quietly, not betraying by word or gesture that he had accurately read her thoughts. So she had compassion and tenderness, as well as guts, beauty and intelligence, did she? But of course she would have; he should have known...

'Thank you; that would be very nice.' Her earlier thoughts made her voice soft. 'Would you like me to show you some facts and figures I've brought with me?' She indicated the briefcase at her feet. 'And I've some financial statements—'

'Not necessary.' He waved the offer aside with the faintly irritable gesture she was beginning to recognise. 'Now I've met you I am quite happy to leave all that in your very capable hands.'

'But I thought—'

'Have tea with me, my dear.' He smiled, a real smile this time, which again was so like Hawk's rarely used but devastating smile that she found her breath catching in her throat. 'And we'll just chat, like two old friends, eh? I have little time for chatting these days, Joanne, and I am finding I want it more and more. You think that perverse?'

'No.' Now Joanne did smile. The old devil could use the Mallen charm when he cared to—he was even more like his grandson than she had first supposed.

'Ah, you think me manipulative.' The white head nodded at her. 'Don't bother to deny it; your face is very expressive. But you are right as it happens, although I am arrogant enough to view that particular facet of my character as an attribute rather than a shortcoming.' Now the smile was a grin, and Joanne actually laughed out loud at the somewhat wicked glee in the distinguished face.

She liked him. She hadn't expected to, not for a minute, but she liked this formidable, irascible old man very much, even as she understood how he had come to be so feared and held in awe by his contemporaries.

It was at the end of the afternoon she spent with Hawk's grandfather, after he had taken her on a slow tour of his fifteen-bedroomed mansion and they had had tea in the sumptuous and stylish drawing room, that he mentioned Hawk again.

'My grandson is wealthy and powerful and often pursued by predatory women; you are aware of this, Joanne?' he asked mildly, straight after a conversation spent discussing his fine antiques. 'Some of them have a mind of sorts, others are nothing more than empty-headed dolls, but they all have one thing in common—a desire to be seen with, and bedded by, Hawk Mallen. You are not like that. You are aware Hawk wants you?'

She had learnt enough during the afternoon about this amazing old man not to duck the question, but her cheeks were pink as she replied, 'Yes, I know he wants me.'

'But you don't want him?

He wasn't hostile, but Joanne still had to take a deep breath before she said, 'I...I don't think just wanting is necessarily enough, not without—without...'

'Yes?' He had moved forward in his chair, and now his voice was quiet and his eyes steady as he said, 'You can be honest with me, my dear, and you can also rest assured our conversation will go no further than these four walls. I will respect your confidence. What more is there beyond wanting?'

'Love,' Joanne murmured quietly, hot with embarrassment.

'Love. A small word but a big concept.' He leant back again, sighing deeply. 'I have loved two people in the whole of my life, Joanne; do you find that hard to believe?'

'No.'

She raised soft honey-brown eyes to his and he nodded slowly as he said, 'No, of course you don't; you have been hurt too.'

She waited, not knowing what to say, and after a minute had ticked by he said, 'I had an unhappy childhood, Joanne. I will not bother you with the details but suffice to say I did not love my parents. I met my wife when I was a nobody and she was a great lady, and we both knew instantly we were destined to be together. Her parents were horrified at the notion, obviously...' His voice was not bitter, merely matter-of-fact.

'She waited for me as I knew she would, and our marriage produced my son, Hawk's father, and took her life. I have often asked myself if my rage and bitterness at losing her so soon affected my relationship with my son, but I truly don't think so. I simply didn't like him. He was very like my own father in nature—cold, shallow, selfish—whereas Hawk's mother was a sweet girl, too sweet in retrospect. She allowed my son to get away with far too much.'

He paused, shifting his position in the chair again before he continued, 'I love my grandson, Joanne. I love him very much and I do not consider that emotion a weakness.'

'Hawk does.' She spoke before she could help herself, all her anguish and pain in the two words.

Jed looked at her for a few moments without speaking and then rose stiffly from the chair, standing with his back to her as he gazed into the leaping flames of the fire. 'I'm going to tell you a modern-day tale,' he said softly, 'a black fairy story if you like, and then it is up to you what you do with it.'

She said nothing, sensing that whatever he was about to do he wasn't doing lightly.

'Once upon a time a baby boy was born to a couple who appeared to have everything. There were no more children, so when the couple die in an accident, when the boy is a man, he has no siblings to stand with him in his grief. His sorrow at this time is not normal, because he has learnt things about his parents, dark, hidden things—things that have rocked his very foundations. Their death increases his already considerable wealth substantially, taking him into the super bracket and attracting women of the more…avaricious type. But he is not a fool, this man; he has lived with riches all his life and he knows their drawing power. However, one female comes along who is more clever than the rest, more…cunning. You follow me so far?' he asked quietly.

'Yes.' Her heart was thudding so hard it was echoing in her throat.

'He falls for her—lock, stock and barrel, as you English say. He needs someone at this time, someone who is wholly his, someone to take away the pain and uncertainty that came with the shock of his parents' untimely death and the subsequent revelations that were even more of a shock. And she knows this—oh, yes, she knows it all right—and she plays him like a virtuoso in the art of love—which indeed she is.'

She couldn't bear to hear it and yet she needed to hear it all; it explained so much.

'He asks her to marry him and she accepts—prettily, of course—and the invitations are sent, the presents begin arriving. And then he visits his best man one afternoon with some details about the wedding arrangements—he has known this friend since boyhood and he is more like a brother—and what does he find but his fiancée and friend flagrante delicto, in fact in the very act of copulation.'

Jed turned to face her then, the sapphire-blue eyes that he had passed on to his grandson blazing with rage in spite of it all being so long ago.

'The ultimate triangle—perhaps even funny if it wasn't so tragic. But worse is to come. Once word gets around about the broken engagement—and word gets around very fast in the sort of high-society circles this man moves in—several of his close friends are brave enough to tell him what they feared to say before—that it is not the first time this lady has been embroiled in a scandal. She has been involved with married men, had many lovers, both before and since knowing this man. It is not something a proud young man of twenty years of age wants to hear.'

'And…and this man—what does he do?' Joanne asked numbly.

'I think you know,' Jed said quietly. 'He becomes disillusioned, cynical, he takes the world by the throat and plays the game by his own rules, and in the process hardens and becomes cold, very much…very much like his grandfather,' he finished softly. 'But there is still the need to love and be loved there, hidden deep in the secret recesses of his heart, buried where no one can see it.'

'You believe that?' Joanne asked with painful directness.

'Don't you?'

'I…I think Hawk wants me because I am unattainable.' Joanne shifted restlessly in her seat. 'You have said yourself he is chased by some of the most beautiful women in the world—successful, rich women, women who are used to his lifestyle and enjoy it. Perhaps he just wants the thrill of the chase for once, to pursue rather than be pursued?'

'The man I was telling you about, the man in the story, is not a fool,' Jed said slowly. 'Perhaps when the one perfect jewel comes along he will recognise it for what it is.'

Joanne stared hard at the handsome face in front of her. Was he really saying he thought she was the right partner for his grandson, or was this incredible conversation a subtle suggestion to the contrary? If she was this 'jewel', Hawk certainly hadn't acknowledged it in

the months she had known him and Jed Mallen must
know that. Oh, she didn't know what to think, how to
feel. She had enough problems struggling to keep her
head above water with one cold, hard, enigmatic man,
without taking on his grandfather too!

'I have enjoyed this afternoon immensely, but I must
be going.' She stood up as she spoke and was going to
hold out her hand for a formal farewell, but something
in Jed's face—a fleeting sadness, a loneliness too deep
and real for words—prompted her to lean forward on
tiptoe and kiss his cheek. 'Thank you for sharing
the...the story with me,' she said softly.

'Think about it,' he countered quietly. 'Please?'

'Yes, I will.'

She thought about nothing else as Jed's chauffeur
drove her back to Hawk's home, but was left with nothing more concrete than a string of impossible questions.

Could anyone break through the ice that encased
Hawk's heart? And if they did, would he want them for
a lifetime, or just for a short while, until he became
bored and restless? Could any female handle Hawk now
that he had become so cynical and cold? She didn't feel
she could, even if he wanted her for more than a brief
fling. She didn't have a stable background to draw from,
a well of family, or even worldly, knowledge. She
wasn't clever or cosmopolitan or wealthy; she was
just...herself. And it wouldn't be enough, *wasn't*
enough.

By the time the long, luxurious limousine glided to a
halt in front of Hawk's mansion she had faced reality.
Dreams were one thing, real life quite another. She was
torturing herself to no avail. She was just a passing whim
to Hawk, a momentary obsession as he would term it,
someone to have fun with as long as the mutual attrac-

tion lasted. And she couldn't be like that. She loved him far, far too much.

The next few days were a subtle combination of wild, fervent moments of happiness, grinding pain, poignant self-analysis and intensely fierce grief for what might have been. Hawk set out to make every minute of her Christmas memorable, and the fact that he succeeded only too well merely added to her turmoil until she began to wonder if she was becoming schizophrenic, especially as Hawk, after that first night, had become the perfect host—charming, attentive, courteous, amusing, and all the time remaining at a very controlled distance.

He had thrown a party for her on Christmas Eve which had begun with carol singers dressed in Victorian clothes and holding lanterns, and had finished, as the clock had chimed midnight, with warm glasses of mulled wine and hot mince pies.

On Christmas morning she had woken to a little Santa sack of presents at the end of her bed—she had no idea what time of the night he had placed it there—and he had come to sit on her bed with her and open the gifts, all the time being warm and friendly...and constrained. He had kissed her and wished her a happy Christmas, but it had been the kiss of a brother and made her want to scream.

They had spent the day with Jed, and Joanne had worn the ruby pendant and matching bracelet Hawk had given her—which must have cost a small fortune—and all the time she had been waiting for one sign, one word, to show she was something more than just— Just *what*? she had asked herself that night in bed. What was she? She wasn't a girlfriend, she wasn't a lover, she wasn't even a straightforward house guest. Jed had asked to see her and she had been brought for the audience with his grandfather post-haste. She'd cried herself to sleep.

It was on the afternoon of her last day in America,

when Hawk was driving her home after a day spent with some old—and, Joanne had discovered to her surprise, very normal and amusing—friends, and the sky was a river of purple and gold and scarlet, that things came to a head.

'Isn't it beautiful?' He had stopped the car on the top of a hill where the outlines of bare trees were silhouetted against the magnificent, colour-drenched sky, and it felt as if they were the only two people in the whole of the world. 'I often come here about this time of night when I'm home just to look at the sunset.'

'Do you?' She had seen this side of him more and more over the last few days—the softer, more vulnerable, gentle side of him. She had discovered he was a man who wasn't afraid to admit an appreciation of scenery and art, who could get on all fours and play with his friends' children like a five-year-old, who loved animals and was tender with anything weak and defenceless. She would rather not have discovered it—it didn't help her love to die—and die it had to.

'My mother used to come here too,' he continued quietly. 'She used to make the excuse she was exercising the dog, but after she died—' He stopped abruptly, taking a deep breath before he said, 'After she died, I understood why she needed to escape sometimes.'

'What happened to the dog?' It was an inane question, she realised immediately after she had said it, but the look on his face was breaking her heart.

'Bertie? He died shortly after my mother was killed.' Hawk turned from the windscreen to look at her then, his blue eyes silver in the twilight. 'He was an old dog; my mother had bought him when I started school—for company, I guess—and once she had gone he just sort of gave up. He adored her.'

'She must have been a lovely lady,' Joanne said softly.

'Yes, she was.' He flexed his long legs in the confines of the low, sleek sports car and turned fully to face her. 'Much like you.'

'Me?' Her breath caught in her throat before she reminded herself it didn't mean anything, not really.

'Yes, you,' he said huskily, his gaze sensuous. 'You—with your hair of fire and your big golden eyes; I want you more than I have ever wanted any other woman, Joanne—do you know that? And I have never trodden so warily, so carefully before.'

'You like the concept of the hunter after the prey?' she asked with painful directness.

'Prey?' The black brows beetled as he frowned. 'Is that how you see this? I don't think of you as a victim, Joanne, just the opposite in fact. I see you as a beautiful, desirable woman, but a woman who is more than able to hold her own in this crazy world we inhabit, and do it with integrity and courage too.'

Words, words, words, but what did they really mean? She stared at him, her face tense and unhappy. He was an enigma, this dark, cynical, cold man who had a drawing power so strong, so magnetic that it pole-axed lesser mortals, leaving them stunned and exposed.

'We would be good together, you know it, and I don't mean just the sex,' he said now, his handsome face shadowed and his hair blue-black. 'I want you with me, Joanne, *really* with me. I want to wake up in the morning and see you lying beside me, and know you'd be there in the evenings so we could discuss our days together. I want to eat with you, laugh with you, share the good times and the bad...'

'For...for how long?' she got out in a painful voice. This wasn't a proposal; she could see the darkness in those beautiful blue eyes that mirrored his soul.

'Does it matter how long?' he asked softly. 'Can't we take each day as it comes and be grateful for it, enjoy each other for as long as it lasts? I don't want to hurt you, Joanne. Trust me.'

'Hawk, I've told you before—'

'I'll look after you, Joanne,' he said evenly. 'You can be as independent as you want. I'll buy you a house, car, and set up an allowance for life that will make you financially secure and allow you to follow any path you choose.'

He didn't see. He really didn't see. She shut her eyes tightly for a moment, finding it was hurting too much to look at him. She didn't want to be independent or have an allowance or be wealthy for the rest of her life. She wanted *him*, she wanted a home they would share together, babies; she wanted—she wanted commitment, and she wanted it to be a willing commitment, because he loved her.

'Joanne?' She opened her eyes to see him watching her, his gaze tight on her face. 'You do care for me a little?'

She couldn't deny it but in the next moment, as his mouth swooped on hers, she realised she should have, because the second their lips touched sensation exploded between them like a raging fire, taking them both by surprise. His arms had closed round her fiercely, her own going round his neck as she pulled him even nearer, and as they strained together in the dim light from the setting sun the air inside the car was electric.

'You are mine; you know this; you cannot deny us both...' His lips were possessive as he murmured against the pure line of her throat before taking her mouth again in a kiss that was all fire and savage passion, and quite different from anything that had gone before.

She knew she had to resist the tide of thrilling sensation that was washing all reason and logic away, but it was hard, so hard, when she was becoming molten in his arms. He had just propositioned her—calmly laid out the ground rules and the benefits that would apply if she agreed to become his mistress. She *couldn't* give in now.

But in his own way he was being absolutely honourable. An insidious little voice was hammering away in her head, doing its part to break down her defences. Wouldn't it be better to take a relationship with him on his terms and hope that it might develop into something more—that one day he might find he couldn't do without her, that he loved her?

His tongue was doing incredible things to the soft contours of her mouth as his hands worked their own magic, and the feeling that was surging through her was so strong, so new and powerful, that she could barely breathe. She knew she was kissing him back with greater and greater passion, that all her body signs were leading him on to more intimacies, that she was stupid, *stupid*; but she couldn't stop.

He twisted in his seat, one hand moving between her shoulder-blades and the other into the small of her back as he drew her hard against the throbbing maleness of his body, her soft breasts crushed against the wall of his chest and her head thrown back to his searching mouth.

She could hear little moans—soft, inarticulate, sobbing groans—and it was with a tiny shock that she recognised they were spilling from her own lips, that her control was quite gone. And Hawk understood what was happening to her—it was there in the guttural growl deep in the base of his throat, in the way his hands moulded her slender frame to his as she clung pliant and shivering against him.

'You want me as much as I want you...admit it,' he murmured huskily against her flushed skin, his breathing harsh and ragged. 'You want me, Joanne; say it...'

But it wasn't just wanting. She froze, the screaming warning her brain had been trying to give her for the last few minutes hitting home with savage force. She wanted him because she *loved* him, and that meant she wanted him a hundred times, a thousand times more than he could ever want her. Her mother hadn't loved like this—she couldn't have—because there was no way she could have gone from man to man if she had. If she couldn't have Hawk, *really* have him, in the only way that would keep her sane—as lover, friend, companion, *husband*—then she would have no one.

'Joanne?' Hawk's voice was questioning, the passion that still had him in its grip making it throaty and harsh.

'I do want you, Hawk.' From some hitherto unknown inner strength she forced herself to say what she had to say. 'I want you very much, in a way I had never imagined wanting any man.'

'Joanne—'

'No, no, wait.' She interrupted his exultant voice flatly, twisting back and away from him as she spoke. 'I know now that you are the reason I've never wanted a relationship with anyone else, that I was waiting—waiting but without knowing why.'

'And now you do?' he asked softly, the tenor of his voice and the look on his face making it clear he knew something was badly wrong.

For a moment, just one fleeting infinitesimal moment, she contemplated preserving her dignity and pride—lying to him and making some excuse as to why she couldn't become his mistress—but she couldn't. It had to be all or nothing—she had known that from the day she met him and fought against it for as long—and so it was nothing because that was all Hawk could take. Commitment, love, sacrifice—they were just words to Hawk; he had torn the feeling that went with them out of his soul fifteen years ago.

'Yes, I've known for some time,' she said quietly, her eyes holding his and a wealth of pain at what she was about to do making them as dark as night. 'I could never become your mistress, Hawk, or your lover,' she continued quickly as he went to speak, 'because if I did it would destroy me, and probably you as well. You have your own moral code, I know that, and I don't think you would want to break someone deliberately.'

'Break you?' He drew back into his seat, his cold, handsome face straightening and his eyes taking on the piercing, diamond-hard sharpness that was so intimidating. 'What the hell are you talking about? I don't want to break you, Joanne. Damn it, you must know that.'

'I do.' She nodded slowly. 'That's the irony of it really.'

'Look, I've had enough of these riddles,' he said grimly. 'I want you and you want me, you've said it yourself, and we're two grown people, not a pair of giggling, groping teenagers,' he added bitingly. 'I've waited longer for you than I've ever waited for anything in my life, and I don't intend to wait a day longer.'

'You'd take me by force?' she asked tremulously.

'If I have to.' He glared at her, the swiftly darkening sky outside the window making him appear like a black silhouette with just the silver-blue of his eyes alive. 'But it wouldn't be by force a few seconds after I touched you, would it?' he continued relentlessly. 'We both know that. Damn it all, Joanne—' his voice had become a groan as his eyes took in the whiteness of her face '—what the hell do you want from me anyway?'

'The one thing you can't give or buy,' she answered tremulously, her love for him causing a physical pain in her chest that was excruciating. 'I don't care about a house or car; don't you see that, Hawk? And I don't want an allowance, or independence, or to follow my own selfish path. I want you, all of you—*I want it all*. I want to live with you, care for you, have your children, grow old together. I want to know you care for me as something more than a body or an attractive appendage on your arm for parties and dinners, that when I get my first grey hairs and my body begins to sag it won't make any difference.'

'Joanne—'

'No, listen,' she said fiercely. 'You listen to me. I don't want to have to wait for the phone to stop ringing, or worry about who you're with or what you're doing when you aren't with me. *I couldn't live like that*, don't you see? I want you to love me like I love you, and you can't, you can't,' she finished on a sob that almost choked her.

'You don't know what you're saying.' But his voice was shaky and he was perfectly still, the last glow from the dying sky outside the car windows strangely poignant to the moment.

'I know, Hawk.' She drew herself up proudly. 'I love you, hard as I know you'll find that to believe. And perhaps another woman could love you and still accept that the way you want it is the way it has to be, but I can't. I don't want you for a few months or a few years, I want you for ever, and to tell you anything different would be a lie. You've told me you always want the truth and that's the truth.'

'You're telling me you want a ring on your finger before you share my bed,' he stated flatly.

Joanne's face went still whiter but she forced herself not to flinch. 'No, that would be blackmail and quite useless with most men, let alone you,' she said shakily, willing the storm of emotion that was threatening to tear loose from the very core of her to be still. 'In fact if you asked me to marry you I would say no,' she continued bravely. 'A ring or a piece of paper means nothing if that's all it is, and it would be with you, I know that.'

'Then what the hell *do* you want?' he ground out savagely.

'I want you to let me walk out of your life,' she said

tautly. 'No recriminations, no bitterness, just a simple goodbye. And…and I want you to look around for another manager at Bergique & Son's. I'll…I'll stay till you've found someone else, of course, but then— Then I want to go.'

'You're telling me on the one hand that you supposedly love me, and on the other that you want to run out on me?' Hawk bit out with a fury that stunned her. 'What the hell sort of love is that?'

'My sort,' she said quietly, lifting her chin as she spoke.

'Then it stinks.' He grasped her shoulders, jerking her towards him. 'If you love someone, you're supposed to want to be with them,' he growled angrily.

'How would you know?' Suddenly there was hot molten rage flowing through her veins and she welcomed it, its cauterising power sealing her bleeding heart and allowing her to throw off his hands with an anger that matched his.

'I know.' He was breathing heavily, his eyes flashing blue fire. 'I was in love once, a lifetime ago, and I wanted to be with her but she had other ideas.'

'And so you let her go?' Joanne said quietly, her rage dying as quickly as it had been born. 'Well, that was love, wasn't it?'

'I let her go because I despised her.' His voice was as cold as ice. 'She betrayed me with a friend I loved like a brother; the two of them had been having an affair behind my back for weeks before I found out. But they lived to regret it; I made sure of that. And it taught me one thing, and for that I'm grateful—love is just another name for a physical act.'

'No.' Her voice was a whisper of pain. 'You loved someone who didn't exist, an image she'd projected. You never did love *her*.'

'What do you know about it?' he bit out cruelly.

'Your mother couldn't stop loving your father whatever he did,' Joanne said huskily. 'I'm sure she tried to—it would have made things so much easier, after all—but she couldn't, just as I couldn't stop loving you whatever you did. I don't want to love you, Hawk—in fact you are the last man in the world I would have chosen to love—but I can't help it. The only protection I have, the only thing I can do not to become like your mother—broken, tortured—is to live without you, to let go. That's what I meant when I said I wouldn't marry you even if you asked me; it would be history repeating itself, and I think you, even more than me, would find that abhorrent.'

'So it is over?' he asked with rigid control.

'It never even began.'

CHAPTER TEN

HER brave words—noble almost, she told herself with bitterly searing self-contempt—came back to mock her desperate misery once she was alone in her suite.

Hawk had driven home in the encroaching darkness without another word, his face as black as thunder and his hands gripping the leather-clad steering wheel so tightly, his knuckles had shone white.

He'd spoken briefly when they'd entered his home, and his voice had been curt and cold. 'I presume you would rather eat here than dine out?'

'Yes, please.' She had tried to match his detachment but failed miserably. 'Perhaps if I could have a tray in my room...?'

'What a good idea,' he'd said grimly. 'I will make sure Conchita is aware of it.' And then he had watched her as she had climbed the beautiful winding staircase, his eyes boring into the back of her head with every step she took.

If she had needed any confirmation that his heart was encased in stone, she'd had it this evening, she told herself miserably as she sat staring blankly into space in the magnificent suite of rooms. She had known he wouldn't exactly be overjoyed to hear that she loved him—still less that his plans to bed her had been thwarted—but surely one kind word, one understanding glance or even a sympathetic silence wasn't beyond him?

It was she who was suffering, after all—not Hawk. It was *her* heart that was broken, *her* feelings that were lacerated beyond repair... She gave herself up to a del-

174

uge of self-pity and despair. His pride had no doubt been dented a little—his ego taking a bit of a hammering in the process—but he didn't *love* her, so her refusal to sleep with him was a momentary hiccup in his life, that was all. And it wasn't as though she had refused him because she didn't find him attractive or that she didn't want him—she had told him how it was. The tears continued to flow, hot and acidic.

She was still struggling for composure when Conchita knocked on her door half an hour later to enquire what she would like for dinner, and she forced herself to listen quietly as the little maid relayed several alternatives the cook had listed.

'I don't mind, Conchita.' The thought of food was repugnant anyway. 'Tell Cook I'll have whatever Mr Mallen is having.'

'But Mr Mallen is having dinner at the Sandersons','' Conchita said brightly, before stopping abruptly and casting a glance at Joanne that clearly stated she was worried she had made a gaffe.

'Oh, yes, I remember now.' Joanne found herself speaking as easily and naturally as though she lied with every other breath, and the fabrication must have been convincing because Conchita relaxed again, bustling away quite happily a few minutes later.

The Sandersons. She remembered the Sandersons: Mr and Mrs Sanderson, filthy rich and full of their own importance, and Victoria Sanderson—elegant, beautiful and clearly crazy about Hawk. They had been at the Christmas Eve party, and Victoria's black looks had left Joanne in no doubt at all as to how the ravishing blonde viewed Hawk's house guest.

So he had rushed off to seek solace with the voluptuous Victoria, had he? She found she was grinding her teeth and it shocked her, bringing her shooting out of her seat as though she were on springs. It didn't matter, it didn't; she wouldn't let it.

By the time Conchita brought the dinner tray at seven o'clock, Joanne had phoned the airport and made a reservation on a night flight to France; mercifully there had been a cancellation and a seat was available. It was the coward's way out—she knew that, she told herself miserably as she forced herself to swallow a few mouthfuls of the delicious dinner—but there was no way on this earth she could endure seeing Hawk tomorrow and travelling back to France with him as he had arranged. Besides, by relieving him of his duty towards her he could spend a few more days basking in Victoria's adoration if he wanted to, she thought painfully, bitter anguish making her as white as a sheet.

She was waiting in the hall when the taxi arrived, and slipped out quietly after leaving a note for Hawk thanking him for his hospitality, but saying in the circumstances she thought it better to leave at once. She also left the ruby pendant and bracelet.

She slept a little on the flight home, but the jangled nightmarish dreams were frightening and more exhausting than trying to stay awake, and by the time they landed, in the early hours of a cold and rainy Paris morning, she felt ill with a mixture of reaction and jet lag.

Once back in her apartment she fell into bed without bothering to undress, but in spite of falling into a deep, dreamless sleep as soon as her head touched the pillow she was awake again within a couple of hours, her brain dissecting every word that had passed between her and Hawk until she thought she would go mad.

She had showered, dressed, and left the apartment before eight, driven by a nervous tension so acute that she walked most of the distance to Bergique & Son, only riding the métro for the last part of the journey.

For the first time since she had been living there Paris

looked dull and dismal, the Parisians colourless and
drab; in fact the very air seemed heavy and lifeless and
defunct. It frightened her if she thought about it—this
inert, joyless stupor that seemed to have taken her over
since the conversation in Hawk's car—and so she was
almost glad when, arriving at the office a day early,
much to Antoinette's consternation, she found Pierre in
her office rifling through the filing cabinet which had
been locked when she'd left, and pure fury replaced the
deadness.

'What are you doing?' It wasn't a time for social niceties and they both knew it.

The heavy-set Frenchman had swung round at her entry into the room, dropping the file he had been holding
so the papers flew in a whirling arc about their feet, but
he recovered himself almost instantly, the ingratiating
smile she had seen once or twice before stitching itself
in place. 'Joanne, we weren't expecting you—'

'*Je suis désolée, Pierre—*'

'Never mind saying you are sorry to him!' Joanne
swung round so violently as Antoinette spoke behind her
that the French girl actually backed away a step. 'It
should be me you are apologising to, Antoinette. What
on earth are you thinking of to let someone have access
to my filing cabinet anyway?' she asked furiously.

'I can explain, Joanne.' Pierre's smile hadn't wavered.
'This is just a mistake.'

'I agree, Pierre, and I think you are the one who made
it,' Joanne said cuttingly. 'You have no right to be in
this building and you know it; I saw the contract Hawk
made you sign and it is crystal-clear about that very
thing. What is this file anyway?' She bent and picked
up some of the papers from the floor, and in so doing
missed the nod Pierre gave to his ex-secretary to close
the office door so the three of them couldn't be
overheard.

Joanne recognised the papers instantly; she had been working on the Netta Productions file prior to the Christmas break, and had begun to be very concerned about the matter before Hawk had whisked her away so abruptly. There had been the smell of something very nasty about the case but the facts had been buried in masses of red tape, and it had required patient and tactful digging to unearth the truth. Looking at Pierre's face as she raised her head, Joanne suddenly had the feeling she was staring at all the answers.

'Well?' Joanne stood up slowly, and it was only then that something very cold and very dark trickled down her backbone as she saw the look in the Frenchman's eyes.

'You stupid, arrogant Englishwoman.' He spat the words out of his mouth, following them with a string of profanities that were all the more menacing for being spoken so softly. 'You poke and you pry, do you not? You cannot leave anything alone.'

'*You* were responsible for that firm going bankrupt, weren't you?' Joanne said slowly, her intuition putting the last piece in the jigsaw. 'It wasn't their managing director who orchestrated the fraud, it was you, and you let an innocent man kill himself when the finger was pointed at him.'

'He was a weak fool.' Pierre's voice held not the slightest compassion. 'Now give me the papers, Joanne, and if you know what is good for you you will forget this conversation ever took place. I have many friends—friends who are invisible and can come and go at will; it would not be wise to cross me.'

'You're threatening me?' She couldn't believe it, she thought wildly. This was the sort of dialogue that belonged to an old second-rate movie, not an up-market publishing company at nine-thirty in the morning of a working day.

'But of course, this is one of the things I do so well.' Pierre flicked his head at Antoinette, indicating for her to leave the room, which she did with an alacrity that told Joanne the French girl was as scared as she was.

'You have only to say nothing and this whole unfortunate matter will die a death,' Pierre continued softly, walking across the room to stand in front of her, his dark eyes gleaming as he looked down into her pale face. 'That is not so hard, is it?' He put out a hand and raised her chin a little.

'Don't threaten me, Pierre.' His touch banished the fear that had had her in its grip, and put steel in her backbone. 'I won't be intimidated by you or anyone else. And don't touch me either.'

'No?' He considered her angry face with a slight smile. 'Perhaps I have underrated the little English girl, eh? Then what would you say to a more…agreeable solution? Perhaps a little thank-you in anticipation? Shall we say a figure of…?'

He mentioned a sum of money that brought her eyes wide open and her mouth slack, before she found her tongue. 'You think everyone is for sale, don't you, Pierre?' she said with icy and scathing disdain. 'Well, this may come as something of a surprise but I am not. These papers will go to the authorities, along with a report of our conversation today, and I think you might be viewing most of the new year from the inside of a prison cell.'

'I can't let you do that, Joanne.' His hands shot out to grasp her upper arms in an iron-like grip that was meant to terrorise. 'Don't make me hurt you—'

'Take your filthy hands off her.'

Pierre just had time to raise his head before he was plucked bodily into the air, and flung across the room with enough force to send him crashing against the far wall, where he landed with all the finesse of a stunned elephant.

'Get up.' Hawk's face was frightening. 'I'm going to teach you a lesson you'll never forget.'

'No, Hawk, no.' Joanne found she was actually hanging on to his back, her arms tight round his neck, as he tried to haul Pierre up by his jacket. 'Leave him, please; he's not worth it—'

'I'll kill the little rat.'

By the time help arrived a few moments later, summoned by Antoinette who appeared to have gone quite hysterical, it was clear Pierre was very glad to be led away and that threats and intimidation were the last thing on the Frenchman's mind, despite the fact that Hawk had told the two burly security men to hold him until the police arrived. Indeed he almost scampered out of the office, pulling the other men with him.

'You frightened him.' Joanne found she had to sit down very suddenly as the room began to swim and dip.

'I'd have done more than that if I hadn't had you round my neck like a limpet.' His voice was soft, very soft, and possessed a deepness that made her raise her head and try to focus on his face, a second before she found herself lifted up and cradled against his chest.

'Hawk, what are you doing…?'

'What I should have done a long, long time ago.' He marched across the room and into the outer office, past a weeping Antoinette and open-mouthed office staff, not saying a word until they were in the lift and going swiftly downwards.

'Hawk, I can stand—'

'Be quiet.' His voice was almost savage and he was crushing her against his body as though he was frightened to let her go, his heart pounding against the wall of his chest with such force it was shaking her frame.

Once in Reception they passed the two security men

and the chastened and silent Pierre without stopping, Hawk shouting a reply over his shoulder as they asked him where he was going.

'But Monsieur Mallen, the police—they will need a statement—'

'Damn the police.'

Hawk carried her over to his car once they were outside the building, depositing her in the front seat as though she were a piece of rare Meissen porcelain, and joining her inside moments later.

'Hawk—'

'In a moment, Joanne.' She subsided helplessly. He drove fast and furiously to a quiet spot overlooking green parkland, before bringing the car to a screeching halt and causing a flock of pigeons to rise in squawking protest. He cut the engine in the same moment and then turned and took her into his arms, ignoring her struggles as he swooped on her mouth in a kiss that seemed to draw her very soul.

'No, no, Hawk...' When she came back into the land of the living from the world of colour and light he had taken her into, she forced herself to try and escape his arms.

'Yes, yes, Joanne.' His tone wasn't mocking; in fact it was painful in its sincerity, his hands moving to cup her face as he stared down at her with the piercing blue gaze that was mesmerising. 'Please, darling, don't fight me.'

Darling? She stared at him, her honey-brown eyes huge. She couldn't be hearing right. 'I...I can't do this, I've told you.'

'Joanne, I love you; I've loved you from the moment I set eyes on you, and I shall die loving you,' he said huskily. 'I don't deserve you, I can never expect you to forgive me for the mess I've made of everything, but believe me when I say I love you.'

'You don't...you can't,' she murmured unsteadily, her ears buzzing as her senses swam again.

'I do, I can.' She hadn't realised she was crying until he caught a teardrop with his fingertip, his hands brushing her cheeks with a tenderness that took her breath away. 'I'm a stubborn man, my love, arrogant, foolish, but when I came home last night to ask you to marry me and you'd gone I got the next plane here.'

'You went to dinner with Victoria Sanderson,' she said shakily, unable to believe what was happening was real.

'No. I refused that invitation days ago, knowing it would be your last night in my home, but I forgot to tell Conchita and when I left so abruptly she just assumed I had gone there,' he said quietly. 'I drove for hours, trying to come to terms with all you had said and my own...my own personal demons. I realised I had been fooling myself, that I had been lying to myself for weeks—months—since the day we met. I didn't want an affair with you, Joanne, I wanted more, much more, than that, but I couldn't bring myself to accept it was love. It made me too vulnerable, too exposed, too much like the next man.'

'If...if that's true, then what made you change your mind?' she asked tremulously, not daring to believe it.

'You.' One word but his heart was in it.

'Oh, Hawk.' As her arms went round his neck their lips fused together in an embrace that brought flames of desire coursing hot and fierce, the world outside the car disappearing as reality became touch and taste and sensation.

'You forgive me, Joanne?' he groaned against the softness of her skin. 'I have no right to ask—'

'Yes, yes, I forgive you.'

'And you'll marry me? As soon as it can be arranged?' he murmured with desperate, hungry lips on her face, her throat. 'I want to care for you, my sweet love, cherish you, protect you. When I saw that gorilla holding you I wanted to tear him limb from limb.'

'I think he got the message.' Joanne smiled shakily through her tears, and then said, 'Hawk, are you sure?' She reached up and took his dark face in her small hands. 'Really, really sure?'

'I have never been so sure about anything in my life,' he said brokenly. 'You are everything I have ever dreamed of, everything I have ever desired. All that rubbish I spoke about love—damn it, Joanne, I was fighting myself, tearing myself apart inside. When you spoke about your childhood, the things you went through, it was like a knife tearing at my guts; I couldn't bear it. And still I continued to fight—'

'Hush.' She kissed the searing self-contempt and pain from his face, covering his skin in soft, burning little kisses. 'I don't care about the past; it's the future that matters.'

'And I promise you it will be a glorious one,' he said softly, his hands stroking her hair as his eyes devoured her face. 'A lifetime will be too short to tell you how much I love you. I didn't love my fiancée, Joanne; you were right about that and I knew the moment you spoke it out loud. It wasn't real love. Perhaps a desperation to belong to someone again, a need for reassurance after all that had happened with my parents, perhaps even the cry of a child in the dark—it was all those things, but not the lasting love of two people who are committed to sharing their lives together. It was never that. I have never loved any other woman before; I know that now. You have my word,' he finished seriously.

'And you never lie,' she said teasingly, her smile tremulous but full of joy.

'Only to myself,' he said soberly, clasping her close again, his arms so tight she could scarcely breathe.

'When you told me how you felt in the car, your beautiful face so white and haunted and your shoulders bowed beneath a burden that never should have been, the disgust I felt for myself was too much to bear. After all the torture of your early years, the pain you endured day after day in a loveless environment, you still had the strength to forgive and go on. It made me feel...contemptible, worthless. You had far more reason than me to shun love, to be afraid to reach out again, but you had done so—bravely and with such courage. Whereas I...'

'Don't punish yourself any more,' Joanne said shakily, distressed to see the pain and anguish in his eyes. 'We've both learnt from life, things we can pass on to our children and their children—'

'But first a time where I have you all to myself,' he said fiercely. 'I am a jealous man, my love; I cannot share you yet. I love you; I need to make you feel that, and I shall tell you every day of your life and beyond. You are mine as I am yours; I will always be everything you need. And our children will be brought up in the light of that love where the smallest shadow will not be allowed.'

Later, much later, when they had loved and touched and tasted and talked and the morning was gone, she moved drowsily in his arms as they continued to gaze out across the park, neither of them wanting to move back into the real world. 'What happened to your theory of women being good for one thing only?' she asked him mischievously, stroking the tanned skin of his chin where a dark stubble was already beginning to show.

'Did I say that?' The sapphire-blue eyes narrowed on her flushed, happy face. 'Well, in your case it is true— to love, worship and adore.'

'That's three things,' she protested weakly, the dark,

sensual glitter in the devastating gaze making her shiver with anticipation.

'I'll just settle for love, then,' he said softly, his hands beginning to coax passionate warmth into every nerve and sinew. 'True love is the greatest thing of all.'

Catherine Spencer, once an English teacher, fell into writing through eavesdropping on a conversation about Mills & Boon® romances. Within two months she changed careers and sold her first book to Mills & Boon® in 1984. She moved to Canada from England thirty years ago and lives in Vancouver. She is married to a Canadian and has four grown children – two daughters and two sons – plus three dogs and a cat. In her spare time she plays the piano, collects antiques, and grows tropical shrubs.

**Look out for
D'ALESSANDRO'S CHILD by Catherine
Spencer in Modern Romance™, February 2002**

CHRISTMAS WITH A STRANGER

by
Catherine Spencer

PROLOGUE

HE WAS on the outside again. On the run. Eventually, of
course, they'd catch up with him, and when they did they'd
put him away for an even longer stretch. But meanwhile
time was on his side. Time in which to carry out the plan
he'd spent nine years perfecting. Time to exact punishment
for the injustice meted out to him.

Oh, he'd been a model inmate! So clever, fooling all of
them with the mealy-mouthed responses they'd wanted to
hear. So eager to be rehabilitated, so willing to admit the
error of his ways. Oozing humility and remorse enough to
make a thinking man's stomach revolt.

But they weren't thinking men, they were fools. Fools
and tools of the system that had rejected him—except for
the man who'd put him behind bars. *He* was an adversary
worth taking on. Outwitting *him* would be a triumph, something in which to take delight when they caught up with
him again.

What else, after all, had he to nourish his soul? No wife,
certainly, and a child who called some stranger "Father".
No home, no job. And no future. Model prisoner or not, his
past would go with him wherever he went. For the rest of
his life.

It was the way things were done these days. Forget all
that nonsense about a man having paid for his crimes. He
never wrote off the debt because they plastered his face and
name on community notice boards and labeled him a dangerous offender, even if he'd been judged guilty of only one
crime—and that vindicated in the eyes of God-fearing people.

5

Vermin, that was what he'd stamped out. A temptation of the devil's making best wiped off the face of the earth. A cheap flirt dolled up to look like decent folk, preying on a man's weakness when he was most vulnerable. Reaching across his desk in such a way that he was filled with the scent of her.

It would have been different if he'd been allowed his conjugal rights, but Lynn had refused him ever since she'd almost lost the baby in her fifteenth week. That had left nearly six months during which he'd been denied his husbandly prerogative. Small wonder he'd fallen victim to the other woman's wiles.

He hadn't meant to kill her. It had been an accident—a panic reaction. She'd made a scene when he'd told her he wouldn't leave his wife for her, and threatened to phone his home, to tell Lynn what a louse she had for a husband, and for a few blind moments he'd lost control and it had just…happened.

He might have been acquitted—at worst found guilty of nothing more heinous than aggravated assault resulting in death. The judge had seemed inclined to sympathy at times, and the jury might have found in his favor—if it hadn't been for Morgan Kincaid.

Kincaid was the one who'd taken everything away and left him with nothing to lose.

Well, Merry Christmas, Mr. Crown Prosecutor!

It was payback time.

CHAPTER ONE

THE snow began in earnest just as darkness fell. Dense, feathery flakes whirling across the beam of her headlights to imprison her in a closed and isolated world.

Jessica hadn't been comfortable with the driving conditions from the start. She was used to a milder sort of winter on the island, one of west coast sea mist and wind-driven rain, not the breath-freezing cold of the high Canadian interior.

She'd spent last night in a small town tucked between a lake and the highway, in a country inn built to resemble a Swiss chalet. There'd been logs blazing in the fireplace in the lobby and a twelve-foot Christmas tree that filled the air with the scent of pine, and French onion soup smothered in melted cheese for dinner. It had been a warm, safe place now some three hundred miles behind—much too far to merit her turning back.

If she wanted shelter from the weather again tonight, her only option was to tackle the eighty miles of switchback mountain road that lay between her and her next stop on the way to Whistling Ridge.

Smearing a gloved hand across the windshield, she squinted through the swirling snow, her heart lurching as the wheels of the car skidded suddenly to the right. Upright poles planted at intervals to measure the depth of the winter snowfall were all that stood between her and the swift, steep drop to the valley below.

This was insanity and only the fact that Selena had been injured in a ski-lift accident could have induced her to abandon her original holiday plans and embark on such a journey. But then, wasn't that how it had always been, ever since they were children? With Selena getting into trouble of one kind or another, and Jessica dropping everything to come to the rescue?

Another forty-five-degree bend loomed up ahead. Cautiously, she steered into the turn. Halfway around, she saw the flicker of headlights below her as another driver navigated the road, but more quickly, with an assurance she sorely lacked.

Once on the straight again, she increased her speed. She had little choice. The car behind was gaining rapidly, there was no room to pass and the snow was, if anything, falling more thickly. In great fat clumps the size of footballs, in fact, that rolled down the mountainside and bounced across the road.

Headlights dazzled in her rear-view mirror. A horn blared, repeatedly, furiously. Panic choked her throat. Was the other driver mad? Trying to run her off the road?

All at once, the open mouth of an avalanche shed yawned blackly a few yards in front, offering a brief haven of safety where she could let whoever was in such a hurry behind get past her.

Clutching the steering wheel in a death grip, Jessica pressed down on the accelerator and shot into the shelter with the other vehicle practically nosing her bumper from behind.

And then the air was filled with thunder and the earth seemed to rock beneath her. And the road, which was supposed to run all the way to Whistling Valley ski resort where Selena lay in a hospital bed, came to a sudden end at the far end of the avalanche shed.

At first Jessica didn't believe it and, pulling as far over to one side as possible to allow the other driver to get by, kept her car idling forward. Until she saw that there was no way out of the shed, that its exit truly was blocked by a wall of snow, and that, far from trying to pass her, her pursuer had drawn to a stop also, and was climbing out of his vehicle and coming toward her.

Incongruously large and implicitly threatening in the light cast by his car's headlamps, his shadow leaped ahead of him on the concrete wall of the shed. Reaching for the control panel on the console, Jessica snapped the doors locked and wished she could as easily subdue the tremor of apprehension racing through her.

Approaching her window, he stooped and stared in at her. She had the impression of a man perhaps in his early forties; of dark displeasure, well-defined brows drawn together in a scowl, and a mouth paralleling the same vexation. Of wide shoulders made all the more imposing by the bulky jacket he wore, and of masculine power composed not just of sinew but of command, as though he was not inclined to tolerate having his authority thwarted by anyone.

The way he rapped on her window and ordered, "Open it," bore out the idea, especially when she found herself automatically obeying the directive and lowering the glass an inch.

"Do you have a death wish?" The question blasted toward her on a cloud of frosty air.

Unvarnished disapproval laced the husky baritone of his voice, leaving her in no doubt that she was alone with a stranger who looked and sounded very much as if he'd like to take her neck between his powerful hands and wring it.

But she wasn't earning accolades as the youngest headmistress ever appointed to Springhill Island's Private School for Girls by cowering in the face of incipient trouble. "Certainly not," she said, as calmly as her thudding heart would allow. "But I imagine you must, if the way you were driving is any indication. You practically ran me off the road."

For a moment she thought she'd managed to silence him. His jaw almost dropped and he appeared to be at a loss for words. He shook his head, as though unsure that he'd heard her correctly, then recovered enough to say, "Lady, do you have the foggiest idea what's just happened?"

"Of course." She gripped the steering wheel more firmly. It was easier to keep her hands from shaking that way. "There has been a bit of a snow slide."

"There has been a bloody avalanche," he informed her with a rudeness she would not for a moment have tolerated in her students. "And if you'd had your way we'd both be buried under a load of snow—always assuming, of course, that we hadn't been swept clear down the mountain."

Embarrassingly, her teeth started to chatter with shock then, and short of stuffing both gloved hands in her mouth, there was little she could do to disguise the fact except blurt out, "That must be why it's so cold in here."

At that, he straightened up and thumped a fist on the roof of her car, sending a clump of snow slithering down her windshield. "I don't believe what I'm hearing," he informed the shed at large, his words echoing eerily. "Is this her way of trying to be funny?"

"Hardly," she retorted, addressing the zippered front of his down jacket, which was all she could see of him. "I plan to spend tonight in Wintercreek and have quite a few miles still to cover before I get there. I'd just as soon not waste time keeping you entertained with witticisms."

He bent down to confront her again, squatting so that his face was on a level with hers. "Let me get this straight. You expect to reach Wintercreek tonight?"

"Didn't I just say as much?" She wished she could see his face more clearly. But everything about him was a little bit distorted in the flare of his car's headlamps, with one side of his features thrown into dark relief and the other silhouetted in light. Like opposite sides of a coin—or good and evil all wrapped up in one package.

She suppressed a shudder. This was not the time for such

fanciful notions. It was a time for positive thought and action. "I have a hotel reservation—"

"I heard you the first time and I hope your deposit's refundable," he interrupted curtly. "Because, as they say in the vernacular of these parts, 'honey, you ain't goin' nowhere any time soon'."

"Are you telling me I'm stuck in here until someone comes to rescue me?"

"That's what I'm telling you."

Her confidence nosedived a little further. "And…um… how long do you think that will take?"

He shrugged. "Hard to say. First light tomorrow, if we're lucky."

"But that's almost twelve hours away!"

"I know." He braced his hands against his knees and shoved himself upright again. "Better turn off the engine before you asphyxiate us, and resign yourself to sleeping in your back seat. Open the trunk and I'll hand in your emergency supplies."

She hadn't thought it possible for anything to make her heart sink any lower but, to her dismay, he managed it with his last remark. "Emergency supplies?"

"Sleeping bag, candle, GORP."

"GORP?" she echoed faintly.

"Good old raisins and peanuts. Trail mix, cereal bars, stuff to keep your stomach from folding in on itself—call it what you like; I don't care. Let's just get you settled before we both die of exposure."

"I don't… I have only a suitcase. With clothes in it," she added, as if that might mitigate things a little.

It didn't. Thumping a fist on the roof of her car yet again, he let out a long, irritable exhalation. "I might have known!"

"Well, I didn't," Jessica said tartly. "They never mentioned an avalanche on the weather report. If they had, I'd have stayed off the road. And please stop bludgeoning my car like that. Things are quite bad enough without your making them any worse.''

She thought he swore then. Certainly he muttered something unfit to be repeated in mixed company. Eventually, he composed himself enough to order, ''Get out of the car.''

''And go where? You already said no one's likely to rescue us tonight.''

''Get out of the car. Unless you were lying a moment ago and you really do harbor a death wish.''

''I'd just as soon—''

''Get out of the goddamned car!''

It was Jessica's strongly held belief that a teacher who wished to retain control of her classes should make clear her expectations at the outset. Insubordination ranked high on her list of priorities. Unless it was stamped out at the start, it flourished quickly and completely undermined a teacher's authority. Related to that were the social graces which, in her opinion, were as important a part of the curriculum as any other subject. She felt it was incumbent on her and her staff to teach by example wherever possible.

Which was why, when she replied to her companion's incivility, she resisted the temptation to tell him to take a flying leap into the nearest snow bank and, instead, said firmly but politely, ''I'll do no such thing. Furthermore, I don't like your tone.''

''I don't like anything about this situation,'' he shot back, singularly uncowed. ''Believe me, if finding myself stranded overnight was in the cards when I got out of bed this morning, I can think of a dozen people I'd rather keep company with than some ditsy woman who doesn't have the brains to travel equipped for winter driving conditions.''

''I'm not seeking your company,'' Jessica snapped.

''But you're stuck with it,'' he said, chafing his bare hands together to keep the circulation going and turning toward his own vehicle again. "So hop out of the car *now*, because it's not big enough for two to stretch out in and I'd like to get some sleep."

Horrified, Jessica stared at him as the import of his words struck home. "You expect me to spend the night in your car...with you?"

"It beats the alternative," he said bluntly. "Life's tough enough without my waking up tomorrow to find a frozen corpse on my hands"

"But—!"

He blew into his cupped palms and, with the first hint of humor he'd shown so far, slewed an alarming leer her way. "Listen, we can debate the propriety of the arrangement once we're under the covers."

He was rude and he was outrageous—but, she was beginning to realize, he was right on one score at least. The cold was seeping through the open window to infiltrate her clothing most unpleasantly.

Still, she wasn't about to cave in to his suggestions without a murmur. "I think I should warn you that I have taken several courses in self-defense."

"Pity you didn't start worrying about your safety before now," he said, his expression at once resuming its former forbidding aspect. "As it happens, I'm harmless, but it would well serve you right if— Oh, what the hell!"

He pushed himself away from her car and seemed to make a concerted effort to rein in the anger suddenly vibrating around him. "You've got five minutes to make up your mind. If you're not out of this car and into mine by the time I've got my sleeping bag unfolded, better say your prayers and write out your last will and testament, because, lady..." he blew into his hands again to emphasize his point "...it'll be the last thing you ever do."

And with that he marched back to his car and doused the headlamps, leaving only hers to bathe the shelter in their glow. She heard a door slam, another open. Saw an interior light go on as he rummaged around at the back of what appeared to be a large utility vehicle. And knew, as the chill already invading the inside of her car crept deeper into her limbs, that she had little choice about what to do next.

He could be a serial killer, a deranged psychopath, a man intent on choking the living breath out of her, but, if she chose to ignore his less than gracious invitation, she'd wind up dead by the morning anyway.

Swallowing doubts and reservations along with what was left of her pride, she rolled up the window and stepped out of the car. As though crouching in wait for just such an ill-prepared victim, the cold took serious hold, knifing through her mohair winter coat as if it were made of nothing more substantial than silk.

Just as she approached, her reluctant knight jumped down from the tailgate of his vehicle, which turned out to be a Jeep whose heavy winter tires were looped with snow chains. ''Smart decision,'' he said, shrugging free of his jacket. ''Take off your boots and coat, then hop in.''

She liked to think she'd outgrown any tendency toward foolish impulse and indeed spent a good portion of her tenure as headmistress counseling her students to think before they spoke, to temper spontaneity with deliberation. Yet the question was out of her mouth before she could prevent it, gauche and horribly suggestive. ''Why do we have to take off our clothes if all we're going to do is sleep?''

He stood before her, the interior light of the Jeep enhanced by the glow of a candle set in a tin can on the floor under the dashboard. Quite enough illumination for her to take in the powerful breadth of shoulder beneath the heavy jacket and lean, athletic hips snugly clad in blue jeans. Was it also enough for him to detect the sweep of color that flooded her face?

If it was, he chose to ignore the fact, instead pointing out what would have been painfully obvious to anyone of sound mind. "I stand six three in my bare feet. Last time I checked, I weighed in at a hundred and ninety-four pounds. For that reason I bought an extra-large sleeping bag but it's still going to be a snug fit for two. I no more want your snowy boots in the small of my back than you want mine in yours. As for the coat, you might want to roll it up and use it as a pillow."

"Of course," she muttered, chagrined. "How stupid of me."

"Indeed!" He rolled his eyes and gestured her toward the Jeep with a flourish. "Climb aboard, stash your boots in the corner, and make yourself comfortable."

Comfortable? Not in a million years, Jessica thought, trying to keep her sweater in place as she slithered into the sleeping bag.

No sooner was she settled than he slammed closed the tailgate and raised the rear window, rather like a jailer securing a prison cell. He then went around to the driver's door, pulled it closed behind him, shucked off his boots and, tossing his jacket ahead of him, proceeded to crawl over the seat and join her in the back of the Jeep.

Inching into the sleeping bag, he turned on his side so that his back was toward her. Why couldn't she have left it at that? What demon of idiocy compelled her to try to make pillow talk?

Yet, "This is really quite absurd," she heard herself remark, in a voice so phonily arch that she cringed.

He sort of shifted his shoulders around and tugged his folded jacket into a more comfortable position beneath his head. "How so?"

"Well, here we are in bed together, and we don't even know each other's names."

"Uh-huh."

"I'm Jessica Simms."

"Are you?" he said indifferently. "Well, goodnight, Jessica Simms."

As snubs went, that rated a ten. "Goodnight," she replied huffily, and went to turn her back on him. Except that, now that he was hogging most of the sleeping bag, there really wasn't room for such maneuvering, a fact he was quick to point out.

"Quit fidgeting and nest up against me," he said impatiently. "Every time you shuffle around like that, you let in cold air."

"Nest?" she quavered, refusing to allow the import of "up against me" to take visual hold in her mind.

"Like two spoons, one around the other."

And just in case she hadn't understood he reached back one arm and yanked her close so that her breasts were flattened next to his spine and her pelvis cradled his buttocks. Truly a most compromising situation and one she could only be thankful none of her colleagues or students was likely to hear about.

"Thank you," she said politely. "You're very kind."

She felt his sigh, rife with exasperation and heartfelt enough that it lifted the sleeping bag and let out a little gust of warm air. "For crying out loud, go to sleep," he said.

Of course, it was an order impossible to obey—for him as well as for her, at least to begin with. For the longest time, he lay next to her, long, strong and tense as steel. But gradually, as the night progressed, his muscles relaxed, and she must have dozed off herself because the next time she became aware of her surroundings he was sleeping on his stomach with his face turned toward her.

In the steady light of the candle, she saw that he was not as old as she'd first supposed and looked to be only in his late thirties. It was fatigue that etched his face, carving deep lines beside his mouth and between his eyes, and making him appear older.

Even as she watched, he seemed to sink further into sleep, so that the grooves relaxed, then faded away until she had nothing left to look at but his long, silky lashes touching softly against the lean austerity of his cheekbones.

How handsome he was, she thought.

What colour were his eyes?

Dreamy brown? No, he was not the dreamy type.

Icy green? Possibly. Despite the warmth generated by his body, she sensed that he was a cool, reserved man. Cold, even.

Her arm had grown numb from being cramped beneath her. She flexed her fingers and, with excruciating care, slid her wrist out and across her waist. But cautiously, without creating the least little draft, so that not even the candle flame wavered.

His eyes flew open anyway, alert and noticeably blue, and caught her staring.

Was the spark of sexual awareness that blazed briefly between him and her a figment of her imagination?

''What?'' he muttered, the word laced with suspicion, and she decided that, yes, it must have been her imagination.

''Nothing. My arm—'' She levered the rest of it free and waggled her fingers, wincing at the pins and needles trying to paralyze them. ''It went to sleep.''

''Pity you didn't,'' he said, his head with its thick, dark hair lowering again to the makeshift pillow.

As suddenly as he'd woken, he fell asleep again. She shivered, less from the cold air lurking around them than from the stark lack of sympathy she sensed in him. She was inconveniencing him terribly, no doubt about it, and even less welcome in his sleeping bag than a bed bug.

Selena's latest crisis couldn't have come at a more inappropriate time, Jessica thought uncharitably. By now she should be lounging beneath a sun umbrella in balmy Cancun and trying to pretend she was more than a lonely, thirty-year-old woman most of whose dreams seemed unlikely to come true, not risking life and limb to be with a sister who had little use for her except when disaster arose.

But the avalanche wasn't Selena's fault; nor was it hers. And if her sleeping partner thought their present arrangement was inconvenient, how much worse would he have found it if she'd sped through the shed fast enough to wind up trapped under the snow at the other end? Or would he have left her to her fate and gone calmly about the business of making himself comfortable for the night without sparing her a thought?

Remembering how irritably he'd reacted to her lack of preparedness, she suspected he'd have left her to suffocate. It irked her enough to want to punish him, enough for her to make no attempt at stealth or silence when she struggled to her other side so that she was facing the deep perpendicular embrasures of the snow shed and no longer tempted to look at him.

He reacted with the same ill temper he'd displayed before. "For Pete's sake settle down," he grumbled. "You're worse than a pair of puppies wrestling in a gunny sack."

And again, just as before, he ensured her compliance by anchoring her in place, but this time so that he was snugly cushioned against her behind, and one of his long, strong legs pinned down hers, and she could feel his breath on the back of her neck.

It was an exceedingly…intimate situation.

Exceedingly!

Her watch showed ten minutes past eight when she awoke to find herself alone in the back of the Jeep. A fresh candle burned in the tin can under the dashboard and the start of another day seeped through the upper sections of the narrow vents on the downhill side of the shed to cast a pale, chill light along its length. Pushing herself into a sitting position and finger-combing loose strands of hair back from her face, Jessica saw him coming toward her from the far end of the tunnel.

Quickly, she shuffled free of the sleeping bag and pulled her clothing into place. By the time he hauled open the tailgate, she had her boots on and looked as respectable as could be expected, given the circumstances.

"Have they come to rescue us?" she asked, putting on her coat.

"No." He reached under the dashboard on the passenger side of the Jeep and pulled out a small knapsack.

"Then what were you doing at the end of the shed?"

He handed her a foil-wrapped cereal bar and raised his dark, level brows wryly. "Same thing you'll probably want to do before much longer," he remarked pointedly.

To say that she blushed at that would have been the understatement of the century. She felt herself awash in a tide of pure scarlet. "Oh...yes—I...um...I...see what you mean."

"Don't let modesty get the better of you. The sun's barely up and I don't hold out much hope of us being dug out for at least another half hour. Too risky for the highway crew, when they can't see what the conditions are like up the mountain. And that's always assuming that there isn't three feet of snow blocking the road between them and us."

Jessica's gaze swung to the nearest embrasure beyond which the narrow strip of sky now showed the palest tint of pink. "And if there is?" She could barely bring herself to voice the question. The thought of being imprisoned another day with him and with such a total lack of privacy didn't bear contemplating.

"We might be here until mid-morning. Possibly even longer. It'd take a bulldozer to cut a path through anything that deep." He hitched one hip on the tailgate and swung one long, blue-jeaned leg nonchalantly, as if picnic breakfasts in avalanche sheds were an entirely usual part of his weekly routine. "So, Jessica Simms, want to tell me what persuaded you to drive up here with nothing more reliable than a set of all-weather radials and a road map to get you where you're going?"

"I'm on my way to visit my sister in Whistling Valley."

"That's another seven hours' drive away. You'd better stop in Sentinel Pass and get yourself outfitted with a set of decent tire chains if you seriously want to get there in one piece."

"Yes." She squirmed under his scrutiny, aware that while he seemed to be learning quite a bit about her she knew next to nothing about him. "You haven't told me your name yet."

"Morgan. If you knew you were coming up here for Christmas, why the hell didn't you plan ahead? BCAA or any travel agency could have warned you what sort of conditions to expect." He took another bite of his breakfast bar, then added scathingly, "Maybe then you'd have chosen clothing more appropriate than that flimsy bit of a coat and those pitiful excuses for winter boots you're currently wearing."

He was worse than a pit bull, once he got his teeth into something. Clearly, he found her apparent incompetence morbidly fascinating. "I didn't have time to plan ahead, Mr. Morgan. This trip came about very suddenly."

"I see." He crushed the wrapping from his breakfast into a ball, tossed it, backhanded, into the open knapsack and unearthed a bottle of mineral water.

She shook her head as he unscrewed the cap and offered her a drink. She wasn't about to let a drop of liquid past her lips until she was assured of more civilized washroom facilities. It was all very well for a man to make do but for a woman....

"Some sort of family emergency?"

"What?"

"This sudden decision to visit your sister, was it—?"

"Oh!" She tucked her hands into the pockets of her coat and hunched her shoulders against the cold, which seemed even more pervasive than it had been the night before. "Yes. She hurt her back in a ski-lift accident and at first it seemed that her injuries were serious."

"But now that you're up to your own neck in trouble they don't seem so bad?"

"No," Jessica retorted, bristling at the implied criticism. "I phoned the hospital again before I left the hotel yesterday and learned her condition's been upgraded to satisfactory." She sighed, exasperation adding to the tension already gripping her. "It's just that Selena's always been prone to getting herself into difficulties of one kind or another."

"Must run in the family," he said mockingly, and took another swig of the water.

She was spared having to field his last observation by the rumble of a heavy engine outside the east end of the shed.

He shoved away from the tailgate and recapped the bottle. "Sounds as if the rescue squad have made it through already. Couldn't have been much of a slide, after all."

They were heaven-sent words.

"Thank goodness!" She scrambled down after him. "And thank you, Mr. Morgan. You undoubtedly saved my life and I'm very grateful."

"I undoubtedly did, Miss Jessica, and you're welcome."

"Have a very merry Christmas."

She thought perhaps a shadow crossed his face then, but all he said was, "No need to race back to your car. It'll take a while before they clear a way out for us."

"It's a miracle to me that they even knew where to come looking."

"They have sensors strung all along the vulnerable stretches of highway. The minute one gets wiped out, they know there's been a slide and they usually don't waste much time getting to it.''

"I see." She pulled the collar of her coat more snugly around her neck. "Well, I think I'll wait in my car, just the same. The cold's making its presence felt again.''

"As you like." He closed the tailgate and raised the rear window of the Jeep. "Just don't fire up your engine until we see daylight. Wouldn't want to die from carbon monoxide poisoning when we've made it this far, would we?''

"I'm well aware of the danger from exhaust fumes, Mr. Morgan," she said loftily, resenting his confident assumption that, because she'd been ill prepared to cope with an avalanche, she must be some sort of congenital idiot.

Half an hour later, however, she was half convinced his assessment might not be far wrong. By then enough passage had been cleared for one of the road crew to come into the shed to check on its occupants.

"Start her up, ma'am," he said kindly, stopping at her window. "You'll be on your way in about ten minutes, but you might as well be warm while you wait.''

After a bit of coaxing, her car sputtered to life and shortly after she heard the roar of the Jeep's engine. Outside, she could see that although the sun had not yet risen above the surrounding mountains the sky was such an intense blue that its reflection trapped hints of mauve in the snow heaped up along the road.

Perhaps if she hadn't been so mesmerized by the sight of freedom she'd have noticed sooner that her troubles were far from at an end. Only when one of the road crew waved her forward did she switch her attention to her car and see the red warning light on her dashboard.

Instinct led her to do exactly the right thing and switch off the car's ignition immediately. The damage, however, was already done, as evidenced by the puff of steam escaping from under the hood.

Behind her the Jeep's horn blasted impatiently, but even a fool could have seen that her car wasn't going anywhere.

With mounting dismay, Jessica watched as her sleeping companion jumped down from the Jeep, exasperation and resignation evident in every line of him, and, in a dismaying rerun of last night's fiasco, approached her window.

"Don't tell me," he jeered, coming to a halt beside her. "Either you've forgotten how to take your foot off the brake or your damned car's broken down."

CHAPTER TWO

ANY hopes Jessica might have entertained that the extent of the problem was not too serious the almighty Mr. Morgan quickly put to rout.

He surveyed her engine, which continued to puff out little clouds of steam like a mini-volcano on the verge of erupting. "It figures," he drawled, rolling his eyes heavenward, and beckoned the road crew to come see for themselves the latest misfortune she'd brought down on her hopelessly inept head.

"Release the hood," one of them called out to her, and, after they had it propped open, they clustered around the innards of her car with the rapt attention all men seemed to foster for such things. There followed a muttered discussion to which Jessica, still slumped disconsolately behind the steering wheel, was not privy.

Eventually, the Morgan man came back and leaned one elbow on the roof. "Might as well face it, Jessica Simms," he announced conversationally, his voice floating through the window which she'd opened a crack. "The only way this puddle-hopper's going to move is hitched to the back end of a tow truck."

She could have wept, with disappointment, frustration, and rage. "I suppose," she said, hazarding what seemed like a reasonable guess, "that my radiator's overheated?"

"On the contrary, it's frozen. Better phone your sister and tell her not to expect you at her bedside any time soon. Sentinel Pass is the nearest place you'll find a service station and they're working around the clock to keep emergency

24

vehicles on the road. Types like you go to the bottom of their list of priorities.''

He bent down and pinned her with a disparaging blue stare. ''Of course, all this could have been avoided if you'd used the brains God gave you and taken your car in for winter servicing.''

''I intended to,'' she spat, terribly afraid that if she allowed herself a moment's weakness she'd burst into tears instead. ''The moment school was out for the holidays I planned to go over to the mainland and have it attended to. Normally, it's something I take care of earlier, but we've had such a mild winter so far this year—''

''Ah, well,'' he interrupted, with patently insincere sympathy, ''they do say the road to hell is paved with good intentions, don't they?''

''Oh, put a sock in it!'' she retorted, consigning good manners to perdition, along with any remnant of seasonal goodwill toward him that she might have been inclined to nurture.

If Satan had chosen that moment to take human form and torment a woman past endurance, he would have smiled exactly as Mr. Morgan smiled then. With devastating, dazzling delight.

A couple of the road crew joined him at the window. ''We're about ready to head back to Sentinel Pass, Mr. Kincaid, so if you want a hand pushing the car over to the side…?''

''I'd appreciate it,'' he said. ''Get Stedman's to phone once they've towed it in and had a chance to assess the damage, will you? As for you,'' he barked, stabbing an imperious finger in Jessica's direction, ''we've frozen our butts off long enough on your account. Into the Jeep, fast, and don't bother to argue or complain!''

She had no inclination to do either. Her most pressing need was to find a washroom in the not too distant future, so the sooner they arrived at wherever he was taking her the better. But he offered not a word of explanation of where that might be as he drove out of the snow shed and, some five miles further along the highway, turned north onto a narrow road that twisted snake-like up the side of the mountain.

As warmth from the heater blasted around her ankles, however, the frozen dismay of Jessica's situation began to melt enough for her to venture to ask, ''Where are we going?''

''To my lair in the hills where I plan to have my wicked way with you,'' he said. ''And if you don't like that scenario I'm willing to settle for driving you to the top of the hill and shoving you over the edge.''

''Very funny, I'm sure,'' she said, refusing to let him rattle her, ''but if that's all you have in mind you could have finished me off last night.''

''Don't think the idea didn't occur to me,'' he warned, and swung left up an even narrower road so suddenly that her suitcase, which he'd flung in the back of the Jeep, rolled onto its side and landed with a thud against the wheel well.

''I think we would both much prefer it if I spent the day at the nearest hotel,'' she replied. ''Perhaps where my car's going, and while it's being fixed I could freshen up and—?''

''There isn't any accommodation to be had in Sentinel Pass. It's a truck stop, not a tourist spot, and they're busy enough without having you underfoot all day. The closest town of any size is Wintercreek which you already know lies two hours east of here, so, like it or not, we're stuck with each other's company until you've got wheels again.'' He drew an irate breath. ''Which will hopefully be later this afternoon.''

Jessica swallowed a sigh and stared through the windshield. Thick stands of pine hemmed the road; directly ahead a snow-covered peak reared majestically into the clear sky. "Do you really have a home up here?" she asked doubtfully, afraid that, unless they arrived very soon, she was going to have to suffer yet another indignity and request that he pull over so that she could make a trip behind a tree. "It seems a very isolated place."

"That's what gives it its charm, Jessica. No nosy neighbors, no TV, just peace and quiet in which to do whatever I please—as a rule, that is."

"But you do have a phone service. I heard you tell the men who dug us out that whoever repairs my car should phone you when it's ready."

"We have the bare necessities," he allowed.

We? "So you don't live alone, then?"

"I don't live alone."

"I noticed," she said, when he showed no inclination to offer any further details, "that the road crew called you Mr. Kincaid, but you told me your name was Morgan."

"It is," he said. "Morgan Kincaid."

She swiveled to face him. "Then why did you let me make a fool of myself calling you Mr. Morgan?"

He flung her another satanic grin and she couldn't help noticing that, loaded with unholy malice though it was, it showcased a set of enviably beautiful teeth. "Because you do it so well, with such strait-laced gullibility."

He wasn't the first man in her life to have realized that, she thought grimly. Stuart McKinney had beaten him to it by a good seven years, and made a bigger fool of her than Morgan Kincaid could ever hope to achieve. "Then I'm happy I was able to provide you with a little entertainment," she replied. "It eases my guilt at having caused you so much inconvenience."

He swung the Jeep around a final bend and, approaching from the west, drove up a long slope which ended on a plateau sheltered by sheer cliffs at its northern edge. On the other fronts, open land sloped to a narrow valley with a river winding through, but it was not the view which left Jessica breathless so much as the house tucked in the lee of the cliffs.

Built of gray stone, with a steeply pitched slate roof, paned windows, chimney pots and verandas, it sprawled elegantly among the fir and pine trees, a touch of baronial England in a setting so unmistakably North American west that it should have been ludicrous, yet wasn't. It was, instead, as charming and gracious as it was unexpected.

To the left and a little removed from the main house stood a second building designed along complementary lines; a stable, Jessica guessed, whose upper floor served as another residence if the dark red curtains hanging at the windows were any indication. Smoke curled from the chimneys of both places and hung motionless in the still air, tangible confirmation that Morgan Kincaid hadn't lied when he'd claimed not to live alone.

"Okay, this is it," he said, drawing to a halt at the foot of a shallow flight of snow-covered steps in front of the main house.

Grabbing her suitcase, he led the way up to a wide, deep veranda and into a narrow lobby where he stopped and removed his boots. Jessica did likewise, then followed him into the toasty warmth of a vaulted entrance hall. Directly in front of her a staircase rose to a spindled gallery which ran the length of the upper floor.

"Go ahead, Jessica," Morgan Kincaid invited, his voice full of sly humor as he gestured up the stairs. "The bathroom's the first door to the right at the top. Take a shower while you're in there, if you like. You'll find towels in the corner cupboard next to the tub."

Beast! Fuming, Jessica grabbed her suitcase and scuttled

off as fast as her stockinged feet would allow on the
smoothly polished pine floorboards.

He waited until she'd disappeared before letting himself out
of the house again and turning to the stables. Clancy was
there, mucking out the stalls. Inhaling the pleasantly familiar
scents of hay, fresh straw and horses, Morgan stood in the
doorway and watched.

Without shifting his attention from the task at hand,
Clancy spoke, his voice as rusted as an old tin can left out
too long in the rain. "'Bout time you got here, Morgan.
Expected you yesterday.''

"I know," Morgan said, a picture of Jessica Simms' narrow, elegant figure rising clear in his mind. "I ran into a
bit of trouble.''

"Oh?" Clancy planted his pitchfork in a fresh pile of
straw, rested one hand on the side of the stall and massaged
the small of his back with the other. "How so?"

"Wound up spending the night in the avalanche shed just
west of Sentinel Pass—with a woman. Her car's out of com-
mission and she needs a place to stay until it's fixed, so I
brought her here.''

The smirk that had begun to steal over Clancy's weathered features at the start of Morgan's revelation disappeared
into a scowl of alarm. "Lordy, Morgan, you got to get rid
of her. This ain't a safe place for a woman right now.''

"What's that supposed to mean?"

"Reckon you ain't been listening to the radio today, or
you wouldn't be askin'. Reckon you ain't seen the mail I
left in the main house, either. You got another Christmas
card, Morgan. From Clarkville Penitentiary.''

"The card I've come to expect," Morgan said, refusing
to acknowledge the unpleasant current of tension that
sparked the length of his spine at the mention of Clarkville,
"but what do you mean about the news?''

"Gabriel Parrish broke out of jail late yesterday afternoon. Heard it on the seven o'clock broadcast this morning."

The tension increased perceptibly, although Morgan didn't let it show. "I'm surprised he's considered interesting enough to make the headlines."

"Heck, Morgan, there ain't a soul alive in British Columbia that don't remember his trial or the man who put him away. Reckon we'd see your face plastered right next to his on the TV, if we had one." Clancy cast him a speculative glance from beneath bushy brows. "How much you want to bet that he'll come lookin' for you, Mr. Prosecutor?"

"He'd be crazy to do that."

"There weren't never no question about his bein' crazy, Morgan. Real question is, is he crazy enough to come lookin' for revenge, and in my mind there ain't much doubt about it."

"Clarkville's hundreds of miles from here. The police will catch up with him soon enough, if they haven't already done so. He's no threat to me, Clancy."

"Get rid of the woman anyway, Morgan, unless you want to risk having her used for target practice."

"You spend too much time alone reading bad westerns," Morgan said. "Parrish isn't fool enough to come to the one place people might be expecting him. He's served nine of a twenty-five-year sentence. With time off for good behavior—and he's been a model prisoner by all accounts—he'd be eligible for parole in another six. He wouldn't blow everything now just to come after me." Morgan shook his head, as much to convince himself as Clancy. "No, he's looking for freedom, not a longer stretch behind bars."

"And what if he's got a different agenda, one that involves settling an old score? What then?"

"If it'll ease your mind any, I'll put in a call to the local police and let them know I'm spending Christmas here, just in case he shows up in the area.'' Morgan passed a weary hand across his eyes. ''Beyond that, all I'm looking for is a hot shower, something rib-sticking to eat, and a nap. I didn't get much sleep last night.''

''Do tell,'' Clancy squawked. ''And wouldn't that just curdle your ex's cream if she knew you'd found someone else to keep your feet warm in bed?''

''Don't let your imagination get the better of you,'' Morgan advised him sourly. ''There's nothing going on between me and Jessica Simms, I assure you. She's too much an uptight copy of Daphne and I like to think I'm smart enough not to fall for the same type twice.''

''Praise the Lord! Because, escaped con on the loose or not as the case may be, this ain't no place for a woman like that, Morgan, any more than you're the marryin' kind. Too wrapped up in your work, too short on patience and too damned opinionated is what you are. Women don't like that in a man.''

''You ought to know,'' Morgan said, laughing despite the anxiety and irritation fraying the edges of his pleasure at being back at the ranch for the holidays. ''Agnes took on all three when she married you, and spent half her life trying to cure you of them.''

Clancy pulled his worn old stetson down over his brow and came to stand next to Morgan in the doorway. ''Had a little chat with her this mornin','' he murmured, nodding to the enclosure atop a small rise beyond the near meadow, where the ashes of his wife of forty-eight years lay scattered. ''Told her I'd put up a Christmas tree in the main house, just like always. Remember all the bakin' she used to do, Morgan, and the knittin' she tried to hide, and all that business of hanging up a row of socks, as if we was still kids believin' in Santa Claus?''

''Of course I remember.'' Morgan slung an arm over his shoulder, a gesture of affection which the hired hand suffered reluctantly. "On Christmas Eve we'll light the fire in the living room, raise a glass to her, and you'll play the organ. She'd like to know we're keeping to the traditions that meant so much to her."

"Always assumin' we ain't been murdered in our beds by then," Clancy said gloomily. "I'm tellin' you, Morgan, Gabriel Parrish is *gonna* come lookin' for you. I feel it in my bones. And he ain't *gonna* knock at the front door and announce himself all nice and polite."

Jessica heard the phone ring as she was toweling dry her hair. Heard, too, the muffled sound of Morgan Kincaid answering, although his exact words weren't clear.

When she came down the stairs a few moments later, she found him seated behind a heavy oak desk in a room which clearly served as some sort of office-cum-library, judging by the bookshelves lining the walls.

"The mechanic from the garage in Sentinel Pass just called," he said, bathing her in a glower. "Not only is your car radiator frozen solid, you've also got a cracked block."

There was no need to ask if he considered that to be bad news; his face said it all. "I gather it won't be fixed today, then."

"Not a chance," he said. "The earliest you'll be on your way is tomorrow—if you're lucky."

In Jessica's view, it was about time her luck changed for the better, but it didn't sound as if it was going to happen soon enough to please either of them. "And if I'm not? How long then?"

"It depends when they can get around to working on your car and how difficult it is to access the trouble. If they have to take out the engine...." His shrug sent a not unpleasant whiff of mountain air and stables wafting toward her. "You could be facing another day's delay."

"But that takes us right up to Christmas Eve! I can't

possibly impose on you and your wife's hospitality for that length of time. No woman wants a stranger thrust on her at such a busy time of year. And my sister needs me.''

''Your sister's going to have to get along without you a while longer,'' he declared, rolling the chair away from the desk and pacing moodily to the window. ''And I don't have a wife.''

''But you said....''

''I said I didn't live alone.'' He spun around to face her, his face a study in disgruntlement. ''I did not say I was married.''

''All the more reason for me to find some other place to stay, then,'' she blurted out, horrified to find her thoughts straying from the very pertinent facts of her dilemma with the car to the vague realization that she was afraid to be alone with this man.

He spelled danger, though why that particular word came to mind she couldn't precisely say. It had something to do with his sense of presence that went beyond mere good looks. Whatever it was, it had expressed itself in the middle of the night before and she knew it was only a matter of time before it would do so again. He exuded a complex and undeniable masculinity that she found...sexy.

An uncomfortable heat spread within her at the audacity of the admission. She did not deal with sexy; it had no relevance in her life. ''I'm afraid,'' she said, ''that you'll just have to drive me to Wintercreek yourself.''

''Forget it,'' he said flatly. ''Even if it didn't involve a three- or four-hour round trip for me, what good will it do you to be in one place when your car's in another, eighty miles away?''

Once again, he was so irrefutably *right* that, illogically, Jessica wanted to kick him. Curbing any such urge, she said, ''In that case, I'll endeavor not to cause you any more trouble than I already have.''

"You can do better than that," he said, and jerked his head toward a door at the far end of the main hall. "You can make yourself useful in the kitchen back there and set the table. There's a pot of chili heating on the wood- stove which should be ready to serve by the time I get cleaned up. Maybe a hot meal will leave us both more charitably inclined toward the other."

Confident that she'd obey without a qualm, he loped off, long legs moving with effortless rhythm up the stairs. Refusing to gaze after him like some star-struck ninth-grade student, Jessica made her way to the kitchen, which would have been hard to miss in a house twice as large.

Big and square, with copper pots hanging from the beamed ceiling and the woodstove he'd mentioned sending out blasts of heat, it could easily have accommodated a family of ten around the rectangular table in the middle of the floor, yet Morgan Kincaid clearly had the house pretty much to himself.

There'd been only one toothbrush in the bathroom, only one set of towels hanging on the rail, and an unmistakable air of emptiness in the row of closed doors lining the upper hall. Did he perhaps have a housekeeper who occupied the rooms above the stables? Was that what he'd meant when he'd said he didn't live alone?

If so, Jessica decided, taking down blue willow bowls and plates from a glass-fronted cabinet, she'd prefer spending the night with her, even if it meant sleeping on the floor. The favor of Morgan Kincaid's reluctant hospitality was no favor at all.

She was stirring the pot of chili set on a hot plate hinged to the top of the woodstove when a man of about seventy, accompanied by a pair of golden retrievers, came into the kitchen from a mud room off the enclosed porch at the back of the house.

Short, stocky and unshaven, his appearance was what one

could most kindly call weathered. "You must be the woman," he observed from the doorway, unwinding a long, knitted scarf from around his neck and opening the buttons on a sheepskin-lined jacket.

Not quite sure how to respond to that, Jessica murmured noncommittally, replaced the lid on the chili pot, and bent to stroke the head of the smaller dog, who came to greet her before curling up in one of the two cushioned rocking chairs near the woodstove. The other animal remained beside his master and it was hard to tell which of the two looked more suspicious.

"You made any coffee?" the man inquired, in the same semi-hostile tone.

"Yes. May I pour you a cup?"

"Cup?" His gaze raked from her to the table and came to rest in outrage on the hand-sewn linen place mats and napkins she'd found in a drawer. "What the hell—? Who gave you the right to help yourself to Agnes's Sunday-best dishes and stuff?"

Compared to the acerbic dwarf confronting her now, Morgan Kincaid's personality suddenly struck Jessica as amazingly agreeable. She made no attempt to hide her relief when he, too, appeared and stood surveying the scene taking place, although she could have done without his smirk of amusement.

"Lookee, Morgan," the old buzzard with the dog spluttered furiously, "we got ourselves a woman with a nestin' instinct taking charge. Makin' herself right at home and pawin' through our private possessions as if she owns the place. Better watch yourself, or she'll be warmin' your bed again come nightfall."

"Put a lid on it," Morgan ordered him affectionately. "Jessica Simms, meet Clancy Roper, my hired hand. He looks after the horses when I'm not here, and keeps a general eye on the place. The dog in the chair is Shadow, the other's Ben. Clancy, this is the person I told you about whose car is being repaired.''

''I didn't figure on her bein' the tooth fairy,'' Clancy returned. ''How long you plannin' to keep her around, nosin' through the house and ferretin' out things that ain't any o' her concern?''

''Not a moment longer than necessary,'' Jessica informed him shortly, then pointedly addressed her next remark to Morgan. ''In addition to taking the unpardonable liberty of laying the table, I found a loaf of bread and put it to warm in the oven. I hope that doesn't also violate some unwritten rule of the house?''

''No,'' he said, a hint of apology merging with the amusement dancing in his eyes. ''And the table looks very nice.''

''In that case, if you're ready to eat I'll be happy to dish up the food.''

''I'm starving, and so must you be.'' He held out a chair for her with a flourish that drew forth another irate snort from the hired hand. ''Have a seat and I'll take over. We're used to doing for ourselves here, though not quite as elegantly as this any more. Clancy, quit sulking and sit down.''

''The dogs needs feedin', or don't that matter now that you got a woman trippin' you up every time you turn round?''

''The dogs won't mind waiting.'' Unperturbed by the irascible old man, Morgan set about serving the chili and slicing the loaf of bread. ''You want coffee with your meal, Jessica, or would you prefer to have it afterward?''

''Whatever you're used to is fine with me.''

''We usually have it with, especially during the winter when the days are so short. We start bringing in the horses around four in the afternoon, which doesn't allow much time for a leisurely lunch.''

''Ain't waitin' that long today,'' Clancy muttered, practically swiping his flannel-shirted arm across the end of Jessica's nose as he reached over to help himself to bread. "Not only ain't the company the sort that makes a man want to hang around, the sky's cloudin' up from the north-east pretty damn fast. Reckon we'll be seein' snow again before the day's out."

Morgan aimed a glance Jessica's way. "Just as well you're not planning to drive all the way to Whistling Valley today, after all, or you might be spending another night on the road and leaving yourself at the mercy of the next person who happens to come along."

"I'm really rather tired of your harping on about last night," she said, the note of reprimand in his remark really grating on her nerves. "I've already told you why I wasn't as well prepared for the weather as I would have been had circumstances been different, and I don't feel I owe you any further explanation or apology."

"Right grateful little vixen, ain't she, Morgan?" Clancy Roper said gleefully. "Reckon that'll teach you not to go pickin' up strange women off the side of the highway."

"Doesn't it occur to you that you were lucky I was the one you found yourself trapped with?" Morgan lectured her, ignoring Clancy. "Or that you have a responsibility to yourself and society at large not to take that sort of risk with your safety?"

"I don't make a habit of expecting the worst," Jessica retorted. "Most people behave decently, I find, given the chance."

He spread long, lean fingers over the table top and shook his head. "Then you're kidding yourself. Good Samaritans are pretty thin on the ground these days, and just because it's Christmas doesn't mean you can afford to indulge in the wholesale belief that all men are full of goodwill."

"Reckon we just might find that out the hard way," Clancy put in with a scowl, "if Gabriel—"

But before he could elaborate further Morgan cut him off with a meaningful glare and a brusque, "Shut up, Clancy. Let's not get into that again."

They ate the rest of the meal in strained silence. Once they were done, Morgan nodded to Clancy. "Feed the dogs while I bring in another load of wood," he said, heading for the back porch, "then we'll get back to the stables."

Feeling thoroughly superfluous, Jessica said, "Is there anything I can do to help?"

"Not unless you're used to working horses."

"Just got to look at her to see she wouldn't know the hind end of one if it was starin' her in the face," Clancy said, shoveling dog food into two bowls.

"You're right," Jessica informed him. "But I'm perfectly able to wash dishes and from the way you've managed to splatter chili all over yours it's just as well. I'm also capable of producing an acceptable evening meal."

"Lordy, Lordy," the old curmudgeon sneered back. "Ain't never before heard a woman spit out such a mouthful of hoity-toity words in one breath."

"Considering we're both lousy cooks," Morgan told him, "I think you'd be smart to button your lip. Jessica, feel free to take over the kitchen. There's a freezer full of stuff in the mud room, and sacks of potatoes and other vegetables. Oh, and help yourself to the phone in the office if you want to call the hospital again."

She did, and afterward almost wished she hadn't bothered. Selena, it turned out, had received a relatively minor injury to her spine—mostly bruising which, though painful, was not expected to create any lasting complications.

Jessica would have thought that was cause enough for any reasonable person to celebrate, but Selena was not famous for being reasonable. Thoroughly put out by the number of Christmas parties she was missing and the fact that the hospital restricted the number of visitors she was allowed, she devoted most of the conversation to a litany of complaint.

Patience stretched to the limit, Jessica finally cut short the call with the suggestion that since there was little Selena could do to change things she might as well make the most of them.

Such excellent advice, Jessica decided, hanging up the phone, also applied to her. She found an apple pie and a package of some kind of stewing meat that looked like beef in the freezer, and potatoes, carrots and onions in the vegetable bins. The refrigerator yielded up butter, cheese, eggs, and a slab of back bacon. Jars of dried herbs and such filled the shelves of a wooden spice rack.

By the time the snow that Clancy had predicted began to fall, shortly after four, the kitchen was filled with the rich aroma of meat and vegetables simmering in the oven, the lunch dishes had been washed and returned to their hallowed place in the glass-fronted cabinet, and Jessica was left with nothing more pleasant to do than await the return of her unwilling host and his uncivil hired hand.

"Hardly the ideal dining companions," she commented to Shadow, who lifted her head sympathetically from her spot in the rocker, then tucked her nose more snugly under her tail.

The men came back about half an hour later. Their footsteps clumped onto the back porch, followed shortly thereafter by the door to the mud room being flung open and the sound of something being dragged across the floor.

"It'll dry out a bit overnight, and we'll put it up tomorrow," she heard Morgan Kincaid say. "Hang up your jacket, and let's get inside where it's warm."

"Where the woman is, you mean," came the disagreeable reply.

"Well, Clancy," his employer drawled, in that husky,

come-hither sort of voice of his, "I'm willing to put up with her company for another night if it means our coming in to find a good hot meal waiting on the table, and after the sort of afternoon we've both put in I'd think you would be too."

"Speak for yourself," Clancy snapped, clearly put out by any such suggestion. "I'll make do the same as usual when we ain't busy puttin' on our party hats for company we ain't asked for. A can of stew's good enough for me—in my own quarters with just Ben for company," he finished, "and where I don't have to worry 'bout strangers pickin' through my stuff the minute my back's turned. See you in the mornin', boss."

A low laugh rolled out of Morgan Kincaid. Low and, to a woman's ears at least, sexy. Jessica put both hands to her cheeks but was unable to control the flush of annoyance conjured up by yet another unwelcome interpolation of that word.

"Gee, thanks!" he said. "I'll remember this the next time it's my turn to do you a favor, old man. You know full well having her here isn't *my* idea of a good time, either."

Pure anger left Jessica rooted to the spot. What did they think? That she *wanted* to be stranded here? Or that she was either too deaf to overhear their remarks or too stupid to understand them?

Well, Morgan Kincaid might like to think he knew what sort of evening lay in store for him, but he was about to discover it was going to be a lot worse than anything he could begin to imagine!

CHAPTER THREE

MORGAN betrayed not a scrap of embarrassment when he came into the kitchen to find Jessica standing by the wood-stove and well within earshot of anything said in the mud room. "Guess you heard that Clancy won't be joining us for dinner," he said, casually batting a few snowflakes from the inside of his collar where they must have strayed when he'd removed his jacket.

"That and a few other choice bits of conversation," Jessica replied stonily. "You've got a lot to learn about being a gracious host, Mr. Kincaid."

"Doubtless, but I'm not interested in taking a lesson right now." He nodded to the enamel coffee pot sitting on the stove top. "Any fresh coffee in there?"

"Find out for yourself," she said, amazed and shocked to hear his surliness rubbing off on her. "And, before you subject me to another homily on your munificence in having rescued me from a plight of my own making, allow me to point out that I have spent the afternoon trying to make up for some of the inconvenience I've put you to. There's fresh wood in the stove, dinner is ready whenever you are, the kitchen is clean—which is more than it was before—and all you have to do is relax and enjoy the evening.

"And," she concluded on a final, irate breath, "just in case I inadvertently say or do something to spoil the occasion, I'll be happy to take a tray up to whatever room you assign to me so that you're not forced to endure my unwelcome company a moment longer than necessary."

"Self-sacrifice doesn't suit you, Jessica," he snorted. "As for your being unwelcome, let's face it, you're no more

41

happy to be stranded here with me than I am to be saddled with you. This is my retreat, a place I enjoy specifically because it's nothing like…'' he hesitated, and a grimace of distaste rippled over his expression ''…the sort of world you undoubtedly prefer. I'm used to doing as I please up here, whenever it pleases me to do it.''

Jessica sniffed disparagingly. ''And what's that, exactly?''

''Whatever takes my fancy—going about unshaven and spending all day ankle-deep in horse manure, or rolling around naked in the snow if I feel like it, without having to worry that some puritanical biddy is going to go into cardiac arrest at the sight.'' He shrugged his big shoulders and unbuttoned the top two buttons of his wool shirt in what struck Jessica as a highly suggestive fashion, considering his last remark. ''I find you a most inhibiting presence, Miss Simms.''

Why, instead of reassuring her, did his words carry a sting that left her feeling drab and sexless? He was perfectly right, after all. She might be only thirty, but she typified the quintessential schoolmarm heading straight into cloistered spinsterhood, and wasn't that exactly the path she'd chosen for herself?

''I won't apologize for being who I am,'' she said briskly. ''You'll simply have to control your unconventional urges until tomorrow when I'm gone. In the meantime, I'd appreciate your showing me to a room where I can spend the night.''

''Oh, hell,'' he said, his husky drawl threaded with impatience, ''help yourself to whichever one you please, as long as you don't choose mine.''

As if having to share a bed with her two nights in a row was more than any red-blooded man should have to stomach! As if he'd rather sleep with a corpse!

Well, she'd known since she was sixteen that she was no

femme fatale. "Poor thing, your feet are your best feature," Aunt Edith had declared wearily, and had turned her attention as well as her affection on the far prettier Selena.

Did some of that old feeling of rejection seep through the indifferent facade Jessica had learned to present to the world? Was that what prompted Morgan Kincaid to add, with more kindness than he'd shown thus far in their relationship, "Hey, listen, I don't mean to come across as such a bear. I'm a bit preoccupied with other things, that's all. The room above the kitchen's the warmest, so why don't you throw your suitcase in there, then come down and join me for dinner? Go on," he urged, when she hesitated. "Whatever you've got cooking smells great and I promise I won't bite you by mistake."

It would have been churlish to refuse. Churlish, silly, and immature. Which explained why she nodded her agreement and made her way up the stairs to the room he'd singled out. Because she prided herself on being a mature, intelligent adult. It was one of the reasons why she'd achieved so much, so soon, in her career.

But how then did she justify the adolescent way she hurried to the mirror above the carved mahogany dressing table at the foot of the matching double bed and pulled the clasp out of her hair so that it flowed thick and full over her shoulders? As if such a simple change were enough to render her glamorous and alluring!

"You can't make a silk purse out of a sow's ear," Aunt Edith had maintained, and it was true. Men did less than look twice at thin, thirty-year-old women with slightly wavy brown hair and plain gray eyes; they didn't see them at all!

Jessica found her brush and drew it systematically through her hair until every strand lay smooth against her skull. With one hand she folded the customary loop at the nape of her neck, then with the other anchored it in place with a plain tortoiseshell barrette. She tucked her blouse more neatly into the waist of her navy pleated skirt and adjusted the starched points of her collar so that they paralleled the row of buttons aligned down the front of her meager chest.

She might not look better, but she looked familiar. And that left her feeling secure enough to brave an evening with Morgan Kincaid.

She walked with the upright, flowing grace of a nun, Morgan decided, his gaze remaining fixed on the doorway leading to the front hall long after she'd disappeared through it. Dressed like one, too, in sober, neutral colors designed along straight, concealing lines. The only piece missing from the picture was the sweet charity of soul one might reasonably expect in a woman of the cloth, but Jessica Simms was a vinegary bit of a thing whose habit of giving a nostril-pinching little sniff of suspicious disapproval around men spoke volumes.

Not that he necessarily held that against her. On the contrary, he applauded her for it. He'd seen enough tragedy resulting from people, particularly women and children, choosing to ignore their self-protective instincts where men were concerned.

Abruptly, he grabbed the empty wood basket and, with Shadow at his heels, strode through the mud room and out into the night, welcoming the sting of the still falling snow against his face, the bite of the wind funneling up from the valley. Anything to distract him from the memories too ready to leap out of his professional past—some of which would, he suspected, haunt him till the day he died.

It was Christmas, for Pete's sake—a time for families to come together in celebration. The trouble was, he'd seen too many ripped apart by violent crime and nothing he'd been able to do in the way of exacting justice had managed to heal them. Not chestnuts roasting, not plum puddings ablaze with rum, not children hanging stockings. Especially not children hanging stockings.

For a while, during the married years with Daphne, he'd hoped she'd become pregnant. He'd needed to know he could look after his own family, even if he couldn't always protect others'. He'd wanted his parents to know the joy of grandchildren. But the children hadn't come, Daphne hadn't stayed, and his parents had died within six months of each other.

So here he was, thirty-seven, with more money than he knew what to do with, a career that promised to elevate him to the Bench before he turned fifty, and spending another Christmas alone, except for Clancy and a woman he felt he should address as Sister!

Flinging enough wood into the basket to keep the stove well stoked until morning, he retraced his steps from the shed to the house. Already, the prints he'd made when he'd come out were powdered with a fresh layer of snow. It was going to be a classic white Christmas, the kind shown on nostalgic cards where women in fur muffs shepherded families to church and children gazed, wide-eyed, through square-paned windows draped in icicles.

Families, children.... Despite his best attempts to shut it out, the whole memory thing came full circle again, threatening to blanket him more thoroughly than the snow.

He shook his head impatiently. He should have stayed in Vancouver where it was probably raining, and those dim-witted ornamental cherry trees along the boulevards and sea-fronts were bursting with pale pink blossom in anticipation of a spring still three months away. Where he had friends who gathered in exclusive private clubs to nibble on Russian caviar and sip champagne. Where the women adjusted their sleek designer gowns and watched him with a certain hunger that, for a little while, he could return.

Instead, he was snowbound with the very proper Miss

Simms who probably wouldn't know sexual appetite if it jumped up and bit her on the nose. Damn!

He kicked open the outside door and dumped the wood basket on the floor next to the tree Clancy had brought in at noon. On the other side of the wall, he could hear her puttering around the stove, opening the oven door, rattling cutlery.

She froze when he came into the kitchen, as if she'd suddenly come face to face with an intruder bent on unspeakable mischief. She stood on the far side of the table, knives and forks cradled in her graceful nun's hands, her big gray eyes all wide and startled, and it irritated the hell out of him.

"What's with the nervous tic?" he inquired.

She stared at him, the way a cornered kitten might. "Is it all right to do this?"

He frowned. "Do what?"

"Prepare the table for dinner."

"Of course it's all right," he snapped, his irritation boiling over. "Why on earth wouldn't it be?"

"It upset your hired hand, when he came in for lunch. He seemed to think I was interfering."

"Oh, that." Morgan selected a bottle of wine from the rack built next to the Welsh dresser and found a corkscrew. "It wasn't you so much as the memories you stirred up. Beyond making sure the plumbing doesn't freeze when I'm not here, he doesn't spend much time in the main house since his wife died. I guess coming in and seeing the place looking the way it did when she was alive took him aback, especially with it being so close to Christmas."

"I'm sorry. I had no idea."

"No reason you should." He took down two wine glasses. "Will you join me, or don't you drink?"

"A little red wine with dinner would be nice."

A little red wine with dinner would be nice, she said,

mouth all ready to pucker with disapproval. Oh, brother, it was going to be a long evening!

While she served the food, he filled the glasses and wondered unchivalrously if his getting roaring drunk might pass the time more pleasantly. She sat across from him and shook out her serviette, her movements refined, her manners impeccable, as if she'd been born with a silver spoon in her mouth and a flock of servants on hand to do her slightest bidding. And yet the meal she'd turned out suggested a more than passing familiarity with the working end of a kitchen.

They had cream soup made from carrots and flavoured with ginger, followed by stew with dumplings and rich brown gravy, and he had to admit the food went a good way toward improving his mood.

"These dumplings," he said, spearing one with his fork, "remind me of when Agnes, Clancy's wife, used to do the cooking. She always served them with venison, too."

"Venison?" Jessica Simms echoed, managing to turn rather pale even as she choked on her wine.

"Deer," he explained, thinking she hadn't understood.

She pressed her serviette hurriedly to her mouth and mumbled, "I was afraid that was what you meant."

"Why, what did you think you were eating?"

"Beef," she said faintly.

He laughed. "Same thing, more or less, except for the antlers."

"Oh!" She pushed aside her plate and forgot herself far enough to plant one elbow on the table as she covered her eyes with her hand.

"What's the matter, Jessica? You're obviously not a vegetarian, so it can't be that."

"It's the image that comes to mind when I think of deer."

"Does this happen every time you eat meat?" he inquired, trying to ignore how her hair gleamed in the lamplight. "Do you see little pigs dancing through the air when you fry bacon, or lambs cavorting when you—?"

"It's Rudolph," she said. "I see Rudolph…maybe because it's Christmas."

The red-nosed reindeer? Morgan leaned back in his chair, dumbstruck. "I'd never have figured you for the whimsical type," he finally admitted, smothering a grin. "Do you believe in Santa Claus, too?"

"No," she said, reverting to her usual prim self. "I learned a long time ago that he was the figment of other children's imaginations, but not mine. And I apologize for appearing to be such a fool. But I'm afraid that, much as I hate to see food going to waste, I simply cannot bring myself to eat…" she ventured another glance at the stew cooling on her plate and turned a shade paler "…that."

"Never mind," he said, oddly touched by this more susceptible side of her personality. "The dogs will love you for it. More to the point, though, is what can we find that you will eat?" He got up and opened the refrigerator door. "We've got eggs and ham and cheese. I could make us an omelette."

"Please don't trouble yourself," she said, the nun firmly in control again. "Please just go ahead with your meal before it gets cold."

"And what will you do?" he asked, irritation flaring up anew. "Huddle in the corner and subsist on bread and water?"

"I'll make a sandwich."

"You'll do no such thing." He grabbed the dogs' scrap bowl from the refrigerator and, picking up both plates, added their contents to what it already contained. "You've hardly slept in the last two days, it's hours since we ate lunch, and you're not going to bed on an empty stomach. I might be a lousy host, Jessica, but I'm not inhuman. We'll eat eggs—unless you see unhatched chickens…?"

''No.'' She got up and came to join him, spine erect, narrow hips swaying elegantly. ''But I do insist on helping, since I'm putting you to so much trouble.''

''For crying out loud, sit and enjoy your wine, and while I'm showing off my culinary skills keep me entertained by telling me why you didn't believe in Santa Claus when you were a kid.''

''I grew up in a very...pragmatic household. My aunt didn't encourage fantasies, not even when my sister and I were very small.''

He paused in the act of slicing the ham. ''Aunt?''

''Selena and I were orphaned when we were kids, and were sent to live with my father's brother and his wife.''

''And Auntie didn't much like being roped in as surrogate mother?''

''She was always very fair. She did her duty the best way she knew how, and so did my uncle.''

Jeez! Morgan reached for an onion and began dicing it with uncommon violence. No wonder she was so bloody repressed. From the sound of it, where she'd grown up wasn't so far removed from a Victorian orphanage! ''And debunking the myth of Santa Claus came under the heading of duty, did it? Does that mean you woke up to empty stockings on Christmas morning?''

''Oh, no.'' She took a dainty sip of wine. ''We weren't in the least deprived materially. There was plenty of money and we always had lots of expensive gifts. They just didn't come wrapped in...magic.''

He broke six eggs into a mixing bowl, added salt, a dash of pepper, a dollop of hot sauce, a pinch of dried parsley. ''What about the tooth fairy?''

She smiled and it transformed her face, suffusing it with life and softening its pale angles with a warmth that left her almost pretty. ''No tooth fairy, I'm afraid, just regular visits to the dentist and new toothbrushes every second month.''

"Well, I don't know...." He whisked the eggs and threw a chunk of butter into the frying pan heating on the stove. "It seems to me everyone deserves to start out with a little make-believe, a little magic. Special times to look back on, memories to treasure. Isn't that what childhood's all about?"

"We had special times."

He poured the omelette over the sizzling butter and swirled the mixture around the edges of the pan, before tossing chopped onion and ham on top. "Like what?" he asked, adding a handful of grated cheese.

She sat and thought for a minute, her face a study in grave concentration again. "I was given a leather-bound edition of the complete works of Shakespeare when I graduated from high school."

"You must have been overwhelmed," he said dryly. "Think of all that lewd material in the hands of an eighteen-year-old girl! It's a miracle you weren't seduced into a life of debauchery."

She flung him a somewhat hunted look and in one gulp polished off half the wine remaining in her glass. "I—"

He divided the omelette, flipped each portion onto the plates warming on the hearth, and waited for her to continue. When she showed no inclination to do so, he put her plate down in front of her and reached for the wine bottle. "What were you going to say, Jessica?" he asked, topping up both glasses.

"Nothing."

The way her mouth clamped shut on the word had his internal radar picking up signals just as it did when he sensed a witness was about to commit perjury. Without knowing how, he'd stumbled on some aspect of her past which troubled her deeply but he knew he'd have to temper curiosity with patience if he wanted to discover what it was.

"In that case," he said casually, touching the rim of his

glass to hers, ''here's to another stab at dinner. *Bon appé-
tit!*''

While he made short work of his share of the omelette,
she pecked at hers like a nervous bird. Attempting to ease
the tension a little, he said, ''I meant to say earlier that the
table looks very nice. It's usually cluttered with stuff and I
just clear a space big enough to accommodate my plate.''

She dropped her fork with a clatter. ''Oh, that reminds
me, I found a stack of mail for you when I came in to get
things ready for lunch and left it on the dresser, next to the
clock. Let me get it for you, before I forget again.''

He started to say, ''There's no hurry,'' but she was already skittering out of her chair and scooping up a miscel-
lany of mail-order catalogues and a handful of cards from
the few people who knew he always spent Christmas at the
ranch.

''Thanks,'' he said, when she dropped the bundle beside
his plate, and would have been happy to ignore it until tomorrow if his attention hadn't been caught by the return
address on the topmost envelope.

Clarkville Penitentiary. The handwriting was unmistakable, as neat and contained as the man who'd penned it. A
jarring reminder that, no matter how much Morgan might
like to fool himself, there was no escaping who he was. The
real world had a way of following him, no matter where he
went to hide.

He sensed her watching him. ''Is there something wrong,
Mr. Kincaid?''

''Apart from this 'Mr. Kincaid' business, no,'' he said
shortly, tempted to toss the envelope in the stove unread.
''Calling me Morgan won't compromise your virtue, you
know.''

''I suppose not.''

''We have spent a night together, after all.''

She flushed at that, the shocked, uptight pink of a virgin

confronted by the nearest thing to original sin she'd ever seen. "But not in any familiar sense," she protested.

"No," he said, pushing away from the table. "Look, I don't mean to appear rude, but there's something here I should have attended to sooner and I'd prefer not to leave it any longer."

"Of course. I'm sorry if I've—"

"You haven't." Annoyed that she assumed his sudden restlessness was her fault and unwilling to explain that it was not, he brushed her apology aside and strode to the door. "I'm likely to be tied up on the phone for some time, so if you—"

"Please don't worry about me," she rushed to assure him. "I'll just finish my meal, then make an early night of it."

"In that case I'll see you in the morning." He nodded and left her to it. Once in the study with the door closed firmly behind him, he slit open the sealed envelope and withdrew the card inside.

A pen-and-ink drawing of Clarkville in winter stared up at him, its walls rising bleakly against the starkness of sky and countryside.

He flipped it open and read the contents inside. And knew at once that Clancy had been right. Crazy or not, Gabriel Parrish was bent on revenge. Other people might not recognize the threat hidden in the words "I owe you so much and hope to repay you very soon" but he did. He knew exactly what Gabriel Parrish was really saying.

Tapping the card against the surface of the desk, Morgan debated his options. They were pitifully few. He could run, which was really no option at all since running was not his style and would solve nothing, or he could go looking for his long-time enemy. Or he could wait for the enemy to come to him.

Briefly, he stared out at a night turned ghostly gray by the still falling snow and knew that of the three only the last made any sense. Which made getting rid of Jessica Simms a.s.a.p. all the more imperative.

CHAPTER FOUR

IT WAS late when Morgan came up to bed. Jessica had expected to be asleep long before then but had found her thoughts revolving around him too persistently for her to relax.

What a strange and moody man he was, charming and open one minute, brusque and reserved the next. She'd watched him in the kitchen, covertly taking stock of him as he whipped up the omelette. Had noticed his hands in particular, how finely shaped they were, how well cared for, with the nails short and scrupulously clean for all that he'd spent the afternoon in the stables.

Had noticed his long, strong legs, too, and remembered last night when they'd trapped hers and held her close to him. Not the sort of memory conducive to relaxation at all!

Then there'd been that other business at dinner. She'd felt like a fool for acting as she had when she'd discovered they were eating venison, and had expected another round of scorn from him. But although he'd laughed at her it had not been unkindly and she hadn't minded. In fact, she had been quite captivated by the way his wide, sexy mouth had curved with amusement.

His glance had met hers and he'd smiled at her over the rim of his glass. Behind him, the snow had swirled against the window, a chunk of wood in the stove had shifted and sent a shower of sparks up the chimney and, suddenly, it was Christmas and despite their being strangers a sort of intimacy had flared between them.

The kitchen had assumed a warmth that went beyond the heat from the fire, the wine had rolled more smoothly down her throat and taken with it the inhibitions behind which she hid so much of herself. She had felt safe; had known that, stranger or not, Morgan Kincaid was a man of integrity and that she had nothing to fear from him.

And then she'd brought up the subject of the mail and that had spoiled everything. He'd changed, become all dark and withdrawn, with a haunted sort of look about him as he'd weighed the one envelope on the palm of his hand.

Instinct had told her the sender was a woman who held the power to affect him, to move him, in a way that she, Jessica, had never enjoyed with a man.

The ambience had altered, become charged with tension, and she had felt herself again the interloper. The intimacy had shriveled, her habitual reserve had come slinking back, and she knew he had neither noticed nor cared that she regretted both.

It must have been close to midnight when his footsteps sounded on the stairs and light from the bathroom next door shone out into the night. Huddled beneath the down quilt, Jessica listened to the muffled tattoo of water running in the shower, and to her horror found visions of him standing there naked, with the water sluicing down his powerful body, springing alive in her mind's eye.

A surge of heat spiraled through her, disturbing, erotic. She remained in thrall to it even after the house sank into silence again; found herself wondering how it would have felt to be under that hot stream of water with him, with his hands gliding the length of her spine to define her buttocks, and his mouth fastening on hers, and his hard flesh fusing tightly within the dark, soft warmth of hers.

Appalled, she shot up in the bed, welcoming the chill slap of air against her bare shoulders. Such thoughts were unconscionable! She hadn't allowed herself such self-indulgent rubbish in over five years—not since Stuart Mc-

Kinney had lied his way into her naive heart and seduced her pathetically grateful body.

Across the hall, a mattress creaked, a small sound in the overwhelming silence of the night, but enough to leave her brain feverish with yet another unpardonable image. Of Morgan Kincaid looming naked above her on the bed, of his hand pushing aside her silk nightgown to caress her naked breast, of his knee nudging apart her thighs.

The blood roared in her ears, scorching, shameful. What was the matter with her? Jessica Simms, headmistress of the Springhill Island Private School for Girls, was famous for the absolute incorruptibility of her morals. What would her board of governors have to say if they could see her now, at the mercy of a sexual fantasy so powerful that she was practically writhing with arousal—and all over a man she'd met only twenty-four hours before and about whom she knew nothing but his name?

Flinging aside the feather duvet, she swung her feet to the smooth pine floor. Not a crack of light showed anywhere as she sneaked down the hall and into the bathroom, with her nightgown whispering around her ankles.

Once inside, she locked the door and crossed to the hand-painted wash basin. Her eyes, when she glanced in the gilt-framed mirror hanging on the wall, stared back at her, their focus glazed.

Aghast all over again, she repeatedly dashed cold water over her face and neck, attempting to chase away with pure discomfort what she couldn't dislodge with logic or propriety. Only when the flush had died from her skin and her pulse approached its normal steady rate did she turn off the flow of water, replace the towel on the brass rail, and let herself out of the bathroom.

He was waiting for her outside in the hall, illuminated by a beam of light spilling from his room. He wore a knee-length navy terry-cloth robe which was tied loosely at the waist, and showed a great deal of strong masculine chest from the top and equally strong, masculine calves from the bottom. Try though she might, Jessica couldn't stop herself from staring.

"Hey," he said, his husky voice washing over her, drifting over her bare shoulders and down between her breasts, "are you sick or something?"

Was she? Had she been infected by some strange virus, and did that account for her unmanageable state of mind? "I was thirsty," she mumbled, refusing to meet his glance.

"You look flushed, as if you might be coming down with something." He flung out one hand in a gesture of unmistakable resentment. "Hell, that's the last thing I need."

"I am not ill," Jessica said firmly.

"It wouldn't surprise me if you were," he said, taking in the thin straps that held up the flimsy fabric of her nightgown. "Don't you own *any* decent winter clothing?"

"If by that you mean flannelette pyjamas, no." She threw a glance at him and without considering the wisdom of her words added, "And you're a fine one to talk. I haven't seen so much exposed skin on a man since dear knows when!"

He looked down and gave the terry-cloth robe a twitch to make sure he was decent, a move that left her wondering if he was stark naked underneath.

He knew, as surely as if she'd voiced her curiosity aloud. "Don't hold your breath, Miss Simms," he drawled. "You've seen all I intend to show."

Evil creature! How could she ever have thought him attractive?

Jessica snapped her jaws together and swung away, intending to put the solid wood of her bedroom door between him and her quickly, before her composure crumbled completely. She hadn't gone two steps, however, when, with the eerie sound of a ghost keening to be free, a mournful howl filled the house, its source so close that it seemed to emanate from the very wall in front of her.

Seasoned students at the school were fond of tormenting homesick newcomers with tales of spooks haunting the halls of the junior dormitory. Pragmatist that she was, Jessica always successfully nipped such ideas in the bud, but, just then, just for a moment, her grip on reality slipped and left her at the mercy of the most bizarre foolishness. Just for as long as it took her to spring back with a startled gasp and come up against Morgan Kincaid's solid, underclothed frame.

At that, *everything* fled her mind except for the fact that, all at once, she was on the brink of realizing her earlier fantasy. She could feel the sculpted muscle of his chest at her shoulder blades, his hand in the small of her back, his breath flowing warmly over the nape of her neck.

But the sad fact was, it was not magical at all.

He didn't pull her protectively close, he moved her away with ill-concealed exasperation. "For crying out loud, it's just the wind in the chimney," he said, his voice about as chill as the night outside. "It means the weather's swung around and is blowing in from the north-east again and that we're in for another storm."

"Really." She tugged the straps of her nightgown firmly into place and, with a haughty little toss of her head meant to intimate that she'd found the physical contact every bit as disagreeable as he had, increased the distance between him and her. "Well, I certainly hope that won't delay my departure tomorrow."

"So do I," he muttered on a heartfelt sigh, before he disappeared into his room. "So do I!"

The next morning, Jessica awoke to find her room flooded with reflected brilliance and the sort of hush that cushioned a world buried in snow. Drifts lay halfway up the window and any trace of a road up to the house had been completely obliterated. Above the trees a pewter sky promised more of the same punishment, although the wind appeared to have died. She didn't need anyone to tell her she wouldn't be going anywhere today.

Morgan Kincaid had left a note propped up on the kitchen table. "Gone out to take care of the animals. Help yourself to breakfast and keep the fire and coffee pot going. Be back in a couple of hours."

It was barely nine o'clock. Jessica discovered that the coffee in the pot too closely resembled used motor oil to warrant human consumption and, while she waited for a fresh pot to brew, took a mandarin orange from the bowl on the Welsh dresser and went on a tour of the rest of the main floor of the house.

In light of the rather spartan decor in the bedrooms, she didn't expect too much and was pleasantly surprised to find, to the right of the stairs, a living room some twenty-five feet long by about fifteen feet wide, furnished in faded rose damask.

A massive stone-faced fireplace flanked by built-in bookcases occupied center place on the east wall. Leaded windows looked out on the valley to the south and the steep hill leading up to the cliffs to the north. Painted molding crowned the walls and framed the glass doors leading to a formal dining room.

Clearly, however, neither room had been used in quite some time. The air was flat and stale. A film of dust covered the occasional tables and the top of the old-fashioned pump organ under the south windows in the living room.

Although the hearth had been swept clean, a spider had woven an intricate pattern across one corner of the chimney opening and cobwebs swayed from the silk shades of various lamps.

In some ways, the dining room had fared no better. Crystal stemware dulled by dust waited at one end of the table. The hearth contained the dead ashes of a fire and drippings of wax had overflowed the tarnished silver candelabra to pool on the fine oak sideboard, as though dinner guests either had upped and left before the start of the meal or simply not shown up at all.

A terrible waste, Jessica thought, popping the last segment of mandarin orange in her mouth and retracing her steps. Rooms like these ought to be used instead of being left to molder. If she were mistress of this house, she'd have flowering plants on the mantelpiece, on the carved walnut chest behind the sofa, on top of the organ and in the middle of the dining table. Scarlet poinsettias, snowy cyclamen, rosy pink azaleas. And sprigs of holly tucked into graceful swags of evergreen over the doorway and windows.

The muffled tramp of boots on the back porch alerted her to Morgan Kincaid's return. By the time she'd made her way back to the kitchen, he and Clancy Roper had helped themselves to the better part of the fresh pot of coffee and were warming their backsides at the stove.

"Good afternoon," Morgan declared sunnily, glancing pointedly at the clock which showed twenty past nine.

Jessica supposed he was trying to be funny and had to admit she was relieved. In view of his parting words the night before, humor, however feeble, was the last thing she expected from him.

"It's not quite that late, surely?" she said, and wished she didn't always have to sound so much like a schoolmarm.

"Day's half over," Clancy Roper informed her, depleting the coffee supply again. "If we slept in till all hours like you, woman, nothing'd ever get done right around here."

He was as difficult an individual as Morgan Kincaid, without the latter's good looks or unexpected bursts of charm to redeem him. "I dare say if I lived here and had chores to do I'd have to agree with you," she said. "But since I don't your point is scarcely relevant, is it?"

"Long as you're here, you've got chores." He jerked his head at the window. "See that sky out there? Loaded, it is. With snow," he added, as if she were too mentally defective to be able to figure out the simplest facts for herself. "And it'll be coming down before much longer. We ain't got time to be fixin' meals, missy, nor keeping fires goin'. We got work to do. Men's work."

Morgan Kincaid filled another mug with what was left of the coffee and handed it to her with a smile. "What Clancy's trying to tell you, in his uniquely subtle way, is that taking care of the horses is our first priority so..."

That smile undid her, seducing her so potently that she'd probably have gone out in her flimsy boots and unsuitable clothes and mucked out the stables for him if he'd asked her to. "So you'd like me to take over in here," she finished for him.

His smile deepened to reveal dimples of all things, one on each side of his mouth. "We'd appreciate it, Jessica." He glanced regretfully at the lowering sky beyond the window. "Especially since there's no way I can get you out of here today. The road is impassable, as I'm sure you must realize."

"I understand that." She shrugged her acceptance of what was patently obvious to the most untutored eye. "But I'd like to phone the hospital and let my sister know."

"Can't. All the lines are down," Clancy said, with manifest satisfaction at seeing her thwarted yet again. "If it weren't for the emergency generator, you'd be trimming oil lamps come sunset."

Morgan shot her a commiserating look. "He's right. I wish I could tell you the line crew will be out to fix the phone before tonight but it's more likely to be several days."

"Surely it's only a matter of joining together a few wires. Isn't that something you could do?"

"If I knew where to start looking, yes, probably. But we're talking about ten miles or more of line, Jessica, and if I could follow that I could just as easily get you down to the main highway."

"Reckon we've got ourselves a housekeeper over Christmas, Morgan." Clancy cackled with malicious delight. "Know how to pluck and dress a turkey, woman?"

"No," Jessica snapped. "So unless you do, Mr. Roper, it'll be cheese sandwiches for dinner on Christmas Day."

Stifling a grin, Morgan said, "Quit needling her, Clancy, and count your blessings."

Jessica stared at him. *"Count your blessings?"* she echoed. "Last night, the only blessing you were hoping for was my speedy exit from your life. Would you mind telling me what's happened—apart from a devastating snow storm— to bring on this burst of seasonal goodwill?"

He and Clancy Roper exchanged glances loaded with mysterious significance. Finally, he said smoothly, "You're not the only one inconvenienced by the weather. The Wrights, a couple from the other side of Sentinel Pass, come up here three times a week as a rule. Ted lends a hand around the stables and Betty does a bit of housekeeping."

A very little bit, Jessica concluded, considering what she'd so far observed about the house. At best, the woman swiped a damp cloth over the most visible spots, but clearly didn't exert herself to do a more thorough cleaning.

"Obviously they're not going to make it up here today, any more than you're going to get to Whistling Valley." Morgan said. "I know you're worried about your sister, but you said yourself she's in good hands and doing well."

He stopped and smiled again, more winningly than ever, then went on persuasively, "So if you're willing to take over in the house—?"

"And what if I break some hallowed tradition?" Jessica cut in. "Or touch something sacred?"

Furiously, Clancy banged his coffee cup down on the table, slopping its contents all over everything. "See what you've gone and started, Morgan?"

Another glance passed between the two men, then Morgan said, "Let it go, pal. We can afford to relax for the next couple of days."

Clancy seemed tempted to argue but something in Morgan's expression deterred him. "As you say," he muttered sullenly. "At least she knows how to cook."

"So," Morgan said, swinging his glance back to Jessica, "what about it? We might as well all try to get along."

"True." Jessica looked around the kitchen, at Clancy's moldy old felt stetson parked on the table and dripping melted snow among the remains of the breakfast dishes, at the bacon grease congealing in the frying pan on the counter next to the sink. "But if you think I'm going to be a lackey to your slovenly habits for the next couple of days, think again."

She flung out her hand in a gesture of disgust that encompassed the entire kitchen. "I'm not used to living in a pig sty, and I refuse to do so when there's no need."

"As long as there's livestock needs tendin' to," Clancy said, "dishes sittin' in the sink ain't exactly a priority."

"I appreciate that and I'm more than happy to pull my weight around the house, but you..." Jessica fixed him with the same determined look she afforded difficult students "...you will mend your ways and show a little appreciation. I will clean and cook and do my best to bring a little Christmas spirit into this house, but I cannot—and will not—do it alone."

Morgan looked uneasy. "Exactly what is it you'd like us to do?"

"Well, for a start, I see no reason for us to be falling all over one another in the kitchen when there's a perfectly lovely room going to waste down the hall. Two rooms, in fact, and neither looks as if anyone's set foot in it in months. So when you come in for lunch I'd like you to light fires in the hearths to take the chill out of the air, and I'll serve the evening meal in the dining room.''

''I gather you've taken a grand tour of the main floor,'' Morgan observed dryly.

''Hah!'' Clancy crowed. ''Snoopin's what she's been doin', Morgan. Didn't I tell you she would?''

''And you'll dress for dinner,'' Jessica went on, unfazed by the interruptions, ''in something other than the blue jeans you've apparently been sleeping in for the last week, Mr. Roper. It is almost Christmas, after all.''

''Dress for dinner because it's Christmas?'' Clancy practically spluttered with rage. ''Confound it, woman, I'm not—''

She planted her fists on her hips. ''Scrooge said more or less the same thing much more eloquently a long time ago, Mr. Roper, so spare me your version of the old 'Bah, humbug'. It's my way or bread and cheese. Take it or leave it.''

''We'll take it,'' Morgan said hurriedly. ''After lunch, we'll set up the tree in the living room and you can go to it. Make the place as festive as you like and we'll put on our party manners. Now grab your hat, Clancy, and let's get that mare settled before we have to dig our way from here to the stables.''

He was almost out of the door when he suddenly turned back. ''Oh, and by the way, stay inside the house, Jessica. It's safer.''

''Safer?'' What an odd choice of word. ''Safer how?''

He paused fractionally and if she hadn't already learned from experience that he was one of the most forthright men she'd ever met she'd have thought he was concocting a lie. ''You could get frostbite,'' he said. ''In this weather it can happen in a matter of minutes, especially to someone dressed so inadequately.''

Honestly, she thought, watching from the window above the sink as the men and dogs made their way back to the stables, the way Morgan acted at times, one would have thought he had next-door neighbors watching from behind starched lace curtains and jumping to all the wrong conclusions about the woman he'd brought into his home.

As for his obsession with the weather and her clothes, it bordered on preposterous.

''You'll be digging yourself out of more than snow at this rate,'' Clancy predicted gloomily as they bent into the wind and slogged toward the stables. ''I'm tellin' you, Morgan, you keep givin' in to that woman and findin' reasons not to get rid of her, and before you know it you'll be up to your neck in more trouble than even you can handle.''

Morgan squinted at the sky. ''It's out of my hands, at least for the time being. You don't need me to tell you there's no way to send her on her way until the weather lets up. For now, she's as safe here as anywhere.''

''T'ain't just her safety I'm worryin' about, Morgan, it's yours as well. You get a certain hungry look about you whenever you clap eyes on her and it gives me the willies. Ain't you learned your lesson yet where fancy city women are concerned? Heck, if she thinks the way you live up here ain't squeaky clean, what do you reckon she'd have to say about the muck you deal with down in the city? Well, I'll tell you,'' Clancy continued, barely stopping to draw breath. ''She'd take a hike, just like the other one did, and what's that gonna leave you with, Morgan, apart from a cartload of heartache you don't need?''

''Not that I don't appreciate your concern, old friend,'' Morgan remarked, ''but in this case it's misdirected. I've already told you, Jessica Simms is no more my type than she's yours and it'll be a cold day in hell before I get myself hooked up with someone like her.''

They were fine words, uttered with enough conviction to silence Clancy, and Morgan might have believed them himself if he hadn't suddenly remembered how she'd looked on the landing the night before. Who'd have expected she'd favor silk nightwear so translucent that if the light had been shining from behind her, instead of in front, there'd be little left to his imagination regarding her surprisingly elegant, fine-boned body?

As for his physical response at finding her suddenly pressed up against him, *that* didn't mean a damned thing beyond the fact that he functioned exactly as any normal man would under the circumstances. Of far greater import was his knowledge that the circumstances were not all that they seemed. Fraught with potential danger, they were about as far from normal as they could get, and that was something he couldn't afford to forget.

Clancy surveyed him quietly for a moment then switched to the subject that was really preying on their minds. "How far you reckon Parrish'll get before they catch him?''

"Depends how much ground he covered before the weather set in.'' Morgan glanced up at the sky. "Wherever he is now is where he'll be staying until things let up.''

"Could be he'll freeze to death and save us all a load of trouble.''

"Unlikely. Parrish is no fool, Clancy, and it would be a mistake to underestimate him. I made a couple of calls last night and from what I gathered his was no spur-of-the-moment run for freedom; it was something he'd planned to the last detail. You can be sure he'd have taken all eventualities into account, including the weather.''

Morgan slid back the heavy stable door and followed Clancy inside, swatting snow from the brim of his stetson. "The point is, he's nowhere near here or we'd know about it by now. Which means that as long as we keep an ear out for the news—and I'm counting on you there, Clancy; I don't want her picking up on anything that might come across on the kitchen radio—we can afford to relax and enjoy the next few days.''

He cast a stealthy glance at his stable hand and chose his next words carefully. ''It also means we can be a bit more hospitable to our house guest. No point in arousing her suspicions any more than we already have, nor in causing her more anxiety than she's already got.''

''Could be you're right. Don't fancy having a hysterical woman on our hands should things suddenly go sour.''

''Exactly. And weren't you the one, yesterday, reminiscing about a woman's touch at Christmas, and how it used to be when Agnes was still alive?''

Clancy reared up like the stallion that had broken his thigh ten years before and left one of his legs permanently shorter than the other. ''Jessica Simms ain't Agnes!''

''But she can cook and clean, pal, and if this blizzard keeps up, knowing the house is warm and that dinner's waiting on the table won't be such a bad thing.''

''She still ain't Agnes.'' Clancy flung the statement over his shoulder, resentment rife in the crooked line of his spine.

Tamping down on the sharp reply begging for air space, Morgan tossed a fresh bale of hay into the nearest manger. Was Clancy getting more obstreperous with age, or was it that his own nerves were more on edge than he cared to admit?

''What do you want me to say? That we'll gang up on Jessica Simms, just to keep ourselves in shape in case Gabriel Parrish shows up? Because if so you're going to be disappointed. It's almost Christmas Eve, for Pete's sake, and I just don't have any appetite for waging unnecessary war for the next couple of days. Because, with the best will in

the world, the road crews are going to take at least that long
to make it up here—''

''Don't need to wait on no road crews,'' Clancy informed
him morosely. ''You got a perfectly good snowmobile in
the garage and could have that woman out of here in less
than an hour, if you had a mind to.''

''And do what with her?'' Morgan snapped. ''Leave her
stranded at Stedman's service station? Use your head,
Clancy! Even if her car's fixed, she won't be driving anywhere until the highway's made passable again; nor will
anyone else. Can't you make the best of what's just as lousy
a situation for her as it is for us, or will it give you greater
satisfaction to have us all at each other's throats?''

''Lordy, Morgan Kincaid, you ain't been this twitchy
since your wife upped and left.'' Clancy slewed a crafty
glance his way. ''Don't like to think what that might mean.''

''Then quit thinking at all! That way you'll jump to fewer
wrong conclusions. A lot of people will tell you I can be a
real bastard to deal with at times, and they're right, especially when it comes to my work, but I'm damned if I'm
going out of my way to be unpleasant just to satisfy you. If
you can't extend a bit of Christmas cheer to a stranger,
Clancy, you're welcome to hole up in your own quarters
until the weather breaks and Jessica's out of here.''

''You ain't spoke to me in that tone in over three years,
Morgan,'' Clancy complained again. ''Not since your ex
took you to the cleaners in the divorce court then ran off to
Mexico with her lover.''

Like a dentist's drill coming too close to a nerve,
Clancy's last remark needled home. Morgan braced himself
and grew very still, a bad sign to those who knew him in a
professional context.

Clancy knew it, too. He sucked in a long-suffering breath
and muttered, ''But you're the boss. If makin' nice is what
you're suddenly payin' me for, makin' nice is what you'll

get.'' He swung around and started for the mare's stall at the far end of the stable, his limp more pronounced than usual as though to underline his resentment. ''Not that I got to like it any. No, sir, I ain't got to like it one little bit.''

CHAPTER FIVE

JESSICA took steaks from the freezer and left them to thaw for dinner, prepared ham and mushroom stuffed potatoes for lunch, then spent the remainder of the morning cleaning the house. A couple of hours of straight elbow grease effected a transformation that was only a little less amazing than the utter satisfaction she experienced as she polished and mopped.

Not that she was inept in such a role. Far from it, as the results of her efforts soon showed. But the lifestyle she'd chosen for herself, solitary and painstakingly professional, didn't call for much in the way of domesticity.

A sense of home and hearth had been a luxury others had denied her as a child and from which necessity had distanced her as an adult. Her residence at the school was entirely self-contained, an austerely elegant little house set in a private section of the grounds, but she spent little time there. In addition to her administrative duties, the endless round of board meetings and other related fund-raising events intruded too frequently to allow for that.

Here, though, she was free to play at what other women took for granted as a routine part of daily life. For however long the weather held her captive, she could create the sort of ambience that had no place in her real life. She could hum carols as she worked, raid the preserves in the pantry and make mince tarts, and plan menus for the next two days.

And she did. With a vengeance. When the men and dogs showed up shortly after noon, the air was filled with the inviting aroma of hot mincemeat tarts subtly underscored by furniture wax and pine-scented floor cleaner.

Morgan and Clancy left their hats and boots in the mud room and she knew that they noticed how the kitchen sparkled from the way they sat gingerly at the gleaming table and sort of examined everything from under lowered brows, but there were no snide comments.

There was no conversation at all, in fact, unless the grunt issuing from Clancy Roper's tight-lipped mouth was to be taken as appreciation of the food he apparently enjoyed, if the speed with which he wolfed it down was any indication. Instead, a miasma of hostility hung heavily between the two men, creating an even more pervasive and disquieting chill than the weather.

Even the dogs picked up on it, slinking under the table and remaining there throughout the meal. The atmosphere was about as cheery as a wake and so thoroughly destroyed the ambience she had worked hard to create that Jessica couldn't keep quiet.

Atypically, she was spoiling for a fight, in part because Clancy put her back up in the way that he sniffed his disapproval of her, and in part to prove to herself that she wasn't in thrall to some misplaced sexual fantasy where Morgan Kincaid was concerned.

It was, she reasoned, impossible to entertain erotic dreams about a man she found thoroughly obnoxious.

"Not that I expect either of you to go overboard with compliments or anything," she said tersely as the last mince tart disappeared and both men pushed back their chairs, prepared to leave the table as taciturnly as they'd sat down, "but a simple 'thank you' would be appreciated. Or is it that, in filling your stomachs with good hot food, you consider I'm merely serving the purpose for which God intended me?"

"I seldom waste time trying to second-guess the Almighty, particularly when it comes to women," Morgan replied with equal brevity.

As if members of the female sex in general and she in particular were an anomaly sent to try the patience of reasonable men! "Very broad-minded of you, I'm sure," she spat. "And what time would you like me to serve dinner, master?"

Clancy snickered and Morgan said testily, "For crying out loud, stop acting as if you're the scullery maid! I thought it was mutually agreed that you'd take care of things on the home front so that we could get through the outside work in reasonable time, but if you think your talents would be better employed in the stables all you have to do is say so."

"Well...no." Jessica had the grace to look embarrassed. "I don't know much about horses and I really don't mind holding the fort in here."

"We appreciate that—and the good food. Don't we, Clancy?"

Clancy inclined his head a fraction and shuffled his stockinged feet. "If you say so."

Morgan sighed in a way that suggested he was shouldering more troubles than Jessica could begin to understand, then spread his hands in appeal. "I know this isn't the sort of Christmas either of you had in mind, and it isn't exactly my idea of a picnic in the park either, but we're stuck with it and each other. Can we please just try to make the best of it?"

"Yes," Jessica said in a small voice. It wasn't like her to be so temperamental. But then, nothing about her behavior had been quite normal since she'd met Morgan Kincaid.

"Okay. It starts to get dark about four, by which time we'll be done with the animals, so why don't we plan to eat around seven? That'll give us time to clean up a bit and do justice to your cooking. We might even go so far as to enjoy a drink before dinner." He swung another glance at his stable hand that was little short of a challenge. "Right?"

Clancy pasted an ingratiating smile on his weathered old face. "Whatever you say, boss."

Morgan's response was edged with steel. "Glad you've decided to see things my way."

"Anythin' else, Mr. Kincaid, sir, before I get back to what I'm bein' paid to do?"

"Not a damn thing." The reply gusted out on a breath of exasperation. "I'll join you shortly, although if something comes up and you need me sooner you know where to find me."

Clancy spared Jessica a direct glare for the first time since he'd come in for lunch. "You bet. Ain't no doubt at all in my mind about where *you'll* be."

"Now what have I done to upset him?" she asked, when the door had slammed shut behind him and Ben.

"More than usual, you mean?" Morgan ran a weary hand through his hair.

Jessica stared at him in surprise. "You're surely not saying he's always this…?"

"Cantankerous?" He let out a bark of a laugh. "Not as a rule, no. Maybe it's just the season. Not everyone likes to make a big deal of Christmas."

But she didn't believe him. The tree had been cut and ready to bring into the house when she'd shown up on the scene. "There's more to it than that. He bitterly resents your letting me stay here, doesn't he? And not just because I happened to bring out his wife's best table linen."

Morgan flexed his shoulders and, hooking his thumbs on his hips, pressed the fingers of each hand to the small of his back. "Don't take offense, Jessica. It's not you personally."

She angled a wry look his way. "I see. He just hates people in general."

At her sarcasm, the suggestion of a grin lightened Morgan's expression. "He leads a pretty solitary life. Goes for weeks sometimes with no company other than the dogs and the horses, except for those days when the Wrights are here. That can be hard on a man's party manners, especially if he suddenly finds himself thrust into the company of a woman.''

''I don't buy that for a minute!'' She scooped up the dirty dishes, piled them in the sink, and began rinsing them. ''For heaven's sake, Morgan, I'm a visitor who'll be gone in a matter of days and who's trying to earn her keep in the meantime, not a permanent threat to his lifestyle.''

''I know.''

''Not only that, he was married at one time and I assume from the way he reacted to my touching her things that he holds his wife's memory sacred and that theirs was a long and happy marriage.''

A grimace passed over his face then, a strange, bitter expression that ironed Morgan's mouth into an unsmiling seam. ''That's because he was smart enough to choose a woman who loved him enough to accept him for what he was and never tried to change him.''

So that was it! The suspicion she'd entertained last night, that there was a woman in Morgan Kincaid's life, sharpened to near certainty. His inexplicable shifts of mood, the sudden edge in his voice complemented by a glacial sheen in his eyes found their origin in a marriage gone sour. If she'd guessed right, the question was, how significant a role did the absent wife presently enjoy?

Jessica itched to know and refused to ask. His matrimonial affairs were no more her business than her single status was his. Except that if a wife *was* lurking in the background, and Jessica could know that for certain, it would be enough to kill her lingering attraction to him. She might be all sorts of a fool where men were concerned, but she wasn't idiot enough to repeat past mistakes.

''Something wrong, Jessica?''

''No.'' She shook her head, as much to dislodge her

thoughts as to answer him. "Shouldn't you be getting back outside to help Clancy?"

"I can spare a few minutes to help you out in here first."

"I can manage on my own," she said hastily, more aware than ever that she was afraid to be alone with him. Afraid that the unholy thoughts she'd entertained the night before would return in full force and that, this time, she wouldn't so easily be able to hide their effect on her.

Even now, she was thoroughly aware of him as he leaned against the edge of the counter and watched her doing the dishes. He had such long legs, such trim hips. He was trim all over, she thought, inspecting him slyly, but with the leanly muscled build of a man who worked off the frustrations of daily life in a gym or on a squash court rather than around horses. In fact, he neither spoke nor looked like her idea of a rancher. But then, most of what she knew she'd learned from movies.

Picking up a dish towel, he began drying the cutlery she'd stacked on the draining board. "No need to tackle it alone when an extra pair of hands will cut the job in half," he said.

"I like to keep busy," she replied, disturbingly aware of his shoulder mere inches from hers, of his elbow brushing her arm as he reached for the soup spoons.

"And you will, if you're serious about our using the other rooms over the holiday. I don't think they've seen the working end of a dust rag in the better part of a year."

"Shame on you," she said lightly, concentrating on the dishes in the sink, which were a much safer subject than his physique. "You should make your regular housekeeper earn her money."

He finished drying the last of the cutlery and flung down the dish towel. "You've rinsed those plates to within an inch of their lives," he chided her, tucking the tail of his shirt into the narrow waist of his blue jeans. "If you're determined you're not going to let me help you finish them, then leave them to drip dry and let's get out of this kitchen.''

''You mean I'm allowed to put my feet up for half an hour?''

''Hell, no.'' He grinned at her, suddenly seeming younger and more carefree than he had at any time since he'd found her in the avalanche shed. ''We're going to light those fires you were asking for, and bring in the Christmas tree. Then I'm going to get my hide outside before Clancy nails it to the wall, and you're going to get busy turning this place into a Dickensian Christmas card.''

But although the fires started easily enough the tree wasn't quite so cooperative. Despite Morgan's best efforts, it wouldn't stand straight in the big brass planter he hauled in from his office. In the end, Jessica had to support the trunk while he jammed pieces of firewood around the base to hold it firmly in place, and by the time that was accomplished she had pine needles in her hair and down her neck, another half hour had passed, and he was swearing fluently.

''Damned thing!'' he muttered, finally crawling out from under the lower boughs. ''Why couldn't Clancy have cut something smaller?''

But Jessica, stepping back to take in the general effect, was overawed by the graceful symmetry of the branches and the way the top of the tree almost brushed the high ceiling. ''It's perfect!'' she breathed. ''Morgan, it's the most beautiful Christmas tree I've ever seen.''

He grimaced at the pine sap staining his hands. ''I find that hard to believe. You don't strike me as the type who'd ever settle for anything less than perfection.''

''That just goes to show how little you know about me,'' she said, recalling the sterile silver foil imitation of the real thing that had been Aunt Edith's idea of Christmas decor. ''Tacky clichés aren't my style, dear,'' she'd sneered, the one year Jessica had dared ask for the kind of traditional tree she remembered from the days when her parents were alive.

"True." Morgan gave the trunk a last nudge to make sure it was standing firm. "We are, as you've already pointed out, virtual strangers, yet here we are playing house together, so don't you think it's time we got to know each other a little better?"

Playing house. That was it exactly. They'd been forced into taking part in a charade, but none of it was real. In a few days she'd be on her way, their separate lives would pick up where they'd left off, and a week from now he'd have erased her from memory. The tree would be tossed outside and discarded, its purpose served. And she would never see this place or him again.

Jessica found the thought profoundly depressing.

"Aren't you going to gratify my curiosity?"

Realizing that he was observing her closely, she sought to distract him by plucking at a strand of dead grass clinging to a lower limb of the tree. "I thought you were in a hurry to get back to the stables."

He watched her a moment longer, then said, "You're right. The story of your life will have to wait until later."

Fascinate him with tales of her hopeless inability to inspire others to love her as they always so easily loved her sister? Hardly!

"The story of my life," she told him firmly, "isn't exactly the kind of thing that makes for riveting dinner conversation."

Unexpectedly, he reached out and smoothed his hand over her hair, removing several stray pine needles as he did so. "Let me be the judge of that."

The contact, though brief, was electrifying. She had a sudden insane urge to imprison his hand against her face, to turn her head and press her mouth to his resin-stained palm. Instead, she shook herself free of him.

He smiled down at her, easy and relaxed in contrast to the stifling tension gripping her. "You look as if you've been dragged through a hedge backwards. Are you sure you can handle trimming this monster by yourself? It's nearly ten feet tall, you know."

"Provide me with decorations and a stepladder, and I'll manage."

She always managed—to repress the craving for love that so easily backfired and ended up hurting her, to hide her fear of rejection, to project an air of cool independence. These were the parameters within which she lived and she would do well to remember that, instead of straying beyond them to weave dangerous romantic fantasies around Morgan Kincaid.

"A stepladder I have," he said, "and you'll find plenty of decorations in the storage closet under the stairs, though I should warn you that they'll take some sorting out. Clancy and I just jammed everything into boxes last year without regard for any sort of order. It was the first Christmas after Agnes's death and post-holiday depression struck pretty hard."

He hadn't exaggerated. It took her the rest of the afternoon to untangle the lengths of colored lights she found in the first box, and check for burned-out bulbs. Finally satisfied that they were all working, she pulled the stepladder close to the tree and began threading the lights through the branches, becoming so absorbed in the task that she barely noticed the afternoon slipping away.

All her concentration was focused on bringing the tree to light and life before the men came back; to have made a start on creating that Dickensian Christmas card Morgan had talked about.

They finished in the stables earlier than Morgan had expected, mostly because Clancy was still sulking and refused to be drawn into conversation. It had started to snow again, bitter, persistent little flakes that stung Morgan's face as he tramped back to the house at about a quarter to four.

There was no sound of activity when he let himself in the back door, no sign of dinner being prepared, and he wondered, with a stab of dismay, if she'd been foolhardy enough to ignore his warning about remaining safely indoors.

Moving on silent feet down the hall, he placed the flat of his hand against the living-room door and nudged it ajar. "Jessica?"

He heard her gasp of alarm, saw the swirl of her skirt and a brief flash of thigh as she teetered atop the stepladder, and was across the room in an instant. "Steady," he murmured, reaching up to anchor her at her waist.

She swayed beneath his touch, and said breathlessly, "Oh, you startled me!"

"Sorry," he said, despising the weakness that made him want to slide his hands over her hips and down the elegant length of her legs. Until that moment, he had not realized how long and shapely they were. "I thought you'd be done by now."

"Heavens, no! I've only just finished stringing lights." She stretched up to secure the illuminated silver star that belonged on the top of the tree, and he instinctively tightened his hold on her, this time aware of how tiny her waist was, how delicately rounded her hips. "There, that should do it."

"Let's turn them on, then, and see how they look." He turned away as she stepped daintily down the ladder and wondered just how it had come about that he no longer saw her as a nun-like creature beyond the pale of a man's unruly appetite.

Dismayed more than he cared to admit by the conflicting emotions she aroused in him, he bent down to plug the electric cord into a nearby outlet and heard her exhalation of pleasure as the room filled with soft light.

"Oh," she sighed, clasping her hands under her chin in pure delight. "Oh, Morgan, look! It's magical!"

But he looked at her instead, and what he saw on her face left him speechless. She looked radiant and innocent and young and beautiful and nothing at all like the severe, up-tight woman he'd so reluctantly accepted into his home a mere twenty-four hours before.

The lights shimmered in the gleam of her hair, in the depths of her eyes, and painted alluring shadows beneath her cheekbones and down her throat. The plain navy skirt hung in graceful folds about her calves and the tailored white blouse, stained with rainbow reflections from the tree, molded itself to her with an intimacy that left him sour with envy.

"You look pretty magical yourself, Jessica Simms," he said thickly, his gaze clinging to hers.

It was as well that the back door thumped open just then or he might have made the colossal mistake of touching her. As it was, there came the slither of wet paws down the hall and the next minute Shadow tore into the room, tongue lolling and tail threatening terrible damage to the tree.

"I guess I should start thinking about dinner," Jessica said, laughingly fending off the exuberant dog.

Morgan cornered the retriever and grabbed her by the collar. "Why don't I take over kitchen duty tonight," he suggested, "and leave you to finish what you started in here? It would be nice to have the tree—as well as us—all dressed up for dinner."

"Your taking over kitchen duty isn't part of our deal."

Nor was finding himself embarrassingly aroused by her proximity! "I'll make an exception just this once—unless you're willing to settle for eating at the kitchen table again."

"No." She spun away from him and surveyed her handiwork thus far. "It won't take me long to finish the tree now, so…" the lights struck a garish note beside the uncertain sweetness of the smile she angled at him over her shoulder "…if you're sure you don't mind taking care of dinner that'll leave me enough time to finish cleaning the dining room."

"It's a deal," he said, and seized the chance to put the length of the house between them before he made a complete fool of himself.

The decorations were an odd mix. One carton contained a glossy assortment of electric-blue glass balls that shrieked designer choice, another held an artificial tree done up to look like a snow-encrusted fir.

But then she found another box on another shelf containing treasures that went back fifty years or more. Delicate spun-glass ornaments spangled with stars, cranberry velvet bows sewn with tiny seed-pearls, hand-crocheted snowflakes so light and fine they'd drift in the air just like the real thing. And lengths of silver bells joined to each other by silver beads which awoke in Jessica a memory of a time she seldom allowed herself to think of any more, when her parents were alive and she was about four, and they'd all gone to her maternal grandmother's for Christmas and that house, too, had been filled with silver bells and beads and a tall, fragrant tree.

Discarding all the others, Jessica took this last box into the living room and set to work. Some ornaments she dangled precariously from the very tips of the pine's branches, others she hid closer to the trunk where they winked shyly among the lights.

Satisfied at last that the tree was as close to perfect as she could make it, she arranged a few remaining blown-glass items in a crystal bowl and set them on the coffee table where they picked up the light from the fire and flung it back in blazing prisms of burgundy and gold.

She polished the tarnish from silver candlesticks in the dining room and fitted them with tall white candles she found in a drawer. She washed the dust from the beveled glass doors and left them open so that the fresh piny scent of the tree could filter through from the living room.

She swabbed cobwebs from the fine brass chandelier above the long oak table, and vacuumed the rugs back to life. And when all the furniture in both rooms glowed from her efforts she searched through the linen drawer in the bottom of the sideboard and found a big white damask cloth and a set of matching serviettes.

"It's quitting time, Jessica. Put your dust mop away and—" Morgan poked his head around the door just as she finished laying out the heavy silver she'd discovered in the silver chest. But when he saw the transformation that had taken place in the two rooms he stopped and stared, and said quietly, "Well, I'll be damned!"

Somewhat apprehensively, she said, "Is it all right?"

He shook his head wonderingly. "It's a lot better than all right." Then, raising his voice, he called out, "Clancy, come in here and take a look at what's happened!"

Jessica heard the stable man's footsteps coming down the hall and braced herself for the silent scorn he'd level at her. But when he, too, saw what she'd done his jaw went slack with amazement and, although she couldn't be certain, she thought that his eyes filmed with tears. "You brought out all Agnes's things," he said huskily. "All the little bits and pieces she made over the years that the other one shoved to one side."

Jessica glanced at Morgan, wondering if she'd inadvertently committed another unforgivable sin, but he shook his head reassuringly as Clancy slowly crossed to the tree and touched one of the crocheted snowflakes with a calloused fingertip.

"Made one of these every year, she did," he said, half to himself. "Used to say they were for the babies God never gave her."

"She'd be glad to see them brought out again." Morgan went to stand beside him and slung an arm over his shoulder.

Clancy ignored him and switched his rheumy gaze to Jessica. "What else you gone and found, woman?"

"I…um…nothing." She indicated the table in the dining room and sent another uncertain glance winging Morgan's way. "Except for the table linens and the sterling. But if you'd rather—"

"Best get the good china out, then," Clancy declared, any trace of emotion firmly under control again. "Ain't no point doing things half-assed."

But Morgan insisted she'd done enough for one day and sent her upstairs to take a shower. When she came down again in a fresh skirt and clean blouse, the table was set, and the men were sprawled in armchairs beside the fire with the dogs at their feet, and chatting amiably. Whatever tension had sprung up between them that morning seemed long gone and they were friends again.

Morgan offered her sherry while Clancy piled another log on the fire. "Shoot, why not?" he said, dusting off his hands on the seat of his pants and accepting the glass of rye whisky Morgan had poured for him. "Reckon we're going to celebrate Christmas whether we ought to or not, so we might as well enjoy it."

The way he said "ought" struck a vaguely discordant note, as though there was something wrong with what they were doing, but Jessica wasn't about to question him on it. It was enough that he'd called off his private vendetta against her. He even unbent far enough to help clean up after dinner—''since you're so persnickety about not leaving a mess behind, woman,'' he said, with the closest thing to a smile yet to cross his face.

He left and took the dogs to his own quarters shortly after, going out by the front door for a change. Morgan and Jessica stood in the lee of the veranda, watching until they saw lights go on in the windows above the stables.

It had stopped snowing by then and a cold moon shone over the land, leaving the air so crystalline that it almost chimed. ''Breathtaking, isn't it?'' Morgan said, gazing out at the frozen grandeur spread before them.

''Yes.'' Jessica hunched her shoulders against the chill penetrating the thin fabric of her blouse.

He noticed and pulled her into the shelter of his arm, in an unselfconscious, brotherly sort of way that nevertheless sent a thrill of excitement charging through her. ''You and your damned wardrobe,'' he grumbled, but there was no real annoyance in his tone any more.

''If I'd known I was going to be moon-watching in minus thirty-degree weather, I'd have brought along my full-length furs,'' she said, unable to control her chattering teeth.

He swung her around and led her back inside the house. ''You don't own any furs,'' he said confidently, steering her toward the hearth.

She crouched before the fire and held out her hands to its leaping warmth. ''What makes you so sure?''

''No woman who sees Rudolph on her plate instead of venison stew would stoop to wearing animal skins on her back,'' he said, selecting a bottle from one of the sideboard cupboards and pouring an inch of cognac into two snifters.

Jessica smiled. ''Perhaps you know me better than I thought.''

He handed her a cognac then lowered himself into his chair again, legs stretched out so that his feet almost touched her. "But not as much as I'm beginning to think I'd like to know you."

When she didn't reply, he nudged her with his toe. "Don't go all coy on me, Jessica. I've never enjoyed playing twenty questions."

"There's nothing much to tell." She shrugged and cradled the cognac snifter in both hands. "I have a sister, which you already know. I'm gainfully employed. I have no known allergies, don't smoke, only drink socially and then not much."

"And you're single."

"Yes," she said, and seized the chance to satisfy the most burning question she had for him. "Are you?"

He smiled lazily. "We're not talking about me and you're not going to wriggle off the hook by trying to change the subject. What line of work are you in?"

"I'm the headmistress of a private girls' school on Springhill Island in the Gulf of Georgia."

"I should have guessed!" His burst of laughter cut her to the quick. "It suits you to a T!"

Deciding she'd rather eat worms than let him see the wound he'd inflicted, she said, "Doesn't it just? Strait-laced spinster schoolmarm all the way, that's me."

He sobered, as though he'd heard something more than the words she'd tossed out so airily. "That's not exactly how I see you, Jessica."

"Why ever not?" She turned her face away from his probing stare and concentrated on the flames leaping up the chimney. "Everyone else does. I'm the plain sister, the intimidatingly sensible one. If glamor and excitement were what you'd hoped to find to brighten the season when you so kindly rescued me, I'm afraid you chose the wrong woman."

"I wasn't looking for any kind of woman," he said, leaning forward to capture her shoulders and pull her back against his knees. "But now that you're here I can't say I regret having found you."

"Because I'm such a good housekeeper," she said, despising the quaver of self-pity she heard in her voice. What a pathetic creature she was, practically begging for his approval.

She felt his breath ruffle her hair, the weight of his chin rest on the crown of her head. "Why do you persist in selling yourself short all the time, Miss Simms?"

Why did he persist in asking questions? In talking, instead of taking advantage of the situation? They were a man and a woman alone in a house for the night, with Christmas lights spilling magic into the room and the scent of freshly cut pine in the air.

It was the perfect setting, the perfect opportunity. If Selena had been the one taking refuge in his house, he'd have kissed her by now. Probably done a lot more than kiss her, in fact. "I'm realistic, that's all. And it's not as if you were overjoyed to have me land on your doorstep."

"No," he murmured, lifting the heavy loop of her hair and caressing the back of her neck. "But that was then and this is now. As for finding you plain...."

He left the sentence dangling, which was almost worse than if he'd ended it by allowing that she couldn't help how she looked. But then, when she'd just about decided she couldn't take his ambiguous silence a moment longer, he finished, "I don't find you plain at all, Jessica. On the contrary, I find you quite irresistibly lovely."

Just for a second everything in the room seemed to hang in frozen tension, in the same way that a concert hall filled with breathless suspense as the conductor raised his baton. The pretty Christmas tree ornaments stopped twirling, the lights ceased their tiny reflective flickerings. Even the flames in the hearth grew still, their crackle silenced and their heat quite unequal to the task of outshining the sudden fire in her blood.

She held onto that moment as long as she could, then came straight out and asked him, ''Are you married, Morgan?''

''No,'' he replied in a low voice, leaving one less hurdle between them. ''Not any more.''

She took a deep breath. ''And do you find me intimidatingly sensible?''

''I don't intimidate that easily, Jessica.''

She dared then to turn her head and look at him, because she had to read the truth in his eyes as she asked him the one question that she simply had to know the answer to. ''Then why haven't you tried to make love to me?''

CHAPTER SIX

MORGAN was blown away, by the question, certainly, and the honesty that inspired it, and by the leap of arousal with which his flesh responded to it, but most of all what moved him was the utter devastation he saw in Jessica's eyes as she waited for his answer.

"Do you think the idea hasn't crossed my mind a dozen times?" he said.

She lowered her eyes then and would have turned away from him, but he forestalled her by holding her chin firmly between his thumb and finger. "No," she whispered, a delicate wash of color flooding her face. "I didn't think you'd even noticed me, except as an inconvenience that suddenly managed to make itself useful."

He looked at her helplessly, at a loss to explain how she'd grown on him over the last forty-eight hours. Could he match truth for truth and tell her that, at first, he'd seen her just as she saw herself, plain and uninteresting? Or that he'd soon recognized that she was simply shy and that, under the somewhat forbidding facade behind which she tried to hide the fact, she possessed a cool beauty, subtle as perfume skilfully applied, and just about as elusive?

He cleared his throat and wished he could as easily subdue the rest of his body. "There is every reason in the world for me not to take advantage of you," he said huskily, "and I'm probably every sort of fool to point it out, but—"

"It's all right." She closed her eyes in humiliation. "I had no right to ask. I don't know what came over me."

"You were being honest with me, Jessica, and I really would be a fool not to feel flattered, but the more important question is, were you being honest with yourself? Are you sure this is what you really want?''

She hugged her elbows, as though no amount of heat from the fire could warm her. ''Not if I start to analyze it. Not if I apply judgement or rational argument. But if I obey....''

The words died on a breath of despair, as though she couldn't bring herself to admit that she was at the mercy of something that refused to abide by the laws of reason.

''What would you do,'' he asked, ''if I said I'd be happy to oblige?''

Her eyes flew open and he saw the panic in them, the uncertainty, and underneath all that something tremulous and fragile and unbearably appealing.

He couldn't bring himself to let her flounder a moment longer. He slid from the chair to sit beside her on the floor and, cupping her cheek in his palm, added, ''But that I'll act on it only if you still feel the same way twenty-four hours from now.''

Her lashes fluttered down beguilingly and if he hadn't known better he'd have thought her a practiced tease. ''I...don't think I could bring myself to ask a second time.''

He took the brandy snifter from her hands and placed it beside his own on the hearth. ''Not even if I show now, like this, how very desirable I find you?''

He tilted her chin up again and fanned the question against her mouth. She shifted ever so slightly, angling one shoulder protectively against his invasion in a gesture that stirred the warm currents of air trapped inside her blouse.

The scent of her flowed out to seduce him, country flowers and summer dawns too alluring to withstand. The kiss he'd intended to bestow as a salve to her pride ran amok with a passion he'd never anticipated and couldn't begin to contain.

Her mouth melted beneath his, so hot and fragrantly erotic that it might never have known the touch of wintry reserve he'd first seen painted there. He felt himself drowning in the essence of her, tasting the texture of her, delving deep to unearth more of her secrets.

She was all silk and sweet compliance, from the soft fringe of her lashes against her cheek to her lips, to her hair slipping free of its clasp and sliding like water through his fingers, to the skin of her throat, to the smooth slope of her breast—

Abruptly he pulled away from her, dropping her like the proverbial hot potato, too shocked by the degree of arousal she stirred in him to consider how she might view his actions.

Confused, frustrated, he flung wide both hands in an attempt to explain himself. "Forgive me. I—that's not what I—"

"Please don't," she said, visibly withdrawing into herself like a flower suddenly deprived of the sun's heat. "Please don't feel you have to apologize. I understand."

"No, you don't!" His answer exploded between them. "Hell, I don't understand myself! I intended to kiss you, that was all. I thought that would be enough and...."

He blew out a breath of exasperation and shook his head. How did a man of thirty-seven, who'd known more than a few women in his time, explain that he'd never before had a kiss sneak up and take him by surprise like that?

"It wasn't enough," he finished quietly.

"But it was very nice," she said, once again lowering her lashes fetchingly.

He almost smiled. "Are you flirting with me, Miss Simms?"

"I don't know how to flirt. I haven't had much occasion to practice."

He sighed ruefully and, picking up the brandy snifters again, offered her hers. "I suspect you'd be a very quick study."

"I'm not sure that I'd want to be," she said seriously. "I think, if ever I were to find myself involved with a man, that I'd rather play it straight. Flirting..." she lifted a disparaging shoulder "...it can lead to trouble, don't you think?"

He leaned his spine against the chair and crossed his ankles. "What sort of trouble?"

"Things can get out of hand. And then, when it's too late, people can find they've done irreparable damage."

Yes, he thought, just as Gabriel Parrish had.

Ill wind that it was, the name blasted across Morgan's mind, scattering everything else before it. Where the hell did he get off even contemplating an involvement with this woman when a madman was on the loose and probably out gunning for him?

She was so painfully honest, and all he had to offer her were lies. But what else could he do? Say "I'd make love to you in a New York minute, sweetheart, but you should be aware we could both be murdered in the bed"?

No. If he cared at all about her—and he was beginning to think he did, more than he wanted or had expected to— he'd leave her in ignorance and, more to the point, ensure her protection.

Draining his glass, he rose swiftly to his feet, gripped by a sudden need to check around outside, to make sure they were all safe, at least for one more night. "I could use some fresh air before I turn in and you must be worn out, the way you've slaved today." Quickly, before the pain so evident in her eyes had him sweeping her into his arms again, he turned away from her. "Get a good night's rest and I'll see you in the morning."

He took all the warmth of the room with him when he left.

Left? Practically ran out, as if he couldn't wait to get away from her, was a more apt description!

Shame and embarrassment flooded through Jessica, leaving her trembling and on the verge of tears. How *could* she have said what she did?

She looked down at the cognac in her glass and wished she could blame it for the words that had escaped her, but the fact of the matter was she'd hardly touched the liquor and had nothing and no one to blame but herself.

Was this what she'd come to? she wondered, standing up only to find that her legs threatened to give out under her. Was she so desperate to feel a man's arms around her again that she was willing to beg?

And yet the way he'd kissed her...the hunger hadn't been all hers. Nor was she so ignorant that she couldn't recognize the desire he hadn't been able to disguise. She'd felt him, hard and powerful against her. Had heard, over the labored thud of her heart, the rasp of his breath as he'd struggled to control himself.

If she had dared trust her instinct, she'd have guessed that he'd told her the truth when he'd said that he wanted her. But intuition, at least where men were concerned, had let her down too badly for her to have much faith in it a second time, especially on so brief an acquaintance.

This hunger, this raw animal magnetism, was a new experience for her and she was terribly afraid it had clouded her judgement. The only other time she'd come close to feeling anything like it had been with Stuart McKinney. She'd believed herself in love with him and thought that justified the physical side of things, only to learn that love didn't necessarily have anything to do with sex.

She'd decided then that she'd never again barter her body to win affection, and she'd never had reason to think otherwise, until now. But Morgan Kincaid...oh, he made her wish she were different, better, braver. He awoke the secret woman inside her and made her yearn and ache and want.

"Idiot," she whispered, and stooped to unplug the tree

lights, then took the brandy snifters into the kitchen before she went upstairs. Leaving the bedroom in darkness, she crossed to the window and looked out at the snow-covered landscape glimmering beneath the moon.

She saw the shadow of him emerge from the dark bulk of the stables, watched as he stood at the foot of the veranda steps and surveyed his quiet kingdom. And knew again a wave of sadness that she could be a part of his life for such a short space of time.

He had already left the house when she ventured downstairs the next morning, and for that she was supremely grateful. It was going to be hard enough facing him, without having to do it over the breakfast table. She was not at her best before her first cup of coffee of the day.

She made short work of cleaning up the kitchen and was on her hands and knees in the living room, adding fresh water to the Christmas tree container, when the back door suddenly thumped open long before the men usually took their mid-morning coffee break.

Her heart almost cartwheeled to a halt but it was Clancy, not Morgan, who appeared next to her with a pile of slender evergreen branches in his arms. "Figured since you done such a fancy job on the tree that you'd want to dolly up the rest of the place," he said offhandedly, dumping his load on the freshly vacuumed rug. "Got some cedar here that I cut first thing. Agnes used to put it on the mantelpiece— left it sort of hanging over the edge—and it always looked real nice."

Jessica sat back on her heels and eyed him cautiously, bowled over by the about-face that had produced such a gesture of goodwill. "Thank you. That's a wonderful idea."

"There's holly growing out back as well. In the corner where the kitchen sticks out, where it's sheltered from the worst of the weather. Not that it's got any right growing at this altitude, but the darn thing's as stubborn as the old gal that planted it.''

''Agnes?'' It seemed a reasonable guess since he was so full of memories of her, but Jessica soon learned her mistake.

''Use your head, woman,'' Clancy snorted. ''Trees don't grow like weeds, 'specially not up here, and my Agnes was only sixty-six when she passed on. I'm talking about Morgan's great-granny. A real green thumb, she had. Got things to sprout that folks around these parts never did see before. Always had holly in the house at Christmas. Thought you might like some, too.''

''I would, but it can wait. You've already got enough to do.''

''That I have.'' He glared at Jessica, as though his bringing her one peace offering had stretched his capacity for seasonal goodwill to its limit.

''Perhaps I could cut some myself later on,'' she offered.

''Not dressed like that, you can't.'' He sniffed. ''Woman, you've been here nearly three days and you still ain't got the first idea what that weather out there can do to a person who don't come equipped to deal with it.''

She sighed. She was getting more than a little tired of being chastised for her inadequate wardrobe. What she wore seemed the preferred topic of conversation, losing out only to the current state of the weather. ''Well, Clancy, I'm learning fast. However, since there's nothing I can do to remedy the situation, I guess we'll all just have to live—''

''Ain't no call for you to get on your high and mighty horse,'' he said, cocking his head to one side and squinting at her. ''All I was goin' to suggest was that from where I stand you look to be about the same size as my Agnes and if you ain't too proud to take hand-me-downs maybe I can fix you up with something so you ain't quite so housebound.''

"That would be very nice," she said, deeming it unwise to take exception to the way he chose to deliver his point.

He left then, slamming the back door in his signature fashion, only to return half an hour later with a large cardboard box which he plunked in the middle of the sofa. "There. See what you can do with what's in here. The boots might be big but that ain't nothing an extra pair of socks can't fix." He nodded and turned to go, then asked, "By the way, what you cooking up for the midday meal?"

"Grilled cheese sandwiches and tomato soup."

"And some of them mince pie things like we had yesterday?"

"If you like. I'll have to bake up a fresh batch, though."

She smiled at him and received a conspiratorial smirk in response. "Better get on with it, then, woman. I'm building up a fearsome appetite running errands for you."

Although she felt better at the improved turn her relationship with Clancy had taken, Jessica still dreaded seeing Morgan again and grew increasingly tense as the lunch hour approached. It was all she could do not to turn tail and run when she heard the clump of boots at the back door. But after all her agonizing he made it easy for her.

"Hi," he said, planting himself at the table and rubbing his hands together briskly. "What's cooking? I'm starving."

His smile was friendly without being intimate, his glance impersonal without being cold, his tone weighted with no hidden nuances. He was so thoroughly and neutrally pleasant that it occurred to Jessica to wonder if she hadn't dreamed the previous night's conversation.

"Heard on the radio this morning that there was another avalanche on the main highway," he commented as the meal progressed. "Just west of Wintercreek this time. They don't expect to have the road open again for at least forty-eight hours."

Clancy, who until then had attacked his meal with the

same silent dedication he'd displayed the day before, froze with his sandwich midway to his mouth. "That ought to put a dent in certain folks' traveling plans."

"I'd say so." Morgan smiled his thanks as Jessica removed his empty soup bowl. "At least until after Christmas Day."

"Speaking of which," she said, producing the promised mince tarts, "unless you've got it hidden somewhere, I don't see any sign of the traditional turkey for tomorrow's dinner."

Morgan intercepted Clancy as he made a grab for the tarts. "We didn't bother with one last year. It didn't seem worth it for just the two of us."

"So what did you have in mind instead?"

"We laid in a good supply of wild duck in the Fall. They're in the freezer but if they don't strike your fancy whatever you decide will be fine." He shrugged apologetically. "Christmas Day's just another working day on a horse ranch, Jessica. I'm afraid you'll be spending a good portion of it alone, doing exactly the same thing you've done so well since you got here."

"Pinch-hitting as chief cook and bottle washer, you mean?" She spoke idly, too deeply engrossed in admiring the lithe male beauty of him to consider how her words might be interpreted.

Unexpectedly, he looked up and caught her staring. "Among other things," he said gently, his gaze holding hers.

Did she imagine that his expression altered imperceptibly, that the color of his eyes suddenly reminded her less of the clear cold of the winter sky than the hazy blue of high summer?

"Well," she said, hoping the confusion churning her blood didn't show on her face, "wild duck sounds fine to me. I'll do my best to make them special."

His gaze intensified. "As you do with everything, Jessica."

"Anybody want to tell me what the Sam hell all the double talk's about?" Clancy inquired, not missing a thing. "Or am I better off not knowin'?"

"You're better off not knowing," Morgan said evenly. "What say we get back to work?"

"Might as well. Sooner we get at it, sooner we're done." Clancy scraped back his chair and snapped the leather suspenders holding up his jeans. "A man sits too long by a warm fire lettin' a woman feed him and next thing you know he ain't good for nothin' the rest of the day."

"Then by all means let's get moving." Standing up, Morgan slewed his gaze briefly back to Jessica and with a masterful stroke of ambiguity that sent a tide of heat sweeping over her added slyly, "You look a little weary, Miss Simms. Why don't you take time out for a nap this afternoon? It would be a pity for either of us to be too tired to enjoy Christmas Eve."

Clancy snorted with disgust, snaked out a hand and crammed the last mince pie into his mouth whole. "Never mind any afternoon nap, woman," he said, heading for the door. "Make more tarts."

By great good fortune, Agnes had been a size eight, too. Her faded blue jeans, softened by many launderings to the texture of doeskin, fit perfectly. Sorting through the other items, Jessica selected a hand-knit sweater that came down past her hips, a cream down jacket with a fur-trimmed hood, two pairs of heavy wool socks to wear under the fleece-lined boots, and a pair of thick leather gloves. But she shook her head at the long red thermal underwear and tucked it back inside the box. She didn't plan to spend any longer outside than it took to gather a few pieces of holly.

The problem was, whatever tool Clancy had used to cut

the cedar was nowhere to be found and the holly branches were sturdy as well as prickly. The kitchen scissors were no match for the job, nor was the steak knife she seconded. Frustrated and out of breath, she surveyed the bright-berried limb dangling miserably but stubbornly from the tree. Obviously, without the proper tools, she wasn't going to have much success.

"Stay inside the house", Morgan had said. But the stables stood a mere hundred yards or so away. Hardly a life-threatening distance, now that she had the right kind of clothing to protect her, surely?

But the cold wind from which she'd been protected by the bulk of the house caught her as she turned the corner and just about froze the breath in her lungs. Hugging the jacket hood closely around her face and wishing she hadn't been so quick to discard Agnes's winter underwear, she struggled across the open ground to the stable and slid back the heavy door just enough to let herself through the opening.

Her arrival went unnoticed at first and for a moment she leaned against the door and simply inhaled the gentle warmth of the place. A window high on the end wall let in what was left of the daylight and two electric lamps suspended from a center beam spilled mellow pools of gold over the scene.

Shadowed stalls lined each side wall, five to the left and five to the right, with a concrete-floored aisle separating them. Steps immediately to the right of the door by which she'd come in led up to a half-loft piled high with bales of bright straw and pale-tinted hay.

To her left, another half-open door showed a small room, the walls of which were hung with the trappings one might expect to find around horses. Saddles and bridles, blankets and liniments, oils and brushes.

The entire place was filled with the scents of hay and

clean straw and the faintly astringent smell of animals. The air was full of soft sound: hooves rustling on straw, contented munching, water gurgling down twin drinking channels, and somewhere out of sight the deep baritone murmur of men at work together.

Something about the place—the hushed tranquillity perhaps, or the far window, stained now with the deep blue of the midwinter afternoon and shot with rose from the dying sun—reminded her of a church. To call out and shatter the peace was unthinkable.

Hesitantly, she moved forward, toward the sound of voices, aware all the time of the horses. Some looked up from their feeding troughs, mildly curious, then dismissed her for the ignorant intruder she undoubtedly was. Others whickered softly and watched her with large, beautiful eyes as she made her way down the center aisle.

She had almost reached the last stall when a low growl issued from an old blanket atop a pile of straw and Ben the retriever rose up to confront her.

"Stop that," she scolded softly, coming to a halt a respectful distance away—not that she was afraid of him exactly, but nor was she fool enough to challenge him on his own turf. "I'm the one who fed you venison stew for the last two days, you ungrateful wretch."

He growled again, loudly enough this time for the men to hear him. There was a moment of complete silence that positively hummed with unspoken threat and then, suddenly, they were there, practically on top of her, Clancy picking up a wicked-looking pitchfork hanging on the end wall and brandishing it fiercely, and Morgan swinging a hammer.

When they saw her, they stopped their headlong rush and froze in their tracks. "Oh," Morgan said, looking somewhat embarrassed, "it's you."

"It's a bit too early for Santa Claus," she said lightly, "so who else could it be but me?"

The men exchanged furtive glances. "Well..." Morgan began.

"Horse thieves," Clancy said, his pitchfork still held at the ready.

"It pays to be careful," Morgan said.

"I'm sure." Jessica nodded her understanding, although in truth she thought their reaction rather extreme, particularly since they both continued to regard her as if she'd sprouted horns.

Morgan took off his hat and drew the back of his hand across his brow. "Is everything all right at the house, Jessica?"

"Of course. Why wouldn't it be?"

"Then what you doin' wanderin' around in here, woman?" Clancy demanded.

"Looking for something to cut the holly with," she said. "And I'm sorry if I'm trespassing, but I thought you might be able to give me something that would do the job."

"Oh," Morgan said again. "Sure. Of course. And you're not trespassing. Not at all. Put the pitchfork away, Clancy, before someone gets hurt."

"You might call off Ben, too," Jessica said.

Signaling the dog to heel, Morgan said, "A better idea would be for the two of you to become friends, then he could keep you company at the house while we're out here."

"I haven't exactly had time to get lonely, Morgan, but if you think a little company would be good for me Shadow seems much more inclined to be friendly and is perfectly happy to spend the day with me. She's asleep in the rocking chair even as we speak."

Again, that silent exchange took place between the men. "Yeah," Clancy muttered, "but Ben's more...."

"Territorial," Morgan supplied.

Jessica regarded them quizzically. "In the event that horse thieves should invade the kitchen in the middle of the day, of course."

"You're right, we're making a fuss about nothing. I guess having you show up so quietly surprised us, that's all." Morgan shrugged and relaxed his grip on the hammer. "I'm about done for today anyway, so why don't I walk back to the house with you?"

"What about cutting the holly?"

"I'll do it. You shouldn't be outside dressed like—" He stopped and seemed to notice what she was wearing for the first time. "Where did you get the clothes, for Pete's sake?"

"From me. They're some of Agnes's things that I'd kept," Clancy said. "Reckon I'll poultice the mare's ankle before I quit for the day, Morgan, 'less you got something else you want me to do?"

Morgan shook his head. "I think we've covered everything."

"What's wrong with the mare?" Jessica asked in a low voice, glancing back over her shoulder as Clancy disappeared into the end stall again.

"Sprained ankle." Morgan took her by the elbow and pointed her back the way she'd come. "Nothing too serious."

"I thought leg injuries to horses were always serious."

"Not necessarily. Come on, let's get you back to the house. This isn't exactly your sort of place, I'm sure."

"Perhaps not, but I can see why Clancy prefers to spend his time here. There's something very comforting about your stable. And the animals...." She turned to him and smiled. "He was right, you know—Clancy, I mean. I barely know the back end of a horse from the front, but even I can see they're beautiful. What do you do with them?"

A grin twitched the corners of his mouth. "Well, I don't

eat them if that's what's worrying you. You won't find horse-meat steaks in the freezer.''

She slapped at his arm with her gloved hand. "The thought never even occurred to me! What I meant was, are they racehorses, or do you keep them just for the pleasure of watching them run about the property?"

"Mostly the latter, I guess." He stopped and stroked the long, soft nose of a horse hanging its head over the half-door of its stall. "They're quarter horses and I do a bit of breeding. And a lot of riding when I can spare the time. But this is a small operation compared to what it was in my grandfather's day, and that's how I like it. With the part-time help he gets from Ted, Clancy's able to manage the place single-handed if I'm not around, although we do employ some of the local kids during the summer."

The horse nudged at his chest and sort of snuffled, a move that had Jessica springing back in alarm. "Good grief, is he going to bite?"

It seemed a reasonable enough question to her, but Morgan just about split his sides laughing. "No, sweetheart, he's looking for something to eat. Do you want to feed him?"

"Not if he's that hungry," she retorted, too fired up with pleasure at the endearment to resent his teasing. "I might lose my hand."

Looping one arm around her shoulder, Morgan reached into his pocket with his other hand and withdrew a carrot. "No chance of that," he assured her. "Not if you do it right. Here, take off your glove and lay this flat on the palm of your hand."

"Can't I keep my glove on?"

"No. You lose half the pleasure."

Taking courage from that casually uttered "sweetheart" and the arm around her shoulder, she removed her glove.

"Now offer him the carrot. Go on," Morgan urged, when

she hesitated. The horse had lost all interest in his owner and was eyeing her with alarming enthusiasm.

"Morgan," she said, "that animal and I haven't been properly introduced and considering how Ben responds to me I'm not sure I'm willing to trust anything quite this big even if he is the most handsome shade of brown I've ever seen."

"He's a chestnut," Morgan corrected her. "His name's Jasper, he's nearly sixteen years old and he's never hurt a fly in all that time. And you're offending him by suggesting he would."

Conscious of the big brown eyes watching her so patiently, and even more vividly aware of the brilliant blue gaze of the man at her side, Jessica raised her arm.

The great head dipped in a bow to her outstretched palm. She felt a touch, gentle as a kiss, the feathery brush of whiskers, and the carrot was gone.

"Well? How was it?"

Her smile completely got away from her, spreading past its normal reserved boundaries with a keen pleasure she rarely experienced. "Piece of cake," she boasted, and suddenly she was leaning against him and they were both laughing.

"I'll make a horsewoman out of you yet," he promised, sliding the stable door shut behind them and hurrying her across the snow-packed path to the house.

He cut the holly while she made tea, then took his cup into his office. "I've got a couple of hours' work to take care of in here before we start celebrating Christmas. Can you keep yourself occupied while you're waiting?"

"Easily," she said, and idled the rest of the afternoon away doing little, inconsequential things. She studded mandarin oranges with whole cloves, piled them in a pewter bowl with pine cones, and set them on the hearth where the warmth from the fire would draw out the scent. She ironed the ribbons she'd found among the decorations and wove them in graceful swirls through the sprigs of holly and sprays of cedar gracing the dining table and fringing the mantelpiece.

She felt it was the sort of thing Agnes would have wanted her to do: to bring the added dimension of a woman's touch to the house and turn it again into a home. And the house responded, seeming to expand at the seams and let loose ghosts from a happier time.

As darkness closed in outside, she basted the potatoes roasting around the leg of pork in the oven, set plates to warm, opened preserved peaches and, in preparation for the ice cream dessert she had planned, left them to marinate drunkenly in a sauce made of brown sugar, raisins and dark rum.

When she came downstairs later, all bathed and perfumed and wearing one of only two dresses she'd stuffed in her suitcase, she found Clancy pumping away on the old organ and filling the room with the wheezing strains of "Silent Night".

In the corner, the lights on the tree winked softly. Beyond the beveled glass doors, candles flickered in the dining room. On the coffee table before the fire sat a fine old silver punch bowl with three matching cups. And best of all there was Morgan, gorgeous in black cords and a white shirt.

She paused a moment on the threshold, wondering a little at the sensation suddenly engulfing her. Airy, translucent and thoroughly unfamiliar, it flooded through her and she realized, with a sense of shock, what it was she was experiencing.

Not satisfaction for a job well done. Not contented gratitude for a pleasant, secure life. But happiness that surged and flowed through her veins with all the verve and delight of champagne sparkling on the tongue.

There were no smartly wrapped packages under the tree,

no uniformed staff hired for the evening. No stream of fashionably clad guests streaming through the front door as they had in her aunt and uncle's house, air-kissing each other's cheeks at the same time that they took covert stock of who was wearing what and designed by whom.

Just Christmas the way it was meant to be: warm, unpretentious, *real*.

CHAPTER SEVEN

MORGAN ladled out hot rum punch but before he could propose a toast Clancy upstaged him. Shuffling around on the organ stool, he clutched the delicate punch cup in his big hands.

"Never thought I'd feel like this again," he began, scanning the room at large. "Never thought it would feel like a home again." He focused his attention on Jessica. "For sure never thought a bit of a woman'd just walk in the door and make the place over in three days."

His expression was almost bewildered and it struck Morgan that his stable hand had aged over the last few months and now looked all of his sixty-eight years.

"'Specially not a woman like you, Jessica Simms," Clancy continued. "Wouldn't have thought you had it in you to pull off something like this." He raised his cup. "Best of the season to you. My Agnes would have approved of you."

"I know I would have liked her, too." Emotion clogged Jessica's voice, undershot her smile, and left her gray eyes sparkling with the hint of tears.

Morgan would have preferred not to notice any of those revealing little details but the more time he spent in her company, the more acute his powers of observation became. And the lovelier she grew.

He continued to observe her over dinner, noticing the thoroughbred elegance of her, her warmth, her patience with Clancy. She'd grown younger somehow, as if she'd shed the weight of countless years of disappointment and unhap-

106

piness. Or, more accurately, as if, since knowing him, she'd discovered joy.

How would it have been between them, he wondered, if he'd met her before? Before a failed marriage had taught him there were some things you couldn't ask a woman to do, such as live with a man who made enemies of creeps like Gabriel Parrish?

He tried to picture her in that world now, and failed. It had proved to be too much for Daphne and, in the end, it would be too much for Jessica, too. She wasn't hard-edged enough.

No. If ever there'd been a time for them, it was ten years ago, before they had each laid out their lives along different paths.

"You've made a conquest," he told her later, slouching comfortably beside her on the couch. Dinner was over and Clancy had retired to his own quarters a short while before, again leaving the two of them alone to finish the last of the wine they'd drunk with the meal. "I don't recall Clancy ever waxing quite so lyrical before."

"My cooking mellows him." Jessica smiled, a shade wistfully, he thought. As if the only possible route she'd find to a man's heart lay through his stomach.

If he could limit his susceptibility to her to such an innocuous portion of his anatomy, Morgan decided, leaning forward and cradling his wine glass in both hands, he'd feel a lot more relaxed about the situation in which he now found himself.

"So I've noticed," he said. "Come to that, I've noticed a lot of things in the last couple of days that escaped me when we first met."

"Such as?" She crossed one knee over the other and swung a graceful ankle. The fabric of her full-skirted dress, something thick and silky printed with dark green ferns on a cream background, flowed onto his section of the couch, begging to be touched.

Fixing his attention on the cedar garland festooned along the mantel, he said, "Initially, I had you pegged as being a bit hare-brained, a bit irresponsible."

"And now you know I'm just a staid old schoolmarm you think differently?"

"It's not your job that changed my mind."

She shifted to a more comfortable position, sliding lower against the cushions and sending a faint whiff of perfumed body talc drifting his way. "What, then?"

The fact that the scent of you drives me mad, he could have told her. That when you stretch out your foot like that, letting your heel slip free of its shoe, I have an insane urge to kneel down and kiss that high, aristocratic instep. That you have beautiful legs, slender, shapely and endless, and I'd like to explore them at erotic leisure. That there's a sliver of French lace showing beneath the hem of your dress and it brings to mind the nightgown you were wearing the other night, and has me wondering what you're wearing next to your skin now—all of which speculation has left me seriously aroused.

"Search me!" he said.

And wouldn't *that* be embarrassing!

Leaping to his feet, he threw another log on the fire with rather more energy than the task demanded. "Your unselfishness, perhaps. You'd never have ended up stranded in a blizzard if you hadn't set out in the middle of one of the worst winters on record to be with your sister. And if we hadn't roped you into housekeeping for a couple of bachelors whose idea of celebrating Christmas runs to propping up a tree in a corner and forgetting to water it, Clancy and I would probably be staring at the bottom of an empty brandy bottle about now, bemoaning our sad and lonely lot in life."

"I can relate to that."

He flung a skeptical glance at her over his shoulder. "What, getting hammered on brandy?"

The way she leaned against the arm of the couch and tilted one shoulder in an unwittingly sensuous shrug of denial that brought her arm into brief and intimate contact with her breast sent a tongue of fire curling through his gut.

"No," she said. "Being sad and lonely. It's just something that comes of being the sort of person I am, I guess."

If she'd evidenced even a shred of self-pity with that remark, he could have dismissed her claim, ignored it, laughed at it. Responded in any number of ways, in fact, but the way he did, which was to ignore his better judgement and submit instead to the urge that had gnawed at him incessantly for the last twenty-four hours or more.

Taking her hands, he drew her to her feet and held her close. "Not tonight it isn't," he murmured into her hair.

She came to him as naturally as if she'd found shelter in his arms a thousand times before. Her head rested below his chin, the scent of her which, across the width of the couch, had spelled faint temptation intensified to vibrant invitation. And the rest of her, every fine-boned, delicately sculpted inch of limb and torso, imprinted itself against him.

It was more than he'd anticipated or planned, yet it left him craving for more. The belief which had served him so long and so well that love was, at best, a transient visitor and not worth the upheaval it created threatened to topple into a great yawning abyss of need.

Love? How the hell had that word slipped through his defenses? He wasn't a good candidate for love and, even if he were, Jessica deserved better. Her life was bound by purer standards than he could afford, her definitions of right and wrong too clearly spelled out in black and white.

How could she understand the many shadings of gray that governed him? How accept the necessity of his sometimes rubbing shoulders with the underworld of crime in order to bring a felon to justice?

She would not. And yet he found himself increasingly enthralled by her. Found himself waiting to hear her laugh; to see amusement shimmer over her face and fill her eyes with light; to enjoy her intelligence and her sometimes acerbic wit. These aroused in him a yearning that would not find ease in sex.

He wanted more. He wanted to take her out in public, show her off to his friends and associates, and to strangers, too, come to that. He wanted to wine and dine her, and proclaim to the world that she belonged to him. The knowledge hit him like a brick wall.

Even as his mind scrambled to absorb the realization, his body again advertised itself with blatant effrontery. Hers swayed in response. She sighed dreamily, lifted her face to his, and any scruples he might have brought to bear on the situation fled.

Sliding his hands down to cup her hips, he brought her more familiarly against him and lowered his mouth to hers. She tasted of sun-ripened grapes fermented to ambrosia, of innocence and sweetness and dark feminine mystery.

She kissed like no woman had ever kissed him before, in a way that had the alarm bells clanging at the back of his mind fighting a losing battle with the pulsing throb of his beleaguered body.

Her lips softened and parted on a whisper. Her tongue, shy as a butterfly, flirted with his, luring him to claim deeper possession of her mouth, and only when it was much too late for him to retreat, enslaving him for as long as it pleased her.

She slipped her arms around his neck and captured his hair in her fingers. Worse, she wove lethal, invisible strands around his heart.

Her flesh was warm and firm beneath his touch, but too

well protected by her clothing. Sinking with her to the couch again, he inched up the skirt of her dress and traced the sweet curve of her knee, discovered the tender inner sweep of her silk-stockinged thigh and then, unexpectedly, a strip of naked skin, enticingly soft, unbearably arousing.

Instinctively she clamped her thighs together, trapping his hand next to the damp, delicious warmth of her, and uttered a little moan of despair—an admission that she was his for the taking.

He'd had his share of women and liked to think there wasn't much that was new or different that he'd yet to learn, but the profoundly erotic effect of that two inches of neutral territory separating him from her most intimate self rocked him to the foundations.

Briefly, lamentably, the atavistic urge to take her then and there, to imprint her with the mark of his possession, blew all other considerations aside. Never mind the wide bed upstairs, never mind chivalry or dignity, and to hell with politically correct. The here and now was what mattered. Urgency raced through his blood, consigning finesse to some other day, some other woman.

But she was not some other woman. She was different, finer. That she was willing to give herself to him was immaterial. Did that give him the right to take her, knowing as he did that, when tomorrow came, he'd have nothing of worth to offer her?

Had he not known the answer, he could have ignored the question. But there was a limit, even to his wilful oversight. Dearly though the effort cost him, he dragged his mouth from hers, grasped her shoulders, and held her at a safe distance.

"This is madness," he muttered, the breath rasping unevenly from his lungs.

Eyes still closed, she leaned toward him. "No," she breathed.

"Yes!" He gave her a shake, just sharp enough to snap her back to reality. "Look, Jessica, despite what you said last night—"

He felt her withdrawal even before she moved, and experienced a perverse disappointment as the magic of the moment disintegrated into a thousand shattered pieces.

"Please let's not spoil Christmas Eve by bringing that up," she begged, backing away from him.

"I think we must," he said, figuring that as long as they were talking he couldn't get into too much trouble. "The fact is, it's altogether too easy to…act on—"

But talking wasn't so safe, after all. Afraid that, unless he phrased things carefully, he'd end up making matters worse than they already were, he stumbled to find the right words—an uncommon occurrence for him. If he could marshal convincing arguments for a jury, why not for her?

But how did a man say, Look, we're here alone, the mood is right, and we've been attracted to each other practically from the word go. I'd very much like to make love to you but you're not my usual type and I'm afraid I can't live up to what you'd expect of me afterwards?

"Yes, Morgan? Go on."

Conscious of her unwavering scrutiny, he floundered on. "Well, it would be easy to get carried away by what we're feeling right now…et cetera."

"Et cetera," she echoed, her breast rising and falling on another sigh. "Of course, et cetera. I understand exactly what you mean."

She turned away, the droop of her head and her profile, illuminated by the fire's glow, a statement in themselves that she accepted his rejection of her. He should have rejoiced at being so easily let off the hook. Instead, the knot of desire tightened within him, leaving him aching for her.

"Do you?" he replied gloomily. "I wish I did."

The ghost of a smile touched her mouth. "It's the loneliness factor,'' she said. ''It can bring the most unsuitable couples together, especially at this time of year, and fool them so that they can't always tell the difference between it and real attraction.''

''True.'' He seized on the excuse as a drowning man might cling to a life raft. ''And being cooped up together like this doesn't help.''

''I know.''

He sneaked a glance at the clock on the mantel, hoping it was late enough that, under the pretext of needing to get some sleep, he could race upstairs and take a long, cold shower. But he saw with dismay that it was only eight-thirty. Too early for bed and much too late to believe they could while away the next couple of hours in idle chit-chat.

Stymied, he paced to the window and stared out. The wind which had wreaked such freezing havoc for the last forty-eight hours had blown itself out finally and taken the clouds with it.

''We could go for a walk,'' he suggested, on a burst of inspiration. ''A breath of fresh air might do us good.'' *Not to mention achieve the same results as a cold shower!*

She looked doubtfully at the silky stuff of her dress, her narrow, elegant pumps. ''I'll freeze to death.''

''Not if you borrow Agnes's long johns,'' he said. ''They'll keep the frost away.''

And him! He well remembered seeing Agnes's red, one-piece winter underwear hanging on the drying rack in the mud room. It was enough to deflate any man's overactive libido.

The night was clear and beautiful. Stars peppered the sky, brighter, larger and more numerous than any she'd ever seen on the coast. A sliver of rising moon showed beyond the lip of the cliff behind the house. Underfoot, the snow gleamed, deceptively smooth and soft to look at, but hard as pavement to touch.

"This way," Morgan said, his breath ballooning out in front of him. "There's a trail through the trees that leads to a lake where we swim in the summer."

Jessica shivered despite the warmth of Agnes's clothing and huddled deeper into the down-filled jacket. "I find it hard to believe it could ever get hot enough for swimming up here."

He laughed. "Temperatures can run into the low thirties in July—and I'm talking centigrade. Believe me, there've been times when the lake's felt more like a bath than a swimming hole."

"We", he kept saying, as if the place was so full of memories of his ex-wife that, divorced or not, she was still a part of his life.

The Jessica Simms who'd set out from the coast a mere four days ago would have refused to gratify the irrational jealousy inspired by such a revealing little slip. But that woman had gone astray in an avalanche shed in the middle of nowhere, and the one who'd taken her place possessed none of her reticence. *She* came right out and asked, "Your wife loved it here as well, then?"

He let out a grunt of sound, too bitter to be called laughter though that was undoubtedly what he'd intended. "Hell, no, she hated it! She hated everything about life with me."

"Then why on earth did the two of you marry?"

"Why does anyone get married?"

"Well," the new, impertinent Jessica replied, "sometimes because there's a baby on the way and, from what I've seen, you—"

"Tend to behave as if I've got no more control over my hormones than I have over the weather?" His laughter this time was laced with self-mockery.

"No!" She drew in an appalled breath. "I was going to

say, you strike me as the kind of man who'd honor his obligations.''

The amusement slipped away, replaced by a gravity that bordered on the austere. ''There was no baby, either before or after the wedding vows,'' he said flatly, ''but there was sex and I suppose we both mistook that for love.''

''That's a terribly cynical thing to say, Morgan.''

He turned a long, level stare on her as they made their way over the frozen snow toward the belt of trees to the west. ''I'm a cynical man, Jessica, at least where romantic love is concerned. It's not a good investment, especially not for someone like me.''

In other words, Don't make the mistake of thinking that my kissing you was the prelude to a serious commitment. She heard the warning behind his words and refused to heed it. ''Just because your marriage went sour is no reason to give up on love.''

''It's not just my marriage that convinced me,'' he said, helping her over a particularly icy patch of ground. ''The private lives of too many of my…associates are littered with the same sort of casualties, some of them involving children. At least Daphne and I didn't add that crime to our list of spectacular failures.''

Jessica knew that the ranch was his home, a place he loved, and she couldn't picture him anywhere else. He seemed so in tune with the solitude, so content with the unchanging pattern of days spent caring for his horses. Yet just for a second she had the feeling that there was another part of his life that he didn't want to reveal to her.

''Is working the ranch a full-time career for you, Morgan?'' she asked.

''Isn't it enough?''

''Possibly. But you mentioned associates just now and I—''

"Well, I'm not the only rancher in the area, so of course I have associates. Don't we all?"

Although he spoke lightly, she sensed a reluctance to pursue the topic further that was borne out when he abruptly changed the subject. "See ahead, where the trees thin out?"

He lifted his arm and pointed. In a clearing lay the lake, a keyhole-shaped body of water whose frozen surface glimmered in the ghostly light. Around its perimeter the dark sentinels of conifers speared the sky.

"It looks magical," Jessica breathed, captivated. "A place of enchantment untouched by the ills of the mortal world."

"It's muddy on the bottom, a haven for mosquitoes in the spring, and the fishing's lousy, but...." Morgan stamped a path through the snow and grinned. "Yeah, I guess you could call it magical. We spent a lot of happy hours here when we were growing up. Learned to swim and water-ski and skate."

"Who's 'we'?" There, it was out at last, the question she'd been itching to ask.

"My sister and I."

She waited for him to elaborate, to fill in the huge blanks of his past for her. Instead, he said, "You skate, Jessica?"

"Not since I was about four. I don't imagine that counts for much."

He took her hand and drew her down to the lake's edge. "Let's find out."

"What—? Morgan, no!" She hung back, realizing what he had in mind. "I can't."

"Sure you can. It's like riding a bike; you never forget how." Slithering the last few feet down the sloping bank, he pulled her after him.

"We don't even have skates," she protested, dragging her feet. "And what if the ice can't hold our weight?"

"You're chicken." Letting go of her, he stuck out his

elbows, flapped his bent arms up and down, and pushed off onto the ice, squawking like a demented rooster the whole time.

"I'm sensible," she called out, laughing. "One of us has to be."

"I'm sneaky," he replied, returning to his starting point with surprising speed. "Come on, Miss Simms. It's lesson time."

Before she could back out of range, he grabbed both her hands and, backing out onto the ice again, towed her after him, willy-nilly.

"Care to dance?" he asked, slipping his right arm around her waist.

Choking with laughter, she said, "I hardly think—!"

He cut her off by breaking into a terribly off-key rendition of "The Skaters' Waltz" and spinning her wildly around the ice.

It was absurd, an adolescent lark that they were both too old to indulge in, and they should both have fallen on their faces. But he kept them firmly upright and the moon shone down on them and another kind of magic took hold.

Slowly his singing and her laughter died and the only sound to split the night was the rustle of their feet on the ice. Slowly, it, too, faded into silence.

His hands came up and closed around her upper arms, imprisoning her far too close to him for safety. Against her will she allowed her gaze to lock with his.

For one long, trembling moment that threatened to outlast eternity, they stared into each other's eyes. The messages, floodlit by the moon's pale radiance, were plain enough to understand.

She saw torment and indecision in those deep blue, soul-searching eyes of his, and a raw masculine hunger that stole her breath away. And she knew that he read longing in hers, and the wanting that refused to go ignored.

The blood thundered in her ears, echoing the frenzied beat of her heart. Her breasts, flattened against his chest, surged alive, the ache that brought her nipples into stark relief spiraling down to clench her flesh in pleasure. And nothing, not even the barrier of heavy winter clothing, could disguise his response to her as he pressed against her, hard, forceful, male.

But mostly it was their breathing that gave them away, erupting in harsh, jagged gasps to mate plainly and deliriously in the cold night air. Writhing, coiling, becoming one.

As she longed to do with him.

As she was sure he longed to do with her. She felt the fight go out of him in the way his shoulders sagged beneath her touch, read the terms of his surrender in the way his lashes drooped and his gaze fastened on her mouth.

The silence spoke for itself, cutting through all the subterfuge to reveal the truth they'd both tried to ignore. It screamed between them, deafening in its tacit admission.

He slackened his grip enough to hold her at arm's length. "You see?" he whispered hoarsely. "This is what I was trying to say, back at the house. A kiss won't be enough. Things aren't going to stop there with us."

"Where will they stop, Morgan?"

He shook his head. "Only you can decide that, because my answer might not be the one you want to hear."

She knew then that what he was really saying was that he could make her no promises beyond today, and that she had to determine if she could live with the fact, afterward, when this special place in time was no more than a memory and they had gone their separate ways.   Why did this have to be so complicated? she wondered, shifting her gaze to the silent, watchful trees. Why couldn't love between a man and a woman be straightforward and mutual, instead of plagued by self-doubt and the insecurity of never knowing for sure the depth of the other person's feelings?

She had thought, when Stuart had filled every corner of her life, that what she'd shared with him was extraordinary, and strong enough to withstand whatever test was flung in its path. But at the end of it all what she'd mistaken for love had turned out to be nothing but an illusion.

"Not that we haven't had fun," he'd told her with charming regret, the day he'd decided she was becoming too much of a liability, "but I can't afford to run the risk of getting fired from this job."

"Fired?" She'd stared at him, too stunned—too *stupid*—to comprehend where the conversation was leading. "We can't be fired for falling in love, Stuart!"

"Ah, well," he'd said, running a paint-stained fingertip down her cheek, "if that were all, perhaps not."

Premonition had cast a chilling shadow over her at his words. "It's all that matters to me," she'd cried, turning her cheek and pressing her mouth to his palm in a desperate kiss. He'd been cleaning the brushes used by his senior oil-painting class and even now, five years later, the smell of turpentine revived the memory of that day in stark and degrading detail. "Nothing else compares."

He'd snatched his hand away and cast a nervous eye at the glass-paned door of the art room, as if afraid a passing student or teacher might happen to glance in and see what was taking place. "But we haven't been as discreet as we hoped. It seems we were spotted together away from the school and the sort of gossip that's given rise to, well...." He'd backed away and his lopsided, careless smile had torn her heart to shreds. "The fact of the matter is, I'm married, sweet thing, and damn me if I don't like the arrangement."

So many little things she'd refused to acknowledge had risen up to confront her then. The fact that they spent almost all their time in the shuttered privacy of her apartment. He seldom took her out in public and when he did it was to some obscure little hole in the wall at the other end of town, or, better yet, out of town altogether.

The fact that they never shared special times like Christmas. "Must pay my respects to the family," he'd say, with such dutiful long-suffering that she'd overflowed with sympathy for him, even though she would have given everything she possessed to have a family of her own to go home to. "Terribly tedious, of course, and I wouldn't dream of asking you to traipse halfway across the continent with me. You'd be bored out of your skull, darling. Best you do your thing and I'll do mine, and we'll make up for it in the new year."

And, perhaps most telling of all, his insistence that they keep their relationship secret from their co-workers. "It's not a good idea to try to mix work with pleasure," he'd said, the first time they'd made love. "Let that lot of busybodies think we're just friendly colleagues. They'll have a field day discussing us if they ever find out differently."

But the other teachers had talked anyway. If their sudden silences when she walked into the staffroom hadn't told her so, their pitying glances had. She'd thought it was because he was so much older than she was, and had turned a deaf ear when a few of the younger staff had tried to involve her in their own social groups. Only when he'd dropped the news that he was married had she understood that they'd known all along what was going on and had felt sorry for her.

She had not been able to bear the humiliation. The day after the affair ended, she'd gone to her school principal and asked for a transfer. He'd agreed to arrange it at once. "I wish you'd come to me months ago," he'd said sadly.

And now there was Morgan, not married by all accounts, but just as much of a threat in his way. What about all the things she didn't know about him, things she sensed but which he would not divulge?

But what about the things you do know? her foolish heart

cried. Don't they count? He's decent and kind and responsible. He took you in, gave you a place to stay, made you
feel at home. And he's brought you back to life, in places
no one else can see. You've learned to feel again since he
came into your life, to want. To *ache*, deep inside, to *melt*.

Helpless to deny any of it, she flicked her gaze back to
his and read the same charged awareness in his eyes.

"Jessica?"

Compellingly quiet, his voice rolled over her, like vintage
port, deep and dark. Like smoky autumn days and rich auburn sunsets. Like love....

Love? her scandalized brain scoffed. Be sensible, for
pity's sake. What can love possibly have to do with this?

Perhaps nothing, but the magnetism or whatever it was
drummed a swift percussion in her blood, leaving her surely
a little insane. Because what she actually did was lean into
him and put her arms around his waist so that not a breath
of the clear, cold air could come between them, and say, "I
think we should stop worrying about tomorrow and concentrate on how we feel tonight."

His breath caught in his throat. "You're sure?"

She nodded. That was all but it was enough.

Dipping his head, he fastened his lips to hers to seal the
contract and let them remain there as his feet retraced a path
to the shore. Her body moved smoothly with his, the uncertainty gone, the outcome assured.

His lips tasted of cold and snow and frosty starlight. Of
passion barely leashed, of scorching hunger and fiery need.
Out there on the ice, with the rest of the world paralyzed in
winter's iron grip, what had begun as a candle's flicker of
attraction burst into flames and all that mattered was that
the waiting was over. Right or wrong, wise or not, she and
Morgan had made a choice and there was no going back.

Finally, he wrestled his mouth away from hers and took
her by the arm. Urgently, silently, he steered her along the

path under the trees, back toward the house. Once he stopped and, pressing her up against the trunk of a cedar, took her face in his gloved hands and kissed her again, as though to reaffirm their decision, to stoke the fire lest it die before they had the chance to warm themselves at its flame.

His tongue spoke impassioned volumes, echoing the urgent thrust of his body against hers. Weak at the knees and utterly breathless, she thought for a moment that they'd never make it back to the house, that he'd take her out there in the shadows, with the snow for a mattress and the stars for a cover.

He didn't. He released her, grasped her arm again and, in a voice rough with passion, muttered, ''For Pete's sake, let's get back to the house before I lose what little sanity I have left.''

CHAPTER EIGHT

THE magic held, speeding them back across the frozen snow, fleet-footed and giddy with hunger for each other. Once inside the house, Morgan shucked off his boots, helped Jessica get rid of hers, peeled her free of the heavy down jacket and flung it with his across the newel post.

"You've got cold hands," he said, chafing them between his.

And I'm getting cold feet, she thought miserably, the practicalities of what they were about to enter into filling her with misgivings.

He'd probably want to strip her naked. He'd see how plain she was then, how straight up and down except for her unremarkable little breasts. Men liked breasts on a woman—lush, ripe, big breasts. Men liked fire in a woman—unbridled passion and a sense of adventure.

Whatever had made her think she could please him?

He dropped a kiss on her mouth and, winding an arm around her waist, led her upstairs. She allowed him to because she couldn't resist. His touch, his kiss, the heated glances he sent her way brought out a lust in her she'd never suspected.

Lust? Her romantic heart rebelled. *Lust wasn't what this was all about!*

What else would you like to call it, dear? the eminently down-to-earth Miss Simms, the headmistress, inquired loftily.

Still she could not free herself of his spell. Blushing, she allowed him to draw her over the threshold to his room. She'd never been inside before. Even during the day the door had always been closed and, curious though she'd been, she hadn't seen it as her right to snoop. He kicked it closed behind them now and flicked on a reading lamp that filled the shadows with too much light.

Like the room itself, his bed, she saw at once, was huge—a marriage bed, plenty big enough for two. And nothing between them and it except a few yards of carpet. She averted her eyes and wished he hadn't turned on the lamp.

Apart from a tall armoire, a set of drawers and two bedside tables, the rest of the room was bare. Short of climbing into the wardrobe, there was no place to which a person might retire to undress discreetly. And she had so many layers of clothes to shed, not the least of which was the long red underwear.

A wave of color swept over her face at the thought of him seeing her in *that*!

"Jessica," he said, linking his fingers through hers and watching her closely, "are you having second thoughts?"

Of course she was! She had absolutely no business contemplating making love with a man she'd known less than a week and, if she were honest, she'd come straight out and tell him she was afraid. But the plainer truth was that, despite the eleventh-hour attack of nerves, her body and soul cried out for him with a fine disregard for moral convention, and she was damned if she was going to turn away from him just because old fears had risen up to haunt her.

"You are very sweet," Stuart had told her, that day he'd shut the door on their affair, "but not exactly a challenge any more, my dear, if you know what I mean."

She'd known only too well. For him, the thrill had been in the chase, in being the first to seduce her. Once he'd accomplished that, he was ready to go on to other conquests.

Well, she had no virginity to lose now, no illusions to shatter. All she had—might ever have—was this moment and Morgan, and the miracle of his wanting her with the same urgency that she craved him. It showed in the molten glow of his eyes, in his clenched jaw, in the tension that held him immobile as he waited for her reply.

"I'm not having second thoughts," she assured him. "I—"

"Because if you are," he went on, "we can stop right now. I won't think badly of you for changing your mind, but—"

"This is what I want," she insisted quickly, before fear that she might disappoint him had her running for the hills.

He laid a finger across her lips. "But I will think very badly of myself if, tomorrow, you decide you've made a horrible mistake."

Out there on the frozen lake she had felt free and strong enough to let her secret self emerge, enough to dare let the romantic in her run free, even if it was only for tonight. She wasn't stupid; she knew her real life was drawn along different, more realistic lines, but just for this one special night she'd come to believe in miracles.

He had made that possible with his kisses and the way he'd looked at her. And now, with his probing questions, he was threatening to take it away. He was resurrecting the headmistress who never acted without due consideration, who never gave in to wild impulses. She didn't want to be that woman. Not here, not now.

"You're trying to talk me out of it, aren't you?" she cried, flinching a little. "Why? Because you've changed *your* mind?"

He slid his hands around her neck, lacing his fingers at her nape and stroking his thumbs along her cheekbones. "No," he said hoarsely. "Right or wrong, I've wanted you practically from the moment I first laid eyes on you. But I'm not sure you...."

"What?" she said, tilting her head so that his hand was captured between her jaw and her shoulder. *"What?"*

He hesitated, his gaze scouring her face. "I'm wondering how much...if this is the first—"

Sweet heaven, he was afraid he was going to rob her of her innocence and that she'd expect him to compensate by making an honest woman of her! "You think I'm some naive, terrified virgin, don't you? But I'm not—a virgin, I mean. I had an affair once...." She drew a sharp, defiant breath. "With a married man."

But he continued to study her with cool dispassion and saw that she'd told only half the truth. "You didn't know he was married at the time, though, did you?"

His insight punctured her bravado, leaving her feeling almost as big a fool as she had the day she'd found out Stuart had been toying with her all along. "No," she whispered miserably. "If I had, I never would have gotten involved with him."

"Well," he murmured, drawing a tender fingertip down her throat with potent effect, "I've already told you I'm not married. That much, at least, I can promise you."

It was, at best, a conditional vow but at least it was honest. And what else could he say? That he loved her? If he had, she wouldn't have believed him. Rational people didn't fall in love in a matter of days and if the realization tore at her heart a little it was because she'd been starving for romance for so long that it was difficult not to want the whole package.

"You don't have to promise me anything," she said, running her hands over the solid planes of his chest. "We haven't known each other long enough to make those kinds of demands on each other. But even if I never see you again after I leave this house I will treasure the memories I take away with me. Let what we share tonight be a Christmas gift each of us gives freely to the other."

Oh, she mourned, hearing the teacher in her upstage the lover, what a pompous idiot he must think I am!

But an expression touched his features then that she couldn't decipher, a spasm of near-grief, almost. He took her face in his two hands and looked so deeply into her eyes that he might have been searching for her soul. Beneath her hand, his heart thumped unevenly. "Where were you when I was young and optimistic, Jessica Simms?" he murmured, inching his mouth toward hers. "And what have I done to deserve you now?"

By design or happy accident—she neither knew nor cared which—his kiss swept them past the awkwardness and re-captured the passion. Suddenly, his hands were everywhere, urging her toward the bed and undressing her every step of the way, layer by layer even to the abominable red under-wear, until all that covered her were her satin camisole, bra and panties.

As if she'd caught his fever, her own hands deployed themselves with shameful abandon, tugging, sliding, strip-ping him too—not quite as expertly as he'd stripped her, perhaps, but with every bit as much fervor.

A trail of clothing marked their haste, her camisole at last slithering beneath his briefs, her bra hooking immodestly into the opening of his cords as they fell to the floor.

Breathless, eager, anxious, she felt the edge of the bed hit the back of her knees and sank to the mattress. He stood before her, naked and indecently gorgeous in the lamplight.

And then he was beside her, the scent of him—his skin, his hair—swamping her senses. The warmth of his big male body next to hers, the probing sensitivity of his hands as they discovered her, the dedication with which he readied her to accept him turned her to liquid fire.

But what made her love him was his gentleness, and his patience. Because for all that she wanted him so badly, she first had to overcome the knot of inhibition that held her hostage—a paralyzing relic of self-doubt, courtesy of the only other man she'd known, which allowed her to partic-

ipate just so far and then no further.   Morgan sensed it
and set about releasing her with an insight that moved her
to tears.

At delicious, excruciating leisure, he kissed her fingertips,
her throat, the soft skin of her inner elbow. He stroked her
face, her shoulder, traced a line between her breasts and
down her ribs, smoothed his hand over her hips and up her
thigh.

And thus, by degrees so slight she barely noticed their
progress, he sought her most intimate flesh, all the time
murmuring words in her ear, calling her sweetheart, telling
her she was beautiful.

And at that moment she believed him. She felt beautiful—voluptuously female and beautiful and desirable.
Enough that she dared touch him, too, cradling the heat of
him, marveling at the silken strength of him, and near melting with the need to feel him buried deep inside her.

But he had further exquisite torture to inflict. Like ripples
in a pond, his touch aroused ever widening rings of awareness within her until, suddenly, she broke free of all restraint
and exploded into arching spasms of response. The havoc
they created to her equilibrium was purely indescribable.

Only then, when she lay quivering with pleasure and calling out his name in a throaty murmur, did he come to her.
Not hastily or covertly, but with a smooth, sure power that
allowed for no regrets, just soaring elation and a shimmering
suspension that she never wanted to end.

He held her close, rocked within her, introduced her to
an intimacy she'd never known before. It was enough. More
than enough. Closing her hands over his shoulders, she
thought dimly that she would remember him and this night
for the rest of her life.

But he had not done giving. "Stay with me," he whispered against her mouth, sliding his hands beneath her hips
and lifting her to meet his suddenly accelerated rhythm.

She gasped at the deeper invasion, fought the old demons again as they rose up to hinder her, but they had lost their power. The confines of her existence shifted, broadened; a new horizon beckoned, and they were together, she and Morgan, riding blindly toward a destination as unavoidable as it was terrifying and exhilarating.

Her hands convulsed, her nails dug into the solid muscle of his shoulders, gouged frantically at his back. She heard a whimpering, a cry that echoed from somewhere beyond eternity, and realized it had come from her.

He answered her and for one endless, trembling moment held them both suspended. In spiraling slow motion, she felt herself expand beyond anything mortal or earthly, felt her heart fuse with his, felt her body aching and yearning and reaching...reaching....

The shattering of release, when it came, fractured her soul.

For a few, passion-drenched minutes, she lay beneath him, too saturated with emotion to move. Slowly, the separate parts of her assumed their separate identities again, though not quite as they had been before—she'd never again be that person! But the mind began to function, the knowledge to unwind.

Wrapping her arms tightly around him, she buried her face in his neck to stop herself from saying out loud that she loved him. Because at that moment, with the memory of his possession still echoing in her blood, she did love him. But she knew that if she told him so she would ruin the perfection of what they'd shared because it was the last thing he wanted to hear.

For a while longer, he remained with his big body covering hers, unmoving except for the diminishing thunder of his heart against her breast. Finally, he rolled to his side and took her with him.

His hair lay damp against his forehead, his skin, still

lightly tanned from summer, gleamed. His eyes had the sated, sleepy look of a man well pleased with the woman in his arms. He had never been more handsome, never more charming.

"Well," he said, pinning her securely in his arms and smiling down at her, "what can I say?"

Coming up with an answer was worse than picking her way through a minefield. "Merry Christmas?" she ventured.

She heard the laughter rumble deep within his chest. "And then some! Jessica Simms, you are quite exceptional and I hope you know that."

But not so exceptional that he could say the words drumming repeatedly in her head. *I love you, even if it is just for tonight.*

Alarmed at the turn her thoughts persisted in taking, she wriggled away from him. How had such a notion managed to creep up on her? Falling in love with a man simply because he'd taken her to bed was a cliché that went out of date in the sixties, one only slightly less absurd than expecting him to reciprocate the sentiment.

"Hey," he said, making a grab for her, "where do you think you're going?"

"Back to my own room," she replied, neatly evading him and swathing herself in the duvet. Never mind that that left him with only a sheet to keep himself warm; she could no more face the prospect of walking out of his room stark naked, feeling his eyes track her every step, than she could remain there and keep her shocking secret to herself. Another minute and he'd see it written on her face, even if she managed to keep her mouth shut. Darn him for turning on that lamp, anyway!

"Why?" he said. "What's wrong with staying here?"

"What would Clancy think, if he knew?"

"Hang Clancy! This is about you and me."

"Nevertheless," she said primly, "I don't care to advertise my private life and I don't imagine you do, either."

Shoving himself up onto one elbow, he watched her, and if she hadn't known better she'd have thought he looked a little hurt at her sudden defection. "True, but that's no reason for you to race off in such a hurry now without so much as a goodnight kiss." Not the least abashed by the fact that the sheet had slipped to reveal more of him than it covered, he beckoned her with the forefinger of his other hand. "Come back here, Jessica. It's not as if I'm expecting company in the next—"

He'd been about to go on cajoling her in the same light-hearted vein. She heard it in his voice, saw it in his lazy, slightly wicked smile. But all at once he bit off the words and flopped onto his back with a scowl. "On the other hand," he finished, one of his sudden mood swings taking hold and souring the moment, "perhaps you're right. Perhaps we are better off in separate beds."

"Exactly." Turning away from him, she stopped to collect her scattered clothing. He must not see the sudden sparkle of tears she dared not blink away for fear they'd splash down her face and betray her.

Good, sound common sense was all very fine, but bringing it to bear on the situation so lamentably after the fact served no purpose at all beyond reminding her that she was a fool and him that she was a temporary diversion.

"Well," she said, making tracks for the door and amazed that her voice sounded so thoroughly normal, "goodnight, Morgan. I'll see you in the morning."

"Jessica?" he said, in a low voice.

She stopped with her hand on the knob but didn't turn. She didn't think she could bear to look on his sleek, male beauty again that night and not grovel at his feet. "Yes?"

"Merry Christmas. It really was special tonight."

*   *   *

It's not as if I'm expecting company…

Morgan lay flat on his back in the dark, cursing himself and the careless utterance that had stripped the evening of its magic and left him staring into the ugly face of the reality waiting for him, if not tomorrow, then the next day or the day after that.

How could he have forgotten it, even for a moment? How could he have allowed himself, besotted imbecile that he was, to become so drawn into the web of attraction she'd spun about him that he'd risked her safety, too?

He should have listened to his first instinct and left her to fend for herself when they'd been rescued from the avalanche shed. Failing that, he should have listened to Clancy and refused to let her remain in the house. She'd have been safer bunking down on a bench at Stedman's service station than here with him.

The damnable thing was, it was too late. A lot too late. No use telling himself he'd known her only three days. Time was relative when emotions interfered. And after tonight it might as well have been a lifetime, because he and Jessica had connected—connected in a way he'd never experienced with Daphne whom he'd known for nearly three years before he'd married her.

A rising wind moaned low around the house. Indication of another blizzard, perhaps, one that would keep Jessica safe prisoner here another few days? What the hell good would that do, beyond strengthening the bond he'd had no business forging in the first place?

Morgan sighed and reached for the illuminated dial of his watch on the bedside table. Almost three in the morning. Another five hours and it would be daylight. Christmas Day in the high country. And somewhere out there Gabriel Parrish waited while, across the hall, Jessica lay alone in her bed.

Cursing again, he sat up and bunched the pillows behind

his head and accepted what he could no longer deny. Things had progressed far beyond the point of his offering a stranger the kindness of a roof over her head until the weather improved. He wanted to keep her with him, explore the wider possibilities of the relationship that had sprung up between them. He wanted to protect her, to preserve her air of unsullied purity, her innocence.

"You want to take on the whole damned world," his ex-wife had accused him bitterly during one of their endless fights about his work, and in a way she'd been right. He *had* been too busy fighting other people's battles to take proper care of his marriage.

But this went beyond the ordinary range of things and had nothing to do with his commitment to sweeping society clean of its human filth. Jessica touched his heart and made him want to rush out and slay dragons for her, a dangerously quixotic fancy that he could ill afford with the very real threat of Gabriel Parrish hovering.

Jessica was precisely Parrish's kind of victim: fragile, vulnerable, gentle. And far from protecting her Morgan had put her smack in the path of danger.

Of course, he could explain the whole mess to her and hope she'd understand. And then what? Have her cringe every time a twig snapped in the cold? Have her looking over her shoulder the whole time she was alone in his house? Have her despise him more than she already did?

Because it was obvious that was how she felt and she'd wasted no time letting him know it, after the loving. If he hadn't heard her cries, felt the helpless contractions of her flesh around his, he'd have thought he'd lost his touch. But just as there'd been no mistaking her climactic response there'd been no mistaking the haste with which she'd departed the scene, once she'd recovered herself, and no misreading the rejection in the erect line of her spine as she'd stood at the door and bid him a cool goodnight.

Thank you for a pleasant interlude, Mr. Kincaid, but now that it's over I see very little reason to prolong the evening.

He'd known a violent urge to argue the point, an unprecedented occurrence for him. He didn't chase after reluctant women; they weren't worth the effort, not when so many others were willing. And heaven could attest to the fact that he wasn't in the market for a long-term affair. Nor, for that matter, was she. A brief encounter they could handle. A dalliance. Something that wouldn't scratch below the surface of their separate lives.

A waltz with a stranger—lilting, briefly and engagingly intimate—but no more permanent than the ice on the frozen lake.

When had the rules changed for him?

A sound penetrated the silence, a creaking that was probably nothing more than the house settling its old bones into the winter night, but which could equally well be a stealthy footfall announcing the arrival of an intruder.

Morgan raked exasperated fingers through his hair. For crying out loud, that was all he needed: to have his imagination run any wilder than it already was!

But once planted the suspicion refused to die. What if Parrish had tracked him down despite the weather and was even now inside the house, searching for his archenemy? What if he opened the wrong door by mistake and discovered Jessica?

Cold sweat broke out along Morgan's spine.

Flinging back the covers, he swung out of bed and pulled on his robe, his feet silent on the floor. Cautiously, he inched open his door.

Nothing. No darting, furtive shadow, no sense of evil lurking, just the quiet hum of the oil furnace and the dim fragrance of the Christmas tree stealing up the stairs.

Across the hall, the door to Jessica's room stood closed. Was she inside, safely sleeping, or had the sound that had alerted him wakened her, too? His outstretched hand froze mere inches from the doorknob.

Hell, Kincaid, he jeered silently, who're you trying to fool? You're just itching to find a reason to go in there and pretending there's a bogeyman haunting the place is about as feeble an excuse as you can get.

But what if…? The spectre of Parrish rose again to haunt him. Grasping the knob, he quietly opened her door and stepped into the room.

Moonlight splashed across the floor and over the bed. She lay in the middle of the mattress, so straight and still that for one wild, irrational moment he wondered if he'd left it too late, wondered if Parrish had found her and she was already dead. And then she turned her head and he saw that her eyes were wide open and watching him.

''Morgan?'' Her voice swam across to him, soft, misty, full of yearning. Like her eyes as they tracked his progress toward the bed.

She held out her arms, silvered with moonlight, and with that simple, eloquent gesture flattened any hope he'd entertained of staying away from her. He could love this woman, he realized despairingly. Love her in ways he hadn't known how to love when he'd married Daphne.

With a muffled groan, he swept aside the covers and strode back to his room, cradling her next to his heart.

They fell on the bed together, mouths devouring each other, hands tormenting, limbs tangling. She was hot and damp and sleekly alluring. Their mating was swift and too frantic to allow for any pretense at finesse or responsibility.

Her body welcomed him, closed around him, caressed him. In vain he tried to hold back, to distance himself just enough to prolong the pleasure for both of them, but it was too late. Without warning she climaxed in a flight of ripples that had him flooding within her in shocking, sudden release.

She was so ready to love, he thought sadly, cradling her sleeping body. So ready to *be* loved. Why had it been he who'd found her? Why not some man whose soul was intact, whose heart had not grown black and bitter, whose energies were bent on something other than a crusade that left him with so little to offer a woman?

Jessica didn't awake until nine on Christmas morning, and even then she might have slept another hour had the sun not crept through the window to shine full on her face.

She was alone in the bed with only the faint warmth where Morgan had lain beside her as proof that she hadn't dreamed the night before. That and her pleasurably aching body.

By the time she was showered and dressed, any hope she'd entertained of trying to pretend this morning was no different from the others she'd spent at the lodge had evaporated. The men were back at the house already, their early chores at the stables completed. "O Come All Ye Faithful" floated up the stairs from the old record player in the living room, along with the smell of frying food from the kitchen.

Securing her hair in its usual smooth loop at her nape, Jessica took a deep, calming breath and prepared to face Morgan, wishing that she could have done so without Clancy there as witness.

It was a far worse experience than she'd anticipated. Morgan sat at the kitchen table, his hands wrapped around his coffee mug. Clancy stood at the stove, swishing something around in the large, cast-iron frying pan, and it was clear from the scowl he shot her way that he'd deployed the last of his Christmas spirit the night before.

"Well, lookee what the cat drug down," he declared evilly.

Jessica resisted the urge to fidget with the collar of her blouse. "I'm afraid I overslept."

"Do tell." He shoveled the contents of the frying pan onto three plates and slapped one down in front of her.

She looked at the greasy mess and swallowed. Chunks of ham floated among half-cooked eggs, alongside hash-browned potatoes swimming in a sea of grease.

Looking up, she found Morgan studying her. "Good morning," he said, a faintly conspiratorial smile warming his eyes. "I hope you're hungry."

Sweet heaven, yes—but not for what stared up from her plate! Picking up her fork, Jessica speared a morsel of ham that glistened with fat. "Not very," she said, suppressing a delicate shudder. "I think I'll just have toast."

"Ain't made toast, and idlers can't be choosers," Clancy informed her sourly. "You choose to lollygag in bed when any decent, self-respectin' woman'd be at the kitchen stove where she rightly belongs, then you put up with what lands on your plate or else go hungry."

"That's enough, Clancy," Morgan warned quietly, keeping his gaze trained on her. "Jessica doesn't need your permission to sleep in. I wasn't up at the crack of dawn myself."

Clancy flicked a knowing glance from her to Morgan and back again. "Hah! Ain't that a coincidence and a half!"

Jessica felt a slow burn climb up her neck to inflame her face and wished she could fall through a crack in the floor. "Well," she said, deciding this was not the time to take issue with Clancy's chauvinistic views on women and their rightful role in society, "I'm sure this is delicious, whatever it is."

And to prove the point she valiantly scooped a forkful into her mouth. Across the table, Morgan continued to watch her, his hands still wrapped around his coffee mug.

Memories floated over, of those same hands covering her breasts, measuring her waist, parting her thighs, stilling her eager hips. "I don't understand myself," she'd confessed, pressing herself to him and reveling in the knowledge that, regardless of what he might be trying to tell her, a certain portion of his own anatomy had an actively rebellious mind of its own. ''It's as if I've got an attack of polar fever or something.''

''Or something.'' His words had slid into her mouth along with his tongue, wreaking delicious devastation.

She'd felt her barriers disintegrating again, melted by the moist heat swirling the length of her and flooding warmly against him, there, in that most private place that he'd touched and stroked and incited to ecstasy.

How embarrassing to remember it now! How shameless!

The color flooded her face anew, so fiercely that it wouldn't have surprised her too greatly to find her forehead emblazoned with a large scarlet WH for Wanton Hussy.

The food in her mouth rebelled furiously and threatened to choke her. Morgan pushed back his chair, picked up her plate, scraped the contents into the garbage can under the sink, then popped two slices of bread in the toaster.

''Coffee?'' he asked her, lifting the coffee pot from its spot on top of the woodstove.

She nodded gratefully. ''Thank you.''

''How about you, Clancy? Ready for a refill?''

Eyes darting observantly back and forth, Clancy grunted acceptance.

Morgan topped up his own mug, too, replaced the pot on the stove and, leaning his hips against the counter, drummed a soft tattoo on the back of his chair as he waited for the toast to brown.

Covertly, Jessica studied him. He had the tall, sculpted build of a telemark skier, she thought dreamily. Sharply defined, clear-eyed. Sexy. She leaned toward him, drinking in the sharp, clean fragrance of him.

The toast sprang up, startling her. Morgan turned to attend to it.

"Lordy, woman," Clancy drawled, sotto voce, "eat him up whole, why don'tcha?"

"Here's your toast," Morgan said, placing a fresh plate in front of her. "Hurry up and eat, then get your coat. I've got a surprise waiting outside."

CHAPTER NINE

AS CURIOUS to discover what Morgan had in store for her as she was eager to escape Clancy's too observant eye, Jessica literally bolted through her breakfast. Nothing, however, could have prepared her for the sight that met her eyes when she stepped out onto the front veranda.

At the foot of the steps stood a sleek red sleigh with a high padded seat clearing the runners by a good two feet. Jasper waited patiently between twin wooden shafts, silver bells gleaming from his harness. ''Thought you might like to go for a spin,'' Morgan said, coming up beside her. ''You've been kind of housebound lately.''

''Yes.'' Jessica stood transfixed, as thrilled as a child. ''Morgan, what an absolutely gorgeous sleigh!''

''Isn't it?'' He stroked a proud hand over the painted side and swung open the little door. ''Hop aboard and let's get going while the sun's still high.''

She climbed up the two narrow steps and settled into the red leather seat. There were hot bricks wrapped in flannel for her feet and a marvellous fur lap rug to keep the chill out.

''Buffalo robes,'' Morgan explained, when she asked. ''Guaranteed to cut the wind, no matter how cold it gets.''

He climbed up beside her, gathered up the reins and clicked his tongue, a signal that had Jasper moving over the snowed-in driveway to the open country beyond.

The scene unrolled like something from *Dr. Zhivago*. Seated beside Morgan, her face framed by the fur-trimmed hood of her jacket, her knees covered by buffalo robes, her feet toasting gently on the hot bricks, Jessica gazed around,

140

eager not to miss a thing as they followed a course along the ridge to the west of the house.

To either side the land dropped away, remote and empty save for the occasional group of snow-laden trees. Ahead, the razor-backed mountains reared up, their winter load dazzling against the deep blue sky.

Except for the soft squeak of the sleigh runners and the jingle of bells on Jasper's harness, the silence was profound to the point of being almost somnolent.

"That married man you mentioned," Morgan said suddenly, the sound of his voice flowing into the still air as smoothly as the hot rum sauce had rolled over the ice cream dessert she'd made the night before, "the one you had the affair with, were you in love with him?"

"Stuart?" Jessica blinked. What had Stuart to do with anything? "Yes. I was very hurt when he ended things between us."

"And now?"

She flung Morgan a questioning stare and found him concentrating fiercely on his driving. "Now?"

His glance flicked briefly over her, then focused on the scene ahead again. "Do you still care about him?"

"No!" she exclaimed. "If I did, I'd never have made love with you last night."

"The two don't necessarily cancel each other out, you know."

"They do for me. I'm not the type to play musical beds." She paused and hazarded another sidelong glance at him. His profile was almost as remote as the countryside. "Are you trying to tell me you are, Morgan?"

"No." He hauled on the reins and brought Jasper to a halt in the lee of a belt of trees. "I like to be able to live with myself the morning after."

The easy relaxation between them when they'd first started out seeped away suddenly, leaving behind a tension as fragile as crystal shimmering in the bright white sunshine. "Then why did you bring up the subject in the first place?"

He sighed and leaned forward to rest his elbows on his knees. "I guess I'm wondering where we go from here. Yesterday, I thought I knew. Today, I'm not so sure."

It was an admission that might have charged her with elation had the darkness in his tone not indicated such a wealth of regret on his part for the fact that they'd made love.

"Well," she said, rushing to fill the silence with an admission more easily borne coming out of her mouth than his, "what happened between us…well, it was a purely physical thing—at least for me."

"Was it?" She could feel his gaze boring into her, seeking to discover truth and fearing, quite rightly, that he'd find only lies. "Then why do I feel like pond scum this morning? As if I've let both of us down and hurt you in the bargain?"

"You haven't hurt me," she said staunchly, because the other option, to burst out crying for something he clearly couldn't give her, would be more humiliation than she could abide. "You've been honest with me and that's what matters."

Broodingly, he studied the distant valley. "Honesty's very important to you, isn't it, Jessica?"

"Yes, especially where feelings are concerned. I lived with the lie of my aunt's supposed affection for years, even though she tried hard not to let it show that she really didn't care much for me."

She drew in a deep breath of the crisp air and prayed it would dispel the sudden urge to bare her soul to him. Wallowing in self-pity was unattractive at the best of times and always dangerous. She no more wanted his pity than she did his affectations of love. She'd endured enough of both to last her a lifetime. "I think there is nothing more insulting than to be the recipient of that sort of deceit."

"Were you very young when you went to live with her?"

"Yes." Jessica pushed back the jacket hood and lifted her face to the pale winter sun. "I was eight at the time and

Selena was five. Of course, I had no idea how my aunt felt about taking us in.''

''How long before you found out?''

''Quite some time.'' Jessica plucked at the fur robe covering her lap. ''In her way, she tried very hard to be a good substitute parent, but it was more a question of noblesse oblige than real affection. She and my uncle had elected not to have a family of their own and I think suddenly finding herself stuck with someone else's small, unhappy children cramped her style terribly.''   ''At least you and your sister had each other.'' He took off his gloves and spread one arm along the high cushioned backrest of the seat. ''No wonder you were so anxious to get to her when you heard about her accident. You must be very close.''

''Not really. As we grew older, we found we had very little in common.'' She shrugged, burningly conscious of his hand draped over her shoulder. ''Selena adapted to her new situation much better than I did. My aunt was a real society matron—gave lots of smart, expensive parties at which she liked to have us put in an appearance so that everyone could commend her for the wonderful thing she was doing. I was a plain, shy child with no social graces at all, but Selena was a party animal from the word go. Pretty, entertaining, amusing. A very easy child to love, even if she didn't have my feet.''

''Your feet?'' Morgan turned toward her and let out a bark of surprised laughter. ''What the hell have your feet got to do with anything?''

''They're my finest feature,'' Jessica said candidly. ''Apart from my brains, they're the *only* feature I have that's worth mentioning, if my aunt is to be believed.''

''Then your aunt is a damn fool,'' he told her, ''and so are you if you believe that sort of rubbish.''

''She did her best in a difficult situation. You have to understand that Selena barely remembered our parents but I did, and I missed them horribly. I didn't want someone else trying to take their place. I wasn't affectionate or...or giving, like Selena. She'd hand out kisses and hugs indiscriminately and loved to be dressed up like a doll and paraded before other people, whereas I was...."

"Yes?" His hand strayed up to stroke her cheek. "What were you, Jessica?"

"Ungrateful, probably. Standoffish, certainly." She gave the buffalo robe an irritable twitch, annoyed to hear a faint whine of self-pity in her voice despite her best efforts to prevent it. "How many poor animals died to make this, do you suppose?"

If he was surprised at the sudden change of topic, he didn't show it. "I've no idea. It was something my great-grandfather gave to my great-grandmother the same year he had this cutter made for her." Swinging sideways on the seat, Morgan brought his other hand over and covered Jessica's, capturing it next to the robe and leaving her trapped in the loose circle of his arms. "Until then, people around here thought she was standoffish, too."

How was it possible that, with winter all around them, just his touch could leave her flushed with rosy warmth? Studiously avoiding his gaze and certain he must be able to hear the uneven thumping of her heart in the silence, Jessica said, "And was she?"

"No. Like you, she was simply different. Born in England, one of four children, affluent parents, private governess, debutante, the whole society nine yards. When the First World War broke out, she became a nurse and went to work in a hospital in London. She fell in love with my great-grandfather when he was shipped there to recover from wounds he suffered in France. They were married in 1918, a big society wedding at her family's country estate, and he brought her home to Canada right after that."

"Home being here, at the house?" So drawn in by the story that she forgot to worry about the effect of how close Morgan was sitting or how snugly his arm had closed around her shoulder, Jessica swung around to face him.

"Not quite. He built the lodge over the next several years.

To begin with, they lived in a cabin with no running water or indoor plumbing.''

"Good grief, talk about culture shock!"

"Exactly." Morgan nodded. "My great-grandmother was homesick and lonely. She gave birth to her first child, my grandmother, in that cabin, with no one to help her, no relatives to fuss over her, none of the comforts she'd been brought up to expect. She had nothing in common with other wives in the area and no friends. Her only contact with the outside world came through the letters she received from home and by the time they arrived the news they contained was months old. Her entire life took place within those four walls with her baby and my great-grandfather who, during the summer especially, spent nearly every waking hour working the ranch."

"She must have loved him very much."

"She did, but even so the marriage almost fell apart when her second baby was stillborn. She was alone at the time and was convinced the child could have been saved had there been someone there to help her."

"I cannot imagine the pain that must have brought her, to lose a child."

"It's not something I would wish on my worst enemy," Morgan said, with such feeling that, if he hadn't already told her there'd been no children, Jessica would have wondered if he and his wife had lost a son or daughter.

"What saved the marriage?" she asked, as much to alleviate the sudden darkening of his mood as to hear the rest of the story.

"She told him she was going home again and taking their surviving child with her, because she couldn't stand the isolation a day longer. Her son lay buried within sight of the house and her daughter was growing up a prisoner of the wilderness, learning none of the social graces that would have been part of her life if she'd grown up in England."

Jessica studied Morgan's profile and thought that, if the old man had been one iota as handsome or one tenth as skilled a lover as his great-grandson, no woman could have walked away from him. "But he talked her out of it?"

"No, he hitched the horse to the buggy, drove her into town and bought her a ticket so that she could catch the next train heading east. But when it came right down to it she couldn't leave him. She had her bags on the train and one foot on the step, ready to climb into the carriage, and then made the mistake of looking down into his big, dumb face, and supposedly said, 'After everything we've been through together, are you just going to stand there and let me walk out of your life, you stupid fool?'"

"Oh," Jessica said, blinking furiously as the silly tears threatened, "I've always been a pushover for happy endings."

"Well," Morgan said, his eyes scouring her face, "it didn't quite end there. Of course, she came back here with him, but the shock of what had almost happened made them take stock. They both realized she needed contact with other people, and a purpose beyond simply being a wife and mother. So, that Christmas, he presented her with the cutter, and she started visiting the other ranchers' wives. Before long, word got around that she'd been a nurse and the next thing she was being called on to help deliver babies, and by the following summer, when the foundations for the house were being built, she'd become something of a legend up here."

He paused for breath and grinned at her. "What was your original question again, Jessica?"

"I asked about the buffalo robe."

"Ah, yes. Well, now you know."

"So tell me the rest."

"There's not much to tell. My grandmother went away to school but came home one summer and fell in love with a neighboring rancher. They married and had only one child, my father. He moved to the coast when he went to university, met my mother there, and settled in Vancouver where I was born. The ranch dwindled, with some of the land eventually being sold off after my grandparents died, and the property lay more or less neglected until I took an interest in it.''

''And your sister?'' Jessica asked. ''You haven't mentioned her except in passing.''

''She married a Frenchman and lives in Marseilles. We keep in touch, of course, but we're not close the way we once were.''

Jessica turned her hand palm up so that her fingers curved around his. ''I'm sorry, Morgan.''

''Yeah, well....'' He blew out a long breath that curled foggily in the still air. ''I guess that happens when another man enters a woman's life.''

''That must hurt. Selena can be a pain at times, but she's the only family I have left. I want to be there for her whenever she needs me.''

His hand cupped her face, sweetly, familiarly. ''I guess you'll be glad when the roads reopen and you can be on your way again.''

Three days ago she'd have welcomed the idea, but now.... ''Yes,'' she said weakly, ''I can hardly wait.''

''It hasn't been much of a Christmas for you so far, has it?''

''It's been....'' A change from the usual, unexpected, novel: the trite responses lined up in her mind, waiting to see which one best fit the occasion, because Miss Jessica Simms, headmistress, charted her life by just such conventions. But she hadn't counted on her gaze slipping to his mouth, so near to hers, so incredibly sexy. ''Wonderful,'' she finished on a sigh.

His breath, sweet as mountain air, fanned her face. His fingers, cool against her suddenly fevered skin, traced a line from her cheek to her jaw and slid around her neck. His head obscured the waning sun as he narrowed the last few inches separating her from him. ''It has, hasn't it?''

''Yes,'' she whispered, and closed her eyes as he lavished kisses on her mouth, first at one corner and then the other, and, finally, full on her waiting lips. Beneath his artful persuasion, she opened herself to him and wondered, as his kiss deepened to claim her soul yet again, how she'd ever bring herself to say goodbye to him when the time came for her to leave.

"I think," he murmured huskily, at last dragging his lips from hers, "that we'd better stop while we're ahead. This isn't making-love weather, even with buffalo robes to keep out the cold."

She didn't know why not. She was on fire for him. But should she say so? Could she even begin to scrape up the courage to tell him that, for her, things had changed, that she wasn't the same hidebound woman he'd rescued just a few days before, that she'd fallen in love with a man because of the gentleness that underlay his strength, because of the humor and passion that marked his life in ways they'd never touched hers?

Of course not! Because, at heart, she hadn't changed. That she was hankering for all the traditional trappings of commitment and happy-ever-after romance to validate what they'd both agreed would be a passing affair was proof enough of that. "I agree," she murmured, with admirable restraint. "And we should be getting back to the house. Clancy will be wondering what we're up to."

"I suspect he's figured it out pretty accurately," Morgan said ruefully, sliding back to his side of the seat and stuffing his hands into his gloves before picking up the reins. "But you're right—we should be heading back. I should give him a hand settling the horses for the night and you've got dinner to prepare."

Why did she allow it to hurt her that, despite the intimacies they'd shared, he was able so easily to assign her to the position of housekeeper again? He'd never promised her a different or more permanent role, after all, and hadn't caring for others and making sure things were done right always been the part that suited her best?

Face it, Jessica, she scolded herself, drawing the hood up

over her head again, you've never been the type that men want to die for. Be grateful for the brief happiness you've found here and let it be enough. Don't spoil it by wishing for the impossible.

And yet, despite knowing all that, she heard herself say, "Why, if this time we've shared has been so wonderful for both of us, does it have to end with my leaving here, Morgan?"

He turned Jasper in a wide circle and waited until they were headed back along the ridge toward the house before he answered. "Because," he said, "I can't commit beyond this time. What you see here, what you think you know, is only part of the man I am."

"And the other part?" she asked, recognizing the absolute truth of what he said. "What about him?"

He sighed and shook his head. "That's the part that worries me."

"You've been honest with me and that's what matters." The words burned themselves into his brain the entire time he was putting the cutter away in the unused barn behind the stables.

The problem was not just that he hadn't told her about Parrish; that could easily be remedied. It was the more difficult truth he was having difficulty with, the one which extended to admitting that he was falling in love with her, that he wanted her to remain in his life after these few days were over. And the hardest truth of all was facing the fact that he had no right to ask that of her.

"Didn't think I'd be seeing you out here again today," Clancy observed sourly when Morgan led Jasper back into the stable. "Kinda thought you'd be so plumb wore out you wouldn't be much use to anyone, seeing as how you didn't get near enough sleep last night."

"Can it, Clancy. I've got enough on my mind without you adding your two bits' worth."

"That sweet woman's falling for you, Morgan," Clancy

persisted, undaunted, "and I want to know what you plan to do about it."

"What the hell do you expect me to do?" Frustrated, Morgan stabbed viciously at the nearest bale of straw with the pitchfork.

"Speakin' the truth wouldn't be a bad place to start."

As if he hadn't already figured out that much! "And tell her what? That she's welcome to bunk down here until the weather breaks but that there's a madman out there somewhere gunning for me and she could end up being murdered in her bed?"

"T'ain't what Gabriel Parrish might do to her in her bed that's worryin' me at this precise moment, it's you. I don't plan to stand by and watch her dismissed as if she weren't nothing more than a servant around here when it's plain—"

"I thought you wanted her gone!"

"Of course I did, you dad-blamed fool! I wanted her as far away as she could get. Far enough that she wouldn't get splattered with the dirt that follows you around, but you fooled around too long and left it too late." He drew an irate breath. "So help me, Morgan Kincaid, if that woman gets herself hurt at this stage because you were too damned selfish to keep your drawers done up, I'll—"

"You're out of line, Clancy! Furthermore—"

The sudden shrilling of the telephone hanging on the wall near the door blasted the rest of his sentence into oblivion. For a second, he and Clancy glared at each other in frozen silence.

"Well," Clancy finally said, after the third ring, "which one of us is goin' to answer that, Morgan? Or are we just goin' to stand here gapin' at it till the damn thing rings off the wall?"

The ducks were in the oven, stuffed with wild rice and basted with a cranberry glaze. The sparkling white burgundy Morgan had set aside for dinner cooled in a silver ice bucket. The tree glowed in the living room, its light augmented by the flames flickering in the hearth. The table was decked out with the fine family silver and crystal.

Stepping into the shower, Jessica let the hot water pelt over her hair and down her body, welcoming the stinging spray. She had never felt more alive, or more complete.

"I guess I'm wondering where we go from here," he'd said that afternoon, and she'd sensed the same bewildered hunger in him that ate at her. "Yesterday, I thought I knew. Today, I'm not so sure."

Tipping shampoo into the palm of her hand, she scrubbed at her scalp, glad she'd have time enough to dry her hair and leave it lying soft and loose around her face instead of taming it into its usual loop while it was still damp.

Regretfully she thought of the elegant midnight-blue dinner dress she'd worn to the board of governors' Christmas cocktail party and wished she had it with her now. But how could she have known, last week when she'd crammed things into her suitcase before flinging it into the back of her car and setting out on the long drive to Whistling Valley, that she'd be wanting to dress up for a man she'd yet to meet? That was Selena's sort of scenario, not hers.

Would he come to her again tonight? Would they make love again? Was she crazy to believe that perhaps their relationship didn't have to end when she left the ranch?

Tilting her head to one side, she squeezed the excess water from her hair and swathed it in a towel. Already it was dark outside, and another night full of stars and promised moonlight upon them. Christmas night, and the most special she'd ever known.

Humming to herself, she patted her body dry. Powdered and perfumed it, and slipped into the ribboned black satin lingerie with its rich edging of French lace. Rolled cobweb-fine silk stockings up her legs and gave an involuntary shiver of pleasure at the remembered touch of Morgan's hands, the first time he'd touched her bare thigh.

The black silk blouse, the straight black velvet skirt, a cameo that had belonged to her mother and the pearl ear studs without which she was seldom seen, and she was ready, except for putting the finishing touches to her hair.

Over the whine of the hairdryer, she thought she heard the back door slam open, signaling Morgan's return. He'd want to shower, too, before they sat down to dinner. Fluffing the last damp curl into place, she swept a final glance at herself in the full-length mirror and left the room.

Not until she reached the foot of the stairs did she realize that he hadn't come back alone. Clancy was with him, still wearing the same blue denim dungarees he'd worn all day. They stood in the doorway to the living room, waiting for her. Was she going to have to scold them into changing for dinner?

Stepping forward with a smile, she said, "You're back early."

"The roads are open again," Clancy said, an odd reply even without the accompanying grimness of tone.

Her heart stumbled a warning which she ignored. "So?"

"There's nothing to keep you here," he said.

Her heart tripped again, an ominous, unsettling occurrence that left her feeling slightly sick. "Are you...am I being...?"

She left the questions dangling and shook her head at the foolish notion that she was being quite literally kicked out of the house on Christmas night. "Morgan?"

He met her gaze unflinchingly and there was nothing in his eyes—no desire, no passion, no shame. "It's time you were on your way," he said, confirming fears that should have been outlandish but which were, suddenly, all too real. "Get your things and I'll drive you to Sentinel Pass."

"Wait a minute!" she cried. "How do you know the road's open again and what's the sudden rush to be rid of me?"

"We got a phone call, woman," Clancy declared. "And, like Morgan said, it's time you got on the road again before the next storm hits."

"Wouldn't you at least like me to serve dinner first?"

she pleaded, and cringed inwardly that she should degrade herself like that. Where was her pride, her self-respect?

"We can serve ourselves," Morgan said bleakly. "Please, Jessica, it's best not to prolong this."

Prolong what? They had been happy together as recently as two hours ago. He had hinted that they might have a future together. What had happened to change things so dramatically?

She looked again from his face to Clancy's and saw the same stubborn determination stamped on the old man's features. "You've done this, haven't you?" she whispered. "You've talked him out of—"

"Clancy has nothing to do with this," Morgan said. "It's a simple matter of making the most of improved conditions while they last. I know how anxious you are to see your sister."

The dismissal was unmistakable, echoing in his voice, reflecting bleakly in his eyes. Had she been deluding herself to think he'd ever shown her a hint of tenderness? Had those unsmiling lips ever softened against hers in a kiss?

"Oh, Lord!" she mumbled, feeling her mouth begin to tremble and seeing Morgan's image blur as her eyes filled with tears. It was the same old story she'd tried to write a hundred times, one in which she insinuated herself into a home, a family. As if baking a few tarts or mopping a floor were enough to earn a place in anyone's heart, least of all a man like Morgan Kincaid who must have women taking a number and lining up to keep him company!

"Bring the truck round to the front while I go get her things, Clancy," she heard him say as she strove to deal with the thudding lurch of her heart as it raced to absorb the blow it had been dealt.

He moved out of her line of vision and left her staring at the teary sparkle of lights on the tree that she'd so lovingly dressed in its best for this special time of year.

She should have chosen the artificial tree with its chichi

decor, she thought bitterly. It might have reminded her that nothing about this Christmas was permanent or real.

Soon—too soon—he came back down the stairs with her suitcase and bag. He opened the front door and Clancy was there, waiting to relieve him of his load. Turning back, Morgan took her coat, the mohair coat he'd dismissed so cuttingly as being no more appropriate than a party dress at a funeral, and held it out for her.

Numbly, she slid her arms into the sleeves, then stood there like a child while he did up the buttons. When he'd finished, he indicated her west coast city boots that had also earned his scorn. "Put them on," he said, and obediently she stepped into them.

"Good." He blew out a breath of relief. "Let's go."

"No," she said, emerging from the almost hypnotic trance that had taken hold. "Not until you make me understand."

"Not here," he insisted. "We'll have time to talk in the truck."

But the time passed too quickly, he saw to that, taking the road at such reckless speed that, if she'd cared a scrap about living to see another day, she'd have thought he was trying to kill them both.

"We've imposed on your good nature long enough," he dared to say, at one point.

"That's certainly a unique way to describe what we've shared," she replied, growing anger reviving some of her fire.

His profile, illuminated by the dim green glow from the dashboard, gave nothing away. "What would you like me to call it, Jessica?"

"Oh, I don't know." She waved a deliberately languid hand but her voice was edged with pure steel. "A wild, explosive attraction based on nothing but proximity, perhaps? Sexual favors in return for domestic service?"

That elicited a response! He swore, spitting out a socially unacceptable four-letter word that crudely described what she'd have called making love until he'd relieved her of any such illusion.

"Yes," she said, Miss Simms the headmistress resurrecting herself too late to reverse the damage he'd done, "I dare say that's how you would describe it. You must forgive me for not having had the good sense to recognize that sooner."

Enraged, he slammed his gloved hands against the steering wheel. "Goddammit, Jessica, that's not what I'm saying."

"Really? You could have fooled me—did, in fact." The last words wobbled embarrassingly. Biting the inside of her cheek, she steeled herself not to break down in front of him. "But that's all right, Morgan. I've been made a fool of before by better men than you."

"Stuart, you mean?" He ground out the question with barely restrained fury. "Hell, Jessica, I don't deserve that."

Ahead, a sprinkling of lights showed in the dark. Subduing the urge to let him know exactly what she thought he did deserve, she said coolly, "Are we almost there?"

"Yes." He swung around a curve that ran parallel to a frozen river winding along the valley floor. "We'll be at Stedman's service station in about five minutes."

Time had never flown so fast. The seconds slipped away from her like her life's blood and there was nothing she could think of to halt their progress, nothing she could say to change his mind. All she could do was try to find an answer. "Why did you ever let me into your life, Morgan?"

"Because when I first started…working, a man murdered a young woman while she was on her way home from seeing a movie with her girlfriend," he said as the first buildings appeared. "She'd walked the last few blocks alone and was killed almost within sight of the house she lived in when it happened."

Ignoring Jessica's murmur of sympathy, he continued, "She was nineteen, the same age as my sister at the time, and the tragedy of it struck home to me in a way I'll never forget. I vowed then that I'd never knowingly let the same thing happen to another woman if I could possibly prevent it."

"So you rescued me for my own good," Jessica said bitterly. "Was that why you made love to me, too?"

He sighed heavily. "No, Jessica. But I thought I knew myself well enough not to contemplate the idea of remarrying. I've never had reason to re-evaluate that decision until the last few days."

Was she supposed to feel better, knowing he'd had to think twice before rejecting her? Don't hand me placebos, she wanted to shriek. I don't want to be your almost-ran!

"I quite understand," she said stonily. "I, too, decided commitment to one individual is a poor investment and made my work my life. And although I am fond of my students I always hold something back." She paused, struggling to contain the pain that howled within her, then uttered the last lie she'd ever tell him. "I never give *everything* to anyone, any more."

The flashing lights in the window of the service station flung red and yellow ribbons out into the road. Steering between the high-banked snow left by the plows, Morgan swung into the parking lot and brought the truck to a halt.

Leaving the engine idling, he turned in his seat to face her. "I guess we both made the right decision, then."

She looked at him feature by feature, committing him to memory and wondering how long it would be before the image blurred enough around the edges for her to forget how blue his eyes were, how thick and dark his lashes, how sexy his mouth. How many nights would she awake from dreaming of him and find herself weeping for the loss?

"I guess we did," she said.

He swung open his driver's-side door. "I'll give you a hand with your suitcase."

"No," she said. "Don't bother. We'll just say goodbye here and get it over with."

"You're right." He pulled off his glove.

Oh, please! she thought. Don't ask me to shake hands and part friends!

He touched her face. He leaned forward. ''Goodbye, Jessica,'' he said huskily, and kissed her lightly not quite on the mouth.

CHAPTER TEN

JESSICA stood in the bitterly cold parking lot, watching Morgan drive away. As his brake lights disappeared around the bend, a spasm of grief clutched her, for the love she had briefly known, for the beauty he had brought into her life.

Swallowing to relieve the ache in her throat, she gave herself a mental shake. Enough! It was over. The real world waited—her world of dependable older sister, of conscientious headmistress. Sober, practical roles for which she was so eminently well suited.

Picking up her bags, she turned toward the service station. Inside, the air was thick and stale with tobacco smoke. On the counter next to the cash register stood a tiny lopsided tree, its spindly branches looped with a dusty foil garland. On the wall behind hung an assortment of flashlight batteries, fishing lures, windshield scrapers and other sundry items. Tire chains and sacks of road salt were stacked to one side on the floor.

A horseshoe-shaped lunch counter filled the other half of the room. Three hefty men, truckers probably, judging by the semis she'd noticed parked outside, straddled stools closest to a serving hatch and joked with the middle-aged waitress busy wiping the tops of plastic ketchup bottles with a damp rag. At the other end, a slender man hunched over a bowl of soup.

From a television set mounted on the wall, a well-known singer hosted her annual Christmas show amid a glitter of sequins and special effects. The orchestra played ''Let It Snow''.

The truckers spared Jessica a cursory glance. The lone

man ignored her, his attention split between his soup and the TV show.

"Ma'am?" A young mechanic in blue overalls appeared from a side door. "You looking for a fill-up of gas?"

"I'm looking for my car," Jessica told him. "It was towed in three days ago for repairs and I believe it's ready for me now."

"Heck, yes, the maroon Taurus. Mr. Kincaid's man phoned not half an hour ago to make sure it would be ready for you when you got here. We're still working on it, but it shouldn't be too much longer." He wiped greasy hands on a rag and shrugged apologetically. "Things are a bit backed up with all the weather we've been getting. Have a seat while you're waiting, why don't you?"

She nodded, too dispirited to argue. Morgan's anxiety to be rid of her, even though it meant her waiting around in this godforsaken outpost of civilization, added fresh insult to injury.

"Hey, Linda!" the young man yelled to the waitress. "Get the lady here a cup of coffee." He glanced again at Jessica. "You hungry, ma'am? Marty, the cook, makes a mean hot turkey sandwich."

The mere thought sent her stomach into revolt. "No, thanks. Just coffee will be fine."

Climbing onto a stool equidistant from the other customers, she propped her elbow on the counter and rested her chin on her hand.

"You goin' far, miss?" Linda, the waitress, plunked a thick mug down in front of her and filled it with coffee from the Thermos jug.

"Whistling Valley ski resort."

Linda pursed disapproving lips. "Rotten night to be driving. You take care, you hear? You'd've been better off to wait up at Mr. Kincaid's place till conditions improved. Road's only been open a couple of hours and littered with more abandoned cars than a scrap yard." She jerked her head toward the truckers. "The boys here say tryin' to get past them all is worse than running a slalom course down a foggy mountain.''

''Maybe I'll check into a motel.'' Jessica poured cream into her coffee.

''Ain't no motel before Wintercreek and that's another eighty miles down the highway. You get that far, you might as well go the rest of the way and be done with it.'' The waitress hitched her bosom onto the counter and leaned forward confidentially. ''You sure you wouldn't rather go back to the Kincaid ranch? Morgan ain't the type to turn a person away on Christmas night, 'specially not a woman traveling on her own.''

''My sister's been hospitalized in Whistling Valley and I'm anxious to see her.''

''Better to wait till it's light out, just the same. Ain't no point in both of you ending up in hospital.''

''Mr. Kincaid didn't seem to think I'd have any trouble getting through,'' Jessica said, wondering why she was even bothering to argue the point. ''In any case, I'm not sure I could find my way back to the ranch in the dark.''

''Ain't no problem, honey.'' The waitress licked the point of a stubby pencil, tore a sheet from her order pad and proceeded to draw a map. ''You're here, see? You just follow the road east till you come to the bridge, then, about a hundred yards past, there's a bit of a rise....''

She droned on good-naturedly. Too weary and heartsick to stop her, Jessica feigned interest and prayed for deliverance. Drumming up a smile of thanks when the discourse finally ended, she placed the completed map next to her coffee cup and heaved a quiet sigh of relief when the waitress turned her attention to serving the truckers slabs of apple pie.

''I'm headed west on the highway and can show you the way, if you like.''

Startled, Jessica swiveled on her stool and realized the man from the far end of the counter had moved and was now standing close behind her.

His jacket collar was drawn up close around his neck and he wore a black wool hat pulled so far down that it almost touched the rims of his heavily tinted glasses. He was well-spoken and looked harmless enough—at least, from what she could see of him—but she'd had enough of accepting kindness from strangers. "Thank you, but I really do have to get to Whistling Valley."

"Suit yourself." He shrugged, a tight smile thinning his narrow lips, and moved away again.

Just then the mechanic reappeared and came to perch on the stool next to Jessica's. "All set, ma'am. Car'll be brought around the front in about five minutes and filled up so you can be on your way."

"Thank you." Relieved, she finished her coffee. "How much do I owe?"

"Not a thing. Coffee's on the house and Mr. Kincaid's taken care of everything else."

Not quite everything, she thought. You couldn't put a price on a crushed heart.

"Hey, Linda!" One of the truckers banged a meaty fist on the counter. "Switch the TV to the news channel, will ya, and let's see what the weatherman's promising for tomorrow? Wouldn't mind getting home before the kids forget what I gave them for Christmas."

"I just need a signature here, ma'am." The mechanic pushed forward a work order and indicated the place. "To say you got your vehicle back with the repairs done to your satisfaction, you understand?"

Jessica scribbled her name, aware of a blast of icy air snaking around her ankles as the outside door opened behind her.

"Might as well stay put where it's warm, honey," the waitress advised, seeing Jessica preparing to leave. "Five minutes, Charlie said, and there ain't no sense hangin' around outside freezin' your butt off all that time." She hefted the coffee Thermos across the counter. "Have another on the house while you wait."

Sweet heaven, Jessica thought wearily, was she never going to sever the ties binding her to Morgan Kincaid's world?

"...conditions expected to hold another day, allowing Christmas travelers delayed by the weather to finally reach their destinations."

Half-heartedly, Jessica turned her attention to the TV newsman, sprig of holly in his lapel, his jovial tone deepening to assume a more somber note as he continued, "On a different front, escaped prison inmate Gabriel Parrish, believed to be headed west in what police are calling a personal vendetta against the man who put him behind bars for the murder of twenty-one-year-old Sally Blackman almost ten years ago, was reportedly seen in the Rosemont area."

The picture on the screen changed to reveal a head shot of the fugitive. Short, greying hair, deep-set, intense dark eyes, and something about the cast of the pinched, unsmiling mouth that struck a strangely familiar chord. Where had she seen it before?

Frowning, she turned her attention to the newscast again.

"...leaving behind a clear trail of evidence. A family planning to spend the holidays in their ski cabin arrived to discover the place broken into and several items missing, including men's clothing, a hand gun, and a small amount of cash," the announcer said. "Their neighbor also reported a stolen snowmobile, since recovered close to Sentinel Pass, a truck stop not far from where crown prosecutor Morgan Kincaid, the man who brought Parrish to justice, owns recreational property. Parrish is considered armed and dangerous—"

Morgan Kincaid, crown prosecutor...the man who brought a convicted killer to justice? Why had he let her believe he was a simple rancher? And what other lies had he told her?

"Car's all ready to roll, Miss Simms." Charlie, the mechanic, swung open the outside door, poked his head inside and waved cheerfully.

A stolen snowmobile, since recovered close to Sentinel

Pass, a truck stop.... Halfway to the door Jessica stopped, a thrill of horror trembling over her.

She cast a frantic glance around the room. The truckers continued to watch the screen. Linda emptied dirty ashtrays into a container. And the man with the tinted glasses and low-slung hat—the man with the disturbingly narrow, pinched mouth?

He had disappeared silently into the night. And so had the rough map showing the Kincaid ranch, which Jessica had left next to her coffee mug.

Except for a solitary light burning in Clancy's quarters, they'd left the house and stables in darkness. That way, it was easier to see anyone approaching the house.

The weather continued to cooperate, flooding the countryside with moonlight. Morgan sat at his bedroom window, unwillingly recalling the night before. Her laughter as he'd pulled her onto the ice, the slenderness of her as they'd danced, the naked desire that had clawed at him until he'd found surcease in her embrace....

He blinked fiercely, willing the images, the ache, to disappear. He was too savvy by far to have been blindsided by love, surely? And yet how else did he define the emotions tearing at him now, when all his energy and attention should be directed on the showdown fast approaching?

"Tell me again what they said when they phoned, Morgan." From his post on the other side of the window, Clancy flexed his arthritic leg.

"That they'd got through to us as soon as the lines were repaired."

"I know that, you damn fool! What else?"

"That they'd found a folder in his cell, collating information from every publication you care to name that ever ran a news item on me or my doings. Photographs, gossip, fact, fiction—you name it, he'd hoarded it."

"Any mention of the ranch?"

"Nothing specific as to its exact location, but enough clues for a man as smart as Parrish to latch onto."

"You sure he'll come lookin' for you here, Morgan?"

"Sure?" Morgan sighed. "As sure as gut instinct and circumstantial evidence can be. He's headed this way, Clancy. I can feel it in my bones."

"You did the right thing, then, getting Jessica out of here as quick as you did."

The ache intensified, spearing him straight through the heart at the memory of her standing alone in the Stedman's parking lot, dumped yet again by someone she'd thought she could trust. "Pity it's the only right thing I did where she was concerned."

They lapsed into silence again, each buried in his own thoughts. The minutes ticked by heavily, a time bomb playing a waiting game.

"It doesn't have to be this way," Clancy said, never taking his eyes from the slim curve of the road as it disappeared beyond the windbreak. "You could call in the law."

"I am the law," Morgan said.

"Reinforcements, then." Clancy stroked the oiled stock of the rifle slung across his knees.

"No. He's out there, watching, waiting. He'd just stay hidden till they were gone. I might as well settle this once and for all."

"Never figured you for a man with a death wish, Morgan."

"I don't plan to die."

"Got something special to live for, have you?"

Morgan felt Clancy's gaze slew sideways and bore into him. "Haven't you?" he said evenly.

"Nothing like Jessica Simms. Reckon you've—"

"He's coming." Morgan's whisper cut into the night as cleanly as a knife blade. "I saw the flash of lights from a car or something as it came around the last bend beyond the pines."

Clancy leaned forward, his gaze raking the inky shadow

of trees on snow. "You sure? Don't seem likely he'd announce his arrival like that, Morgan."

"I'm sure." Silently, Morgan stepped to the corner of the room and lifted the shotgun from its resting place by the wall. "He's here, Clancy."

"Son of a gun!" Clancy exhaled sharply. "Someone's here all right, driving right up to the front door bold as brass, so it can't be Parrish."

Swinging back to the window, Morgan cursed as a familiar maroon sedan slid to a stop at the foot of the steps. "That's Jessica's car."

"God Almighty," Clancy whispered in horror. "You're right, Morgan. And she ain't come alone."

She brought the car to a halt at the foot of the steps. It had been easy to find the house, once she'd made the turn from the main highway. Morgan's tire tracks were plain to see in the bright white moonlight and all she'd had to do was follow them.

"That's right, dear." The pleasant, cultured voice filled her with terror. "Slide out of the car slowly and remember I'm right behind you. Morgan will be so surprised to see us, don't you think?"

He was mad. She had realized it from the moment his voice had floated from the back seat, just as she'd headed back along the highway to warn Morgan and Clancy. "How kind of you, my dear," he'd crooned, "to chauffeur me the last few miles of my long journey."

As if the realization that she had an escaped felon for a passenger hadn't been fright enough, he'd kept the cold tip of a gun pressed to the back of her neck throughout the journey and spent the entire time it had taken her to drive the distance to the Kincaid ranch spewing out in silky tones his venom for Morgan, and for her.

"Slut," he'd said, as pleasantly as any other person might have said "Have a lovely day". "You slept with him, didn't you? I could see it in your eyes, back there in that disgusting greasy spoon of a diner where we met, when that pathetic fool of a waitress mentioned his name. You had that look about you, of a woman scorned.''

Now, as she stepped out of the car, she searched for a way to distract him just long enough to escape into the house. ''What are you going to do next?'' she asked, clinging to the door frame as her feet slithered on the packed snow.

''Why, we're going to pay a little visit to your lover,'' he said, his breath drifting revoltingly over her face as he sidled up next to her and took her other arm. ''Oh, look, he's come to welcome us! Isn't that sociable of him?''

A sudden blaze of light accompanied his words. Morgan stood silhouetted in the open front door of the house, a large gun held loosely in his hands. ''Let her go, Parrish,'' he said coldly. ''You've got no quarrel with her.''

''Put the shotgun away, dear boy,'' Parrish cooed, jabbing the nasty little revolver to her temple, ''or I'll be obliged to shoot your little whore.''

Carefully, Morgan laid his firearm on the floor of the veranda and started slowly down the steps.

''Stay away,'' Parrish warned, his voice rising dangerously. ''Come any closer and she'll die, Kincaid, just like the other one did.''

''You don't want to kill her,'' Morgan replied calmly, continuing his descent. ''You'll never be a free man again, if you do.''

''I'm already free,'' Parrish said, raising his arm and pointing the revolver straight at Morgan's chest.

''Not for long,'' Morgan assured him, reaching the last step.

''For as long as it takes,'' the madman squealed, his grip on Jessica's arm slackening as his voice ran manically out of control.

It was at best a slender chance, but it was the only one to present itself. Desperately, she flung herself forward, catching him off guard and swinging the front door of her car toward him with all her strength. He saw it coming and let her go as he tried to fend it off and at the same time retain his footing on the treacherous ice.

Simultaneously, Morgan leaped the remaining distance between them, landing half on top of Jessica, with enough impact to knock the breath out of her, and half on top of Parrish.

She was aware of a scuffle, of grunts of pain. Of bodies rolling in the snow and the glint of cold metal in moonlight as Parrish swung his revolver in the air. She saw Morgan lunging after it, saw Parrish's insane grin as he aimed straight for Morgan's head.

She heard the sickening impact of a bullet hitting flesh, and her own scream of agonized fear as both men slumped to the frozen ground.

"Morgan!" she wept, crawling forward on her hands and knees, beside herself at the pool of blood staining the snow where he lay beneath Parrish.

"Stay where you are, woman, till I'm sure I've disabled the critter."

The words came to her from a distance, fogged by an overwhelming sense of misery unequalled by anything she'd experienced at Stuart or her aunt's hands.

Slowly she looked up to discover Clancy's familiar scowl hovering above her, and thought it was the second most beautiful sight she'd ever seen. The first was Morgan, heaving Parrish aside and retrieving the revolver which had slid half under her car.

"Wonder where he got this little beauty?" he remarked, as casually as though he played Russian roulette with his life every other day of the week.

"What does it matter?" she shrieked, reaction setting in and sending the tears streaming down her face. "That lunatic almost killed you! For pity's sake, Morgan, he almost killed both of us! Why didn't you tell me what's been going on? Or didn't it strike you as being any of my business?"

"I did my level best not to make it your business, Jessica.'' He poked at Parrish with his foot, at which the injured man let out a howl of pain. ''You got him right in the shoulder, Clancy. Just enough to put him out of action till I get him locked up again.''

''Intended to,'' Clancy said with pride. ''Not that I had much choice, seeing as how you were about to get yourself blown to kingdom come. Hell, boy, if I can shoot a rat's ass at a hundred yards, I can nail scum like Parrish *exactly* where it'll do the most good. Don't reckon he'll be giving anyone too much grief for the next little while.''

''You got through to the police?''

''RCMP are on their way. Stop your sniveling long enough, woman, and you'll hear the sirens,'' he added severely to Jessica, who leaned against the hood of her car, openly sobbing.

''What the hell,'' Morgan said softly, pulling her into the shelter of his arms. ''You're in shock, sweetheart. Let's get you inside and away from this mess.''

He led her up the steps and into the living room and seated her tenderly on the couch. Dazed, she stared around her, at the unlit Christmas tree, at the dying embers in the hearth, at the table she'd set for three…how long ago?

Morgan brought her a glass half-filled with brandy. ''Here,'' he said. ''Drink this.''

She looked up through a sparkle of tears—at the shimmering crystal in his hand, at his long, lean body that had come so close to being torn apart by violence.

What if she hadn't heard the news report? What if she'd gone on her way, full of bitterness and wishing that the misery he'd doled out to her would come back to haunt him threefold, then found out when it was too late that the man she'd fallen in love with had sent her away so that he could play hero in a drama guaranteed to have no happy ending? What if he'd been killed and left her to cope with the guilt of knowing she'd come close to hating him for the way he'd hustled her out of his home and his life?

How dared he? The tears rolled down her face afresh, hot

streams of them, fueled by anger. "How could you do this to me?" she sobbed, dashing the glass from his hand. "How could you have lied to me, over and over again?"

He slumped beside her on the couch. "To protect you," he said bleakly.

"Protect me from what? From falling in love with you?" Her voice rose in anguish. "Is *that* why you slept with me, Morgan? To protect me? Well, excuse me for not appreciating the gesture!"

"Honey," he said, trying to draw her into his arms. "Sweetheart—"

"Don't touch me!" She scooted to the far end of the couch, her body racked by violent shivers. "I was just a diversion, something to keep you amused until the real action began, wasn't I?"

"No," he protested, refusing to keep his distance. "Jessica, honey, if I'd realized when I met you what sort of trouble was waiting, I'd never have brought you here. By the time I knew the score, it was too late—there was no place else I could send you. I thought, as long as the roads were impassable, you'd be as safe here as anywhere."

He lifted his hands to touch her, then let them drop helplessly when she flinched away from him. "I knew that Parrish couldn't get very far as long as the snow kept up, and that the police would be looking for him, but I never expected that we'd...that you and I would—"

"What?" she spat. "Climb between the sheets? Roll in the hay? *Screw?*"

Sweet heaven, where had socially correct, morally upright Miss Simms gone, and who was this shrew screaming obscenities at the man who'd just saved her life?

"It wasn't like that, Jessica," he said, "and I'm sorry if I handled myself in such a way that that's the impression I gave you. I know all about society's misfits and the ills they confer. I'm expert at unraveling other people's truths from the web of deceit behind which they camouflage them, but

I guess I don't know squat about showing a woman I love her.''

"No, you don't," she sobbed, stoking her anger with a fury born of heartache and delayed fear. "I should have let that madman blow your brains out...."

"Yes, sweetheart," Morgan said soothingly, circling his arms around her despite her best efforts to elude him.

"Except he'd never have been able to find them...."

"No, darling. Hush now and let me hold you."

"Police have arrived and want to talk to you, Morgan," Clancy said from the doorway. "Shall I bring 'em in here?"

"No," Morgan said, releasing her and standing up. "I'll see them in the office."

The chill left behind where his arms had been cut her to the bone. "Woman," Clancy declared wrathfully, throwing a handful of kindling into the fireplace and stirring the embers to life, "we could all use a fresh pot of coffee. And if you really want to make yourself useful you could make more tarts."

"I am not your kitchen lackey," she retorted, umbrage reviving something of her usual starch.

He grinned at her over his shoulder. "But you're Morgan's woman, ain't you?"

"No," she said. "I most certainly am not."

He grinned for the second time in a minute, an unheard-of occurrence in Jessica's limited experience. "Try tellin' him that," he advised.

She was a fool to let his words warm her the way she did, an even bigger fool to let her hopes rise from the ashes of her earlier despair. But then, she'd suspected as much, practically from the moment she'd first set eyes on Morgan Kincaid.

"I'll make coffee," she finally agreed, "but you can forget the tarts."

"What the hey?" Clancy snickered. "At least it's a start."

* * *

It was the better part of two hours before the police completed their business and Gabriel Parrish had been shipped by ambulance to recover from his wounds in the nearest maximum security penitentiary.

Not long after that, Clancy pulled his usual disappearing act, leering evilly over his shoulder as he left.

"It's his way of saying he approves of our being a couple," Morgan said wryly. "He's quite the romantic under that crusty exterior."

"What Clancy does or doesn't approve of is immaterial," Jessica said sadly. "We are not a couple, Morgan. Couples don't offer protection as an excuse for deceit, they trust each other to cope with the truth."

Spreading his arms wide, leaning both hands on the mantelpiece, he stared at the fire. "And what if the truth divides them, Jessica? Then what?"

"Then they were doomed from the outset. Lies don't strengthen a relationship, Morgan, no matter how well intentioned they might be. They undermine it and eventually they destroy it."

His shoulders sagged at that and it took all the resolve she could muster not to go to him and wrap her arms around him and tell him that none of it mattered as long as they were together.

She hated the fact that her body and heart held such sway and tried to pretend differently, but the awareness, the sheer physical longing, never let up. It growled and paced within her, gnawing away at her defenses no matter how diligently she tried to subdue it.

"I lied to you," he said eventually, his voice weighted with regret, "for your own good. To keep you safe, to leave you free of fear."

"The blow you dealt me in doing so far exceeds anything Parrish could have done to hurt me," she replied.

He spun around, his face blazing with sudden anger. "You say that now but if I'd told you I was falling in love with you and wanted a future with you how long would it have been before you'd decided I wasn't worth the risk?''

''Never,'' she said. ''Because love involves risk. It means trust and acceptance and passion all bound together by truth. No games, no artifice, no promises that can't be kept, just the pledge that tomorrow or next week or fifty years from now the feelings will still be there—stronger, surer, no matter what.''

''There was a time, when I was first married, when I'd have agreed with you but the rot set in anyway, so subtly that I never knew for sure just when it started.''

''There must have been signs, Morgan. Marriages don't fall apart overnight.''

''Oh, there were signs, all right. My work became the other woman, at least in my ex-wife's eyes. She resented my involvement with what she called 'the seamy underside of the law'. Suddenly, what she'd once perceived as respectable and even honorable became a lifestyle liability, a threat to her peace of mind. And who's to say she wasn't right?''

An explosive sigh burst from him, seeming to tear its way free. ''You say you want the truth, Jessica? Well, here's the truth of my life when I'm not kicking back up here and breathing the clean country air: I put criminals away. If I'm ever appointed to the Bench—and there are rumors I might be—they'd probably call me the hanging judge because *I do not believe anyone should break the law with impunity*.''

''You're shouting at me and there's no need,'' Jessica said. ''I happen to agree with you. You don't have to convince me.''

''But what if you were married to me? Could you handle the occasional hate mail, the vicious, anonymous phone calls that would find our home no matter how often we changed to another unlisted number? Could you survive hearing the insults hurled at your husband by a man facing a prison term? Because Daphne couldn't. 'No woman should have to live with this kind of harassment,' she told me, when she finally bowed out of the marriage.''

''Didn't you try to talk her out of it?''

''No,'' he said. ''By then I no longer cared enough to try. So don't tell me that love means acceptance or the pledge that it will survive, no matter what, because I'm here to tell you it doesn't always work out like that.''

Jessica felt a profound sadness then, for him, for them. He might profess to be falling in love with her but how did they stand a chance of finding happiness if, from the outset, he expected they'd fail? He seemed so strong, so confident, and yet he was as lonely and isolated in his way as she was in hers. When had he stopped believing he deserved some satisfaction for a job well done?

''Doesn't anyone ever take the time to tell you you make a difference?'' she asked him. ''Or that the world is a better place for having men like you in it?''

''Oh, I have my fans,'' he said wryly, ''but the people I'm most likely to hear from are those who feel I've ruined their lives. Gabriel Parrish is a case in point and I wish I could tell you he's the last, but I can't. The world is full of wing nuts, sweetheart, and the best I can promise any woman is that I'll stand between her and danger whenever I see it headed our way, but that's hardly a guarantee likely to inspire her to making a lifetime commitment to me.''

Could she, if he were to ask her? Jessica looked down at her hands, knotted together in her lap, evidence that the trauma of the last few hours still lingered.

She hadn't coped very well tonight. She didn't think she'd ever cope well with that kind of situation. What if he was right and the odds were against her? Did either of them need the burden of another failed relationship?

''Tell me what you're thinking,'' he said, when the silence grew too oppressive.

She gave a little shrug and sighed. ''I think we're making a mistake even discussing the possibility of such a commitment when we've known each other so short a time and clearly have much more to learn.''

He smiled. ''Well, you're a lot more sensible than Daphne ever was; that I have to admit.''

Sensible. The word had dogged her from childhood and she hated it. But it was hard to shake off its influence after so many years and follow a different course.

She wanted to go to him, to have him sweep her up in his strong arms and carry her up to his room. She wanted him to strip away her clothes and cover her with kisses. She wanted him to unleash her sexuality again and make her forget every other consideration but that they needed each other in a way that defied sensible or proper or logical.

She took a deep breath and screwed up her courage to tell him so. But how? What were the right words? *Where* were they? ''May I stay here tonight?'' she said, praying he'd hear what she was really asking.

He searched her face, then looked away to the moon-streaked darkness beyond the window. ''Yes,'' he said. ''Of course. Your room's still here and it's much too late for you to think of driving any further tonight after all that's happened. You'll face the journey much better in the morning when you've had some rest.''

''I suppose.'' Still, she lingered, longing for him to argue her point, to convince her that time didn't count when two people shared something as rare and beautiful as they'd found.

But he didn't. Instead he looked at her with a wealth of sadness in his eyes, as though he could read exactly what lay in her heart.

''You have a life, Jessica,'' he said. ''A nice, ordered life, with everything laid out and run according to rule. I don't. I never know what tomorrow will bring and, to be honest, I'm not sure I want to. I'd like to tell you I can change, that I'm ready for something less hair-raising than what happened here tonight, but I'm not sure I can do that, either.

"I'm falling in love with you. I'd like to think we have a future together. But I have no right to try to sell you a bill of goods until I know for sure exactly what it contains, so please don't ask me to do that. You deserve better. You've been cheated enough."

CHAPTER ELEVEN

WINTER dragged its heels into a late spring and Jessica went through the motions of running her school. But the routine that had sustained her for so many years had lost its power to heal. She was the custodian only of her students; they were not really hers to love, and even if they had been they would not have eased the ache in her heart.

Only Morgan, whose memory refused to fade, could have accomplished that and he, apparently, had no urge to do so. He had let her walk out of his house and out of his life and made no attempt to stop her.

Selena had been scandalized when she'd heard. It had been her considered opinion that only a complete nincompoop would allow such a "stud muffin" to escape, and that the only thing left to do was go back and fight for him.

Jessica hadn't thought herself capable of finding anything amusing just then, but hearing Morgan described as a stud muffin had elicited a smile. However, she'd refused to follow her sister's advice, determined that, as long as Morgan was the one with all the doubts, he must also be the one to resolve them.

She would not go begging for love again. Actions spoke louder than words and he was the one who'd talked about their finding a future together. If he was serious, he must come to her.

But the days had become weeks and now it was April, with the magnolias in the academic quadrangle in early bloom, and not once in all that time had there been a word from Morgan.

She stared out of her office window, watching as the last few students left by family car for the Easter break, and could have wept all over again for what she had let slip through her fingers.

It seemed that frivolous Selena, who'd barely managed to scrape through high school, won more prizes where men were concerned than her supposedly clever sister could ever hope to acquire. Pride, Jessica had come to appreciate, was a poor substitute for love.

Squaring her shoulders, she turned to the paperwork waiting for her on her desk. But scholarship grants and budget restraints held no fascination for a mind morbidly curious to know if another woman had leaped at the chance to fill the spot she'd so foolishly vacated.

Was it worth the risk of further heartache to find out?

Yes, she decided. Anything was better than living in a vacuum of uncertainty. Of waiting for the phone to ring, for the mailman to deliver a letter, for a sign, however small, that Morgan had not found he could live very well without her. There had to be closure, one way or the other.

She glanced at the clock above the fireplace and reached a decision. If she put her mind to it, she could finish up what had to be done here and still make the five-thirty ferry sailing to the mainland.

There was no putting things off any longer. Real love didn't conveniently go away. It refused to die, no matter how firmly one ignored it. That much she'd learned over the last three and a half months and if Morgan hadn't, it was time she taught him.

The daily grind of upholding justice regardless of personal cost went on, but the spark, the drive, the caring commitment had grown dim. For years Morgan had successfully looked outside himself to find fulfillment but now, when he needed it the most, satisfaction eluded him. Without her he felt only half alive.

"For a guy who's a shoo-in for promotion, you're looking pretty grim these days," one of his colleagues observed, the week before Easter.

He wasn't the only one to notice the change. "What's curdlin' your cream?" Clancy inquired, when Morgan phoned to say he'd changed his mind about spending the long weekend at the ranch. "Time was you couldn't wait to drag your sorry hide up here."

"I have other plans," Morgan said, arriving at a decision he should have reached weeks ago.

He cleared his appointments by eleven the next morning and arrived at the ferry terminal shortly before noon. It was a fine day with light winds and too few clouds to obscure the sun.

As the stretch of water between the boat and the mainland grew wider and the low-rising hills of the islands took on more distinct shape, he paced an isolated section of the ferry's upper deck, rehearsing what he'd say to her.

He still wasn't sure he'd got it right, even when the announcement came over the loudspeaker that the ferry was approaching Springhill Island and those passengers disembarking there should return to their vehicles.

He was a man used to being in charge, a man who acted and got things done. The nervousness gripping him now was so foreign to him that he hadn't the foggiest clue how to go about dealing with it.

Impatiently he waited for the long line of cars ahead of him to move out of the cavernous hull of the boat. At length he was waved forward and emerged into the sunshine again.

Even as his deck was being cleared, a lower deck was already loading vehicles leaving the island. Just as he left the ramp and pulled onto the road a sleek blue bus with the words "Springhill Island Private School" scrolled on its side inched its way down toward the belly of the boat.

Ahead of him a traffic light turned red. Slowing to a stop, he took down the sunglasses clipped to the visor above the windshield and studied the map on the seat beside him. The school lay about thirty miles away, at the southern tip of the island.

He settled back for the drive, the blood which had moved

so sluggishly through his veins in the last weeks pumping with tense anticipation. He passed farms, golf courses, yacht basins, old inns and gracious country houses. Offshore, the neighboring islands snoozed in the afternoon sun.

At any other time, he would have found the spectacle delightful. Today, he was too preoccupied trying to control the nervous tension, the like of which not even the most hardened criminal had ever managed to promote in him.

Suddenly, the split rail fence of a dairy farm to the left gave way to a high stone wall and at last—too soon—he was there, passing between iron gates bearing the same gothic scroll as the bus, and following a curving drive lined with flowering dogwoods.

Occasionally, beyond the trees, he caught glimpses of a lake, playing fields, several small houses, and finally came upon the school itself, a dignified ivy-covered Victorian building.

The domed foyer was empty but he could hear women's voices coming from the door marked "GENERAL OFFICE" and also from several of the classrooms surrounding a central courtyard. Feeling oddly out of his element, he approached the office door.

It swung open before he could knock. "Oh!" the pretty young woman facing him exclaimed. "Sorry, I didn't mean to run you down."

"That's okay," he said, and had to clear his throat before he could continue. "I—er—I'd like to speak to...."

He stumbled to a halt, too far removed from his own milieu to feel comfortable, too out of sync with the stomach-churning state of nerves in which he found himself to project his usual air of authority.

This was Jessica's turf. Here, she wasn't the woman who'd filled his life and his bed too briefly but who'd stolen his heart for ever. She was the boss, the one in charge. She could—and might—have him thrown out.

"Yes?" The woman with the books was staring at him,

clearly wondering if she had some sort of lunatic on her hands.

Jeez, Kincaid! Get it together!

"I'd like to see the headmistress."

"I didn't know she had another appointment today. Is she expecting you?"

"No," he said apologetically, and wondered how in hell a man of his years and experience could suddenly regress to the maturity level of a boy hauled up on the carpet for breaking the rules. "No, I'm afraid she isn't."

The woman smiled kindly, the way a nurse might before handing over a patient to a sadistic dentist. "Hang on, and I'll see if she's still here. She did say something about catching the last ferry to the mainland."

"When does that sail?" Morgan asked, deciding that if he and Jessica had passed in the lineup of cars at the terminal the gods were definitely having a good laugh at his expense.

"Five-thirty." She dumped an armful of books on a nearby chair and poked her head inside the office again. "Has Jessica left yet?"

"No," an unseen voice replied. "She's in her office as far as I know."

"You're in luck." The pretty woman turned back to him and smiled again. "I'll warn her she's got a visitor. I'm Deirdre Bayliss, grade ten home room teacher and head of the math department, by the way. Whose father are you?"

"I'm not," he said.

Ms. Bayliss's eyes narrowed slightly and her smile wasn't quite as warm when she asked, "Then who shall I say is calling?"

To his disgust Morgan realized his palms were sweating and his shirt collar choking him. "Um…I'd like to surprise her. Pleasantly," he added hastily, at the suspicious glance this aroused. "I'm her…friend. She spent Christmas at my place."

She'd probably kill him for making that little tidbit of

news public knowledge, but he'd geared himself up to come here and confront her, was putting himself through hell now he'd arrived, and he wasn't about to be thwarted at this late stage by being refused permission to see her.

"Well, I'm not sure...."

"I know. In this day and age, you can never be too careful." Reaching into his wallet, he withdrew a business card and offered it for her inspection, along with his most winning smile. "I'm harmless, as you can see, but you're welcome to stick around and see for yourself if it'll make you feel better."

He knew Jessica well enough to realize she'd walk barefoot over hot coals before she'd air her private life in front of any member of her staff. If he could just get a foot in her door, she'd allow him to stay and say his piece, no matter how much she might want to kick him out on his rear.

"Well," pretty Deirdre Bayliss allowed, visibly impressed to find herself talking to the senior crown prosecutor of the lower mainland, "I'll see you to the door at least. Follow me."

The budget proposals were read, the mid-term reports signed and her desk was clear. Apart from a couple of minor items she was finished, and should make it to the ferry terminal in plenty of time.

She was at her filing cabinet, with her back to the door, when it opened. "A gentleman to see you, Ms. Simms," Deirdre Bayliss announced, her use of Jessica's surname indicating that the visitor was not someone either expected or known.

Probably another well-heeled parent wanting to see his daughter pushed to the head of the admissions waiting list, Jessica decided resignedly, sneaking a glance at her watch. He'd pretend otherwise, of course, dangling the offer to underwrite a scholarship or contribute vast sums to the construction of a new wing, but there'd been too many such bribes in the past, usually occurring with a new term about to begin, for her to expect anything different this time.

Well, she'd give him exactly five minutes before she showed him the door. Expression neutral, blood pressure normal, emotions under control, she turned to greet the visitor.

He filled the doorway to the extent that Deirdre had to stand on tiptoe and peer over his shoulder to catch Jessica's eye. And suddenly, after months of hoping and wanting and, finally, of despairing, she was face to face with Morgan again.

Astonishment left her swaying on her feet. She felt the blood drain from her face, bleaching her features with shock. This wasn't happening the way she'd planned! She needed time to prepare herself, to decide how best to approach him.

"Would you like me to stay, Ms. Simms?" Deirdre said, alarm threading her voice.

She feared her knees would give out under her. How she heard the question over the roaring in her ears defied explanation. "No," she said weakly. "That's quite all right, Ms. Bayliss."

He smiled at Deirdre, who looked far from reassured, and practically shut the door in her face. Jessica wobbled to her desk and virtually collapsed into her chair. "Well, Morgan," she squeaked, with a pathetic lack of originality, "it's you."

"In the flesh," he said, his gaze swinging around the room to take in the mahogany furnishings, the credentials hanging on the wall, the magnolia framed in the French windows that led to the quadrangle, and coming to rest finally on her.

Oh, in the flesh, indeed! Every gorgeous, formal inch of him! No blue jeans today, no stetson, no leather boots, but a tailored navy blazer, grey pants, white shirt and ultra-conservative burgundy tie. The dark, unruly hair was combed into submission, the jaw freshly shaven. And the face, the eyes, the mouth....

Jessica swallowed helplessly and pressed her knees together so hard that the little bones on the inside of her ankles ground painfully against each other. "Well," she said again, and followed that up with the most inane question of all time. "Are you here to register your daughter?"

He subjected her to a long, level stare. "No. To the best of my knowledge, I don't have a daughter—or a son, either."

"Of course not," she said. "I remember now you told me there were no children from your marriage."

"Is that all you remember about me, Jessica?" he asked gently.

"No," she whispered, the same old awareness arcing between them again, a high-voltage wire dangerously alive. "I remember everything. *Everything.* Especially your fear that commitment to your work would prove an insurmountable obstacle to our finding happiness together."

She chanced another direct glance at the handsome, unsmiling face and all her self-protective instincts converged to shield her from yet another disappointment. From habit, the headmistress supplanted the lover—unimpeachably correct, starchily aloof. "Which makes me wonder, Morgan, why you're here now. Have you decided to give up the law and be what you once led me to believe you were—a simple rancher with no hidden agenda?"

He paced to the window and stared out. "I've thought about it," he said, his smoky, sexy voice playing sonatas down her spine. "I've indulged in endless games of 'what if' over the last few months."

He swung around to face her and she marveled that she somehow managed to stop herself from rushing to him and flinging herself into his arms. But she dared not, not until she knew for sure....

"I wondered if we could handle a long-distance marriage, with you here and me someplace else—the ranch, or private practice, perhaps. Such marriages sometimes work,'' he said, at her small exclamation of protest.

"Not for me," she said firmly.

He drummed his fingertips on the window ledge. "I see."

"Really?" She moistened her lips with the tip of her tongue. "And what is it that you see, Morgan?"

"You've done what I haven't been able to do. You've put the past—our past—behind you."

"And how," she inquired, the headmistress still refusing to bow out and let the woman who loved him speak from her heart, "do you arrive at that conclusion?"

"Well, hell," he said, his voice raw with misery, "I think I just proposed. And I know damn well you shot me down before I barely got the words out."

The warmth that was melting her heart stole into her face, softening her features and thawing the tears damming her eyes. She blinked them away. "I didn't mean to do that. What else did you wish to say?"

He heaved a great sigh. "That I was wrong to let you go, wrong to think time or distance would solve anything. That neither of those things has anything to do with love."

He flexed his shoulders and loosened the knot in his tie. "That the few days we shared, Jessica, have overshadowed every waking minute of the last three and a half months for me. That I tried to forget you—for your sake, for mine—"

He stopped again and raked his fingers through his hair, disheveling its tidy perfection. "Hell, I don't know! And what does it matter anyway, if you don't feel—?"

She couldn't bear it a minute longer, not the pain they'd both suffered, not the time they'd wasted, and most especially not the stretch of carpet separating them that neither dared to cross. They were both so tentative, so cautious, so protective—of each other, of themselves.

One of them had to be brave and he'd already laid himself on the line for her. It was her turn to take a chance.

"I won't settle for a long-distance marriage," she said, at last finding the strength to do what she'd wanted to do from the moment she'd seen him standing in her office doorway. Pushing herself out of her chair, she went to him and put her arms around his waist. "If I love a man enough to marry him, I want to be with him all the time."

"Do you still love me, Jessica?"

"Oh, yes," she whispered, leaning her head against his chest. "I thought the feelings might die, especially when I didn't hear from you, but they didn't. I've missed you so much, Morgan."

"Me too," he said, wrapping his arms around her. "Me too, sweetheart."

"If being a rancher full-time will make you happy…?"

"It won't," he said. "That's Clancy's idyll, not mine. Speaking of whom, there's one man who'll happily dance at our wedding. I think he'd marry you himself if he had the chance. But about that other 'what if' I mentioned—the one about going into private practice—"

"Is that what you really want, Morgan?"

"No." She felt the shuddered intake of his breath, sensed the battle he was waging within himself. He tightened his arms around her. "You're a remarkable human being, and I love you for who you are, for the way you think. But more than that I need you. Don't make me go the distance alone, Jessica. My work—it's not always pretty, it's seldom polite and it's almost…" he drew a deep, despairing breath "…almost never clean. But it's who I am, what I believe in, and if I'm to go on making a difference—trying to make things better—I have to have someone to come home to who believes in me. I have to have you."

"You already do," she said. "I've been yours for the taking for months."

"But I don't have the right." He gestured at the elegant office with its white-painted classical fireplace and high coved ceiling. "How can I ask you to give up the ordered, exclusive life you've carved out for yourself here? Because that's what it really boils down to, sweetheart. I can't be effective as a crown prosecutor living on Springhill Island."

"But I can be a wife anywhere."

"You'd do that? You'd give up your job just to be with me?"

She would have laughed if she hadn't been so close to tears. "*Just* to be with you? Morgan, my dearest love, I left here at Christmas believing I was a whole woman but I knew, by the time I came back, that I'd brought only half of me home."

She touched his face, tracing loving fingers over his cheek, his jaw, his mouth. "Teaching, running this school—I made them my life because they were all I had and for a long time they were enough. But then there was you, and everything changed. With you, finer dreams didn't seem so impossible any more."

"Why didn't you tell me? We've wasted so much time."

"I wasn't willing to risk having you turn away from me. I thought, on Christmas night when you left me outside that service station, that I'd never felt such heartache, and I made a vow I'd never leave myself open to that sort of pain again. But I've learned there are worse things."

"Are there?" he said tenderly, lowering himself to the chair she'd recently vacated. "Such as what?"

"Such as being a prisoner of one's pride. Such as being afraid to live. Would you believe," she said, allowing him to draw her down onto his lap, "that I decided this afternoon that it was time I stopped being such a coward? I was going to come to you and refuse to go away unless you could tell me you were happier without me. Because you can't turn off love, no matter how ill advised it might seem, no matter how inconvenient."

"There could be other Gabriel Parrishes, sweetheart."

"If there are, we'll face them together. It's time to close old doors, Morgan, especially with so many new ones waiting to be opened. I'm not Daphne; you're not Stuart."

He took her face between his two hands. "I don't know how I lived without you, my lovely Jessica, but I do know

I can't go on that way. Will you marry me, despite everything?''

''No,'' she sighed as his mouth inched toward hers. ''I'll marry you because of everything.''

EPILOGUE

"HELLO, gal. Sorry I haven't been up to chat the last few days but I've been away to the coast, to a weddin'. Morgan's weddin', Agnes, and you ain't seen nothin' like it. More fancy folks in fancy clothes than you could shake a stick at. An' queer food like you wouldn't believe. Weren't at all sure a man were meant to put it in his mouth, let alone swallow the dad-blamed stuff. Nothin' like your good home cookin', gal. And the drink—hah! Fizzed up a man's nose worse'n that mornin' brew you used to concoct to keep me regular through the winter.

"But it were worth the trip, just to see Morgan so happy. And that Jessica! Why, Agnes, she looked darn near as beautiful as you did the day you married me. All in white, she were, with the rear end of her dress trailin' behind her for half a mile. You'd've loved all the flowers, gal. Roses and sweet-smellin' foreign things, and little white misty bits of stuff like the wild baby's breath you used to grow, 'cept this were bigger and come from a greenhouse.

"As for Morgan, well, he'd've looked just fine if he could've kept the sappy grin off his face. Embarrassing, it were, watchin' him. Good thing he got himself a sensible wife this time. She'll do, Agnes. She's a good woman—could've been your daughter if God had seen fit to send us one. Feet planted on the ground and good-hearted, that's the new Mrs. Kincaid. She'll not be runnin' for the hills at the first sign of trouble. She'll deal with it, just the way you would've.

"Reckon there'll be young'uns before long, gal. Jessica turned all red in the face when I asked and Morgan told me to hush my mouth. Said it weren't something he wanted broadcast just yet, as though a little foal were already bakin' in the oven. Wouldn't surprise me a bit, Agnes, the way he carried on at Christmas, sniffin' around her all the time. Thought I was goin' to have to hog-tie him to the stable door a couple of times.

''He and his new missus is comin' up to the ranch in September. I'll introduce you then and, come next spring, I'll bet my last dollar there'll be a baby to show off.

''Anyway, gal, there it is, all the news that's fit to print. I missed you. I always do when I'm away from you. Reckon I can understand how Morgan feels. When the right woman comes along, she makes a man feel whole.

''Best be gettin' back to work now. The wild flowers is bloomin' all around you, all red and orange and purple, just the way you always wanted. You rest easy and I'll stop by again tomorrow, same as always. I've loved you for nearly fifty years, darlin'. I ain't about to stop now.''

Modern Romance™
...seduction and
passion guaranteed

Tender Romance™
...love affairs that
last a lifetime

Sensual Romance™
...sassy, sexy and
seductive

Blaze™
...sultry days and
steamy nights

Medical Romance™
...medical drama on
the pulse

Historical Romance™
...rich, vivid and
passionate

29 new titles every month.

*With all kinds of Romance for
every kind of mood...*

MILLS & BOON®

Makes any time special™

MAT4

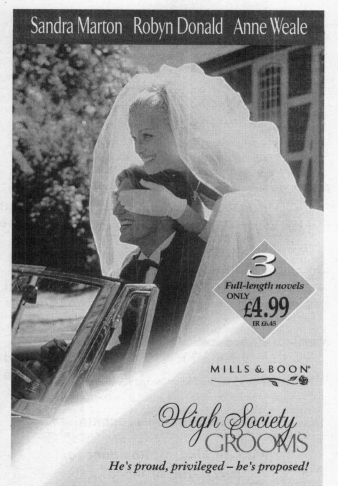

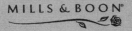

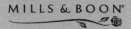

Modern Romance™

FORGOTTEN SINS *by Robyn Donald*

Aline was in bed with a stranger! He claimed she'd made love with him. Her mind couldn't remember—but her body was on fire. He accused her of faking amnesia, of deliberately holding something back. But his passion for her was undeniable!

HIS TROPHY MISTRESS *by Daphne Clair*

Jager had been a boy from the wrong side of the tracks when he'd made heiress Paige his bride—now he was a self-made millionaire. Had he returned to claim Paige as a trophy, to show how far he'd come, or did he truly care for her?

THE THIRD KISS *by Leanna Wilson*

Though uninterested in 'temporary marriage', Brooke couldn't refuse when Matt Cutter, Texas's most eligible bachelor, promised funding for her favourite charity. And besides, acting the loving couple was remarkably easy. But maybe that was because they weren't acting anymore!

THE WEDDING LULLABY *by Melissa McClone*

A wager had meant a one-night marriage for innocent socialite Laurel Worthington and handsome tycoon Brett Matthews. On discovering she is pregnant, Laurel finds Brett and asks for his help. He vows they'll marry again, but this time Laurel wants her husband's heart.

On sale 4th January 2002

Available at most branches of WH Smith, Tesco, Martins, Borders, Eason, Sainsbury's and most good paperback bookshops. 1201/01b

MILLS & BOON
FOREIGN AFFAIRS
A captivating 12 book collection of sun-kissed seductions.
Enjoy romance around the world
DON'T MISS BOOK 4
outback husbands–
The fiery heart of Australia
Available from 4th January
Available at most branches of WH Smith, Tesco, Martins, Borders, Eason, Sainsbury's and most good paperback bookshops.
FA/RTL/4